# THE PHOENIX FEATHER III:
## FIREBOLT

## ALSO BY SHERWOOD SMITH

# THE PHOENIX FEATHER

## 3

## FIREBOLT

## SHERWOOD SMITH

BOOK VIEW CAFE

Published by Book View Café Publishing Cooperative
304 S. Jones Blvd., Suite 2906
Las Vegas, NV 89107
www.bookviewcafe.org

ISBN: 978-1-61138-998-2

Cover Design by Victoria Davies
Interior Design by Marissa Doyle

# ONE

THIS CHAPTER IN THE Story of the Phoenix Feather begins with the remainder of the Redbark companions — Ryu, Matu, and Petal — left watching in distress as the imperial army marched off with Shigan.

Who had, to Ryu's horror, turned out to be Imperial First Prince Jehan Jion.

Of all those listeners inside and outside Madam Swan's entertainment house, only Ryu understood ancient Imperial, and how the sinister imperial ferret Fai Anbai most unfairly staked everyone's lives against their imperial prince's. She was wild with anger and grief — but so tired after talking nearly all night, then only a brief sleep, that she stood there beside the window staring into the rapidly emptying square as everyone in the world burst into question and comment around her, mostly variations on, "What were the imperials saying? Why did they take away the dancer?"

"They went to their knees, did you see that?"

"He must be a runaway noble."

"Why would anyone run away from riches and anything you want?"

"Who understands anything nobles do? Thank the gods it was his bad luck that brought the imperials down on his head, and not mine, that's all I know."

And everyone judiciously made signs warding bad luck.

Ryu roused when Madam Swan's voice rose to an almost piercing level. "Oh, yes, that must have been the *infamous Firebolt* who *left last night*. I am *so shocked!* Why, if I had known he was so infamous, I would *never* have taken his custom. I have to think of the reputation of my house, you know!"

Then she was there in a swirl of pink silk and rose fragrance, saying, "Yes, these might be the Redbark Sect companions, but I believe Firebolt left them behind."

Only then did Ryu remember Matu and Petal on the other side of the room. They had been whispering fiercely, but they looked up when confronted by a man dressed like an ordinary traveler. This man then turned to glance at Ryu, as an armored imperial wearing the feather-and-tassel hat of a captain entered the room, flanked by guards who shooed everyone else out.

The civilian gestured to the three of them as the captain stood by, holding a sheathed sword. Even in her misery, former cadet Ryu noted that sword gripped in his left hand — ready for a fast draw with his right.

The civilian said, "I have a few questions."

Matu's usually pleasant face hardened. For a sick moment Ryu wondered if he was going to turn on her for lying about her gender . . . but then she saw that his angry gaze was not on her. She remembered that Matu's father, laboring in some imperial mine on an island named Benevolent Winds, was an eternal knot in Matu's heart, never far from his thoughts whenever he saw, or heard, imperials. He was not going to give these imperials anything they didn't already have, no matter what they threatened.

But the questions turned out to be brief. It was clear that to the imperials, the important action was over. Did they know his name, Shigan Fin, did they know where he was from, no, Redbark asks no questions, all are welcome . . . Petal did the talking. Ryu tried to follow, to think ahead, but her thoughts stumbled, nearly paralyzed by the overwhelming emotions, and exhaustion, that pressed down on her soul. Her heart. She drooped miserably, wanting to curl up in a ball and cry.

She blinked when the captain's voice sharpened. ". . . you answer me, boy?"

Petal said hastily, "Matu here is a loyal member of our sect, but he's a little slow."

The captain looked from Matu to Ryu hunched there by

the window—and she felt herself dismissed in the way adults dismiss children. Never before had she been glad to be short and round-faced as the captain said to the man in plain clothing, "I believe we are finished here."

As soon as the imperials were seen out the door by deferential staff, Madam Swan went through the entire house, and anyone she didn't recognize she smilingly escorted to the common room, offered free food and drink, then gestured for the Redbarks and her staff to meet her in the kitchen.

"You three," she said to Ryu, Matu, and Petal, "ought to go before they decide to come back and take you along for further questions. The rest of you, you know nothing at all, and offer free drinks. Let's get this past us as quickly as we can."

"Why did they take the Comet?" the lead dancer asked.

Madam Swan raised her hands, looking upward—and in that moment Ryu suspected that the woman also understood the ancient tongue, or enough of it to hazard a guess. "Who knows? One thing I am certain of, anything with the imperials is political in nature, and politics is a den of tigers. Do you really want to poke a straw up a tiger's nose?"

"No!" everyone agreed, and dispersed.

The three remaining Redbark companions packed up their new things and left.

They passed by the Five Heroes and up a randomly chosen side street, to another smaller square. Here they stopped.

Ryu looked uncertainly at Matu. For it had been Matu who blurted out *her* after Shigan's *Stay with him*.

Ryu braced herself to face the consequences of having lied to them all, from the beginning—but Matu was not thinking about that. "What was wrong with Shigan?" he asked, low-voiced. "They knelt down. But then they took him away."

Long habit prompted Ryu to let Shigan tell his own story.

If they ever saw him again.

Fresh grief knotted painfully in her heart, and she sighed heavily. "Madam is right. Imperials mean something political."

"Just like my father," Matu said bitterly. "I always suspected Shigan might be a noble. But I thought . . ." He shook his head. "Doesn't matter what I thought." Then, after a deep breath, "Before that feather-hatted army noser butted in. We were talking about what to do."

"It's all right. You don't have to include me," Ryu said,

eyeing his not-quite-at-her gaze. "Ayah! I'm sorry I lied. About my . . . not being a boy, I mean."

Matu sidled uncomfortably, but before he could speak, Petal said firmly, "That's your business." And to Matu, in a low voice, "You ought not to have told Shigan."

Matu studied his boot tops. "I don't know why I said what I did. It—it just seemed wrong for Shigan not to know," he mumbled.

"And so you grabbed a boiling kettle," Petal said. Matu flushed as Petal turned to Ryu. "You've been such a good leader, I for one would be glad to keep following you, girl, boy, or whatever you want to be."

"Thank you." Ryu held out her hands, palms up. "Unfortunately, I don't have any idea what to do. If you've got ideas, I'd be glad to hear them."

A brief silence ensued, then Petal, who seemed determined to speak the truth even if it frightened her, said, "I would rather not spend another winter in the far north. Too many rumors of trouble up there."

Matu looked up long enough to say, "I'm not ready to go back to Ten Leopards yet."

Ryu ducked her head. She'd been about to suggest that. Not that she was thinking of his large, sometimes bewildering family. The lure—and it was increasingly strong—was Grandfather Ki, and his knowledge of Essence. Now that Yaso had left them, she had no guidance whatsoever.

Ryu turned to Petal. "What would you like to do, if you could go anywhere?"

Petal's chewed lips pressed to a line. Then she said in that same high, gritty determined-to-speak-the-truth-voice, "I want to at least check at Te Gar." She twisted her hands in the old way at the mention of her one-time home. "I keep worrying about my sister. If that marriage ended, or something happened, and she was forced to go back to *her*. I need to know. If I can. Before I go anywhere else. If it was up to me . . ."

Matu interrupted that morass of conditions to say in a low voice, "I'd go with you. If you want me."

Petal's smile brightened her entire countenance.

Ryu looked down at the ground. She did *not* want to go south, which was into imperial territory. Shigan—an imperial prince—the imperials showing up so suddenly—she felt as if a tiger had leaped toward her out of the blue, but then passed over her head to chase an unseen prey behind her. She would be foolish to turn around and begin chasing the tiger, and going south felt like it would be chasing the tiger. But if the others wanted to go there, maybe she ought to go too, to protect them — and to try to mend whatever it was that she'd broken between Matu and her.

Matu said, "If you will consider a suggestion . . ."

Ryu stared at her feet, the knot in her heart twin to the one in her stomach when she realized that Matu had stopped calling her Redbark Brother Ryu. "What is it?"

He looked away, then back, his shoulders straightening. "I know the Ki clan owes you nothing, nor you the clan. But you ought to understand what it means when Grandfather Ki said he was waiting for you. He never did that for any of *us*."

Ryu looked up, hope in her face. She said truthfully, "You're wrong about my not owing them. If you and Petal hadn't brought them to that Shadow Panther lair, Shigan and I would be dead by now." And when Matu flushed, but didn't deny it, she asked tentatively, "Do you think Grandfather Ki would still welcome me?"

"From everything the elders say, he would like nothing better. He won't care about . . ." Matu blushed even redder as he made a vague gesture toward the front of his clothes. "It's your skill. He can teach you about Essence. I can draw a map how to find the island."

Ryu looked at the pair, aware of herself as an awkward third. "I'd like that, too," she said.

And saw a quick look of relief in Matu's face — no more than she felt herself. The decision seemed to be made. Everyone looked at everyone else, and saw agreement.

Ryu slid her hand into her pack, and pulled out the bag of cash. "Let me split this three ways while you make the map."

Both things were soon done, and the three of them faced one another once more. Petal spoke up, her voice husky with conviction. "Wherever I go, I will always take Redbark with me."

Ryu bobbed awkwardly, though she was sure Redbark was a bubble that had quite thoroughly popped. She did not say so because this was Petal, always a good person who meant well. They walked together down toward the wharf, relieved to see that the imperial ships were mere silhouettes on the horizon.

Matu and Petal found a ship going south, and Ryu one going north. Theirs was leaving on the same tide, so they went straight on board after a subdued farewell.

Ryu's was still loading supplies. She was told it would sail on the late tide, which left her with time to spare — and nowhere to go. She was so very tired, but the emotions of the day were immediate, like ghosts crowding around her. Among the many lingering regrets and jolts of hurt was Madam Swan's brightly false tone when she had entered that room ahead of an imperial spy.

An imperial spy! Ryu had believed herself safe from any such person, far, far from the sinister reach of that emperor who had tried to kill her parents. She was so very glad she had never given in to the impulse to tell anyone The Story!

What to do now? She had to stay awake — and to make sure there were no more imperial spies around.

In reaching for the cash in her pack, her fingers encountered metal — the silver feather pin she had stuffed inside her sleeve when she and Shigan escaped the Shadow Panthers. First thing she could do was keep a promise she had made, and see if she was being followed while she did it.

She looked at the rooftops and spotted the pagoda of a temple. She remembered the smaller Snow Crane temple near the large one, and made her way there, stopping once to get some wine.

As soon as she walked in, the familiar smell of incense, the very old, weather-worn, well-beloved statue of Suanek still with a trace of a beatific smile in the age-furrowed face, threw her spirit back in memory. Not to a place — there had been no temple at Sweetwater, which was too poor, and too small. But the incense, the sutras, the stillness when everyone gathered before the shaman, that she remembered. For a moment she was small Mouse again, kneeling between her parents, who were so very tall and strong and safe at her sides . . .

She blinked very fast, fighting tears. Not now, not here. She was supposed to avoid attention, not draw it.

She lit incense, offered a prayer for her family, and for Redbark, each now following a separate path. That included Yaso, who she hoped to see again.

Then she poured out the wine before the altar, and as she did, she prayed silently to the gods that if First Brother Banig was to be sent back into the world, his soul might choose a family that loved him, as hers had; that he would choose a teacher like Ul Keg, who would give him respect as well as knowledge, and friends who would help him toward justice.

Her last thought, as she laid the silver feather pin on the altar beside other gifts, was of Shigan. Keep him safe, she whispered to the Snow Crane, God of the Abandoned. He walked into the grip of the enemy rather than see anyone dead—keep him safe.

When she rose, she cast a quick look around. She saw no one suspicious, but she still felt as if unseen eyes followed her.

She went to one of the street vendors and bought hawthorn candies, then wandered to a shady place squeezed between a girl her age selling charms and a gaunt, patched scholar offering to calculate birth lines and divinations, or to write letters. The charms were simple luck talismans, badly drawn. She sensed no Essence in them. Any serious scholar of Essence, Mother had said when Ryu was small, knows that you don't really "catch" good luck. Just as you can't truly ward bad luck—the warding gesture is a mental turning away from evil. Wards have to be specific. At least the luck charms are harmless—at most they are like putting out a tea cup in hopes of catching a specific raindrop.

The charm vendor's owl-like call, "Booo-Sisi! Boooo-Sisi!", for the charms to invoke the demon to eat nightmares, clashed with the vendor across the way bawling, "Shoes! Shoes!" At least the nightmare-eater is specific, Ryu thought. Though how much Essence was in those charms? She couldn't sense any from where she sat hunched down, back to a rough stone wall as she slowly ate the hawthorns and watched every person. Every wandering vendor.

When she'd eaten the last hawthorn and licked her fingers, she drifted up the street behind a group of noisy apprentices until she found a shop through which she could see to the back door. She dashed through and bolted up a narrow alley, then charged through the open door of another shop as laborers carried heavy trunks out.

She skipped through the shop and out again, repeating the pattern until she spotted a complication of roofs, gathered her fading strength, and leaped up. She crouched there, making sure she could not be seen from any windows. There were no upper stories to the buildings here, only on the hill, and those were too far away for her to be seen, though she spidered her way over the slant of the roof to the other side, overlooking the sea, just in case.

Here she sat, trying to figure out what to do. A disguise. As what?

She looked down into a minute court no bigger than a blanket, where a girl watched two or three very small children toddling about.

A girl.

A disguise hiding a disguise? Or was it time to go back to being herself? Except who was she, really?

Ayah! She had often complained to herself about living as a boy. There was no more Redbark before whom she had to maintain her disguise. There was no Redbark—no more Ryu.

The realization made her shiver. She felt so . . . strange, as if she had slipped and the world had changed around her. Were the gods laughing?

She slipped down from the roof and made her way to the more modest shops on side streets. She first changed one of her gold coins, as more than one of those always raised eyebrows unless you were a noble. Then, loaded down with strings of cash, she went to different vendors. From one she bought a girl over-robe and under-robe like the things Petal had worn. From a stall at a crossroad she bought a ribbon, and from a vendor her own age a little silken purse.

From another vendor she bought a bigger shoulder carryall, into which she could fit her other clothes, and her staff in its two pieces. She then bought a pair of indoor slippers. She kept her nice new boot. Women in the gallant wanderers wore boots, too. The robe would cover them anyway.

That done, it was time to assume her new . . . disguise? She was done with disguises. Except she didn't know who she was when she wasn't Ryu. Could she be Afan Arikanda? But that felt like a disguise!

Perhaps it was the right idea but the wrong way to think about it. The imperials did not know who Afan Arikanda was, so she was free to find out. As for the name Ryu, she could leave that to Muin now, and there would be no danger any- more of someone hearing of Ryu of Redbark and connecting it to Ryu Muin of the army, which might cause him trouble, and impede his path.

She made her way to an alley between two buildings, overshadowed by an old cypress. As she looked at her new things, she suddenly remembered the morning after Ul Keg had told her The Story, how her mother had talked about guilt, and beauty, and half a dozen things that she now understood, more or less: men still mostly ruled the civilized world, because the oldest laws and traditions had been made by them.

She grinned. Though she had never seen a mirror, she knew from others' reactions to her that she was not, and never would be, beautiful, and as for the rest, thanks to Father, she could very well take care of herself. She had escaped many of the problems other women faced by living as a boy. It was time to join those proving that girls could do just as well in the wandering world. Even if at first it felt far more false than Ryu or even Orderly Mouse.

She held out her rose-colored new robe, aware that she had never actually owned any girl clothes. Mother had been saving her own carefully preserved things for when she grew; meantime she'd been like a third brother . . .

Yes. There was a rightness to this decision.

First she tied the ribbon to the silken purse, then transferred the two Restoration Pills from her sash to the silken purse. Over it she whispered a water-warding charm, and pushed Essence into it. She hung it around her neck.

Then it was time for the clothes.

She kept her underthings, at first leaving off, for the first time, the binding that had flattened her small breasts. But it felt strange not to wear it. She disliked the way she felt — as if she were unclothed. She put it back on, but looser, and made a mental promise to herself to find out what girls actually wore under their clothes. Then came the outer clothes — the under-robe, the over-robe. She still wore trousers, but the flowing panels of the robes effectively hid them.

She folded the left panel of the over-robe to her right hip, then tied everything in place with the plain sash she'd bought. Ready! No — there was her hair. What to do about that? She'd worn the boy's topknot all her life, and the headband of a warrior.

She pulled off the headband, her forehead feeling strange — cool. She took out the hair clasp she had chosen for its plainness. Her heavy hair whumped onto her shoulders and back, flyaway bits immediately getting into her face. She held it out in both hands. It was thick, and so heavy that the old wild curls had lengthened into waves. She knew how to braid strings, but when she tried to braid her hair, it kept escaping, snarling and flying all over the place.

She sighed, then remembered that common girls wore their hair down at least in part, though of course warrior girls wore topknots or braids and headbands. But right now she did not want to look like a warrior, until she was well away from any imperials still slinking around.

She tried gathering the hair growing over her ears, added it to that on the top of her head, and pulled it up. Her fingers knew how to make a topknot, so she did that, and then, with the strangest sensation, she secured it with Shigan's tiger-eye pin. Her mind shot her straight back to Shigan's first day at Loyalty, and his drunken mess of a topknot. She heard his voice again, so close to her ear the night before, warm with laughter as he admitted to not knowing how to dress himself before he came to Loyalty Fortress.

She felt again the warmth of his fingers as he pressed the tiger-eye hairpin into her hand.

She shivered. He was gone. Forever. Maybe even dead. Who knew what that emperor would do.

She gritted her teeth against the knot throbbing in her heart, the ache of her throat, the sting of tears along her eyelids. Life was full of farewells and sorrows, so those old poems always said. It was also full of joy and surprises, and Ul Keg had insisted that a person had to look for those.

Therefore she would not think of him dead.

She looked down at herself. Everything seemed all right, and was definitely different from the way Ryu of Redbark always looked. She pushed the bottom part of her loose hair off her shoulders to hang down her back, then touched the tiger-eye pin once more.

She closed her eyes, faced east, and wished Shigan joy.

Then she faced southwest, bowed, thanked her parents for her birth, and promised to go forth into the world as Afan Arikanda again—

Ayah, no, there was still the danger of that emperor whose terrifying reach had taken Shigan away, and nearly snatched her. She would go into the world as Ari. Yes. The rest could come.

She bowed a last time, picked up her carryall, stuffed the boots and clothes into it, then set out, intensely self-conscious.

The shadows had begun to slant. Time to make her way

back to the wharf.

People! She held her breath . . . They passed.

That was another good thing about not being beautiful, she thought with weary relief as she made her way downhill. No one gave Ari a second glance.

.

# TWO

TWO DAYS OUT TO sea, Fai Anbai, chief of the emperor's ferrets, stood at the rail of the flagship, which was flanked by two
fully armed warships as well as three fast couriers. He
breathed in the summer wind scouring over the gray-green,
tossing waves. Oh, success was so sweet. He and his team had
done the impossible: tracked down and rescued — captured —
*liberated* the emperor's first son, and without a hair harmed on
the worthless prince's head.

Fai Anbai stood alone because he knew he had to wrestle
his (quite natural) emotions under control. Every eye watched,
every word was listened to by the ship's crew and the imperial
guards who came along as adjuncts to protecting an imperial
prince. The emperor would want it all, to the last detail. Fai
Anbai could not betray by so much as a flicker of an eyelash
his determination that, should the emperor decide to execute
said son, he meant to be there to see it, even though it would
never last as long as had this damned search. But he'd relish it,
oh yes, he would . . .

Until that justly deserved fate, he and his elite ferrets
would scrupulously observe the protocols, affording First
Imperial Prince Jion the respect due to his rank. Equally
important, they would exert themselves to see that he reached
the imperial palace intact. There would be no hurling himself
over the side to drown in a fit of petulance at having his years-

long spree of self-indulgence curtailed.

Fai Anbai walked along the rail and gazed out over the water, reminded of a time when he was very small, before he left his home in the imperial city to begin the grueling training that had led to where he was now. He'd had a garrulous old auntie who'd often said, "Children of nobles, and royals . . ." She'd raised her fingers to her lips and dropped her voice on the word *royals* as if someone (like him) lurked in the shadows of the family home, ready to arrest the family for disrespect to rank. ". . . they're brought up so delicately that their bodies cannot tolerate the slightest hardship. Especially if they are spoilt. When families spoil their children, it overloads their luck."

Your luck certainly ran out, Fai Anbai thought mordantly as he cast a scorching glance back toward the other end of the deck, where the prince walked about, dressed in silk and jade ornaments, his braided hair glinting with gold and pearls.

The slight sound of soft slippers on the deck caused Fai Anbai to turn.

The only person on board who dared to approach him (for they all sensed his mood, though his face remained inscrutable) was Whiteleaf, the gentle little graywing who had been the prince's steward from childhood. It was impossible to know how old Whiteleaf was: the denaturing charms that left graywings effectively castrated without resorting to the knife guaranteed the smooth, round face of youth until suddenly their hair whitened and their skin sagged like soft dough, at extreme old age. His general age could be guessed by his name, Whiteleaf, which meant he belonged to the "tea generation" of graywings — those graywings who had care of the emperor's generation.

Fai Anbai had not wanted to bring Whiteleaf along for what he knew would be a strenuous, stressful search. The graywing had nearly died of illness a few years before, and previous to that had been raised to palace duties and all its comforts. Unlike the ferrets, who were inured early to long days of arduous travel and the extremes of hot and cold. Yet Whiteleaf had endured without complaint, and more to the point, had proved to be crucially important in this search, not just once, but twice.

"Steward Whiteleaf?" Chief Fai said.

Whiteleaf looked unhappy. "The prince is not eating. I am

so worried. If we could stop somewhere for things I know he once liked."

Heat and fury corroded Fai Anbai's throat. He managed an even tone as he said, "Is he refusing to eat?" And he let himself envision tying the spoilt prince up and forcing food down his throat.

"Oh, no," Whiteleaf said earnestly. "He always thanks me for whatever I bring, and he eats a bite or two, and even praises it, but then he seems to lose his appetite, and it all goes cold before he apologizes and says he's not hungry."

Apologizes? That did not sound like First Imperial Prince Jion in the least. In the sweetness of much-prolonged victory, Fai Anbai permitted himself a little sarcasm. "Are you certain we have the right person?"

Whiteleaf looked startled, then disconcerted, and Chief Fai forced a smile. "I'm joking, Graywing Whiteleaf. I know you identified our imperial prince correctly — and all credit will go to you. And to Agent Tek Banu for setting us on the right path."

Whiteleaf flushed, and bowed, his smooth, callus-free hands pressed together. Then he said, "May we stop?"

Fai Anbai said diplomatically, "The emperor's orders were clear: we must return with all speed. But we can speak with the cooks aboard the other warships, if you like, and see if they might have what you require."

Whiteleaf thanked him and trotted off, pausing only once to bow before the prince, who had grown so very tall in the years he had been missing. "May this lowly servitor beg forgiveness for interrupting your imperial highness's reflections?"

For four glorious years, Jion had lived as Shigan, an ordinary mortal, first as an ordinary army cadet, then as a gallant wanderer of the Redbark Sect. Now finding himself forced back into the constraints of imperial princedom, he suppressed a sigh. He longed to tell Whiteleaf just to talk, but the graywing's humble words were a reminder that Jion could no longer expect the easy speech of the gallant wanderer world. Furthermore, to assume it would be dangerous. "Please rise. What is it?"

"This lowly incompetent has gained permission to inquire of the other ships for different foods, and wishes only to beg his imperial highness to inform this worthless servant if he has new favorites?"

"Anything is fine, Whiteleaf."

Whiteleaf knew that was not true, or he wouldn't have the question, but he dared not begin what might sound like an argument. Promising to do better, he took himself off to make his list.

Jion watched him go, knowing that Whiteleaf was upset that he hadn't done justice to his cooking. Once again the invisible obligations tightened around him. He could say that he was not hungry, but he could not say, though it was true, that the sight of food upset a stomach already churning with regret and disappointment. Impotent fury. Because he had that very first day, in spite of the haze of exhaustion, become aware of the wall of moral outrage shared by every single person aboard this ship—with him as the target.

The first sign had been when he walked out of the entertainment house to say to Fai Anbai, "The people I was with know nothing. I hope you will let them be."

Chief Fai had regarded him with the flat, unwinking gaze of cold loathing before giving a nod to a squad, then raised his hand in the signal to bow. And when that mockery had reminded Jion who truly held the whip-hand, the entire formation had closed around Shigan, an even more effective reminder that once again he was utterly powerless.

On the march to the harbor, and as they came aboard, he had looked into familiar faces of imperial guards who used to give him a smile as they saluted, and saw utter dispassion above those salutes.

Ironic, wasn't it, he thought later as he lay down at last to try to catch up on lost sleep. He did not want to be here. They clearly did not welcome him back. But all was as it was because of the will of the emperor, felt throughout all the Empire of the Thousand Islands.

And so, here he was, trying to fit back into the identity of Jehan Jion, First Imperial Prince. As a gallant wanderer he had been able to command himself. As an imperial prince, he did not even have that.

When he woke, there was a graywing waiting beside his bedside with tea to rinse his mouth. He had a wooden bath waiting—the water having been boiled somewhere and lugged in by the bucketful, the labor for which he never would have given a thought before his days as Shigan—and waiting hands to scrub him and wash and oil his hair, and to scrape the hairs off his chin and upper lip, as noble parents still expected their young men to go cleanshaven until they married.

After the bath he had to stand while those hands dried and dressed him in silken clothing—the graywings must have sewn through the first night as he slept, his gallant wanderer clothes no doubt used for measure, and then whisked into nonexistence. Then a heavy belt of jade and silver, from which depended a beautifully carved jade ornament with its long silken tassel. As those soft hands dressed him, he willed himself to submit to it, thinking back to his first exhilarating, and exasperating, and frightening days of freedom, when he'd had to learn how to dress himself.

Then he had to sit while those patient fingers braided his hair, and placed his old golden hair clasp in it. No longer could he wear the headband of the warrior. All he had left to him of Shigan was the necklace Ryu had given him, which Whiteleaf had not touched—more surprisingly, had paid no attention to.

What even was a Restoration Pill? Probably an antidote to poison. It might even work. But no pill, he thought with bitter humor, would restore his head to his body. Or fix crushed and wrenched joints and flesh, if the death was to be especially salutary for the spectators.

He touched the necklace through his clothes, then dropped his hand, not certain who was watching, though he knew he was watched. And no doubt every word he spoke, every move he made, was being written into some report.

At least he was permitted to feed himself. Except that he couldn't eat. He was confined to this ship, restless and unable to do anything but walk about on the deck. He couldn't even do Redbark drills.

That is, he could. For a moment he let himself imagine it. Then he imagined his father hearing about it . . . That reunion was already going to be bad enough. Possibly even fatal, depending on Imperial Father's mood. Doing Redbark in front of all those watching eyes would be extra wood on the fire, as the imperial children had, by the emperor's decree, been forbidden to train in arms.

He gazed moodily out at the sea. Of course they had to have some idea what he'd been doing. Fai Anbai and the imperials showing up when they had was no accident. Their appearance had been carefully calculated, which meant that the ferrets had to have heard at least some of the rumors about Firebolt and Redbark Sect. But he'd have to pretend to know nothing, at least until he understood his status when they got back to the imperial palace. Just as ministers at court began some criticism or suggestion with statements like, "I am a mere ignorant person of no talent, but . . ."

Only he did not get to have a *but*.

While Jion sailed inexorably back toward the imperial palace, Afan Yskanda, already confined there, hugged to himself the dream that Ul Keg had given him by offering to aid him in escape if he could just reach the Phoenix Moon God temple in the imperial city.

Of course the dream always began with Yskanda somehow managing to reach the streets of the imperial city without being noticed. That was all right. He knew it was just a dream, and would remain so. He could not endanger this good, generous, kindly monk — or the unknown acolytes. If he were to gain his freedom, it must be by his own efforts.

And so life went on, but it could not be called bad. He worked through the portrait of the first consort, who was unexpectedly talkative. And inquisitive. He answered questions with harmless anecdotes about Master Bankan's lessons, or about life in the forest as a child — nothing about his family, ever.

She was a kindly woman, but it was a relief when he finished her portrait.

Then came the very minor problem of how to sign it. In class he'd signed his full name to differentiate himself from others, for he'd encountered a few Afans, all south-islanders. Until now he'd left his name off the imperial portraits, aware of his lowly position as an assistant. It might be regarded as presumptuous. But now that he had been appointed as portraitist of the imperial family, it would be considered remiss if he did not sign those portraits.

He thought about it for a time, until he remembered his initial encounter with fine brushes and ink, when he and First Brother and Mouse ventured to the harbor city in the boat they had made themselves.

Since then he had often recalled the sheer pleasure of discovering what good ink and brushes could accomplish. And then he had it. Of course it had to be a feather. If anyone noticed, they would take it as a symbol for Afan. That was fine. But only he would know that it also stood for the phoenix feather, which symbolized their parents' faith in First Brother's eventual greatness. Yskanda had no doubt whatsoever that as soon as Muin discovered where he was, he would swoop in to rescue him, the way he'd rescued Yskanda from the bullying twins when they were small. And the feather would also signify little Mouse, always so inquisitive, leaping from branch to branch in trees like a small bird.

By now he was well practiced in the stroke that would convey the effect of feathering. A single stroke — just so — and there it was, his new signature, down in the corner.

That portrait was now finished. He sent a formal message to the second imperial consort, begging her to choose a time convenient to her. This was granted through a message from a graywing, making it plain that the second imperial consort assented because this was the emperor's wish.

No doubt the message was intended to remind Yskanda of his humble place in the world, but he was already well aware of it, and his only reaction was relief that she cooperated.

A relief only in one sense: she remained utterly silent, clearly tolerating his presence only because the emperor willed it so. She was very beautiful, but her portrait was his least successful, for, like her daughter, there was no discerning the person behind the exquisitely made up features. He confined himself to reproducing all her jewels and embroidery with equally exquisite detail. And, like her daughter, she approved of this utterly lifeless portrait, with its realistic depiction of jewels, embroidery, and dangling golden chains, the accoutrements of power.

Between those sittings, he attended court with the court artist. By now he was getting very good at picking up the old man and carrying him to and from his cart. They were back to their regular schedule as much as possible, Yskanda serving as legs for them both as Court Artist Yoli's old bones slowly mended.

Yskanda had begun the third imperial consort's portrait when everything changed.

# THREE

THE DAYS BLENDED SWIFTLY into one another for the ships conveying First Imperial Prince Jion back to the imperial island.

Jion remained mostly in the spacious, airy cabin that had been set aside for him, only he was never alone. Whiteleaf was always there, striving to anticipate his prince's every wish, though the prince seldom spoke.

His appetite returned, which made Whiteleaf happy, at least. And Fai Anbai could almost have forgotten he was even on board, so quiet he was, making no demands except early on, for something to read. The irony did not escape Jion when he was given a copy of *The Five Elements* and *The Dialects of Enlightenment*, but he sat at the desk he'd been provided, ground his own ink, and began recopying them as a way to get through the long days. His hands, four years accustomed to wielding staff and sword, had to relearn the subtleties of calligraphy. His handwriting was worse than it had ever been.

Fai Anbai knew they were a week or so out from the imperial island by the behavior of the pigeons in the cages. He had spent some nights writing his report for the emperor, considering what was best left to be spoken aloud in the expected interview.

He also wondered, for the ten thousandth time, whether his first child, born during the chase, was boy or girl: other than the word that had come of his wife's pregnancy (the scribe on pigeon duty at that time being her cousin), there had been no personal news for anyone.

As expected, not quite two days later, a pigeon fluttered down to its cage on the deck. Around its leg was fitted a tiny scroll covered with minute handwriting. No surprises in those orders.

He considered what to do first, then summoned Tek Banu, his senior investigator. He was always scrupulously careful dealing with her; he knew she resented having been passed over for command of the ferrets. Most especially as in this case, there was no question of gender preference. The ferrets had been started by a woman, and women had been chiefs.

When Tek Banu appeared, blank of face and crisp of salute, he said, "I just received word. As promised, the emperor has granted the elites an immediate liberty, to make up in part for three years of effort with no time off."

Her face did not change—as usual. "How long, sir?"

"How long do we have?"

"Yes, sir."

"I don't know. I would think a Phoenix Moon month, two at the outside if there was something special in a family. I know that Reneg's wedding was put off twice first because of the search to Imai, then this chase."

She gave a curt salute. "I will forgo liberty if I may request a private interview with the emperor, sir."

Fai Anbai's heart sank. This could not be anything good, all his instincts clamored. But there was no possible reason to deny her request. After all, it might not be granted.

Summer was waning when they came into sight of land. After a stretch of beautiful days, they woke to gray skies and seas, and a cold wind, a taste of the winter to come. As if, Fai Anbai thought, the gods themselves were passing judgment on that spoilt prince.

Who came up on deck when the shout echoed around the ship that land had been sighted.

He was perfectly appointed, outwardly at least the ideal imperial prince. When Fai Anbai made his bow, the imperial prince nodded, then surprisingly came to stand beside the ferret chief at the rail. They had not exchanged a word since the day the prince was recovered.

"You know he's probably going to kill me," the prince said

conversationally.

Rightly deserved, Fai Anbai thought—though with less heat than he'd begun this journey. He said stolidly, "That's between your imperial highness and his imperial majesty."

Color ridged Imperial Prince Jion's splendid cheekbones, but he said only, "I mention that in case I do not get a chance to speak. I overheard talk by Screaming Hawk, about their leader Master Night, that he might find interesting—"

Here Fai Anbai bowed as he cut in, his words at the most formal and distancing third person, his tone flat as a blade. "This servitor of his imperial majesty must observe, in spite of his imperial highness's gracious deigning to speak, that military matters are not his purview. And it must be added, surely those into whose custody Screaming Hawk was surrendered will know how to extract any useful information he possesses."

First Imperial Prince Jion gazed out to sea, his hands behind his back, apparently impervious to thundering snubs. "I don't think torture will work on him," he observed, as if they were discussing the weather. "Especially to reveal who's behind him. I suspect it's a noble, one who makes even him fear."

Then he turned away. They both remained on deck as the ships drew into the harbor, which had been cleared of other vessels. Rain began spitting, cold and stinging, but the prince stayed where he was as gigantic splotches marred his embroidered silk.

The flagship drew up to the wharf, where a palanquin waited, surrounded by guards, all ignoring the increasing rain.

The imperial prince was the first off the ship, two huge guards leading the way, bare steel in hand, ready for anything. More guards lined the wharf, and were poised with crossbows on walls and rooftops.

But nothing happened as the two bodyguards, the prince, then Fai Anbai, proceeded down the ramp and up the wharf to where the palanquin awaited: it was the emperor himself, they saw, as the curtain drew aside.

The guards fell to their knees as one, as rain pounded helmets, backs, bared swords.

First Imperial Prince Jion bowed low.

"Look up," said the emperor.

Father and son regarded one another for a few heartbeats, the son wet through, the father pale as death, except for dark red along the splendid cheekbones so like the son's.

"Through the west gate," the emperor said curtly to Fai Anbai.

The prince said nothing, but paled to a deathly shade: the west gate was the military gate, giving onto the prison and the execution ground.

Then the emperor slightly mitigated the order. "You, to the ancestral shrine for reflection," he said to the prince. And to Fai Anbai, "Bitternail will bring you to me for your report." Meaning merely the emperor did not want a public entrance, as no one but military (and ferrets) used the west gate.

The curtain fell, the bearers picked up the palanquin, as the imperial guard rose. They silently accompanied both imperials toward the west gate, leaving Fan Anbai to dismiss his ferrets to their well-earned rest.

He thought of his wife and child. But that must wait; Bitternail held out a towel, and Fai Anbai slid the last of his gold into the graywing's hand.

Once again, Fai Anbai walked along byways, out of sight of the enormous population of the imperial palace, though he strongly suspected that word was winging its way about in whispers: the imperial prince had returned, and entered on the west side.

The emperor awaited him with thundering heart. The joy he had felt when that first report was brought: *He is alive, on his way* had been so fierce it was painful.

So fierce, that the anger sparked by the sight of Jion in person — tall, strong, exuberantly healthy — had been equally incandescent. How inexplicable, that he wanted nothing more than for Jion to be alive and well, yet he when he actually saw that Jion was not at all in a wretched, pitiful state, his temper had ignited.

He awaited Fai Anbai in the private interview room, mentally ordering the questions that had tormented him over the past nights as pigeons winged from ship to shore and back again.

Fai Anbai followed Bitternail, mentally rehearsing the report that had kept him awake for nights.

When at last he made his bows, and the emperor bade him speak plainly, he said, "The credit for closing the trail goes to Senior Agent Tek Banu and Graywing Whiteleaf respectively, your imperial majesty. Graywing Whiteleaf was recommended by Graywing Chief Bitternail, and proved his value by sorting various rumors we received. It was he who insisted we ought to follow anything having to do with musicians, music, or dance — "

"Music?" the emperor repeated. "I thought he was chasing those outlaws — no, go on."

"Tek Banu discovered, and Graywing Whiteleaf identified, a poster that he believed depicted the imperial prince, your imperial majesty. His imperial highness was identified as a dancer named The Comet. He appeared to be traveling with members of an obscure sect called Redbark, under the leadership of a criminal known as Firebolt. They were on their way to a martial arts competition in one of the northwest islands. So far, we have not been able to discover much about this Redbark Sect. We began moving very fast once we discovered that the prince had been captured by scouts from another sect, the Shadow Panthers."

The emperor said, "Understood. There must be as many obscure sects as there are islands. If this one is not on any watch or capital list, it can wait unless there is some other reason to pursue it. Go on."

"The full report is here, you imperial majesty," Fai Anbai said, holding out a sheaf of papers to Bitternail. He'd copied it over no fewer than five times, deleting and amending each time, as he decided what was to be spoken verbally (leaving no tangible record) and what could be written. "It lists all our false trails and resifting of information — our goal being, as you ordered, as covert an investigation as possible, given the lack of success during the initial search."

That, he thought, was neutral enough, passing no comment on the futility of the army's previous strongarm tactics at ramming through cities (sending all criminals scuttling for hidey holes) and pouring out silver for what had proved to be completely faulty information. The army ought never to have been entrusted with a search; however, that had been an imperial order, made in the heat of a moment. It was this tact that Fai Anbai's father had inculcated in him, at least as important as investigative skills, if one was to be facing the emperor.

"I've heard of the Shadow Panther Sect," the emperor said grimly. "They were put forth as possible suspects in the assault on Loyalty Fortress some time back."

Fai Anbai was too well-trained to agree with that assumption without seeing the evidence — and too experienced to deny it. "By the time I got a detachment from Emerald Bay to reinforce my elites, your imperial majesty, we were half a day late: we arrived on the horizon to discover the stronghold burning, dead and wounded sect members scattered over that end of the island, and the Redbark group, with his imperial highness, on the run."

"How many in this Redbark Sect against how many Shadow Panthers?" the emperor asked.

"The initial information was confusing, your imperial majesty. Some insisted Redbark is three, sometimes five, at most, but that the fight involved twenty or thirty outlaws against the Shadow Panther criminals, a force at least twice in number. We believe an allied sect came to the Redbarks' aid, then vanished again. We also discovered that the chief of that arm of the Shadow Panthers was leading the pursuit on an adjacent island. While the criminals did the searching, I put together a plan to round them up, as well as our target, thus protecting his identity."

"Excellent," the emperor said. "Did you corral this Firebolt as well?"

"We did not, your imperial majesty," Fai Anbai had to admit. "Information was confusing as to the identity of the Redbark Sect chief, and our main concern was with his imperial highness Prince Jion, who might be constrained against his will. When my scout discovered that he was traveling freely with three youths and a young man who carried an herbalist's satchel, we turned our attention to the Shadow Panthers, who were mounting a vigorous chase."

The emperor waved a hand, dismissing these nonentities. "Well done — very well done. Anything else can wait. You may leave now, and be sure to let me know what you would like as your reward. I did promise."

Fai Anbai bowed, knowing what to say to that: "Nothing, your imperial majesty. It is my honor to serve." He then had to keep his promise to Tek Banu. He'd decided to wait till the end of his interview in hopes that the emperor would be finished with them all. "There is one more matter, your imperial majesty."

"Which is?"

"My senior agent, Tek Banu, requests a private interview

with your imperial majesty." And waited for irritation—
impatience—an acerbic comment on presumption.

None of those came. The emperor was in an expansive
mood: Jion was alive. And home. "Tell Bitternail I am at leis-
ure," he said.

Fai Anbai had to bow himself out. He found Bitternail with
Tek Banu, who had not been offered a towel; Fai Anbai realized that Bitternail knew Tek Banu, who had never been
known to tip graywings, though she did disperse money for
information when in the field.

"He is waiting," Fai Anbai said—and wanted to add, *Keep
it short*, but Tek Banu was senior to him in age, though not in
rank. In any case they had never had any relationship except
the most formal, strictly duty.

He walked away, mentally shedding the entire matter:
now, at last, to see his wife, and meet his child.

Tek Banu was escorted into the interview chamber, where
she prostrated herself. "You asked to speak to me," the emper-
or prompted.

Tek Banu's world was made up of lines and squares, dark
and light. All constantly threatened to shatter into chaos unless
the forces who upheld order were vigilant. Order equaled
justice, dealt with steel and blood. Order was built upon the
sturdy foundation of hierarchy.

Dis-order was evil.

Chief Fai Senior had had her utter loyalty until he retired—
and instead of appointing her as new chief, as was her right as
senior agent, he had handed the ferrets off to his son. The ferrets were not a hereditary body. Ever since that miscarriage of
justice, order, and right, she yearned for one thing: her proper
place. The place she had *earned*.

She said, "Your imperial majesty has granted us liberty."

That flat, slightly strident voice—the emperor remembered now why he had agreed to bypass her in favor of Chief Fai's
son Anbai. This was the agent the former chief had likened to
a hungry wolf in pursuit of a cricket, the kind of wolf who
always ravaged, and always won. But unlike wolves, she did
not work well with others, preferring to hunt alone.

"I have," he said. "Did you want to ask for another reward?"

"This lowly agent desires only to serve, your imperial majesty," she stated flatly. "Before we were ordered to find First

Imperial Prince Jion, I saw the assistant court artist. I know that face. That is the son of Danno, the traitor captain of the guard at Pear Tree Garden Pavilion. Once I rip the truth out of him, I will not return until I bring you Danno's head. And the woman's, if you so order."

The emperor had stilled when he heard Danno's name spoken. He did not, at all, like any reminder of what he had come to regard as his private game. "I believe," the emperor said, "that what happens or does not happen to Assistant Court Artist Afan Yskanda is my decision."

Tek Banu blinked once or twice as she struggled to assimilate the fact that she had made a misstep. Then she had it — did she sound like she had superseded the proper chain of command? "This agent will not act except on orders, your imperial majesty." She bowed stiffly, rather like a wooden puppet.

The emperor was about to point out that she had already superseded orders in bypassing Chief Fai Anbai, then shrugged that off. Perhaps he could make use of so straightforward an individual — if he was precise in his orders. But first, "What do you expect in trade?"

And there it was. Without hesitation, she stated flatly, "Restoration of my right as senior agent: give me command of the ferrets."

The emperor had by now subdued — or thought he had subdued — his anger. He clapped his hands onto his knees. "Very well. Leave Afan Yskanda alone. I have plans for him. Use the initial investigation from Fai Anbai to begin your search. If you bring me Danno — preferably alive — you will have what you ask. I much prefer alive, understand. Do what you like about the woman, if they are even still together," he added belatedly, having no particular desire to see Alk Hanu again, whether or not she was now known as Ugly Iley.

Tek Banu, having come this far, said, "I would like to ask one thing more, your imperial majesty — "

"You want this to be a secret mission," the emperor said. "I think that was implied from the moment you walked in here, or you would have gone through the chief you wish to replace." He waved a hand, and Bitternail stepped to her side.

She was less amazed at the emperor's apparent omniscience than at having gotten all that she wanted. But then, she ought not to have. Who would understand proper order more than the emperor?

# FOUR

"ANOTHER SET OF SCREENS?" Yskanda asked as he lifted Court Artist Yoli from his cart and set him on his cushion, then helped him settle his still-healing leg. By now he was so used to lifting and carrying the old man that he didn't even grunt.

"You haven't figured it out?" Yoli asked, bristling brows raised. "Ayah! I keep forgetting you were not raised to palace life. All the new screens and decorative scrolls will soon be followed by an army of young apprentices repainting walls and everything else. There is talk of an imperial wedding."

"Oh?" Yskanda asked, turning to survey his table of colors. "Who?"

"First Imperial Princess, of course. She's of age. Has been for a year, but no one refers to that." He observed Yskanda's air of distraction as he counted over his colors, and smiled wryly. "No reaction? You're not in love with the beautiful princess? You must be the only young man in the palace who isn't."

"She is very beautiful," Yskanda said readily.

Yoli grinned at the lack of ardency. "But?"

"But in the way of a killing frost. Bright and glittering, yet ..." *Deadly.* He couldn't bring himself to say that about so beautiful a person who everyone praised as a loyal, well-behaved, ideal imperial princess.

"Yes. Exactly like her mother, who was known as one of

the Three Beauties of the capital in her day. What you don't seem to realize, or be interested in, is that this marriage, when it happens, might very well determine the future of the empire. The Su clan of course will want any potential consort to adopt into the imperial clan. Which will only happen if she is moved into the Pavilion of Sun's Grace as the imperial heir. If she marries out, then someone else will be regarded as heir." He added under his breath, "But I wouldn't plan on that." And in his normal tone, "Notice that many of these older screens are in the peony and golden phoenix mode."

Yskanda was scarcely listening—he was wondering if the period of the Three Beauties was before or after his own mother had been so briefly in the capital, and were there any pictures? Suddenly he wanted very badly to go to the archive, but this he kept to himself. "Shall I get down the ground oyster-shell? It seems we will need more white." He climbed onto a stool to reach a jar on one of the overhead shelves. "Oh no," he murmured as he stepped down. "This is nearly empty."

"Send the page—no. Run yourself. If there's a line, you'll get it faster. Make certain you get extra safflower red, red powder-gold, and at least 200 sheets of gold foil."

Yskanda repeated this list to himself, mentally added to it from his own desk, and departed, taking a route that kept the rain off him. He took a shortcut through Bright on his way to the supply building, outside of which he nearly ran into a group of ninth rank scribes talking in low voices.

They broke apart when they saw his hat and robe, then Senye Tan exclaimed, "It's Handsome Afan! *He's* close as a clam. Afan, have you heard the news?"

After their time together, Senye Tan still had not learned that Yskanda would never answer but with a cautious, "What news?"

"The prince is back!" Senye Tan lowered his voice and looked around for spies.

"Which prince?" Yskanda asked.

Senye Tan laughed, and several gave Yskanda incredulous glances.

"Afan's always got his head in the paints," Senye Tan said to them, then turned back to Yskanda. "Remember the First Imperial Prince? Oh, but he was sent off around the time you came, I remember. But even you have to remember word going around that he'd vanished. Ayah, he's back!"

Yskanda's first thought was, oh no, another imperial family drawing—just as he was finishing with the third consort. But the way Senye Tan's countenance turned serious sent faint alarm through him.

Senye Tan stepped close, saying low-voiced, "You really didn't hear about the harbor cleared of all vessels this morning, before the rain? Gen Xunek swears he saw the prince at the west gate."

"Does that mean . . ." Yskanda grimaced. Wasn't this prince his own age? He loathed the thought of any execution, but the idea of it being someone his age was somehow more . . . immediate.

"No one knows. But be on your best behavior at court tomorrow."

As if Yskanda was ever not on his best behavior! But he knew Senye Tan meant well, and thanked him.

Senye Tan gave Yskanda a proprietary pat on the shoulder, and walked on, whispering to his followers.

Yskanda carried on, retrieved his supplies, and started back. Two or three times he spotted, or heard, whispering knots of people who kept an anxious eye for guards or graywings. When he got back to the court artist's workroom, he said, "The entire palace seems to be whispering about the return of the first prince. Not through the imperial gate, or even ours, but the military one. What does that mean?"

"Nothing good." Court Artist Yoli's expression tightened, uncharacteristically grim. "The degree remains to be seen." He said no more than that; of all the imperial children this one had been his favorite, a rascal, but one with a good heart.

They worked through the hours of Phoenix. Noon came and went, Yskanda going to fetch the meal for the court artist as well as himself. They often shared meals in the workroom; because Yskanda was to lose the afternoon to the portrait of the third imperial consort, he and the court artist ate while they discussed the screens and considered marriage and fruitfulness symbols.

The Horse hours passed, until the warning gong before the last, the signal for Yskanda to lay aside his work and collect his implements for what he hoped would be his last hour with the third imperial consort. The weather had worsened.

He passed from awning to awning, head bowed against

the rain. At a grand moon gate carved of pale stone, he sent a glance into the isolated courtyard before the imperial ancestral shrine. It had been empty every time Yskanda passed, save on New Year's Day, when the entire imperial family gathered for the ritual.

Today it was not empty. Yskanda caught sight of a single figure kneeling on the streaming flagstones. Yskanda checked, staring at that sodden figure with black hair hanging in snake-locks down his back, to his feet placed precisely together, toes of his slippers just visible beneath the rumpled hem of his sodden silk robe. He was taller than Second Prince Vaion, straight-shouldered and muscled like a feline, judging by the silk clinging to his body. As Yskanda watched he began to topple, then jerked himself upright. The weariness in that rigid figure snapped into a muscle-locked stiffness that caused Yskanda to wince.

He felt odd, as if he had peered into a room to witness what had been intended as a private moment, and bustled away, keeping his steps silent.

The third consort was ready for him, though distracted. She seemed to want to talk about something, but Yskanda knew better than to respond to any of her hints for gossip among the staff.

Second Imperial Princess Gaunon popped in and out several times, fussing about her mother then whispering to her, with many backward looks at Yskanda. This effectively prevented him from finishing the portrait as each time the princess claimed her mother's attention, the mother altered her pose.

Yskanda bit down his exasperation, and when the welcome gong rang at last, he rose, bowed, claimed that his incompetence prevented him from finishing and begged for a last session. Then he surrendered the unfinished portrait into the hands of the waiting graywing, who gave him what Yskanda suspected was a sympathetic glance. Though with the graywings you could never be sure.

And he walked out. This time, he avoided so much as a glance at that figure still kneeling in the courtyard, though the image of the rain-soaked, weary first prince remained painted against his eyelids for the remainder of the day.

As for Jion, he was not aware of anything beyond the numbing pain in his knees, and the chill as the rain steadily beat down. At first he'd knelt there, thinking how easy it was after all the hard work he'd put into his martial arts. Before he'd left, there had been a lot of kneeling in this very spot. He knew the exact spot where the contours of a particular flagstone most easily fit a pair of knees. He'd thought an entire hour was torture when he was fourteen.

As the last of Phoenix watch passed, rain steadily pouring down, he worked up a suitable speech. He did not want to lie, but he wasn't going to say that being away had been a bad thing. It hadn't, and to say so would be a betrayal of Ryu, of Redbark, of them all.

The gong rang at noon, signaling the beginning of Horse. His legs had gone completely numb, and he began to regret having walked all through the previous night in his cabin, back and forth, instead of sleeping. As the first hour of Horse advanced at a cruelly slow pace, he let himself sink into memories. But those brought up Ryu, and . . . how could he not see?

But he—*she*—had worked hard not to let him see. He understood that now. For whatever reason, she had lived her life as a boy. As his little brother, who never seemed to grow. He had never questioned that. He'd never thought of her as a man—she had not thought of herself as a man. She had strutted along like the boys at Loyalty Fortress, had used their mannerisms. And it wasn't all mimicry. He had noticed, often, that when she was brooding, she'd rub the callus on her thumb against her upper teeth. That was not at all what he thought of as a girl gesture, but what really was "girl" or "boy" after all? So much of it was learned, like the ribbons and the fragrances, the coy look under lashes over a shoulder. The perfectly arched moth brows to enhance the almond shape of eyes . . . Ryu had done none of that. And yet, now that he thought about it, there was *girl* revealed in a thousand little ways.

How had Matu found out? He remembered the tension between the two before they reached the Sky Alliance competition—and that came after Ryu spent some time following Matu around, and choosing him first for sparring.

Jion's numb lips twitched in a grin. He had no idea how old she was, but he strongly suspected she had begun to reach the age of interest. And who but Matu would be the safest object of desire? Only it obviously hadn't gone well . . . oh, so much he hadn't seen!

The memories began to slide into sleep and he started to fall, then gasped, jerking himself upright. This wouldn't do. He was stronger than that. This was no duel with the likes of Screaming Hawk; it was mere kneeling. Anyone could do that. The rain didn't help, but at least it was not snow . . .

And so began the battle against his own body, as Horse gave way to Dragon, and then, as the sun slowly vanished, Dragon gave way to Turtle.

The first time he fainted, he woke up to the gong signifying mid-Turtle. He hauled himself up again, shivering uncontrollably. He braced his knees apart, gripped his thighs, and began Redbark breathing, concentrating on bringing warmth into himself. Now he wished he'd paid attention when Ryu and Yaso did their Essence tricks. But wasn't Essence a lot of trickery? The greater powers were uncontrollable — inaccessible to ordinary folk such as he. Even Ryu, who seemed to be closer to whatever it was, obviously struggled with it.

The breathing did help. For a time. A trickle of warmth, of strength, flowed through him, and he resumed the correct position, head bowed slightly, his gaze on the memorial tablets inside the shrine — pale oblongs whose lettering glinted in the candlelight. He looked at the group representing the generation above him, the ones who had killed each other after the empress died. Their silent testimony to why he ought not to learn martial arts. Except he had learned them. Yet he didn't want to kill his brother or sisters any more than he ever had. *The sword does not wield itself . . .*

Control slipped again, and the second time he woke up, the rain had stopped, revealing the stars of Tiger Watch, the moons having vanished altogether.

He was shivering again, but by now he understood enough about weather to determine that it was not cold enough to kill him. This had become a silent battle of will with his father. What was he supposed to do, fall to the stones sobbing and pleading? He'd pull out his own tongue by the roots before he would do that.

He forced himself upright, and began Redbark breathing; the next thing he noticed was the gongs signaling the assembling of the ministers at Court. That meant that his father was on the move.

So it was — after a largely sleepless night, during which the emperor had often paced alone, in the dark, to peer down through the back windows of the Golden Dragon Pavilion at that solitary figure in the courtyard below.

Jion had lasted longer than he had before his own first faint all those years ago, though not by much. The weather had been largely the same. He imagined Jion down there arguing mentally with him the way he had argued with his grandmother before she had made him kneel there through a day, and a night. *If the girl refused you, you should have sent her home. And killing her family? How could you be so short-sighted? You are lucky the Alk clan was at its end, or we'd have wolves in the city walls and rats in the temples right now. As it is, I'm going to have to face Young Su in court, and probably elevate him to Right Counselor because he'll insist you insulted the entire Su clan by choosing that useless girl over his daughter . . .*

He fought his own memories, imagining Jion reliving all his mistakes, what he'd say.

After the second faint, he nearly sent Bitternail out there. Jion looked so . . . lifeless. But he gripped himself, and presently, after an eternity, Jion stirred, and hauled himself upright. The emperor was aware of a spurt of admiration: he had given in by dawn, calling for the graywings . . .

Would Jion beg? He found himself wishing he would — and at the same time hoping he wouldn't. It was with such an internal debate that he submitted to the long process of getting ready for Court.

Melonseed entered once the emperor was bathed and his hair ordered. He bore, with his usual reverence, the Dragon Robe. "I suppose the entire palace is talking?" the emperor asked.

Melonseed bowed his head, murmuring, "Your humble servant is —"

The emperor sighed. "When you start with that tone I know you're going to admit to nothing. Which I suppose means yes. It was probably inevitable from the moment the harbor patrol cleared the bay. But I was not going to risk some sort of attack," he finished grimly. "There are still too many questions unanswered."

With that he fell silent as Melonseed critically watched the silent graywings adjust the Dragon robe, then fitted the headdress to the emperor's head before saying softly, "Her imperial highness the first imperial consort awaits your imperial majesty in the outer chamber."

Nothing the emperor hadn't expected; at least she was alone. The one he rather dreaded was his mother. Jion was her favorite, too.

He went to the first imperial consort, with whom he had shared so many of the bitter winds of change, his gaze searching her reddened eyes. Yes, there was the fear he'd expected to see. He leaned down to kiss her, for he had been fond of her ever since their first, honest talk so long ago, when he was isolated in the palace by imperial decree, and she a grief-stricken, pregnant eighteen-year-old, her exalted descent from the most ancient noble family in the empire notwithstanding. He took her trembling hands and murmured, "I'll talk to him. He needs a good scare first."

She bent to press her lips to his fingers, dripping tears onto them, her shoulders shaking as she tried valiantly to smother a sob. He kissed her forehead and passed on, leaving her to recover in the quiet room.

He knew the answer to his question the moment he entered the throne room. The atmosphere caused the hairs on his neck to lift. It was that sense of lightning to come in a building storm. His gaze snapped to where the Easterner ambassador usually stood, then he recollected with a short sense of relief that the ambassador had withdrawn for the appropriate fifty days of mourning—and to await new instructions, once the new ruler secured the throne. He had his spies, watched in turn by the ferrets, but he would be unable to interfere for now.

As the ministers went through the opening ritual the emperor sustained a brief, visceral memory of his brother stalking him through this pavilion—and then his thoughts arrowed to his son still kneeling in that courtyard.

Of course he was going to bring him in, but when? How could he get across what a *stupid* thing Jion had done? The emperor's eyes cut to that old snake Su, standing there so sanctimonious in his purple robe. He had no doubt whatever that the elder Sus were poised to hold a celebration at the first beat of the execution drums: with Jion gone, they'd assume Manon would be the undisputed heir.

And so it might be even if Jion lived . . .

His attention returned to the court when the Left Chancellor stepped out, and the morning began with sonorously delivered reports from various chief counsellors, followed by the Minister of Military Affairs.

He knew everything they would say, which allowed him to watch the others for subtle signs; he then remembered the court artist, specifically Afan Yskanda of the observant eyes and revealing brush. Yskanda sat below, beautiful as the Morningstar God, his hands busy with his ink. No doubt it was that cagey old Yoli Jiwa who had discovered the emperor looking through Yskanda's drawings (and why should he not?), for recently Yskanda's work had been technically brilliant but absolutely wooden. But that would not last . . . the emperor fully expected expression to creep back into those drawings, a brush stroke at a time. Artists need to make art, and the best art captures forever the essence of things, the truth.

Should he—

The last of the counsellors was finishing his report on naval action in the northwest (was that Jion's Shadow Panthers?) when the doors opened, and in strode a striking figure: she was alone, barefoot, her face veiled with floating white gauze. She wore the pure white of mourning as she advanced up the aisle, head bowed.

Sheer annoyance, mitigated slightly by reluctant acknowledgment of an inspired move, woke the dragon within the emperor's temperament. Of course it was Manon. Her veil was long, as modesty demanded, but it was so sheer that her pure profile was visible the length of the room. Her unbound hair had been brushed until it shone, a veil like midnight hanging down the back of her train to her knees.

She halted the requisite steps before the throne and then sank gracefully to the floor, forehead pressed to the ground as, in a high, clear voice, she said, "I beg you, Imperial Father, to heed my plea, for did not Kanda say that family is the root of humanity?"

And she went on, in a measured voice that she had to have been rehearsing half the night, to throw out the quotations about families, brothers, and loyalty that everyone in this room had surely written a thousand times as children.

The emperor cast a fast glance at Old Su—who stared at his great-granddaughter, his pouchy eyes wide and his heavy lower jaw not quite hiding how appalled he was. Then this was not a Su clan ploy, but Manon's own idea. The emperor remained quiet, the dragon within swinging its fiery gaze this way and that as he considered the situation: he had lost the luxury of giving vent to his temper before the world's eyes the day he impetuously set out, with all his guards, after Danno and Alk Hanu.

Manon was the most obedient daughter he could have asked for. Quick, smart, studious, beautiful. But the more she grew to be like her mother, the more he disliked her, an emotion that disturbed him. No one should dislike his children—and if the Su clan ever whiffed a hint of his true feelings, the never-ending power struggle with them that had been part of his life since the day he was crowned would shake the ground and rend the skies.

He was aware that he always judged in her favor, afraid that he might let his emotions show. It was easy enough, for she was so very good . . . or good at appearing good. He knew the essence of the problem: the more she sounded, or looked, like her mother, the more he distrusted her as a tool of the Su clan, in spite of telling himself—quite reasonably—that she could not avoid resembling her mother. He had to remind himself that she also carried half his blood.

She went on to offer her life in exchange for taking her brother under her wing until he could restore himself in the eyes of Imperial Father. As she modestly offered to be responsible for Jion's future actions, the emperor was very aware of ambivalence. He could tell from most of the ministers' expressions that they were seeing in her a blend of the Morningstar God for beauty and for heroic daring, Erku the Hero come down from Heaven. Even Su's enemies appeared to be moved and amazed. Did they not see that what she effectively asked for was Jion's demotion in rank behind her . . . which would put her a step closer to the crown?

Ah, Old Su (who had been Young Su during his grandmother's reign) now saw it—his expression had smoothed to the humble, downward gaze that characterized him at his most deadly. But that jowly, potato-nosed old snake was not Manon, who was proving that indeed she had the emperor's own blood running in her veins.

What was her real motivation here? A move on the imperial Circle board for the Su clan, or for herself as his daughter, and loyalty to her brother as a prince of the imperial Jehan line? Whatever it was, he had to admit her gesture was a dragon's strike. Maybe that was what was needed for the empire in future. Not necessarily the person he loved most . . .

She had come to a close. He must act now, to preserve the imperial face, which was fundamental to the order of the empire. "Rise, daughter," he said, descending the steps to hold out his hand. "Rise, my child, and be at peace, for has Kanda not written that the strength of a nation is reflected in the integrity of the home?"

Her gaze behind the veil lifted to his, searching. He returned his most benevolent smile, and gave the waiting graywings the signal to call court to a close. Then he tucked Manon's arm under his, and walked with her down the length of that long aisle, providing his own quotations from Kanda as he went. At the door, he spotted her maids outside, waiting with a palanquin, probably with shoes inside, and a warm cape.

He lifted his hand, she bowed low, and withdrew, each reflective. He faced the fact that hitherto he had avoided: his two smartest children were in fact adults, making movements of their own. And she reflected that he had neither acceded to her plea for her brother's life, nor denied it.

.

# FIVE

THE EMPEROR RETURNED TO the Golden Dragon Pavilion, and, postponing the usual meeting with the consorts and his informal interviews to follow up on various depositions, he ate a little, then lifted the heavy crown, revealing his hair caught up in a pearl-and-diamond encrusted golden clasp. Still wearing the Dragon Robe, he said to Bitternail, "Bring my son."

Bitternail knew which son was meant; the entire inner palace, from the dowager empress to the sweepers, had been on the alert, as if they all felt the dragon's mood.

Bitternail bowed and withdrew. With a flick of his hand the emperor sent the rest of the waiting servitors out, and then, alone, paced to the back room. Jion had fallen over again, either asleep or in a faint. He looked pale as death.

The emperor found himself holding his breath as Bitternail himself, and Jion's steward Whiteleaf, went out to the court-yard, and bent over the waterlogged figure. Jion stirred after what seemed a protracted time, and the emperor let out that breath. He then retreated to the most private of his interview chambers, as the graywings dried Jion hastily, rubbed some life into his limbs, and then pressed a healing draught to his nerveless lips, medicine that Whiteleaf had been refreshing each half hour all through the long night and longer day.

Jion was still wet but looked much more alive when he stumbled painfully—held up on either side by two of

Bitternail's stronger assistants—into his father's interview chamber. He took one glance at the Dragon Robe, and fell forehead to the floor, without speaking a word.

"Rise, Jion. Come here. Sit, so I can see your face."

Jion stumbled a little—his joints and muscles still felt like badly made stick-and-paper puppetry, except for his knees, which were agonizingly swollen.

He dropped abruptly onto the waiting cushion at his father's feet.

"What," the emperor asked, "did you learn from this escapade?"

How many imagined conversations had Jion held through that horrible, nightmare-ridden night and day? This question had occurred in another form: *Why didn't you surrender yourself to a garrison?* To which there were many answers, among them: *I thought you wanted me dead.*

But he had not really believed that, and when he looked into his father's searching gaze, he intuited how very much the emperor would hate hearing that.

But he could not say the foremost reason: he loved his freedom.

What was another truth? "I . . . I wanted to see, and understand, how ordinary people in the empire live. What they think."

The emperor lifted his brows. "But from what I have heard, you were mostly at the borders and beyond. What can you learn of the empire's people from outlaws?" He spoke mildly enough.

Jion knew he ought to speak with the most abject humility and formality, but he scarcely had the strength left to speak at all.

He made a try. "This unworthy son . . ."

"It's a little late for that," the emperor cut in—mildly enough.

"Wanted to . . ." Jion drew in a deep breath. "Learn why they are not a part of the empire." He lifted a callused hand to push back his dripping hair.

Some of the emperor's fury eased. That was actually a good answer. Or good enough. Even if it had been a motivation dreamed up over the past week, it exhibited some semblance of thought.

His gaze still on that callused palm, the emperor said, "Tell me about this Firebolt you were running with."

Jion's heart beat fast. That afforded him a trickle of strength, though he knew it would not last. "We didn't talk about our pasts. Which is why no one knew who I was. All I learned was that he came from the Redbark Sect, which sustained some kind of attack. He was the sole survivor."

The emperor had no problem with lawless sects killing one another off, and waved his fan to and fro. "What I want to know is this: is he likely to lead some kind of rebellion? In the name of justice, or Redbark, or whatever he might conveniently call it."

Jion's eyes closed as he uttered a voiceless laugh.

His father, watching closely, said, "You find the topic of rebellion humorous?"

The humor vanished. "I do not," Jion said, opening his dark-circled eyes. "It's the idea. The image of Firebolt leading one. It just won't come. I guess you could say that his methods are the dispensation of justice one person at a time. Nearly always rescue of the defenseless. Monks. The old. Poor people. He *hates* leading, even as small a group as four. As for rebellion, I don't know how much the ferrets told you about the situation I was in when they appeared, but we had recently escaped a Shadow Panthers attempt at forcible recruitment."

"I heard that you left ahead of a pursuing army of criminals, smoke rising from the remains of their stronghold behind you."

"True. The important part is — and I tried telling the chief ferret this — I had occasion to overhear a lot of drunk talk while I was playing the guzheng for Screaming Hawk. The stronghold leader. There's someone they call Master Night leading. Some things that were said made me think that this man is a noble. And further, he has some plan for invasion of one of the wealthier islands, the way they talked constantly about treasure and riches. No idea which one."

"Chief Fai Anbai," the emperor said, "is not a part of the military command tree."

Jion bowed his head — he should have remembered that his father's mind was more like a series of locked vaults than like a great open space in which all things are connected.

The emperor went on, still in that same deceptively mild tone, "I'm curious. What would you have done with this information had not Chief Fai caught up with you?"

Jion looked up, to meet his father's bland smile and inscrutable gaze from long phoenix eyes — the same black as his own, under the same winged brows. "I don't know. Had not thought that far ahead yet. We were forcibly recruited, as I said. By which I mean we were given some kind of sleep poison in goldwine. And when we woke up, we were surrounded by Shadow Panthers. They said join or die. We joined until we could escape."

"Just ahead of pursuit," the emperor said, and his head tipped, as he studied his son from another angle. "I gather that before your encounter with the Shadow Panther Sect you earned your daily rice by playing the guzheng?" His father's teeth showed in a flash of distaste. "Or dancing for the pleasure of the criminal world?"

"I only danced a few times, and one of those was a ruse to escape the Shadow Panthers. The ferrets will no doubt have told you that," he added.

The emperor's face tightened in disgust, and Jion saw that pursuing the subject would only make his father angrier. Imperial children did not perform for vulgar eyes. Making music might be tolerated because the musicians sat at the side, sometimes hidden altogether. "I also played the guqin, as well as the pipa," he said.

"And how did you like being commanded to perform for coins? More to the point, how long did you expect to carry on in such a manner?"

Jion spread his hands. "I don't know. I was living day to day. Observing, learning things. Like how to repair my own clothes. Laundry. How long boots last when you walk up and down mountains. Cooking — I know how to catch and grill fish. I also got to witness how fine porcelain is made, when I stayed with a set of Ghost Moon monks."

A pause became a silence, then the emperor's tone lightened. "The oddest thing is that I find I almost envy you — how many islands of my empire have you seen that I only see through others' eyes? But I suspect the experience of walking up and down mountains and catching and grilling fish would be endurable for maybe a week. Did it ever occur to you that if you wished to learn how to mend your own clothes, or to grill fish, you could order someone to come to your pavilion and demonstrate it?"

Jion sighed. "It did."

"And?"

"My answer, Imperial Father, I fear will only make you angrier with me than you are already."

"You should have considered my anger," the emperor retorted, "before vanishing four years ago. It seems you never did reach the Silk Islands from what I can gather . . . Never mind. We will come to that. You did not send for demonstrations on grilling fish and the rest of it because . . ."

"Because whoever came would either have one eye out for promotion, or competition, or else be terrified. And so they would say whatever they thought I wanted to hear. I wanted to see people . . ." He avoided the word *free*. "In their everyday lives."

"You don't think there isn't competition, or terror, or ambition, in commoners' lives?"

"I know that the common people experience those things. They also experience droughts, floods, pirate attacks. Thieves close to home. But you asked for my motive." The borrowed strength was giving out, and Jion's voice had diminished to a husk. He made a visible effort, and said, "I gave it to you. I know it was poorly considered, that I was woefully ignorant. That I am extremely lucky to be alive. I know all those things now, Imperial Father."

"And so, if you see a chance, you will not hare off again?" He saw Jion hesitate, and the anger flared again, to be suppressed. "Never mind. Of course you will, as you so cogently pointed out just now, say what you think I want to hear. And I won't believe it, because I know it's the prudent answer, which may or may not be true. I once was proudest of you, out of all my children. You destroyed that in one act. But you are still my son, the most like me in significant ways. Including stubbornness. I find myself wanting to give you one chance to prove yourself. Go on back to your pavilion. You will be confined there until I say otherwise."

"Might your grateful son ask if anyone can visit?"

"Such as?" The emperor's brows rose again.

"This son desires —"

"Speak directly."

"Thank you, Imperial Father. I was thinking of my brother. My sisters, too. I heard Gau-Gau," he added. "Or maybe I dreamed it. I didn't actually see her. But I thought I heard her voice echoing from somewhere. Trying to wheedle one of the graywings into sneaking me a steamed bun."

The emperor smiled at this small sign of affection between his children, so very different from the armed truce he himself had grown up with. "I would not be at all surprised. As for your elder sister, she made quite a commendable speech before the ministers today, quoting pages of Kanda and the poets, and offering to educate you into obedience under her sheltering wing." The emperor finished on a slightly acid note, but if Jion heard it, or understood the implications, there was no evidence in his sudden smile.

"Manon! That sounds like her."

The emperor waved a hand in dismissal, thinking that if Jion turned out to be unable to see Mt. Lir over his head, well . . . time would tell. "Oh. That reminds me," he added, remembering his other project. "Your grandmother expressly desired a portrait of you. Your siblings, and your mothers, have already sat to the new assistant court artist. I will send him along presently."

Jion tried to rise, and fell back, paling.

"Bitternail!"

Graywings appeared, and gently helped Jion to his feet. He clearly was on the verge of collapse, and yet from somewhere he mustered enough strength to bow. The emperor had to admit, stupid as this escapade had been, Jion did not lack for courage.

Jion was aware of none of this as he straightened up, Ryu's necklace banging against his ribs.

Bitternail handed off responsibility to Melonseed with no more than a glance. As the graywings helped Jion away, he closed his eyes, letting the soft hands guide him. The gods all must be smiling—he'd come out of that alive.

But the danger was far from over. As he covered the last agonizing distance to his manor, weary as he was, he noticed guards at every corner. There was probably a perimeter five rings deep.

Watching for him from Grove of Serene Wisdom Pavilion, Jion's manor, was Steward Whiteleaf, and the rest of Jion's household, most of them new promotions.

"There he is," said Yarrow, the new body servant, long and thin with a narrow head. He reminded Whiteleaf of a bamboo shoot. His brows contracted. "It looks as if he cannot walk. Steward Whiteleaf, you did not say the criminals Out There had harmed him . . ."

Whiteleaf silenced Yarrow with a glance. Yarrow was patient and thorough, but he could also be a little giddy. "Because nothing of the sort happened," Whiteleaf said, raising his voice slightly so that the rest of the staff heard. That ought to take care of gossip. "Come."

It would never do to wait for the emperor's graywings to bring the prince all the way inside. They hurried out, bowing to their superiors, then offering silently to take their precious burden.

Melonseed gave Whiteleaf a brief nod, and the steward understood then that the interview had not gone badly.

"Whiteleaf," the prince breathed. "Ah. Where's Bluetwist? Who is this?"

"If it pleases your imperial highness, Yarrow will have the honor of tending to your personal needs. Bluetwist did not recover."

The prince sagged in their grip, then straightened with an effort that both Whiteleaf and Yarrow could feel. His bruised-looking eyes narrowed. "You didn't tell me that. On the ship."

"This incompetent deeply apologizes," Whiteleaf said as they eased him inside the door and through to the waiting bedroom.

"You probably don't want to say I was pouting too much," the prince said with a hint of his old laughter. "I really thought old Bluetwist would be right here, grumping at me about how dirty I'd let my clothes get . . . Dead?" He winced.

Yarrow remained silent. Between them they got the prince out of the sodden, muddy clothes, and into a hot bath. When he was entirely disrobed except for the locket, Jion quickly lifted it over his head, watching the two graywings as he did. Neither pair of eyes followed his hand — Whiteleaf was testing the water, and Yarrow folding the sodden clothing.

Jion could not bend. He fisted the locket, realized he would not be able to bathe with one hand outside the water, and dropped the thing onto the gilt table, words of deflection forming behind his lips. But they were unneeded. The graywings either were pretending not to see the locket, or really did not see it.

Very well. That was for later contemplation. Jion hissed in pain when his swollen, bloody knees first immersed in the water. Both servants held their breath, but then the prince let out a long sigh. "Oh, that is much better. Though I don't think I'll be able to get out again."

"I'll fetch the salve," Yarrow offered, and sloped off, his long legs below a very long torso making him look like he leaned into a wind.

The prince dropped his head against the back of the tub, and turned his gaze to Whiteleaf. "You know, in the gallant wanderer world, I had to dress myself. I even learned how to sew up holes in my robes. I learned to cook. A little. There were no graywings."

Whiteleaf smiled, thinking that the prince had spoken more words in this past turn of the little hourglass than he had during the entire ship journey. Was that due to gaining his imperial father's mercy and forgiveness?

"No graywings," the prince mused in a slow, sleepy voice. "I never considered before . . .Why did you become one?"

Whiteleaf stilled, the question utterly unexpected. Unprepared for. Always, a wall existed between servers and served.

How to answer? Memory had always been a gate of swords, though the decades had blunted them a little: the weak clasp of his mother's hand, her skin hot and dry; the high voice of his new "aunt" insisting that her favorite shaman cured everyone; the funeral rites, and his older brother helping him to bow to the floor for the first time. Then the wedding, and his aunt living with them; her caresses and coos until the cry of an infant, then the slaps, and always being hungry, and Father's hand hot and dry with the same illness.

Then the cooing again, and the caresses, as his aunt said over and over, *You'll bring honor to our house, Little Second. Only you can save us by going into the palace.*

And then his brother's whisper, *Don't say yes. They'll denature you.*

*What's that?*

*It means you won't marry or have sons to worship at your ancestral tablet.*

*I'm hungry,* he said. *Aunt says I'll never be hungry again if I go into the palace.*

Then standing with a lot of other little boys as the tall ones in gray with the big hats gave him a new name, and new gray clothes, and began lessons . . .

Whiteleaf blinked the image away, and its remembered grief and bewilderment, to find the prince's exhausted gaze still turned his way. "It was deemed best for my family for me to come into the palace," he finished.

"How old were you?"

"Five."

"Five," the prince repeated, on a husky note of horror, and Whiteleaf knew that the first imperial prince had crossed that threshold that he never would approach.

He knew what was coming next, and forestalled the question. "They don't permit us to do the denaturing ritual until we turn ten. By then we know something of what to expect. Not all choose to stay," he added. "I never looked back."

Jion heard beneath the gentle, dignified voice a firmness that made him wonder if asking had been as a breach of Whiteleaf's dignity. Life among the gallant wanderers had opened his eyes to the fact that everyone had face, from beggar to baron. Except that he was now back in the realm in which everything a prince did was right. Even when it wasn't.

"This low servant prays that your imperial highness will find Yarrow a satisfactory replacement," Whiteleaf said, and Jion took it as a gentle attempt to end the subject.

"I'm sure he'll do—ayah! Look at these knees. I can't even stand up without wobbling like a leaf in a high wind."

Yarrow and Whiteleaf got the prince to his bed, wrapped in a soft robe, his knees treated with salve. He couldn't bear anything touching them, even silk, so he lay with his legs on pillows as they got hot tea into him, and a dish of congee.

He didn't remember eating the last bite.

# SIX

JION HAD SCARCELY SLEPT for an hour when the sound of voices brought him up and up and up to consciousness again; his time with Redbark had made him a wary sleeper.

"What is it?" he muttered.

Whiteleaf said softly, "Her imperial highness the first imperial consort is here."

Here? If Jion's mother had come to his manor, it would be unfilial to deny her. He forced his eyes open, and a short time later entered his interview chamber, a graywing at his elbows on either side.

There was his mother, with the Imperial Physician in tow. "Jion, my son! You've grown! Quick, quick, quick, put him back in his bed at once. Cannot you see how it pains him to stand?" She was very pale, having stayed awake praying while her son knelt in the shrine court before the Jehan ancestors.

"Not their fault," Jion whispered, for it was excruciating to stand again. ". . . filial . . ."

"Very filial it will be if you drop dead at my feet," his mother retorted, and made shooing motions until he was safely deposited on his bed again.

Only then did she give in to the luxury of pent-up sobs, alternately expressing her thanks to all the gods and exhorting the physician to hurry — what medicine should he take — did he need charms, moxibustion, needles, tea?

Jion submitted to the examination, and promised his mother to do everything the physician required as a prescription was dictated: incense to purify and rectify the air, medicine twice a day, diet, and massage for his sadly bruised knees — after the swelling subsided.

Once the physician departed, she sat beside him, sobbing harder at how much he had grown — and were those whiskers on his chin? He held her hand and soothed her, his heart knotting deeply with remorse in a way that no punishment could ever elicit, aware that he was not sorry he had gone, but he was very sorry his mother had suffered for it.

She was barely finding her voice when Dowager Empress Kui Jin then showed up, the long phoenix eyes she had bequeathed to son and grandson glistening with the sheen of tears she did not let fall.

Both son and mother immediately started to rise, but she made a sharp gesture that kept them in place. She took one look at Jion's knees, and her daughter-in-law's tear-stained face, and sent her entourage outside to wait, except for Topaz. This graywing at a gesture carried in a heavy food box from which she triumphantly brought out exquisite, expensive dishes such as bird's nest soup, congee made with green plum syrup, lychee, and healer's tea made from aged ginseng and longevity root.

"There is enough here for the both of you," she said quietly, kindly. "Renyi, cease your lamentations, lest the gods think you are unsatisfied with our good luck. He has returned, as you see. And surely you do not wish to pain me and your son by harming your health?"

The first imperial consort did her best to swallow her tears, but she never ceased trembling as she looked tenderly on her son, reassuring herself that she was not dreaming. He was here, alive, and though so very changed, there was the glow of health under too-pale skin.

Imperial Sister Lily quietly entered, a tall person with a dome of a forehead counterbalanced by a strong cleft chin. Midway in that unprepossessing face a pair of wide-spaced, narrow eyes looked compassionately on the world.

"Dearest Young Brother Jion, I am so happy to see you are safe," she exclaimed.

He managed a brief grin. "Senior Sister Lily! I notice you don't say you're glad to have me back."

Her eyes searched his as she said in her careful, conscientious way, "If you are happy to be back, that *would* gladden me. But seeing you alive and well *does* gladden me."

There was no more chance for her to speak; though Whiteleaf and Topaz set out the food, with Yarrow hovering in the background in case he was needed, Jion could scarcely get a bite to his mouth for all the questions his grandmother asked. He deflected these as best he could, saying no more than what he had told his father, until at last the dowager empress stated that the food she had brought would congeal soon, and they ought to let him eat it, and rest.

"I'm so glad you're safe," Lily said again as she obediently rose, and Jion briefly wondered if there could be extra meaning in that. No. A pang of remorse reminded him that before he left he had been more troublesome than not. It was merely the sort of thing people said.

With Yarrow's aid he walked them to the door — the imperial guards outside were a silent reminder he could go no farther, even if bending his knees to walk hadn't felt at this point like stabbing knives — and once he was able to lie down again, he thought about his two elder sisters.

Lily had always been so quiet, so calm. Well, so was Manon, but her quiet was so very disciplined, every move one of grace. Jion knew the cost of that. He had shared all those dancing lessons with her, but where he had shrugged off the poses, she had made them part of her.

Lily, however, just *was*. Only now he realized how very little he had seen of her in the year or two before he left. It had been so gradual — the more time he spent with Manon, the less he saw of Lily.

He obediently forced down as much of the food as he could, knowing that a report would be duly carried to the elders, and then, at last, he was able to sleep.

The next sibling to visit was Gau-Gau, dancing in late the next morning, her maid bearing a skillfully carved food box. "Look what I brought you," she exclaimed proudly. "I ordered all your favorite things!"

Jion lifted the lid. "Sesame balls with bean paste . . . sun cakes . . . pine-kernel rolls . . . Aren't these your favorites?" he asked.

She shrugged. "Maybe you changed your mind while you

were gone, so I thought I'd get what we both like!"

She sat down and began eating them herself, as she chatter-ed about everything she could think of that had happened while he was gone, incidents so minute that each drove home to him the inescapable truth: the silken cage had bound him again, more tightly than before. ". . . Oh, and the most exciting thing is, we had our portraits done. Assistant Court Artist Afan is so *handsome*, and so *kind!* Manon despises him, of course, because he's common, or maybe because he's more beautiful than she is. *I* think so, anyway."

Jion marveled that the entertainingly crabby old Yoli Jiwa had finally assented to an assistant, then shrugged off the unknown assistant court artist.

The third day, Vaion appeared at last. Jion's heart leaped when his brother sauntered in, tall at near sixteen, his voice no longer a bat squeak. He looked almost shy when he came in and saw how tall Jion was, and the way the silk of his robe did not hide the contours of his arms and legs. "They wouldn't let me come until today, Senior Brother, or I would have been here first thing. What happened to you?" Vaion asked. "I don't mean your knees. We all saw you out there. I mean . . . all this time?"

Jion had been thinking about how to answer that. "It's probably best if I say as little as possible," he replied wryly.

"Did anyone threaten your life?" Vaion asked.

"Gau-Gau asked as well. Is that a hint you two wish I hadn't returned?"

"No!" Vaion retorted, stung—then saw his brother's grin. "How can you say that, when I've missed you every day!"

"I missed you, too. But as you can see, I'm here. Tell me about what you've been doing."

"Study," Vaion said on a long-suffering sigh, and then proceeded to describe everything he loathed about dull, strict old Master Zao and about the carefully chosen noble-born boys who came to study with him, and what fun he and his particular friends had in spite of studies.

But! "It's all boys now," Vaion complained. "They took the girls off to their own study when Old Fox-Whiskers caught Cousin Zuinan writing love-poems in his copybook to show Toutu Rin, and she started giggling loud enough for them to hear at the South Gate." He was going to add that the boys got justice in that Toutu Rin was now stuck with Manon in the first chair (which meant she led the study along with the presiding scholar), but he remembered that Jion *liked* Manon. She had never treated him the way she treated the rest of them.

He shrugged off the subject and got to what interested him. "Did you learn sword-fighting?"

"Vaion —"

"Just yes or no. I won't beg you to show me. I still remember the beating I got from when I sneaked over to watch the imperial guards at drill. I still believe it was Manon who blabbed — but I know, I know, she was only doing her duty." He scowled and rubbed his backside. "I don't understand why Imperial Father thinks you and I will suddenly try to kill one another. I don't want to kill you! Do you want to kill me?'"

"No. But then I don't want the throne," Jion said.

"Nor do I! Just *think* of having to sit there sweating in that Dragon Robe, and having to smile at that potato-nosed old weasel Great-Grandfather Su!"

"You don't dream of having the power to kill people you don't like, and to make changes?"

Vaion brooded. "No. I'd rather run away, not go stalking you through the inner palace the way First Imperial Uncle is supposed to have done to Father, according to the whispers." Vaion looked down. "They hated one another, that's what Gau-Gau overheard Second Mother saying once. And Lily once told me she could point out all the records proving that when the throne is empty it suddenly changes people." He sounded like the boy Jion remembered who'd loved the duels in hero tales, but there was a narrowing of question in his eyes that Jion had never seen in Vaion when his brother was small.

"Maybe one changes on coming of age." Jion settled back against the pillows. "When does ambition set in? Ayah, Manon has it, but that might be Second Mother's doing. All I know for certain is, you don't have to dig far in the archives to be aware that there are a lot of bloody battles over the throne in our family. And in past dynasties."

"I know. I made a list," Vaion said unexpectedly. He really was growing up — but then so was Jion himself. "I don't like Manon," Vaion added, sounding twelve again. "But I can't see wanting to kill her."

"You still haven't gotten past resenting her?"

"If she wasn't so *perfect*." And when Jion laughed, Vaion made a wry face and muttered, "She uses it as a weapon to make me lose face."

Though a lot had changed, this old argument obviously had not. Vaion got to his feet, yawned, then strove to sound casual as he said over his shoulder, "They started sending me pillow maids after Cousin Zuinan got caught writing erotic poems in his copybook. If you want some suggestions about who is best, say the word."

Jion thanked his brother without telling him that he had already been offered a visit from the pillow maids, and he'd refused, claiming too much pain from his knees.

That wouldn't have mattered if he'd really wanted them. How to explain that once he might have accepted the skills of the pillow maids without thinking about the minds behind the soft hands and sweet voices — or about who was in the room or just outside of it, listening, watching, reporting.

He'd learned a preference for mutual attraction over what the women in Madam Nightingale's had called a purely business arrangement. At least in a business arrangement they could say no, unlike in history, but he liked attraction going both ways. Also, he was not certain that imperial palace pillow maids could say no even if he asked, which made the prospect repellent. The very idea brought those wretched women on Screaming Hawk's island to mind, and Ryu's fervent vow to rescue them. Knowing now that she, too, was a girl unsettled him the more. Until he knew more about those pillow maids, and how much freedom they had, he wasn't going to be sharing anything with them.

But explaining that to Vaion meant getting into his life over the past few years, and he knew every word would be reported.

Besides, what he really wanted was to go back to Madam Swan's upper room, and lie next to Ryu again . . . and then what?

Now that he knew he was a she, it changed everything — and yet it changed nothing.

After Vaion left he forced himself to his feet. He could stand, which meant he'd heal faster if he didn't lie around. He prowled his manor restlessly, ignoring the pain in his knees, until it was late. And when he couldn't sleep, he got up in the darkness and moved slowly through the simplest of his dance exercises, which cut his mind free to reach back through memory.

It was an easy guess why Ryu and her brother had entered the army — they were talented, but wouldn't get any training on some obscure dot of an island. And though the imperial army took women, they were invariably sent to guard noble and imperial women, or else sent to the navy to train as navigators. A few generals used them as scouts. All a waste of Ryu's talents.

Also, men and women trained separately, and clearly brother and sister had wanted to stick together. Until Ryu's talents erupted at the mercenary attack — there would have been no keeping her identity secret then. So she deserted, but she still didn't trust Jion enough to tell him the truth. Salutary!

He wanted so very badly to see her, to ask why he'd never earned her trust, but he could only talk to her in his imagination, while dancing slowly in the dark to music heard only in his head.

The next morning he woke before dawn, the old Redbark drill time. Dressed only in loose pants, he padded barefoot into his tiny courtyard to warm up with dance drills. And then he moved slowly through a mixture of the easiest Redbark drills and dance, ignoring the twinges and aches in his still-bruised knees.

Slow as it was, the exercise got his blood singing in his veins again. He bathed, dressed, and sat through Yarrow applying salve to his knees as he ate breakfast.

He was finishing when Manon glided in next to her mother, their silks flowing. "Jion!"

"Honored Second Mother," Jion cried gladly, bowing to the second imperial consort, who smiled at him as she enfolded him in a soft, scented embrace. "You honor this wretch," he said, his delight warming his voice.

"Of course I had to come to you, once I discovered you could not come to us. Welcome home, dear boy," she murmured. "Heaven! How you have grown!"

She let him go, and he turned to Manon. "Senior Sister! I hoped you'd come," he said as she stepped into his arms.

"Welcome home, Younger Brother. I knew that Imperial Father had released you from kneeling at the shrine, but I just found out that you are confined here — I was at my pavilion, and I even had all your favorite foods ready and waiting, before I thought to ask. Honored Mother found out, and so here we are."

He hugged her again, then stood her back, hands on her shoulders as he looked her up and down. She was beautiful, of course—always had been. She was a lot less changed than Vaion, except she somehow looked more like a young woman than a girl. Inscrutable. "Are you happy?" he asked.

Her eyes widened briefly. She had clearly not expected that—and she flushed, which made her look younger. "I am now, with you back," she said softly. "We did not know if you were alive or dead." She blinked twice, then her gaze lowered, eyes hidden by her long lashes.

"How did you survive?" Honored Second Mother asked, looking amused as she settled into the chief chair, Manon and Jion at either side. She waved off Whiteleaf's offer of tea, and the servants withdrew.

"It was not easy," Jion said, thinking rapidly. While Honored Second Mother had always been the most indulgent toward him, she was still very strict, and scrupulous about the rules. Words said could not be unsaid. Why not a small test? "I earned my daily bread by playing the guqin, and when my left hand got tired, I played the guzheng." He leaned forward, adding conspiratorially, "Once or twice I earned a meal by dancing."

Honored Second Mother brought her crimson-and-peach sleeve up to hide the lower half of her face as she uttered a soft laugh. "Impudent boy!" she murmured—with no remonstrance, but there was a shade of complacent distaste in her tone that surprised him. Was that new, or had he missed it in the past? Either way, the impulse to say more withered.

"This unworthy son begs to be told what he missed," he said instead.

Between the two, Honored Second Mother and Manon described the latest plays, and praised a new pipa player, a truly jadewood-hafted Talent. At the end of that, Honored Second Mother rose and shook out her silken robes. "We shall have to celebrate your return," she murmured. "If you wish to resume dancing lessons, you are always welcome to come to us—ayah, once His Imperial Majesty returns your privileges to you," she amended, bending to kiss his cheek. "It is still Manon's form of exercise. I'll leave Manon and you to catch up with one another."

He and Manon saw her to the door, then returned to his

sitting room, where he looked around, then said in the ancient tongue, "I wrote to you. At your bookstore."

Manon lowered her head. "I can no longer go there."

"Why not? When?"

"After it was discovered that you had disappeared."

He winced. "I'm sorry, Non-non. I never thought you'd be made to suffer for my decision."

"I'm just glad you are back."

"Did you get my letter?" he tried to remember when news of his disappearance might have reached the imperial city — and had no idea.

"I did not," she said.

"Maybe it's just as well." He shrugged off the matter. "I doubt it made any sense. I was trying so hard to make it sound general, and yet hint that it was from me. All I could think of was putting in quotations from the plays and poems we used to read. I'd first thought I ought to write in a code, the way gallant wanderers do in the stories, but once I actually had to produce one, I had no idea how to go about it."

She smiled, the light from the open windows reflecting in her dark eyes. "I surely am too stupid to catch your hints. As for books, they send me lists now, so I am not without resources."

"Good. I'm glad of that, at least. Though I know you liked getting away. I sure did," he added wryly, remembering his bratty escapades in the capital city.

She made a graceful gesture, and he added, "Father told me what you did at court. Thank you, dearest, good Elder Sister Manon. Considering how I managed to ruin your one escape, that makes your gesture doubly important."

"'Escape,'" she repeated, then uttered a soft laugh. "How was your 'escape'? Was it what you wished?"

He opened his mouth to let out some of his pent-up feelings, then he heard a slight noise from the other room. It was only Whiteleaf, putting away clothing, but it brought back to him that every word he spoke was listened to. Dangerous, how during his Redbark days he had become so accustomed to the luxury of privacy, granted by others' indifference. "It was different from anything I expected," he said, and laughed. "Father told me you offered to educate me. Shall you do that, Manon, educate me? Will I earn back a little face becoming a studious scholar in your image?"

"I would like nothing better." She smiled. "What touches cinnabar turns red, and anything near ink gets smudged. You must make up for the lost time. I'll bring you a stack of books tomorrow."

Her assurance that he'd smudged and smeared himself in his time away stung a little, but after all, she had no idea what he'd experienced. What he'd learned. He accepted her offer with a smile, assuming that this supposed study would be their excuse for them to go somewhere alone, so he could truly talk.

She returned the next day with a pair of graywings laden with books and scrolls. The weather had cleared, the air fresh with a hint of autumn. And warm again, though the lower angle of the sun was a reminder that winter would soon be nigh.

She suggested moving out to the tables in his tiny court. There, under the unseen eyes of the servants, she said, "Now we may speak. What truly happened to you?"

He hesitated, wondering how to remind her that though no one was in sight, everything in this tiny court was easily heard from the windows. How could she not know that?

He began a couple of words, then the thought struck him that of course she knew it. She might even have been ordered to interrogate him. In which case he was putting her in an impossible position. He couldn't know without asking — yet here they sat in listening range.

Then it hit him that during his time away, though she had changed little on the outside, her awareness, her perception of herself and her place in the world, might have altered as much as his had. Perhaps she had become Father's favorite. And she deserved it. She certainly had suffered no ill effects from interrupting court, something he never would have dared to do without invitation from Imperial Father, even when he was the favorite. Of course he never wanted to go to court, but that was beside the point . . .

All right, he could not tell her. Yet. If she wanted to know the details about what he'd done and thought, she would have to find a way for them to be without witnesses.

She watched him during this hesitation that had lengthened into silence, aware of how much he had grown. It was more of a change than mere height, though he had that, too. Completely gone was the sulky boy. What could possibly have caused such a change while he was mucking about in the filthy outdoor world?

He flashed a smile and leaned forward, stuttered a few words, blinked and frowned a little, his brows so like Imperial Father's drawing inward, then his expression eased.

"I learned how to earn my daily meals," he finally said with a laugh.

"And how did you like that?" Her humorous, slightly exaggerated tone made it clear she was expecting the complaints to begin.

"It was a very . . . different life. Which is over now."

"We shall have to see if you picked up bad habits playing music for undiscriminating ears," she said.

He laughed. "A challenge. I'll take that challenge — I expect you'll find me woefully behind you in skill. But I mean to catch up. What did you bring me?"

Ah, now was the time to establish leadership. In a calm, poised voice she began discussing the books, beginning with the oldest treatise on Kanda's *Conversations*. She kept that up until the gong rang, and she had to go.

That established their pattern for his period of confinement. With little else to do, Jion began reading those books — he even finished up the copy project he'd begun during the journey back to the imperial island. He decided the prudent thing to do would be to give his watchers nothing interesting to watch.

And it was interesting to read the ancient wisdom again, especially Kanda, whose thoughts the ancient philosopher had written down as he wandered from island to island. Confined to the inner palace and made to memorize the most didactic exhortations, Jion had had scant interest in Kanda. But now he found himself absorbed in seeing the underpinnings of empire life so long ago. There were times when, in his imagination, he tramped alongside Kanda, who had slept outside during all weathers, and had gone hungry, too. Kanda had had his followers to talk with, making the trek bearable, even enlightening. The way Jion had had Redbark.

The way he'd been able to talk with Ryu. If that was even her name. It had to be her family name, at least; he remembered the brother, distantly seen now and then at Loyalty Fortress. He could not recollect her first name. Wait, it hadn't even been a name, had it? Wasn't it Mouse? Maybe

"Mouse" was a name in those outer islands, for boy or girl. They hadn't talked about personal things—and now he understood why on her end—but they had talked about every other subject under the sun.

Only, he thought, laughing at himself as he lit another candle, nobody would ever write any of it down.

# SEVEN

DAILY REPORTS WENT OUT just as expected. The emperor got the most detailed report each morning as his servants bathed and dressed him.

"Yesterday as the day before, your imperial majesty. His imperial highness woke before dawn, and went into the court to do exercises—"

Since this seemed to have become a pattern, the emperor asked, "What exercises?"

"His dance exercises," Whiteleaf said confidently, remembering those from the prince's boyhood. "And then some martial ones."

The emperor remembered those callused hands. "What kind of martial exercises?"

Whiteleaf knew nothing of martial exercises, and cared less. His life in the palace had been dedicated to making life clean, gracious, and elegant, as befitted those with imperial blood. Even if he had an interest, he couldn't see well enough to distinguish much. "This ignorant, unworthy servant observed only that they were martial—waving his arms in a way that was not like his dance poses. But there are no weapons in use, or even present in the pavilion." He ended on a firm note—rules were rules.

"Waving his arms around." The emperor suppressed a desire to laugh, and shrugged off the martial exercises, which had to be sloppy and full of bawling bravado, typical of the criminals who called themselves *gallant wanderers*. If they had any self-discipline, they would have made their way to the army or navy.

"... bathed and breakfasted, after which he sat down to his studies." Whiteleaf went on in a wealth of detail about what the prince was reading, glad to be giving such an unexceptionable report about the charge he had been fond of since babyhood.

"Second Imperial Prince Vaion comes by every day after his studies. He left yesterday before the evening meal. After dinner, the prince played the guzheng for the entire evening watch, and when he rose from that, the new pillow maids Bitternail sent over came to offer their services, but again he turned them down."

The emperor's brows lifted. A few days, while recovering, was understandable. Had Jion been damaged in his wanderings? But the emperor had received a precise report on his son's physical well-being after that first bath. "Did my son say anything?"

Whiteleaf's gaze dropped. "His imperial highness said to this lowly servant when he bade me send them away that he could wait until he did not have an audience."

Audience? Since when were servants an audience?

Whiteleaf went on, "Should this stupid servant try pillow boys for his imperial highness's comfort?"

The emperor waved that off. "Pillow boys won't secure the imperial bloodline," he said with a shrug. "He's young. Being a hermit won't last long. Give him a few days. Boys that age, he'll soon forget all about his 'audience'."

The emperor was mildly intrigued, especially about the studying. But wasn't that Manon's idea? Jion was following her lead? As he had apparently been following the lead of some criminal out on the border islands.

The emperor considered his conflicting emotions. Jion had shown such promise! But on the other hand, a brilliant son well ahead of his peers might be impatient to inherit his throne before his father was ready to relinquish it—the old records were full of sanguinarily inauspicious tales of this sort, and the emperor had done what he could to circumvent that by allowing the dancing lessons. And what a mistake that had been! He'd put an end to it, and turned his mind back to the fact that the future ruler had to be educated. It might already be time for the eldest children to be given tasks, if they did not find ways to serve him and the empire that one or another might one day rule.

He was still pondering that as he went off to morning court.

Fai Anbai, chief of the ferrets, also received a report through his own channels, and was not pleased. Nor was he displeased—so he told himself. His extreme ire had lessened over the course of the journey to a tightly controlled disgust; he'd left the ship no long wishing to personally witness the young prince put to death. He had no wish to see him at all, or hear about him, ever again.

But that was impossible. He received regular reports on the entire imperial family, as a matter of course. He just hoped the imperial offspring were done interfering with important matters—matters of empire. Spending the better part of two years chasing a spoilt runaway prince had become a state matter only because the emperor willed it so.

Of more far more interest was catching up with the mountain of reports that he would have to peruse one by one. It was going to take even longer now, with Tek Banu off on her own. She had been the best at reading everything, and spotting anomalies that others missed.

He turned his attention to the most recent report, from the agents he left behind at the end of the pursuit. The arrival of that report occurred moments before a visit from his father, ostensibly to see the granddaughter who Fai Anbai was just now getting to recognize him. Once in a while she even smiled, instead of staring at him like a stranger invading their rooms and then howling for rescue.

"You did not just turn up to see Little Treasure," Fai Anbai said to Grandfather Fai as they watched the toddler intently studying a bee bumbling about the chrysanthemums her mother was carefully harvesting for chrysanthemum tea.

"No more than you have taken your earned liberty," his father retorted. "I've seen your window lit at night, when everyone else is asleep."

Fai Anbai's wife, Yan Yian, slanted a smile their way; five years ago, he had returned from a long chase to discover that his father had arranged a marriage for him with the Yan family, who were connected to the mighty and numerous Ze clan. Yan Yian, a fourth daughter, had been employed by the ferrets as a translator and researcher. She had agreed to the marriage before he had any idea of it.

Whenever he saw her after time away, he was grateful for his good luck.

"Do you have any idea where Tek Banu is?" Grandfather Fai asked.

"Precisely, no. She has communicated with no one. But I have a guess."

Grandfather Fai shook his head. "You ought never to have let her go to him directly."

Fai Anbai knew that, but he'd seen no way around it at the time. He said, somewhat stiffly, "If the emperor finds me unworthy of my position and seeks to replace me, I exist only to serve."

Grandfather Fai gave an irritated grunt. "Son, she surely remembers the events of thirty years ago. And as surely intends to use it to her advantage. Did you discuss the matter with her?"

"No," Fai Anbai stated. "Without orders, I won't bring up that matter at all. I certainly don't want to demonstrate an interest, and have her use that as an excuse to burn out Afan Yskanda's eyes, or cut off his right hand, in order to ascertain the details of a personal matter three decades old. I see no threat to the empire in any of that sorry tale—she would be of far more use pursuing the matter of the mercenaries who attacked Loyalty Fortress. She still has what little we've collected about that. I refuse to believe that was a random attack. An attack on some civilian island, possibly. What could they possibly get from a training fortress? Someone very powerful wanted the son of someone else of equal or superior power dead, and did not care how many died in order to accomplish it. Cavalry General Falik's boy is just one of the many sons of high rankers there! Surely some minister or other is spoiling to present a memorial about it before court, at the worst possible time for the emperor." He sighed sharply, glaring at the pile of reports. "We're behind everywhere. I need her *here*. Working under my eye."

Having said that, he remembered why his father asked, and sighed again. There was that buried deep in ferret archives that Tek Banu, with her determined fixation on the emperor's personal infallibility, should never see.

He lifted his gaze to his father's. "She has always been regular about reports from the field. We should have warning."

A glance from his wife toward the open window was enough to end that subject, though both father and son had been trained in keeping their voices low. But the conversation was bordering onto exceedingly dangerous territory.

Grandfather Fai sighed. "I suggest you send Peony to follow up on the mercenary attack. She could probably use a break from spying on the Su clan."

"Good idea. I'll do that. What is the news from the north?"

Fai Anbai was aware that his father still kept his own sources. That was fine with him. Whenever they had occasion to compare what each had heard, it inevitably turned up something worth knowing.

"No changes up in the far north that I am aware of, but then most of my time was taken up with the search for the prince, and then the matter of the Shadow Panther Sect. The captain Screaming Hawk was impervious to questioning, but one of his newer recruits wasn't."

"Ah," grunted the older man.

Neither liked torture, though it was recognized as a tool of the trade. Torture was rarely reliable. Anything you heard had to be checked exhaustively as people in extreme pain would tell you whatever they thought you wanted to hear.

Grandfather Fai had taught Anbai that torture was most effective at a remove. Fai Anbai's usual process was to outline in graphic terms the fate awaiting criminals, and watch for signs of fear. Those whose terror was already anticipating pain were (after a few days of silence, darkness, and terrible noises in the distance) taken by when one of their fellows, preferably a thoroughly guilty criminal, was undergoing interrogation. The promise *You're next* almost always produced a stream of confession.

Which again had to be investigated. But that was work for his agents.

"Which reminds me," Fai Anbai said. "The prince foretold that result, almost word for word."

"Ah?" Grandfather Fai said. "Did he know them well? He joined them?"

"According to his and others' testimony, he was their

prisoner for weeks. I did not expect insight from him."

"Could he have been lying about not joining this sect?"

"No, our talker made it clear that he'd been guarded, he and the one they call Firebolt. No one quite trusted them. With reason, as it turned out. The prince and Firebolt between them seem to have led the escape, burning the place down behind them."

"Quite a feat for a spoiled prince," Grandfather Fai observed.

Fai Anbai shrugged. "He probably just did what he was told — if he were a leader like this Firebolt, why did we not hear of it before? Or, why were we not hearing of the 'justice'" — Grandfather Fai could hear the sarcastic twist his son gave that word justice — "of Shigan, the false name the prince went by? I wish we'd known more about Firebolt when we surrounded that square. I would have issued orders to secure him. But he's bound to turn up again. To resume, Master Night is purportedly raising an army, which of course becomes an army matter. I've given them everything we know. That brings me to what the confession didn't reveal, but the prince did: the Shadow Panthers might be connected to a noble family."

"How?"

"That's what I need to find out, *if* it's even true, of course. I gave the prince little opportunity when he tried to tell me."

The older man grunted. "You denied him face, didn't you."

"I did. Two years, Father. Two *unnecessary* years," Fai Anbai added, suppressing a spurt of venom; about the time he had finally caught the prince's trail, Little Treasure had passed that all-important first birthday. He reminded himself that at least the baby had reached for the ink-stick rather than gaudy but useless trinkets. A very auspicious sign.

Wrenching his thoughts back to his professional grievances, he dropped his fist onto the pile of waiting reports. "This is only a part of the ongoing matters that I was forced to put off while I chased all over the islands after a spoilt prince."

"How did he react when you snubbed him? Did you publicly deny him face?"

"No, no. Only when he came to me aboard the ship. No witnesses."

"Then you didn't completely lose your mind."

Fai Anbai felt a protest forming, but he quashed it. His

father was anxious on his behalf, and Fai Anbai knew his own impulse that day had been nothing but spite. Justified or not, it came close to betraying his oath. He said reluctantly, "I don't know how reliable a source he is. If anything he said proved true, I might have to follow up. Though this line of inquiry impinges on military territory."

"That last is true enough," Grandfather Fai said.

"I will drop the matter entirely, unless I receive orders. There is enough to catch up on . . ."

It was a relief for Yskanda and the court artists when life seemed to settle down to a more or less even keel within a week after the first imperial prince returned. Of course no one saw the imperial prince, so gossip ran in the usual circles — people asking questions of one another about where he'd been and what he'd done, then speculating on scant evidence. Rumor's restless flow moved back to the autumnal festivals, and conjecture about who First Imperial Princess Manon would marry. Word ricocheted from palace to city and back again as various go-betweens presented trains of magnificent gifts before court, accompanying petitions to seek a betrothal. The most important being an envoy from the new king of the Easterners, who sought a trade treaty to replace the tribute treaty from previous centuries.

The quieter atmosphere enabled Yskanda to finish off the portrait of the third imperial consort. He hoped to just hand it off, but he was summoned once again for the viewing, this time not to the third imperial consort's residence, but to the emperor's own interview chamber, the sumptuous one seldom glimpsed by any but the family, and a few honored subordinates.

On the walk there, kindly, austere Melonseed informed Yskanda that he was to be rewarded, and how he was to respond: full formal bows, as always, and formal gratitude as well. Yskanda obediently rehearsed the properly abject words of gratitude, but as he hurried behind the swaying robe of the graywing, he was distracted by the sight of drawn steel and armored helms. Were there more imperial guards on duty than usual?

There were. Apprehension hummed in his blood and

knives churned his stomach as they mounted the narrow servants' stair then emerged at the back of the fine hall with all its gilt furnishings. Yskanda's greatest fear, ever since his brief encounter with Ul Keg, was that his father would try to come to rescue him. He was terrified by the prospect—his only hope was that Mother would prevail, and convince him it would be an act of madness that would get him killed.

It was far too easy to imagine the emperor summoning him in order to brandish his father as a prisoner, the promised reward merely a cruel sort of bait—but his first glance afforded no such terrible sight: he saw only the entire imperial family gathered there.

The emperor, watching from the throne, saw the extreme anxiety Yskanda could not hide, then the easing of relief. He had no time to wonder what that was about: the graywing and the assistant court artist made their bows, and here was the third imperial consort, exclaiming her praise and delight over the portrait, her words tumbling over the dowager empress's own praise.

Yskanda responded properly, and bowed to the ground again when the dowager empress bade her graywing to bring him a reward. Yskanda rose to accept, felt the heavy weight of gold in the exquisitely carved little box, and bowed yet again.

He was obviously very ready to retreat when the emperor's voice halted him with a jolt. "Don't run away quite yet, Assistant Court Artist Afan. There is one more member of the family remaining. Her imperial majesty the dowager empress specifically requested his portrait."

The dowager empress, sensing undercurrents, murmured, "We are so glad to have our dear first prince returned to us."

Yskanda bowed yet again. He didn't so much as look for the once-missing prince among all the others, as he knew by now that graywings would tell him when and where to appear. His duty was to accommodate, no matter how busy he was elsewhere; in the meantime, he decided that this year, his letter to Master Bankan would look the same on the surface, but would make it very plain where he was, his current position, and that he was doing all right, in case anyone in his family thought to check there before attempting a rescue in the imperial city.

He offered his humble thanks, and then he and Melonseed withdrew, leaving the rest to sit down to dinner, as musicians played, and Jion looked about appreciatively, glad to be let out of his cage. (Though he didn't miss the number of guards around, silent reminder that he was still very much under interdict.)

But on the surface all was harmony and mutual praise. The third consort and her daughter chattered fulsomely about the gorgeous portraits; the dowager empress smiled on them all. The first consort and her daughter admired the music. The emperor praised Manon for her beneficial influence on her first brother—for the emperor had noted the positive stream of knowledge being carried to Grove of Serene Wisdom that Jion had, ever since he could read, felt an especial misnomer. Jion himself bowed and smiled, bowed and smiled as Manon accepted their father's praise with her usual modest, self-effacing reserve. And at the end of the successful evening, Vaion and Jion exchanged muted glances of relief.

As the second consort and her daughter exited, silks rustling, the emperor wondered if this appearance of scholarly effort was a sign of a fresh alliance between Jion and Manon, submission on the part of Jion, or possibly the beginnings of a silent competition. He could not control what would happen to the throne after his death. But that did not mean he ought not to exert himself to try.

He withdrew to his private room where his current favorite was waiting to distract him. His grandmother's acerbic voice spoke in memory, not long before she died: "Remember, Enjai. If you manage to succeed me, as I hope you will, your task does not end there; it merely begins. The common folk cannot do anything to imperial monarchs until after death, but they can get revenge for bad government through a thoroughly smirched reputation, and that lasts *centuries.*"

# EIGHT

ONCE AGAIN, GRAYWING WHITELEAF brought up pillow maids. "Or would you prefer pillow boys, your imperial highness?"

Jion gave his head an emphatic shake, laughing a little. "A couple of years of nothing but the smells and sounds of boys around me convinced me that I much prefer girls." He stopped there, reminded that Whiteleaf was perhaps not the one to share hilarity about the matter.

Yet here they were. It was at that moment he realized his own foolishness in forgetting dynastic thinking. His father — and no doubt his mother as well — would be concerned about the future of the Jehan line, and needed reassurance that he was capable.

What would Ryu say?

She would duck her head and growl something about boys and their toys. Ayah, *how* he longed to see her — there was so very much to talk about, to be understood between them!

But she was somewhere else in the world, and he was confined to his manor. And here was Whiteleaf, yet again, which meant there was imperial intent behind him.

Time to resolve his own questions about the prospective sharers of his imperial highness's favors, he decided in a burst of self-mockery. "Let me meet a few."

Over the next few days, he did. It turned out that their

personalities were as varied as their appearances. All were pleasing to the eye, dressed much as the girls and boys at courtesan houses dressed, to attract. Otherwise they were tall and short, plump and willowy, all shades of skin, some with the lighter, sometimes reddish hair of easterners, others with blue-black hair similar to his own.

The girls who lisped in babyish voices or assumed a cringing submissiveness he turfed right out again, shuddering. There was one on the second night who met his gaze directly, if a little coyly. She was quite pretty, about eighteen, with charming dimples beside her smile. She was also chatty, talking in a fluting voice that was more pleasing than not.

Three exchanges into their acquaintanceship, she brought up Empress Emerald — she who had come into the palace a pillow maid, ended up married to a besotted emperor, and began a singularly bloody reign by having all her once-rivals strangled. She was only stopped by civil war — precipitating one of the few times the ministers united in a single cause to get rid of her.

But romantic stories about her persisted in songs and plays, and while Jion sympathized with ambition, he was taken aback by the sheer avarice in this girl's wide gaze. Emerald (she had taken the name of her idol) seemed surprised, even hurt, when Jion sent her away again, claiming a stomach upset.

The fourth night, he conceived the idea of setting up a Circle board, both as something to do, and as a kind of test. He hoped to find someone like the girls he'd met in gallant wanderer entertainment houses on his travels. The ones he liked had been far more experienced than he, self-assured, and enjoyed life in the wandering world. The best of them had taught him to give pleasure as well as to get it.

On the sixth night, Graywing brought a pillow maid who appeared to be a few years Jion's elder. She was adept at Circle, though he could see immediately that she had no passion for it — no more than he did. After he won, he cut through her conventional flattery of his skill and greatness and asked her name.

"This lowly one is named Sia Na, if it pleases his imperial highness." Conventional manner, but her words were straightforward, neither cloying nor cringing.

He made sure his bedroom door was firmly shut, though

he knew he could not control who might be listening outside it.

"Is seducing me something you're constrained to do?" he asked in a low murmur, hoping that bluntness would disclose truth.

Her eyes widened, then crinkled in mirth a heartbeat before she lowered her head.

"What's so funny?" he said. "You can be straightforward in here. I wish somebody would," he added not quite under his breath.

Sia Na studied him for a moment, then said frankly, "Ayah! Your imperial highness, if you had *any* idea the competition to be picked to come to your manor, you would not ask that question. You don't know how very much you are admired from afar . . ." She saw in the tightening of his mouth and his sideward glance that flattery repelled rather than compelled him She reminded herself that her fifteen years in the palace was nearly done, and there was no gossip about him being the type to order beatings or worse. And he'd said she could be straightforward.

Why not be straightforward—a little?

"We all come from poor backgrounds," she said, answering the question behind his question. "We're not supposed to talk about ourselves, but that's the truth. We give ten years to the palace, and if we do well we go away with golden dragons in a pouch, more than some whole clans could hope to see in a lifetime. If we stay fifteen years, they promise us either a respectable marriage, to set us up with a business, or to forgive any crime in the family under capital offences."

"'Us' being . . ."

"All of us—that is, maids, serving boys, which includes those of us picked for the comfort arts. Such as this lowly servant, your imperial highness."

"Comfort arts," he repeated.

"I assure you, we're very well trained, your imperial highness. It's not merely seduction. Some are better than others with aromas, or with teas. Some with music. My art is massage." Her eyes narrowed. "I can see, if your imperial highness will permit me, that you are tense here." She touched the muscle between her own right shoulder and her neck. "And probably lower down your back. I could take those knots out."

As soon as she spoke, he was aware of a tightness, the

unpleasant twinge of a knot, right where she'd pointed. He'd been subliminally aware of it, but shrugged it off as part of the aches and twinges of not getting to spar.

He rolled his shoulder, and there it was. He stretched out on the bed. "Try it," he invited.

She was very good at her arts, and knew exactly what sort of effect her clever fingers would have on a strong young man of twenty.

After an encounter equally satisfying to both — for he'd learned some surprising skills himself — she was pretty certain she knew how to please this elusive prince. "This servant can pick out some of my companions who might please his imperial highness," she offered. "All of them are good at some skill — and two of them play like tigers at Circle."

"Good," he said, with a far more natural smile than he'd had at the beginning. "I'm not looking for favorites. But fun, why not? Bring at least two or three next time."

She left as noiselessly as she'd come, leaving him considering what he'd learned. In future he might or might not want anything more than some competitive Circle, but the noise and laughter heard outside his room would be more or less the same. And an ever-changing crowd would lessen the chance of one being assigned to get close to him to spy on him at his most private moments. A crowd! He smiled to himself as he imagined what sort of reports would be duly winging outward.

Yskanda and Court Artist Yoli plunged back into the glorious world of color and symbol. When they were left alone by the rest of the palace population, they were both content.

But there was no leaving them alone.

A week later a graywing appeared and Yskanda had to set aside his brushes and inks to go once more to the inner palace, this time to the pavilion of the first prince. Again, there were more imperial guards around than usual.

Jion, imprisoned in his pavilion, found any distraction welcome. At first Vaion had visited every day, but study, family expectations, and his usual pursuits had become quick visits now and then, usually to complain about how excruciatingly dull lessons with Master Zao were — which Jion fully sympathized with.

Then there were Manon's visits; her servants brought her flute, or pipa, and he was very hard put to perform adequately. Her musical tastes had become far more sophisticated while he was away. She introduced something new each visit, never anything he was familiar with.

One day Whiteleaf brought out a court robe of silvery gray silk embroidered with cranes and day lilies, to be worn over a deep green under-robe, and beneath that, black silk undershirt and trousers.

Jion looked at the court clothes in puzzlement. Wasn't he still confined to his manor? He picked up the fine jade belt, and the exquisite jade pendant with its silver tassel knotted in the Eternal Treasure style. "Day lilies, honor to grandmother," he observed. Ayah! He remembered. "The portraitist is coming?"

Whiteleaf bowed, and supervised the preparations. Jion submitted to having his hair elaborately braided and fixed with golden ornaments, and a diamond put in his ear. When the servants withdrew, he said to Whiteleaf, "Who is this assistant court artist? He seemed familiar at first glance, but I'm fairly sure I've never met him."

"He is a newer arrival," Whiteleaf said.

A few more questions elicited the sparse information that this Assistant Court Artist Afan appeared the Year of the Rooster during harvest season, which Jion recollected was about the time he and Ryu left Loyalty Fortress. Afan Yskanda had subsequently passed the Imperial Examination, and been promoted, although he'd looked no more than twenty when seen across the room in Imperial Father's interview chamber.

When Yskanda entered, Jion had to revise his estimate yet again — this assistant court artist could not be any older than Jion himself. If that much. A heartbeat or two passed unnoticed as both took in the other; Yskanda's drummed against his ribs when he saw how very much this first imperial prince resembled his father. His nerves fired with warning.

"Rise, rise," Jion said to the top of the modestly tasseled loaf on Afan Yskanda's head. There was barely any fuzz on his upper lip, though his face was beginning to show the planes of manhood.

"This individual of no talent wishes to inquire where your imperial highness would prefer to sit," Yskanda said to the floor, then dared a quick glance of assessment.

"That's easy enough." Jion was struck yet again by a brief sense of familiarity with the assistant court artist's searching gaze. But he was equally certain they had never met. Surely he would have remembered that face. "I've only got one room that meets your requirements."

He led Yskanda from his receiving hall to the next room, which was the most formal in the pavilion, the furnishings the same ones that had seen his father win the duel with First Imperial Uncle Hojai, and emerge as emperor.

The furnishings were the finest jadewood, with vases of blue and white full of autumnal flowers, but Yskanda saw none of it. His gaze arrowed straight to the great silk painting hanging behind the fine south-facing chair. He stopped short, his eyes wide—and once again, briefly familiar. Very briefly. Jion shook his head, reminding himself that this boy had arrived while Jion was gone, so it was impossible they had met.

"You follow the Snow Crane?" Jion asked after the pause became a lengthy silence.

Yskanda jolted into awareness, then his face flooded with color as he hastily bowed, sputtering apologies until Jion held out a hand, protesting. "Stop, stop. It's all right—really. Go right ahead and look at it, if you find it inspiring. I grew up with it there, from the time I was very small. All the furnishings in here changed around it, you might say, as I grew. It's so familiar it's become effectively invisible to me."

Yskanda's gaze strayed back to the silk, which was larger than the usual, the colors, the execution so brilliant his throat ached with wonder.

Central was the goddess Suanek, whose sutras were often heard at rituals of great importance. She was larger than life size, finely rendered, her eyes peering over the heads of viewers, her smile benevolent as she balanced gracefully on the back of a golden fish with water foaming all around. Her robes and hair rippled in the wind as she rode toward the rising sun; in one hand she carried a live willow twig, and in the other the blue and white vase from which she sprinkled the waters of immortality over the souls of humankind.

Jion stepped up beside him. "What is it that you see that I can't?"

Yskanda turned to study him doubtfully. Jion gazed back at that face that was in its own way as stunning as any painting. He wondered if the girl scribes on the east side of the palace found errands near old Yoli's lair, as Yskanda hesitated considering what was safe to say.

Jion waited. After all, he had nowhere else to go, and nothing much to do.

Finally Yskanda said, "This beginner of no talent ventures to inquire of your imperial highness . . ."

"Please," Jion said, pressing a thumb to one eye and his forefinger to the other. If Yoli's assistant would be running off to Imperial Father to report everything he said, well, what would be the harm in attempting to bypass the extremes of formality? Jion knew quite well that his father sometimes did just that. "I just spent time away from the ways of court, and it was a relief to be free of the flattery and self-abasement. Just tell me what you see."

Yskanda said slowly, "Is your imperial highness familiar with the Six Principles of Painting?"

"I'm sure something or other was unsuccessfully dinned into my unwilling ears by my tutors when I was small. I do know that there must be a balance between life and traditional figures, and I recollect a lot about the art of brushes during the time they tried to get me to paint an endless series of bamboo stalks and leaves, in order to train my hand. Go from there."

Yskanda bit back what could have been a very long lecture, and said, "It . . . it is a very old style, meticulous in execution, your imperial highness. It is a perfect balance between all six requirements. At least to this lowly assistant's eye."

Jion turned to study the goddess's benign face gazing out over their heads, his hands behind his back as he rocked from heel to toe. Then he grunted. "I don't remember much about Suanek except that at one time her worship was everywhere. She gave the last part of her name, *ek*, in some dialects *eg*, to the language."

Yskanda thought of Ul Keg—who would have been born with a family name, relinquished when he became a monk. He was a worshipper of the Phoenix Moon God, but the Snow Crane way included all paths to wisdom.

Jion watched Yskanda's gaze diffuse, and wondered what was going on inside his head. More natter about brush strokes and the Six Principles, most likely. "Ayah, shall we get going on this portrait? What do I do? This is a first for me. I know old Yoli used to sketch us, but that was at festivals and the like, never posed portraits."

"Your imperial highness must sit wherever is comfortable. If it is possible, a place where the light is good," Yskanda added diffidently, aware that he never would have made so much of a demand of the second consort or her daughter.

"How about in here?" Jion said, leading to his bedroom with its west windows. The afternoon light slanted in, highlighting the old painting on the east wall. "This pavilion is misnamed the Grove of Serene Wisdom," he said casting himself into the low chair behind his desk, and crossing his legs. "As you probably noted, there isn't any orchard or grove. This pavilion was apparently the royal residence before the palace was expanded, overlooking an orchard, but the peach trees vanished, or died, or were moved. The manor itself was cut in half, my brother's pavilion being the other half. It's not very serene, and I've yet to discover any wisdom in it. Except of course that contributed by others long dead." He smacked a pile of old books. "Imperial princes live here, princesses on the other side, until someone is moved into the imperial heir's manor across from the emperor."

Yskanda was finding this First Imperial Prince Jion completely unexpected, but he was not about to relax his vigilance. He murmured apologetically, "Might this unworthy intruder into your imperial highness's peace . . ."

Jion cast an assessing eye at the modestly lowered head, looking for irony. There was no hint of it.

". . . beg your imperial highness for a more traditional pose?" Yskanda's hands suggested a higher chair.

Jion had noticed that no servants were in sight. Whiteleaf of course would be somewhere within call, but the old graywing was fragile—probably too fragile to struggle with a heavy wooden chair. To test who and how many were listening, Jion did not raise his voice at all as he said, "Bring in a suitable chair."

And the oak chair carved with chasing water dragons appeared, almost immediately, brought by a new, husky graywing whose name he didn't know. Yes. That was interesting.

Jion shook out his robe and sat down, emulating the posture of the emperors in the official portraits. "How is this?"

"It is perfect, your imperial highness."

Yskanda knelt on the floor—which seemed to Jion to be an exceedingly uncomfortable posture for painting—spread his materials on a low table, and began to work rapidly. For a time Jion was satisfied to glance down at the edge of his vision to watch those long hands moving so assuredly. But when his neck stiffened and he had to move or get a permanent knot there, the assistant court artist instantly began putting his things away.

"I'm just stretching. Go on."

"This unworthy servant shall return when your imperial highness commands," was the answer, and Jion gave an internal shrug. There was no keeping someone who would probably turn out to be a bore. Or worse, a tale-bearer.

The assistant court artist was back again a few days later, apparently according to some internal schedule that Jion was not privy to. Before then he'd had regular visits from his mother and his siblings, Gau-Gau bringing good things to eat, as if he were in prison, and not perfectly capable of ordering his own pastries and cakes.

Manon stayed longest, questioning him closely on Kanda's writings, and then the commentaries. It was only after she left and Afan Yskanda showed up that Jion recognized an attribute the two shared: guardedness.

Instantly intrigued, of course he had to find out why. Manon was easy enough to guess—Imperial Father had no doubt given some sort of orders to the siblings about him, and she was always scrupulous in her obedience. Right now she was here in the guise of tutor. He'd have to wait until she was herself again.

The next time Afan Yskanda came began quietly, Jion sitting in the chair, trying to remain still, as the assistant court artist sat cross-legged at the low table, only the top of his hat visible as his hands worked with assured strokes. Interesting that his hands appeared to have more confidence than he did, judging by his diffident voice, his expression. It really was guarded, a different quality than the impassive blankness of the trained servants.

Jion found sitting tedious in the extreme, so he'd planned to work on his memorization as a way to pass the time, and perhaps earn back his relative freedom. The problem was, he'd never been any good at memorization. Once he'd understood a text enough to restate it in his own words, maybe with a scrap of poetic allusion, his tutors in the past had praised him for his comprehension and diligence, his study partners had been careful not to show him up . . . and he remembered distinctly balking even at that at age fourteen, and bribing his cousins into cheating for him because everywhere he turned, he was gently but firmly guided right back to his beribboned box. Which included the carefully selected classics he was supposed to know by heart.

He understood now that his resistance, petulant as it was, had led to the "opportunity" of "governing" one of the smallest and most peaceful of the Silk Islands for a period, to—he was told—experience statecraft while he studied. But he'd understood it to mean only that he was to say what he was told to say, to read what he was told to read, and to believe what he was told to believe about the world.

He still had not discussed with Manon any of what happened instead of this planned stay in the Silk Islands. Her visits were witnessed by all his servants, who had been chosen by his father.

And so, here he was, trying to make up for lost time in order to win back the limited freedom he'd had at age thirteen.

As the subtle whish of brush on silk continued, like the trickle of a tiny stream, Jion began mentally running through the tedious texts. After a time he wasn't aware of, he shifted gradually to murmuring them aloud as he kept bumping up against one sticking point, until a voice offered the words his stubborn brain would not furnish.

Afan Yskanda's voice was so soft that at first Jion thought there was a ghost at his shoulder. Absurd, of course—he'd never seen so much as a hint of a ghost. Why would one be quoting Kanda now? Then he looked about for Whiteleaf, but he was not in sight.

Jion had been staring into space. Without dropping his chin as he held his pose, he lowered his gaze, and began again, "Propriety is exhibited in *respect*, which is deference toward elders and those in authority, with specific reference to . . . to . . ."

"Rituals," came the soft voice, as Afan Yskanda's hands did not pause in their work. "Rituals, ceremonies . . ."

"Rituals, ceremonies, and the etiquette of daily life," Jion finished. "Ayah, I can't remember what comes next. Give me a hint!"

Afan Yskanda glanced up, coloring to the ears. But he bowed from where he sat, and murmured, "The character for the virtue of *propriety* is rooted in the character for *ritual*, reflecting the natural correlation between them."

"Go on," Jion said, intrigued.

"Kanda stated that the exigencies of ritual place legitimate ethical demands on us, but Empress Lan taught that they could be overridden by obligations of demands of an urgent necessity . . ." He laid his brush down carefully. "Shall this unworthy assistant continue, your imperial highness?"

"How much," Jion asked, "do you know by heart?"

Yskanda bowed again. "How much would his imperial highness desire to hear?"

Jion laughed. "Now I see why you passed the Imperial Examination. Were you the First?"

Yskanda murmured almost too softly to hear, "This unworthy individual of no talent was nearly last."

"I'll wager anything you were the youngest."

Yskanda bowed again, wishing he'd kept quiet. Except that the prince had obviously been struggling to get past that one word. Yskanda had spoken half-expecting punishment for presumption, but it was so frustrating to listen to, he'd thought it well worth the risk—and (supposing he survived said punishment) perhaps he would be deemed unfit for any more encounters with the imperial family. That would have been worth one of those terrible graywing beatings.

But this first imperial prince grinned—and there was a flash of mirth, utterly different than the cold smile Yskanda had glimpsed in the emperor. He bent over and sketched quickly, as the prince said, "How about 'manifestations of benevolence'?"

Yskanda quoted that passage as he worked.

"The three prerequisites for extension!" The prince's tone was part challenge, part laughter.

Yskanda looked up, and there was that mirth again. His sketching became surer as he supplied the requested passage.

Jion continued to throw random terms and words, each of which Yskanda answered in pages of remembered text, until Jion finally gave a laugh. "Don't you ever falter?"

"This unworthy—"

"You really don't have to keep up the self-abasement while in here," Jion broke in with a sigh.

Yskanda went right on, ". . . lack of talent is wholly ignorant about scholarship concerning statecraft, your imperial highness. It was on such a question that, ah, nearly failed this untalented servant." Yskanda's awkwardness with courtly speech patterns betrayed how little training he'd had.

Jion found him more interesting by the moment—and he certainly had nothing else to do. "You had a monk as a tutor, I'm guessing? Phoenix Moon, mostly likely—aren't they the most common wandering teachers?"

Yskanda bowed.

"Is there a trick to learning off so much written text?"

The impulse to demur, to say that there was no trick, that he and his sister had both found it easy from early childhood while their brother found it impossible, almost made it to Yskanda's lips. He squashed it, of course, but was appalled at himself. It was far more dangerous to be around so seemingly friendly an imperial than it was to be around the icily superior second consort or her daughter!

He glanced up, to find Jion leaning over, watching him with unhidden interest. "There really is a secret method? Or is it some sort of Essence charm? Why do you look at me as if answering will get you beheaded?"

Yskanda's face drained of color. Jion understood then that whether his casual joke was true or not, this Afan Yskanda believed it to be true as he put his forehead to the cool floor and spoke the most abject apology he could muster.

Jion sighed, quite aware that he was walking a very thin sword edge; telling the complete truth with those listening ears behind screens and walls might get them both killed. Yet he was really intrigued because it did look as if this assistant court artist feared the same fate.

Then the apology to the floor ended with, "It apparently comes easily to some, but in no way does it confer wisdom. Your imperial highness."

Jion sat back. "I have a cousin who always had to show us up by blathering the exact wording of a lesson almost as soon as he heard it. Until one of the tutors set him to write a commentary. I don't think it could have been a very good commentary, because the tutor later made a comment about how parrots could quote pages of poetry with about as much comprehension."

Again there was that elusive expression of genuine mirth, but with the shifted gaze of mixed emotions—a trouble Yskanda intuited the prince tried to keep hidden. Mirth was straightforward.

Yskanda looked down at the sketch, and discovered that he had tried so hard to differentiate this face from the father's face that he'd created a distortion. Being around this prince was dangerous. He seemed different from his father, but that made him no less a threat. Yskanda kept having to bite back comments — which, even if not revealing in themselves, might lead to conversation, which could be disastrous. He had come to trust Court Artist Yoli in a limited sense, for they mostly spoke about art. But conversing with one of the imperial family — that could only lead straight to the execution square if he let slip anything about his family, his father, or their whereabouts.

He took his small brush and adjusted minutely here and there. The mirth smoothed into a more general blandness, which was good enough for now. The painting was far more conventional, though it wasn't *right*. He wished he could finish it in the safety of the workshop —

Safety? He remembered finding the evidence of a search, and mentally shook himself. There was *no* safety in the imperial palace. Just the illusion of it. To trust to that would get him killed.

# NINE

FOUR DAYS OUT FROM Ten Eagles Island, the good weather changed overnight. Water and sky dragons fought in a storm that sent Ari's ship climbing up impossible waves to plunge down into equally impossible valleys.

Ari had seldom been sick while sailing, but the violence of this storm forced her to the side, clinging to the wood as the only stable thing in a world of chaos. She began her Essence breathing to keep her body from submitting to chaos, gulping in the cold air and stinging raindrops. Her blurred vision lifted, perceiving three blue dragons hanging in the sky, whiskers trailing in the clouds, claws—four talons, not imperial dragons—smacking the tops of the waves into foaming spray.

Then she blinked, and the dragons blended with clouds and the rain. What did that mean? She had already learned that different augurs would interpret sightings in different ways. She knew she wanted to hear words of safety—she thought of Yaso, surprising herself with longing for the safety she had felt in Yaso's presence.

At last the prayers of every person on the ship prevailed. The sky cleared but the chilly wind blew hard, searching every crevice of summer clothing to make the humans shiver. The King of Hell had sent the winter demons on the wind far too early, Ari thought grumpily, as she shrugged her robe up closer to her ears. Of course she hadn't thought to buy a coat — who wanted to carry one when it had been so very hot?

But she stayed on deck anyway, bringing her inner Essence to a roaring fire that didn't quite reach fingers and toes. It was better to remain a little cold than stay in that stuffy atmosphere, with a lot of people who were, at best, unfriendly. And at worst —

"There she is."

Ari sighed. She'd noticed immediately there were only three women on board. One had a husky husband along with her, and both jealously guarded their cargo. The other was about forty, thin, tired-looking, with three children gamboling about her, and a gray-haired auntie with her to help watch them.

Ari was the only teenager, and alone. Which three young men with skimpy mustaches and beards thought of as an invitation to talk to her.

"Talk." She had spent enough time around young men to know exactly what they were thinking. She had avoided them as much as she could, staying close to the other women uninvited. But now she was alone on the deck in the cold wind — except for a couple of sailors, who paid no attention to the passengers. And here came the three, who spread out, crowding her against the rail.

"You shouldn't be traveling alone," said the leader, who was short and brawny. He looked from side to side, and as his friends made encouraging motions, he added, "But we can protect you."

"We can," said the tallest one, his jug-handle ears ruddy in the cold. "We like protecting friendly girls."

"If they are friendly," echoed the third one, who was almost handsome — except for that leer.

"I can protect myself," Ari said.

And, as she expected, out came the "Oh, ho!" laughter — knowing, jeering. She sighed again, more loudly. Why were barely grown boys so very predictable?

Hoping to avoid the scene she knew she wasn't going to avoid, she turned her back and gazed out at the deep blue sea with its tossing whitecap sprays. Until the heavy hand landed on her shoulder.

"All we want is a little friendly — "

Elbow, palm-heel to the chin, side-kick to the knee.

Number one dropped to the deck, howling curses. In the three heartbeats it took his friends to recover from their total surprise and then come at her, she'd yanked her staff from the carryall she kept with her at all times and snapped it together.

Three pairs of eyes rounded (one pain-hazed). They stumbled back a step as she advanced, gaining space. She swung her staff, glad to have it in hand again, then set it humming. If possible their eyes widened even further.

"I could really use a scrap," she said evenly — a little wistfully. Definitely non-threatening. But as she whipped that staff around then grounded it on the deck with a crack that echoed off the masts, her would-be protectors backed off another step.

"Really," she said conversationally — for she didn't see any purpose in making enemies of them. "I haven't drilled for days, and it actually *hurts*. How about it, boys?"

"Who trained you?" the tall one asked. The leer was gone, replaced by anger.

"Redbark Sect," she said, and her voice was very wistful now.

"Redbark!" one repeated. The affront was gone, at least. "Isn't that . . ."

"Do you know Firebolt?" the third asked, and all three were now overgrown, shuffling boys.

She considered what to say, then decided against the fun of seeing those wide eyes fall out of their heads if she admitted to the name. Firebolt was supposed to be somewhere else, as far as the imperials were concerned. She no longer trusted them to remain at a safe distance.

"Yes," she said.

"What's your name?"

"Ari," she said.

"'Peace,'" the brawny one cracked, *haw*ing with laughter. "That's a good one, with those skills!"

Ari put her hands together in the gallant wanderer bow as she said, "I only fight to protect those who can't protect themselves. For justice."

The three stared at those straight, earnest brows, that young face innocent of malice or coyness, and remembered the tale of the burning ruins of the Shadow Panther lair.

One by one they bowed back, mumbling their names, not without a few sheepish sideways looks. The angry one was the most uncertain, still feeling he'd lost face, she sensed. He was silent as the other two spoke.

"Do you know Redbark style? You must."

"Will you teach us?"

"What would you like to learn?" Ari asked, and saw the anger recede in the one.

The rest of the day went much better. They had the rudiments of training, relying as big boys did mainly on strength. She taught them the Earth warmup, then put away her staff and scrapped with them in hand-to-hand. They were easy to defeat as they had no real idea how to work together beyond crowding a target, and then when the target was down, kicking and punching until it stopped moving.

She worked them hard, and by the time darkness closed in and the rising wind drove them below, entertained them with a few stories about Firebolt's actions in the name of justice.

The next morning was even colder, gray sky and sea. She leaped up to the deck—followed by the three in fumbling bounds. They chuckled uncertainly, joking back and forth in a way that veered between bragging and challenging, so she invited them to stretch with her.

After three of Shigan's dance tortures, they gave up, and all the rest of the journey they showed a tendency to follow her around. She worked them until they could barely stand, talking always about justice for those who couldn't fight, and defense, unaware of the looks of approval from the sailors, who had been readying for trouble. She was only aware that she, in working them, got a good workout herself.

When Ten Eagles was sighted, one asked her what she was doing there, and she replied, "Going into the mountains to cultivate."

The three tried to hide their disappointment. They respected that—oh indeed—but it sounded both difficult and dull, and they were seeking adventure.

She gazed into their faces as she dropped into the boat, and hoped that their idea of adventure had moved away from picking fights to be fighting. But she wasn't going to assume that a couple days of sparring would change someone's path in life.

Again, she completely misjudged the effect she had. As a small child she had been Little Third, the tag-along; after her tenth birthday, her thoughts had bent toward helping First Brother on his road to greatness. He would be able to make the right decisions for the good of all, just as he had protected her and Second Brother in their Sweetwater days. She was comfortable with the idea that she slipped in and out of people's lives without a ripple. Without consequences.

But consequences there were. Of the three whose lives she was now leaving, one had stomped through life looking for fights to win because the winning might . . . make something better happen? But as that little boat headed for Ten Leopards, taking one of the mysterious Redbark Sect away toward cultivation, he stood at the rail remembering everything he'd heard about Firebolt from *winning* to *winning what?*

Defense for the defenseless did not seem so bad a place to start. "Listen," he said, turning to his two followers. "I was just thinking . . ."

And so he said the words that would set their lives in another direction, which is where we shall leave them.

Ari discovered she was the only one going ashore. The sailor who took her there pulled up beside the single pier, and then to her surprise he bobbed a short bow, for he and the crew had decided that she was Firebolt in disguise. She bowed back, polite though puzzled, then clambered onto the makeshift pier. When she turned back to ask, the sailor was already rowing back, aware of the tide about to turn, and shaping in his mind how the story would be told once they reached their next harbor.

She continued on to the building she remembered from what felt like so long ago. There, she changed back into her Ryu clothes and tied on her headband once again for the journey up the mountain. Though she liked the Ki clan, she felt unaccountably shy about going to them in her girl clothes. It seemed easier to dress as Ryu again.

Once again she ran up the mountain, exulting in her strength. When she reached the plateau, the sun had gone down behind the western peaks. Twinkling not far away, like a necklace of fireflies, lay the Ki village.

She was welcomed with enthusiasm, and a little puzzlement, quickly hidden. Ari understood then that Matu had told his family that she was a girl at some point when they came to Redbark's rescue at the Shadow Panther lair. No one said anything, but when it came time for sleep, she was no longer relegated to the attic with all the children. She had a little room between two of the girl cousins.

She washed out her robes before she slept, hung them on the clothes rack to dry, and the next morning she changed into them. But she left her hair in a topknot, which was so much easier to manage than the messy way she'd been doing her hair before. She used her old clasp, but secured it with Shigan's tiger-eye pin.

"Broth—Sister Ryu," one of the cousins exclaimed as soon as she emerged. "Breakfast is ready!"

"Please call me Ari," she said, feeling her way into this new identity. Even if it felt a bit like new skin, tender to the touch.

"Sister Ari," responded the cousin with a gallant wanderer's bow.

Ari decided she might as well get used to it, and asked, "Could one of you teach me to braid hair?"

The cousin's eyes flashed wide, then she grinned. "I will, after we eat! Braids for fighting practice or decorative braids, it's all easy once you get the way of it."

She was right.

The Ki clan was as friendly as always, noisy, everyone talking at once. They kept Ari the center of attention, not just as a guest, but out of respect for Redbark's reputation. That reminder of Redbark, which no longer existed, saddened Ari, but she accepted their effort as kindness.

Grandfather Ki presided, benign and smiling. At the end of the meal he said, "We will leave in three days."

Those three days passed quickly. During those days, Ari experimented, deciding that for morning drill she preferred her Ryu clothes, and the rest of the day, she did her best to get used to her flowing sleeves and heel-length robe. She tried to get used to having a braid dangling down her back. It was good to wear a headband again, which kept sweat from dripping into her eyes.

At the end of the three days, the entire family gathered to see her and Grandfather Ki off. They pushed the little boat into the lake, which lay still in the quiet air. A wide wake rippled out behind the boat in the arrow reflective of geese in flight. Ari looked at that, then at the white-crowned mountains, then back at Grandfather Ki, who smiled at her and said, "Your first lesson: how to row a boat."

But she already knew how to row a boat; she just never talked about when she had learned, and where. And Grandfather Ki did not ask.

The lake was gray and restless, so the going was slow, but by early afternoon they reached the other side. She and the old man together dragged the boat up onto the shore and turned it bottom side up. Then she hefted both her own carryall and Grandfather Ki's.

"I can carry that," he said.

She eyed the steep trail leading up the slope, and shook her head. "I should do it. I am your apprentice . . ." She looked around the quiet lake, the high mountains, the sky, and knelt right there on the shore, wet as it was. Putting her head to the ground, she said, "Will you accept me as a student, Master Ki?"

"Who is my student? I do not care what your background is. I will never investigate it or exploit it. I ask who you are, not who you were, unless you wish to tell me."

She hesitated, then resolved to speak: if she could not trust him, then she ought not to accept him as a master. "I was born Afan Arikanda," she said softly — very aware that she had never actually spoken her entire name out loud since she'd left Sweetwater. "Right now I'm trying to be . . . Ari."

"Peace," Master Ki said, and laid his hand on her head. "Rise, Ari. I see question in your face. I asked my question; now you ask yours. It is good so to begin, with trust between us."

She scrambled to her feet. "When I was here before, I saw some of the Ki elders doing a martial art, with fans. It looked like fans. But the rest of the family didn't do it, and when we went off to the competition, you said to me maybe you'd teach me someday, so I knew I wasn't good enough." All that came out in a pent-up, breathless rush. "Am I good enough now?"

Grandfather — now Master — Ki laughed. "You have drawn some strange conclusions, my child. First, you were with . . . ah, Yaso. Who was teaching you something of Essence, am I right?"

Ari's eyes widened. Most people had never seemed to notice Yaso. "It's true. But Yaso went away."

"Secondly, I wanted you to see the fan form, and to think about what you had seen. It is very dangerous, though very effective. What dangers occur to you?" he asked as they began to walk.

"Ayah! I did not see what it did, but it seems the goal is to tap acupoints where the nerve-conduits meet."

"Very good. And?"

"The real danger is that they moved right within sword's reach."

"Excellent. No one can learn it without already being an expert at the sword, or staff. I believe you demonstrated your ability there. But also, one must know the conduits and their acupoints. Have you studied such?"

"My mother is a village healer," Ari said. "She was teaching me affinities, herbs, and healing when I left home. I do know about nerve conduits, and I know a few acupoints, mostly the ones in head, hands, and feet, for curing headache, and the like."

"An excellent beginning." He chuckled, a breathy sound. "Come. We have a long climb ahead of us, and while my little valley should still be warm, the path might not be so congenial. I will test your knowledge as we go."

He led the way into the mountain, first asking what she had read and studied, and then, once he had a thorough understanding of what she knew and what she didn't, he said, "Now I want to hear the history of your use of Essence."

When she got to the attack by the mercenaries on Loyalty Fortress, he held up a hand, and sat on a nearby boulder so that he could watch as well as listen.

Troubled, she still related everything, including Yaso's words much later. At the end, she waited anxiously.

He said, "Are you thinking I will judge you? Not so. It seems your Essence is shaped by different elements than mine. It has to do with all that fire and heat coming suddenly into conflict with air and water in the sky. Your instinct was to knock those mercenaries flat to keep them from killing those villagers, which in itself was protective. But you did not shape the blast of heat. It went up as well as outward, which incidentally helped drain you."

"I've been afraid to try experiments ever since Yaso told me I caused that typhoon. I still worry that I might have hurt someone."

"If the storm went out to sea, then it would be all right, except for any passing ships, until it spent itself. At least ships are built to withstand bad storms. You don't know, can't know, what the result of your storm was. Accept that it happened, and that you must learn to control your Essence."

She clasped her hands gallant wanderer-style and bowed.

"I will," she promised fervently.

"Now, let's go back to the fan form, which will greatly help your control, as well as give you a very useful new martial art."

He rose with a grunt of effort, and they began climbing once more. He began teaching her the names of all the acupoints. It was all verbal teaching, with demonstrations on his own limbs, rather than requiring her to memorize a drawing and lists. She had always been a fast learner, but with demonstrations, she found learning far less arduous.

At the end of each day, when they camped, he tested her by requiring her to tap the pressure points on herself, both to settle them into memory and to train her control. The lightest tap for some shot a slightly unpleasant sensation through her, as if invisible bees with tiny stingers jabbed her nerves. A slightly harder tap was like the agony that bumping the pressure point in the elbow shot through her.

They continued to climb, each day the air colder, the east side of hill and cliff more barren. Ari woke each day shivering, a chill that persisted in spite of the heat caused by the climb, but Master Ki had her concentrate her Essence breathing on each acupoint, then outward through the conduits until warmth kindled from within.

When they reached a peak, the narrow trail led gradually downward and the journey became easier. A day later they walked into a sheltered little valley like a cup between peaks, except on the southwest side, where the sun shone on the rich soil. "It's warm here," Master Ki explained. "The fire dragon beneath the mountain is closer to the surface. You will see that everything grows here in abundance."

It was true. Her first sight of Master Ki's home was brilliant splashes of white and red and green, lush lotus and climbing hibiscus, around a small pond fed by a waterfall. Cinnamon woods lined the ridge in one direction, and bamboo in the other, so very thick that as the path led through them, she chanced to look down at her hand and saw that her flesh had turned green from the filtered light.

They emerged to find small terraced patches planted with vegetables, melon vines curling up bamboo stakes, and above, fruit trees: haw, pear, apricot, plum, orange. Master Ki's home was not quite a house nor a mere cave. It had been built into the side of a rocky cliff by long-ago hands, having possibly begun as a cave. It had been hollowed out, a floor hewn flat, and a wall with a window and door built in stone across the front. Calligraphed Essence charms hung like little banners on all walls, warding moisture.

Between the lattices of the window was not paper, as in the south, but several thicknesses of silk, and here, too, Essence charms had been appended, Ari guessed to keep warmth in.

The stone cooking area in the center of the floor was both for warmth as well as food. A narrow shelf at the back was for Master Ki's bed, the bedding stashed neatly in a woven basket next to it. Ari supposed she would be spreading her bedding on the floor, which would soon be swept and scrubbed clean.

At a sound she peered through the open door.

A fern rustled, and deer walked through the little cup valley, glancing their way with mild-eyed placidity. When Ari caught her breath, Master Ki laughed. "If you like animals, you will find many visitors. Especially in winter, when the snows come to stay. Which is why we will spend a couple of weeks harvesting and laying in supplies not just for us, bur for our four-footed and winged visitors."

She set down the bags and her staff. The bulk of the bags provided by the Ki family turned out to be stuffed with things they could not forage: blocks of tea, a roll of good, sturdy hemp cloth, candles. "Though these last we really do not need, but my daughter never seems to believe me."

"You can make Essence lights that last?" Ari asked. "I can make weak ones, but they are as dim and brief as fireflies."

"Brighter light is easy enough, especially if fire is your natural element," Master Ki replied tranquilly. "But first, now that you know your acupoints within and without, I shall teach you the fan forms while the air outside is still relatively warm."

"Why a fan? Can it only be done with a fan?"

"Of course not," he said, giving his husky, dry laugh. "Fans are easy to carry, and often at hand. We make the fan sticks with decorations at the top that serve well in reaching pressure points. It was a defense developed centuries ago, before the Sage Empress outlawed slavery, and specifically, the selling of women. The entertainment house women used it first, and it spread to the nobles through a princess who led a very interesting life. Monasteries adopted and adapted it. It has never been widespread, as first one must truly understand the nerve-conduits, as well as how to avoid getting inside the range of a sword."

And so, over the following days she worked hard. She cleaned the inside of the hut of the summer dust and leaves blown inside. Then she labored in the garden next to Master Ki, getting in the last of the vegetables, berries, and roots, gathering, shelling, grinding and storing nuts, and learning how to prepare meals. In the afternoon they worked through the fan form, which required impeccable precision. She was so busy that for a time she didn't even get to Redbark martial form.

In the evenings, the Essence lessons began. First, breathing. Master Ki had her begin anew, working on how she sat; then he instructed her to touch the tip of her tongue to the roof of her mouth and breathe. At once she felt her throat opening, and air flowed more easily.

Why didn't Yaso teach her that? Because Yaso was not used to human shape? Again, she felt as if she had brushed against another world, one she had not perceived. The idea made her shiver.

Once the new breathing discipline became more natural, she was told to empty her mind of memories, worries, calculations, and expectations. Only then, Master Ki taught her, could she maintain Essence vision.

"We are human," he reminded her tranquilly. "We walk through a human world. There are some who find the human world too harsh, too chaotic for their spirits, and they crave the world of the unseen. Some for contemplation; others try to live wholly there. To remain solely in the Essence world, which is not the world our flesh and bone bodies are born into, sometimes is to be regarded as mad by the humans around us. And there are those who seem to see both worlds."

"Oh," Ari exclaimed, and remembered some of the neighbors' whispers about Second Brother Yskanda. "Is *that* what madness is?"

Master Ki gestured outwardly as he said, "Madness is many different things, so many that it is a useless word, except as a name to separate off a portion of humanity from the rest of us. Do you need such?"

Ari considered the names, or labels, she was used to: mother, father, child, sister, brother. Monk, warrior, artisan. Master, apprentice. Beggar, thief, criminal. Gallant wanderer.

Dancer. Prince.

Emperor.

People could be more than one of these things, as she was herself. Except for that last one.

Master Ki leaned forward. "Do not think I am saying that such labels are evil. Some find them necessary, for they are a part of the order of the world. You must decide if separating someone, or yourself, from the rest of humanity is useful or harmful."

"Oh."

Once again she shut her eyes and emptied her mind. Her senses flooded with impressions, but she let them go without trying to identify them, much less react.

Master Ki said, "Now open your eyes."

Ari opened her eyes, and there was the now-familiar dell, but the air scintillated ever so faintly with thin drifts of color — Essence. She sucked in a breath, delight blooming inside her — and it was all gone.

Master Ki said that that was enough for now, they still had work to do. When Ari had cleared a space from rocks and stumps of harvested vegetables, she began her stretches. The dance moves brought Shigan near again, so near that she fancied she could shut her eyes and feel him next to her, effortlessly and elegantly doing the over-head leg stretch that had her grunting and breathing hard. How was he — where was he? That is, still in the world?

She touched the tiger-eye hairpin, then dropped her hand. It hurt so much to think of him, for there was so very much more to talk about now, but all she had of him was this piece of wood.

She swung into Redbark form, whirling through three times, which got her blood singing. But it did not banish the hurt.

The days passed, then the first snow arrived, lazy flakes drifting down to stipple the now-empty garden with pure white. That day was the first time she heard what she soon began to think of as the heaven flute.

While she gazed out at the white sky, white trees, and white garden, the sound floated down from somewhere above. Initially it was so soft she thought she imagined it. Except she could never have imagined such sublime sounds.

Gradually the flowing melody strengthened from breathy lightness to a liquid clarity as the rise and fall of notes searched out all the corners of her heart, and made her eyes sting. She remained where she was, not daring to move lest the music go away, until it ended as softly as it had begun.

She ran to Master Ki. "Did you hear that?"

"I did. I hoped you might be able to hear the hermit play. But no one knows when it will happen."

Ari had been about to demand an identity, and a location. Hermit? Then whoever it was would not want visitors bursting in to demand more. Ari bit her lip, thinking of Yskanda—how much he would enjoy it. He'd told her when they were small that he was trying to draw music, and while she still had no idea what that meant, she knew that at least Second Brother did. Shigan was another who loved music. He'd go still as a cicada in winter when he heard skilled music, as if he were alone, just himself and it. And when he danced, it was akin to all the Sun Sutras in the world.

Ari accepted that the music would come when it came. The valley was peaceful, her Essence control was getting a little stronger, and she was learning so much!

Two days later, they were hit by a sleet storm. Ari and Master Ki spent more time inside, and Ari gradually began expecting to see Essence in the air. Not just Essence, but the forms that lived in that world that overlapped our world like the tide slipped up onto the strand and back again.

She could see the wind imps now. They were actually rare—not every wind was imp-driven. She also had to learn not to "see" eyes on them merely because she had eyes. It was too easy, Master Ki warned, to impose familiar lineaments on an unfamiliar form.

The next time the hermit's music came, sky dragons eeled with sinuous grace through the air high overhead, their scales a silvery gray-blue that made them nearly invisible against the sky. Ari gazed upward, entranced: she had no idea if the dragons caused the music, or the music the dragons. Or if they were entirely unrelated.

Ari watched as they played and tumbled ahead of a snowstorm, until they vanished in the snow, and the music stopped. Then she exclaimed, "Those dragons didn't have eyes! I thought I saw them, but it was just ridges, really, with eyebrows of those rippling . . . whiskers."

"That is how this type of sky dragon—the weather

dragons— experience their world," Master Ki said. "They are made mostly of mist and cloud. What use have they of eyes?"

Ari remembered the dragons she had seen in the typhoon, and exclaimed, "There are different types of sky dragons?"

"Different types of all dragons," Master Ki replied. "When you get stronger, you can try to follow them. Some do that instinctively. Others never manage it."

"I can fly?" she exclaimed in a squeak of joy.

He laughed softly as he glanced at one of the baskets containing tools, and his old sword. "Some can, but it is very rare." Then he touched his head. "Equally difficult is sending your soul outward. But you must practice certain exercises first, to ensure your soul knows its way back to your body."

Ari thought of Shigan—and her mother and father. And Ul Keg. "Can I go to people?"

Master Ki tipped his head. "Again, some do so easily, others never."

"Sometimes in my dreams, I talk to my mother," she admitted. "And sometimes, when I bow to the south, I feel her next to me. If I do it properly," she amended. "But I thought that was my imagination."

"Hard to say, right now," Master Ki replied. "And then there is the fact that one can reach for another, but that second person is not able to reach back. It's easiest in dreams, for then our minds have fewer expectations than our awareness in the waking world. Expectations," he added, "can be as effective as stone walls and tile roofs. If people do not believe what they see, they will deny what is before them, or insist it has to be something else."

"Like seeing eyes on weather dragons." Ari bowed in thanks for the lesson, then got back to work.

Flying was not impossible? She remembered very distinctly how it felt when she leaped from the high front wall of Loyalty Fortress, some fifty paces from the ground. But she had landed as lightly as if she had hopped over a puddle.

She *had* to learn at least one of these skills, if she possibly could, to reassure her parents—and maybe to find out if Shigan was still alive.

# TEN

SECOND IMPERIAL PRINCE VAION'S birthday fell on the first
day of the tenth Phoenix month, ten days before Sky Wishes
Day, when people sent their wishes for the remainder of the
years sailing toward heaven in sky lanterns.

Before the imperial children collected their birthday gifts
there was the usual birthday ritual to be got through. Vaion
came to Jion to complain about it.

Jion laughed, though sympathetically. "I do understand.
Believe me. I do, little brother. Unfortunately, things being as
they are, I can't get you any kind of gift."

Vaion brightened immediately. "Spend the day with me!
That's better than giving me more things I have to find a place
for. I don't want anything else. Except maybe a better race
horse," he amended. "Cinnabar was old when I first sat in the
saddle, and that was ten years ago. He's a good horse, but a
real snail now. If you can bear to see the ancestral shrine again
after being stuck kneeling there for days, come with me."

"I was there just a day and a half. My being there is not the
fault of the ancestors. But I'm still confined here, you know. If
you want my company, you'll have to ask permission on my
behalf."

"I'll present it as evidence of filial respect," Vaion said.
"You know Imperial Father will always give in if a thing
somehow reflects Kanda."

Vaion pestered his devoted graywing for filial wording to carry to his Imperial Father, and received the expected permission. This he carried triumphantly back to Jion, saying, "You'll be riding with me again in no time."

Of course the day was a cold, wet, miserable one, but at least Jion did not have to kneel out in the courtyard. Jion and Vaion dressed in their most formal clothes, which, being five layers, were pleasantly warm. Imperial guards accompanied them to the shrine, where they set out the sacrificial foods, lit incense, and performed the formal bows to the ancestors, giving thanks for Vaion's life and asking them to watch over him.

All along the wet walk, Jion peered about, checking the positions and movements of the imperial guards. This he did not mention to Vaion. If, no, when he decided to test the limits of his boundaries, he wanted the risk to be only to himself.

The pair proceeded to Third Imperial Consort's pavilion, where they made their formal bows to Vaion's mother. Thence to the Imperial Dowager's Residence, and finally to the Golden Dragon Pavilion, as it was not a court day.

Vaion made his bows to his father as he recited the ritual words of gratitude, taking precedence in this one instance of Jion, who knelt behind and to one side.

Then the formal part was over. Vaion rose, smiling with relief and anticipation, ready to retreat to his pavilion to receive the expected greetings and gifts. To his surprise (and quickly expressed thanks), the emperor decided to accompany them.

Jion wondered if it was because of his own presence, and if so, what it might mean. Or maybe it was Imperial Father's way of signifying approval of Vaion, a son who managed to reach sixteen years without running away.

Jion remained in a subordinate position as they all proceeded to Vaion's pavilion, which had once been part of Jion's. It was much smaller, but with an actual garden built around a pool. Jion waited to see if he would be peeled off and sent home like a recalcitrant toddler. His father gave no sign—the imperial guards remained impassively in the back-ground—and so they all entered Vaion's hall in a semblance of amity.

The emperor, of course, took the south-facing chair, but Vaion knelt on a cushion at his right, and Jion sat below him.

Then in came the family, bearing their good wishes and

gifts: Gau-Gau, not surprisingly, with delicacies, but also with something new, a fan she had painted herself.

Vaion's mother brought bolts of fine silk and brocade; then First Imperial Consort and Imperial Princess together gave him some very rare and beautiful fish for his garden pool.

Manon and her mother, Second Imperial Consort, appeared, and Jion could not help but notice and regret that the note of genuine mirth in the conversation at once died to correct politeness.

The second consort spoke sweetly to Vaion and gave him a jade ring. Manon spoke affectionately, praising Vaion for what she had heard as excellent reports from the tutor, and gave him an exquisitely copied book that the young artists over at the scribe wing had been working on for three weeks. Vaion's cheeks reddened with mortification when he saw that it was an ancient text on law—the very one he had failed an examination in recently—but he strove to look gracious as he spoke his thanks, acknowledging that it was a very fine gift involving the labor of so many.

The second consort looked on approvingly at her daughter as the emperor said, "A very well considered gift, Manon."

Jion wondered to himself if anyone else heard how ambivalent that comment was. Or he could be wrong. Imperial Father looked pleased, his tone was kindly, Manon smiled, and the mothers bowed to one another.

There remained only the emperor, who had his gift brought to the front court: a pure white, prancing steed whose parentage was two famous racers. Vaion could scarcely express his happiness, but he tried, after which everyone departed—Jion too, after a single glance from his father as he said the words, "We shall leave you to enjoy your gifts."

All the maternal cousins and other schoolmates showed up soon after, dressed in their formal clothes. They bowed to Vaion and gave him the expected rings, jewels, books, and a pair of fine boots, ate the refreshments Vaion's servants had set out in preparation, and then most of them took themselves off.

Vaion's particular friends remained—Cousin Zuinan, a year older than Vaion, and good-natured, joke-loving Lu Fan, who knew every poem about being drunk in the classics. Kui Zuinan, being a year older, had experienced everything before the other two, and told them what to expect as they reached each landmark. All three had admired Jion the way boys admire an older boy good at everything, ever since they were small.

"He's really back," Lu Fan said, eyes goggling.

"And he looks . . . different," Cousin Zuinan said. "Did you see the calluses on his hands? What did he do? Where was he?"

Vaion shook his head. "Doesn't want to say." And he flicked glances from side to side, their old signal meaning the schoolmaster was watching—and they understood that whatever had happened, Prince Jion had gotten into trouble for it. Which made him even more interesting, even if they couldn't pursue it, lest someone report them.

"Can't leave his pavilion," Vaion added. "Unless it's for a celebration like this."

"So . . . no horse races?" Cousin Zuinan sighed. "I wanted to show him my Cloud-Eagle."

"Why would he want to leave his manor?" Cousin Zuinan snapped his fan, hiding his raised brows.

Lu Fan pursed his lips. "You think the rumors about First Imperial Prince Jion and a nightly revel of pillow maids are true?"

"I had it straight from my cook, whose nephew is one of the sweepers along the Princes' Row. According to him, they all come out laughing afterward."

Impressed looks semaphored between the young scholars, then Lu Fan said suddenly, "We ought to hold a poetry party."

"Poetry?" Zuinan groaned. "We get enough of that at lessons."

"Poetry games," Lu Fan corrected. "Bird sticks, flower sticks, either one would give us a fun game—and plenty of hot wine."

The other two both turned wondering gazes to Lu Fan.

"I'll petition Imperial Father if you host it," Vaion said.

"Nothing easier," Lu Fan replied, with the careless confidence of a very wealthy young man—the Lu family being connected to the Ze clan. For him there would truly be nothing easier. He had only to mention it to the house steward, and the army of Lu servants would ready everything. "We can invite Prince Jion. Perhaps he'll share his harem. If not them, maybe some advice?"

Vaion sighed, eyes skyward. "He's confined to his manor, remember?"

"Ah. Yes."

The two took their leave, and Vaion walked over to Jion's, from which emerged the shimmering sound of guzheng chords. Jion alone, playing his music, no evidence of a harem.

Vaion walked in, and Jion set aside the guzheng and reached for a pipa to strum as Vaion began talking about his new horse, then ended with, "Except for that snake Manon, it was a good enough day."

"What's wrong with her gift? She almost always gives books," Jion reminded him.

"If you can't see it, there's no hope for you," Vaion retorted. "It's not just that I failed the examination on that boring, fusty, old-fashioned snore; it's the way she's assuming she can be my tutor, though she is my elder. You can let her do that to you, but I *hate* her doing it to me. My mother says it's all part of her campaign to be made crown princess."

Jion lifted a shoulder. "But she wants to rule. Do you?"

"I don't know," Vaion said, looking away. "Sometimes I don't, sometimes I do. What I *don't* want is her giving me orders." He scowled as he picked up the fan that Gau-Gau had painted. "But we've argued about Manon so long, and it never goes anywhere. It's boring — *she's* boring."

"Whatever else she might be, Manon is not boring," Jion said in an easy voice. "I just don't understand why you hate her so much."

Vaion gave his elder brother a sarcastic look. "She's sweet to *you*. But even Gau-Gau, who was just a baby, saw how she became your best friend when she noticed you and Lily always studying together. And crowded her out."

Jion waved that off. "What I remember is Lily trying to study while I whined about sword fighting and freedom," he said with a humorless laugh. "No blame to her for wanting to study on her own. I bored myself."

"She might have," Vaion said. "But she wouldn't have said so. You know Lily. She is never mean. The way Manon treats her whenever the elders aren't around . . ." He saw the old impatience returning to Jion's face, and changed the subject. "This fan. Is this supposed to be a peony, or a cabbage? Or a turtle?"

"I thought it was a rose," Jion admitted.

"Ayah! At least Gau-Gau made it herself." Implication: Manon gave orders for someone else to do the labor on that book. Jion was grateful he left it unsaid. "I wonder how long her passion for painting will last — especially if they don't force that poor assistant over here to tutor her."

"What assistant — ah, you mean Assistant Court Artist Afan?"

"Yes. Isn't he doing your portrait?"

"Nearly finished. Is he always as skittish as your race horse out there?"

"You saw that, too?" Vaion asked, throwing the fan down. "I met with him for my first posing out in the garden, away from everyone, and he wasn't quite as jumpy."

"Why is he that way, do you know? I can't get him to talk. I try and try and all I get is face-to-the-floor, this unworthy wretch. I once joked about beheading and he reacted like the executioner was on the way to fetch his sword."

"My mother thinks Grandmother Empress believes there's some mystery."

"Oh? Why is that?" Jion set aside the pipa and regarded his brother with interest.

Vaion shrugged, his long sleeves embroidered over with moon-flowers rippling like water. That was another change, Jion noted: when he'd left, Vaion had hated bothering with clothing, but now he seemed to be developing a taste for fine embroidery and long tassels on his jade belt pendant, knotted in the Butterfly style. "All I know for certain is that it was Imperial Father who put Afan Yskanda in as Yoli's assistant. Though he'd only been here a year."

"That sounds like he might be a ferret. I thought they trained for years before they started being ferrets. He can't be any older than I am."

"I don't know. What I do know is that he's a Talent, and the rules for Talents are different."

"A Talent," Jion repeated. Not a ferret, who would never look terrified. A Talent, and a mystery. Oh yes, this he had to poke at! There was little else to do except miss Redbark, and Ryu, and that made his nights restless enough.

He went on to talk about horse racing until Vaion left.

Jion, alone once again, resumed playing the pipa as he contemplated that conversation. He'd waved Vaion off, and still hoped he was wrong. Because if he wasn't, then Jion had completely misunderstood Lily. He had always loved and admired his elder sister — and had thought her quiet withdrawal a silent reproach. Manon had contributed her mite, always referring to Lily's pretense of goodness, her assumption that her shadow was larger than a tree — and always those reminders that Lily's blood was half common. He'd tried to ignore that talk, but maybe he'd let more of it influence him than he'd been aware. He couldn't mend the past, but he could pay more attention to Lily now.

When he was permitted to leave his manor again.

He turned his mind to the days ahead. First, his own plans, like waiting for a cloudy night, preferably with rain, to test the perceived holes in the imperial guards' field of vision. Which were very narrow indeed. This was the time of year when the moons were drawing together again, so night maneuvers had to be in the rain.

Meanwhile, he needed another distraction during the day — something that would gain approval as well as give him a chance to see more of Lily — and got an idea. He carefully composed a request of his father, couched in the most abject language, suggesting that the entire family come to his pavilion for Sky Wishes Day, for which he requested permission to gain the expertise of Assistant Court Artist Afan in preparing the lanterns.

Much to his surprise, he woke to a verbal message the next morning: permission granted. That promptitude seemed to suggest that Afan Yskanda might be Imperial Father's creature, even if he wasn't a ferret, and therefore would be reporting everything Jion did and said. Ayah, that was nothing new.

The second surprise occurred later that day, when he dashed into another room to fetch an old poetry book, and saw a new servant busy dusting the shelves. In the past he never would have looked twice, but after his time at Loyalty Fortress, and with Redbark, he immediately recognized the martial arts readiness in the man's lineaments. This was definitely a ferret. To report on Jion? Why would Father need two spies . . . or had Jion got it completely wrong, and this ferret was here to report on Afan Yskanda? Who had looked terrified the first time Jion laid eyes on him.

Jion sat down and wrote a note to Lily, explaining his Sky Wishes idea and begging her to help him select appropriate poems. He sent a page off with that as the assistant court artist showed up to complete the last of Jion's portrait.

Jion said, "As soon as that's done, there's another project."

Yskanda bowed, his face hidden. When he came up, his expression was utterly blank, but Jion could read the reluctance in every line of his body. Jion pushed on, wondering if he'd blundered somehow. "This is for Sky Wishes Day—what I want is a hundred lanterns. More. Painted cleverly, to rise into the air all at once. Fireworks, only with lanterns. After which of course everyone can send up their own lanterns."

As soon as he said the word "fireworks," Afan Yskanda's expression lengthened into a genuine, if brief, expression of wonder. Spy or not, Jion had guessed correctly: this Afan Yskanda delighted in the world of color.

Yskanda got to work on finishing the portrait, then surrendered it and bowed himself out, promising to return the day after next court session. Then he bent into a cold wind and hurried back to the court artist's workplace and relative safety, as Jion considered with satisfaction that now either of two things would occur: he and Afan Yskanda would be putting the entire house of servants to work, during which he was certain he could winnow out whatever mystery there was—or else old Yoli would intervene, which might get Jion out of his manor.

A note appeared, and he recognized Lily's hand. She would be honored and delighted to aid him.

Yskanda found Yoli hobbling to the storage cupboard on a crutch, muttering curses under his breath at every step. Yskanda sprang to help him, and when they had between them replenished the supplies and sat down again, Yoli eyed his assistant as said, "You didn't finish that portrait?"

"Oh, I did. But there's a new assignment." Yskanda repeated what Jion had requested.

The court artist leaned back. "You should know by now this is not a position where you can sit around and catch sparrows in the doorway. I can even say that it was far busier when I was young."

"And you had assistants," Yskanda pointed out as he glanced regretfully at the half-finished screen on its frame beside his own desk.

"Which we shall have as needed. An army of them as soon as they negotiate a wedding treaty for the eldest imperial princess, and an auspicious date chosen. And when those assistants arrive, our conversations will be entirely upon matters of ink and silk." The court artist used the end of a brush to scratch one of his white, bristling brows, then said, "You only have a week and a handful of days to get this project done for the prince. You shall have assistants for it. Get you used to being in charge."

# ELEVEN

PETAL RARELY SPOKE ABOUT her nightmarish life with her stepmother.

She told Matu there was no use in it, and to talk about it made her relive it. But when Te Gar emerged on the horizon, the wind was soft enough for the ship to glide slowly, which made its motions nearly bearable for Matu. He was able to sit up, but he was far from comfortable. "Let's talk. Anything to keep my mind off the water."

"What shall we talk about?"

"We're coming to Te Gar and your old life," Matu said gently. "Will it help or hinder you to talk about it?"

"What do you want to know?"

He said, "I don't really know anything. Just that Ryu insisted on bringing you with us, even though there might be a risk of you being written up as a runaway."

Petal flushed. "I never did anything wrong. I was not a bond-servant. And if she had reported me, I was of age, for I know girls can leave by their sixteenth year, and I was near eighteen—though First Mother beat me every time I said my real age. She insisted I was younger so she could get an extra year out of me. But after Ryu said to come, and said I could learn Redbark, and said at that island, that I was . . ."

"A hero," Matu said. "Ryu is right. And ought to know," he added loyally, still feeling a pulse of guilt for how badly he had handled Ryu's confession.

"Ryu is the hero." Petal blushed, her gaze lowered as if bad luck would come flying up from the underworld to punish her for such temerity. But the day remained clement, sea birds squawking overhead, sailors calling to one another as they brought the ship about. No one paying the least heed to them.

Neither she nor Matu yet had the words for the self-worth Petal had been learning, though they understood it instinctively. Further, they both understood that Ryu had given Petal this gift by being the first — outside of Petal's half-sister — to see worth in her.

"You *are* a hero," Matu said.

"No," she denied quickly, for at the very least such a claim was inauspicious. But then it struck her that perhaps she was denying the gift Ryu had given her. She had to explain, and once she began talking, she could not seem to stop, especially about her half-sister.

"She was named Autumnal Beauty from some old poem, but everyone except First Mother called her Autumn," Petal told Matu as the uneven juts resolved into the rocky hills behind the harbor, picked out in the low light of impending winter.

"She was like you? Kind," Matu asked.

"*Truly* kind," Petal stated, doggedly honest. "I learned how to pretend to be kind from her. Though I was always resentful and angry. I learned from her that others could hurt the way I did. But I didn't mind getting back at someone who hurt me, if I could. Kindness was in her heart. She got that from Father."

"As did you," Matu said.

Petal looked away, as above, sailors called out to one another, bringing the ship in line with the harbor entrance. Sometimes it harrowed her soul, how good Matu was to her — it was like a summer's day, yet she feared the sun might become too bright and warm. She had gone without love for so long that she knew not how to accept it; however, enough of her father's love remained buried in memory, as well as her sister's, for her to crave it, to want to learn it again.

She gulped in air, then said, "I was barely four when Autumn was given over to me to watch — there were three years' difference between us. I thought she was my baby, and so I treated her as my own. Father was alive still, so I was able to learn how to tend her without the beatings I got later if she cried or got hurt. But she cried when I cried, and when she got old enough to talk, she tried to shield me. And to help me when she could sneak away from her lessons in being a lady, for First Mother kept telling her that her duty was to make a great marriage."

"Why was this woman called First Mother? Did you not have a mother before her advent?"

"Mine died when I was small," Petal said. "She was old, like father. When at last she was with child she had terrible trouble having me, and when no other child was forthcoming, though they both went to shamans and augurs, he married that woman as a side-consort. My mother was dead within a year, and in looking back, it seems to me First Mother had something to do with it, if only in nagging her into the underworld to escape. At any rate, she became the first wife, and insisted both of us call her First Mother, as if my mother had never existed."

"Did your father marry another side consort?"

"There was talk of it. He wanted a son. But in another year, he, too, was dead of old age. He aged ten years for each one after my mother was gone. I became less than a bond-servant, and First Mother reserved all comfort and delicacy for Autumn, who she expected to make a grand marriage—the inn would be her dowry, for First Mother kept bragging how Father had left the inn solely to Autumn once they both were gone. I was nothing."

Matu's fists clenched. He liked to face the word with a peaceable front, but he was beginning to fear he wouldn't be able to keep his temper around that woman. Maybe it would be better for Petal to go alone, and he could wait.

". . . learn to bow with grace, so you make a grand marriage, learn calligraphy, for no nobleman will look twice at a woman with bad handwriting, so she always heard. But no one was better at embroidery—everyone on the street said so, not just me." Petal smiled proudly. "I had to get my nose right up next to it in order to see her stitches, but I assure you, few could make more delicate stitches, even in the imperial city itself. Everyone said so."

"You said she was married off to someone old?"

Petal shivered, and when the anchor went down, she staggered, and Matu held her against him to steady her. "She was fifteen, and he was old, with seven consorts already. She cried to me about how his watery eyes followed her about," Petal said, her gaze distant. "How he smelled of stale wine. She cried and cried — it was the only time she was ever punished. First Mother locked her up until the wedding on her sixteenth birthday, and then made her drink a potion. When Autumn came out of her room in her red gown, with a golden bride crown on her head, her eyes were rolling, and First Mother had to hold her up. She was put in the bride palanquin, and I never saw her again. I am haunted by the fear that she might have been sent back to First Mother, and made into a bond-servant like me. For it would be unlikely she could make a second marriage of the sort First Mother wanted."

When Petal spoke in that soft, tremulous voice — the voice of someone making a vow — Matu knew that nothing would sway her. And so he kept his misgivings to himself, and when the ship landed at Te Gar, he waited to see what she wanted to do first.

His own wish was to take her to the cousin who lived inland, or if Petal did not like that, he had several destinations in mind, all either Ki relations, or allies. But this quest must come first.

Petal held his hand tightly when they descended the ramp. They reached Prince Ratha's Miracle Victory Way, the main street. Most of it had not changed, except gone were certain vendors who had been a regular sight. Including Old Rock, the scarred gallant wanderer who had offered fights for wagers.

As they walked past that spot, Matu looked at the rain-swept stones where the platform had been, and wondered yet again why Ryu had lived in that disguise. And here was another pulse of regret at how badly he had reacted to her confession. He still had trouble adjusting his mind away from the thirteen-year-old boy he'd thought her. But Petal had never seen Old Rock's setup, so he kept his observations to himself.

Not long after they passed that spot, Petal stopped dead, causing a vendor behind them to let out an oath as he sidestepped, his tree of ready-made Sky Wishes Day lanterns swinging dangerously.

"Sorry, sorry." Petal and Matu bowed.

The man's irritated gaze went from Petal's abject posture to Matu's brawny shoulders and direct gaze; there was no intimidating this one. He nodded curtly as he passed on by, and Petal clutched Matu's hand. "I can't go near. I thought I could, but I can't face First Mother."

"You never were a bond-servant," Matu reminded her.

"Yes." But she swallowed, her shoulders up by her ears, head bent.

He tried again. "You've been free all this time."

Her lips parted, but no sound came out.

"And I'm here. She can no more put a bond collar round your neck or take a stick to your back than she can fly. I'll see to *that*."

"I can't let you do anything that would get you arrested." Petal's eyes squeezed shut, but tears of shame leaked out anyway. "I'm so *afraid* she'll do it, that she has evil Essence charms waiting for me, and next thing I know a boiling kettle will fall on my head, and I'll find myself . . ."

Matu took her hand, an idea evolving in his head. "Petal. Let me go check. Please."

She stilled, her gaze downward. She was hating herself as a coward, and he knew it.

"Please, Petal. You took care of me on that ship. On *every* ship. Cleaned up my puke without a word or a sigh. Let me do this easy thing for you. I'm not afraid of that woman. In fact, there are some things I'd like to say to her—and no one gets arrested for speaking their mind about ill-treatment. You go to that tea shop over there." And when she hesitated, "Your stepmother won't even remember me. I was only there the once, when she turned me and my cousin away. I'll go, I'll only stay long enough to see if Autumn is there, and come back. Then we can plan. All right?"

Petal clamped her lips tightly against asking for reassurance that he would not disappear on her. If he did, it would be no more than she deserved—it would be her fate. Ryu had taught her that she could survive.

He pressed her hand once again, said, "I'll be right back," and when she knuckled her eyes and nodded agreement, he continued the last distance as he mentally prepared a brimstone of a speech once he got inside the inn.

But there was no getting inside. He found himself confronted by a locked door, with crossed bands over it, declaring the Blue Hibiscus closed by order of the Department of Registry. Registry instead of Justice?

He turned away, and after some thought, jogged down the

street to the bakery where Tenar had worked. The owner recognized him at once. "You're back—and so grown!"

Matu bowed, spoke polite greetings, said that Tenar was well, and then asked about the inn.

The baker's brows knit. "That woman! A rat with four eyes, she is! It was some time last year—she was arrested for mistreating bond-servants. She'd had warnings, but always lied, and we all think she paid off the old inspector, the snake, though the umbrella-maker says she reported her at least five times. Always said there wasn't any evidence. But the *new* inspector caught her in the act. There was quite a scene, everyone saw it! She was hauled away, and last I heard was handed off as a scrubwoman for Imperial Works." The baker spat in the street. "*I* would have put her to hauling slops."

"What about the inn?" Matu asked. "Confiscated?"

"We expected that, but no." The baker raised her hands. "The officials wrote off to her married daughter, so I heard from my younger brother, whose wife has a paternal uncle as is cousin to the second assistant to the Registrar. But this married daughter wrote back saying to give it over to her elder sister, the one who ran, though I assure you, no one blamed her. Certainly not I! But she was gone, so the inn was closed up for a year and a day, and unless she, or some cousin with a claim, shows up, the place will be turned over to the tax department. That was full three seasons ago."

"Thank you," Matu said.

He retraced his steps at a run, and found Petal anxiously awaiting him. She had not gone into the tea shop, but mindful always of her meager funds, stood outside in the cold.

He told her what he'd discovered, and she stared around as if stunned.

"What should I do?" she whispered.

"What do you want to do?" he asked—and was ready to put forward his travel ideas, when she turned to him, her chin jutted resolutely.

"I want to go to the prefecture, and claim my father's inn," she stated.

It was his turn to stare.

"Yes," she said. "If there is one thing I know how to do, it's to run an inn. That comes of having had to do all the work pretty much by myself, with the bond-servant hauling the things I could not lift, and the heavy repairs, and chasing those who tried to leave without paying. And Autumn *gave* it to me! It would be unfilial as well as inauspicious to refuse such a gift." She took Matu's hand in her own callused, rough-skinned hands. "I could make it a gallant wanderer inn. We don't have to go to them. Let them come to us. Especially Redbark—if any Redbarks come, they will stay for free. And I can keep training, in the back court."

"You?" he asked, smiling—inside he was thinking, *No more ships?* "Is there any place for me in this plan?"

He was teasing, but even after more than a year with Redbark she still struggled to understand teasing. "There will always be a place for you," she said, then lifted her head to search his face. "Are you wanting to go?"

"No," he said, and remembered to speak plainly. "I want to stay with you."

Petal's thin lips vanished in a white line. She trembled all over, and her eyes filled with tears for the first time since she had vowed never to cry again. She dashed them impatiently off her cheeks as she said in a low, flat voice, "I know things don't last. All those pretty songs mourning after love that's spent like a rose, and the rest of it. I don't expect anything from you. But I want to say, you can be with me as long as you like."

He felt the word *forever* hovering there—and it felt real. But he could not predict the future, and to try to do so would be the kind of pretty lie she hated. He would have to prove it to her, day after day.

What a good life that would be!

He smiled, and she gave him a tiny, wistful smile back as he said, "Though I'm thankful for Yaso's medicinal pills, I don't want to be on a ship anytime soon." And after he won from her a slightly watery laugh, he rubbed his hands. "It's still early in the day. Shall we go to the prefecture?"

"Yes." Petal endured a flare of anxiousness, but tried not to show it. Ryu had told her she could be strong. Ryu was shorter and younger and he—that is, she—was strong. So very strong. *I can be Ryu,* Petal told herself. "Yes, let us go while it is still Horse watch. I need to know."

They backtracked down the street, past familiar shops. One or two people recognized her, and called out greetings, which surprised her; she had no idea that many had discussed her situation, and pitied her for it, but there was no interfering with families.

She returned bows, and kept going, though inwardly she quaked as if going directly into the tiger's den.

When Matu took her hand, she gripped his with her sweaty fingers, holding tight as they approached the prefecture adjacent to the garrison, with the grand Justice Building facing the street. Out in front of it stood the giant drum with the red-tied mallet, for any subject who wanted to demand justice.

But she was not here to demand justice. It seemed that had already happened.

They went around to the side gate and waited in line outside the Registry office. Matu remained right by her side, even when she was called into a long, stuffy office stacked to the ceiling with shelves and shelves of ledgers, bagged scrolls in the very back.

"State your business," said a robed and hatted assistant.

"I came back to . . . that is, I returned to discover that First Moth — that my stepmother," she restated firmly, "was arrested. Which I am — " the words *glad of* died. They would think her unfilial. "I am here because Blue Hibiscus was my father's inn — "

"Ayah!" The man's furrowed brow cleared. "Blue Hibiscus! The inn left to a sister. If you can prove you are she, we will be very glad to have that case closed. Very glad."

"How do I do that?" Petal asked.

"Have you any identifying papers? A letter, perhaps?"

"No." Petal flushed. "My stepmother . . ."

The assistant to the registrar remembered the woman, and cleared his throat. "Let me consult the registrar."

He whisked himself away in a flare of robes, and presently returned with a tassel-hatted, round graybeard who eyed Petal doubtfully as she bowed politely. He said, "Yes, we shall be glad to close this case. Let us proceed." He held up a sheet of paper on which they could see a red stamp. "Age?"

Petal lifted her chin. "My stepmother tried to say I was born the year of the Water Snake, but I know I was born in the Year of the Horse."

The gray-bearded registrar looked down at the sister's testimony, which said: *My mother always insisted she was born in the Snake year, but it seems to this sister she was really born the Horse year.*

The assistant caught a significant glance from his chief, and knew what must come next. The other facts listed were daunting—"thin, fawn-brown skin, dark hair," which could be approximately half the population—but at the last was "blind in one eye"—which could be faked. But they had a test for that.

It was easy to see which eye was purported to be the blind one. The assistant tiptoed around to that side, then, brandishing a seal opener, stabbed it toward Petal's face from the side. She did not even blink. Matu jumped, and was about to protest when the assistant held up his hand to halt him. He moved to the other side, and had just raised his hand when Petal flinched, staggering back a step.

Matu scowled at the assistant, who bowed, saying, "Blind in one eye: proved."

The registrar laid aside the paper. "We will now proceed to the inn."

And so, as the denizens of the street watched, the registrar himself trundled importantly along the very middle, enjoying his moment of drama. His office ordinarily was not one of excitement, unlike the judiciars.

Everyone gave way as the little parade passed: the registrar, two assistants, both carrying writing implements, and two guards with their staffs. Petal and Matu followed behind, Matu glad that his knives were wrapped up inside his carryall. He was as apprehensive of officialdom as Petal.

They stopped outside the inn, and the registrar waited while the guards removed the seal paper across the doors, then opened them.

Dusty air whooshed out, carrying the smell of dried plants. The hibiscus plants in their pots that First Mother had been so proud of had all dried for lack of water.

"Now, we shall proceed to the second step in the establishment of your identity," the registrar said, giving Petal's scruffy, travel-worn appearance a dubious eye. "We have broken the seal upon the outer door. Describe for us where the papers of import are kept, and any details of said room."

In a voice that only slightly quavered, Petal told him where the ledgers were to be found, and even how the household accounts were kept, for all that had been her job. Her stepmother had only watered the plants, and counted the money as well as kept it.

Petal knew where her stepmother's room was, of course,

though she had never dared to set foot in it. No one but
Autumn had been permitted past the doorway.

Shaking with trepidation, Petal described the room as last
she saw it; then the registrar led the way. The room smelled
musty. No trace of her father remained — it was a fine room
with silk wall hangings dominated by a painting of a plump,
smiling God of Wealth, a small altar below it. The fruit in the
bowl had rotted to dust, and the incense holder was long cold.

Petal looked about at the rumpled bed, untouched for
three seasons, the clothes tree with an outfit still hanging there.
Petal's insides clenched at the sight of the familiar garment,
and she wondered whose hands had been forced to wash it
after Petal escaped.

From there to the trunks behind the bed. Both were exactly
as she had described them, though she never had been
permitted to see the insides.

The registrar said, "The description matches. Third and
last proof, witnesses. If any of the neighbors recognize you,
and they are virtuous, tax-paying members of the community,
we shall declare your identity established.'

Every one of the neighbors recognized Petal — and were
more than ready to add extra vilification of the former
innkeeper should it be wanted — but the registrar said, "You
will have to take that to the judicial office. My responsibilities
extend only to proving ownership of this property, for the
benefit of public order."

The umbrella-maker from two doors down elbowed her
way in, determined to add her mite. "Yes, this is Bing Petal,
old Master Bing's eldest girl. I knew him well," she added —
skipping past the fact that she had unsuccessfully tried to catch
Old Bing's eye, until she gave up and married the shoemaker's
younger brother. "Yes, I'll sign and thumbprint that paper."

Then the little parade trod back to the registrar's office,
where he performed mysterious things with papers, stamps,
and the like, offering free advice in a scolding voice. "Prince
Ratha's Miracle Victory Way is a reputable street," he finished.
"An inn will benefit the community as well as contribute merit
to public order. All entertainment has to be properly
registered."

And though his next words were an official welcome to the
new owner of the Blue Hibiscus among the dignified ranks of
merchants, he kept her lingering as he delivered a great deal

of advice about the responsibilities and expectations of so exalted a position.

Through all this Petal waited, head bowed. She scarcely heard a word he said. Instead, over and over, she heard her name, Bing Petal. He saw her lowered head and moist eyes as a sign of her humble reception of his admonishments and wound up his speech a lot sooner than his assistants expected. He even unbent enough to say, "Any questions, Madam Bing?"

Madam Bing. She had become a person in the eyes of the law. A person of ownership. The enormous task of cleaning, repainting, and refurbishing did not daunt her. She was used to that work. What did . . .

"If . . . my stepmother finishes her sentence," she asked softly, "can she take my father's inn away when she returns?"

*My father.* Pleased with this filial respect, the registrar positively smiled. "Only if you give it to her," the registrar said, pompous again—he remembered dealing with that woman, who had argued over every tinnie of city fees and taxes. "As a criminal, she forfeited ownership. The inn would have been confiscated, but she produced a will from the former owner Bing Pan—"

"My father," Petal whispered.

"—which stipulated the inn was to go to his second daughter in the event of their demise, or judgment. Since he died a respected citizen, and the daughter was not implicated in the crimes, the chief justice ruled that his will was to be honored. We showed you the sealed paper on which the daughter left all to you. All is in order and correct. My seal there establishes you as the proper owner now." He ended on an interrogative note, eyeing her as if doubting she had listened after all.

Petal hastened to bow three times, thanking him in a torrent of broken words, and the registrar stroked his mustache and smiled again.

They were free to go.

The two walked out, and Matu, who was gnawingly hungry, waited for her to speak as they traversed the long street back again, past Old Rock's place, and many sights that brought Redbark vividly to mind.

When they neared the inn, Petal spoke. "He did not let me inside, but I saw a letter on one of the trunks. It might be from

Autumn. Before we do anything, I must see it."

With trembling hands she led the way inside, and to her stepmother's room. She picked up the sealed letter, broke the seal, and held up the paper nearly to her nose.

*Dearest elder sister:*

*I am writing this before I return to Hawthorne Hill. I am living there with Izu Ranu, who was our husband's sixth consort. I was widowed the night of my wedding, my husband never getting up from the wedding chamber table at which he ate a vast meal which included tiger liver and deer antler and toad venom. It might have been the toad venom that caused his heart to stop, but I believe Suanek heard my prayers. The only thing my mother ever did for me was to make him permit me to keep my dowry, with which Izu Ranu and I have set up an embroidery shop. If you return, you must come to Hawthorne Hill to see us. I am very happy here, and my only desire in this life is to see you again.*

*They made me come here after First Mother was arrested. I am going to sign the papers to leave you the inn, which I always hated. I would not know the first thing about running an inn, but I remember well that you did. It is the least I can do, who was never able to help you when I was a girl.*

*Your loving younger sister*

*Bing Autumnal Beauty.*

Petal pressed the letter to her heart. The paper crackled as her hands trembled, and she looked around, dazed.

Matu was full of questions, but suppressed them. He could wait.

"I am now *Madam* Bing," she said at last.

The corner of his mouth lifted. "Respectable merchant-owner of the empire." He looked a question that he could not quite speak, and asked the question next to it. "Is that what you want?"

She turned a frown of decision his way. "No. Yes. But the way Madam Nightingale and Madam Swan do it, paying taxes

and perfectly reputable to the empire, but they welcome gallant wanderers. We can get advice from that relation of yours,
the healer."

Matu brightened at that.

Petal propped her hands on her hips and looked around.
"The first thing to change is this room. All her things must go,
and I will hire a shaman to exorcise it. I want no sign of her
bad luck to linger. Then . . . I know just how to do it all. Was it
not my hand turned to most of the work? We'll make it look
proper for the imperial inspectors, and then we'll get two trees
in pots for outside, and hang wishes and blessings on the
branches, but among them will hang the gallant wanderer
white. This can be Redbark's new home, since their old one
was destroyed. And when Ryu returns, she will find Redbark
ready and waiting."

# TWELVE

JION HAD TAKEN TO climbing onto his roof, late in Turtle watch, once all the servants thought he was asleep. The time to be sneaking around would have been Ghost Month — though the nights were still summer-short, they were darker, with both moons barely clearing the horizon, especially when new. But it was too late for the new-moons nights, so he was going to have to settle for a rainy night, cold as it would be, for sneaking out.

At first he had been very obvious about coming out onto the roof, wine in hand, with a lamp, brush, ink, and paper, midway through Dragon, once he'd sent Sia Na and the girls away. He always noisily returned at the first gong of Turtle. He either wrote out poems or tried to write new ones, and the servants (and his watchers) had become sufficiently used to him on the roof that they returned to their regular watches.

During the past couple of nights, it had been cloudy enough for him to venture out again late in Turtle, when the servants thought he was asleep. This gave him the opportunity to observe the night guards. He was fairly certain he had found a single weak spot in their overlapping fields of vision. Only one, and that was narrow, but one was all he needed. If he was careful.

Two mornings after Vaion's birthday, Afan Yskanda turned up again, just as Jion was picking up his inkstick.

He set it down, smiling in welcome. "This four-century-old commentary on Kanda can wait another day. There's a great deal to do before the tenth, so let's get right to it. We'll have to work until lighting time."

"This unworthy begs forgiveness of his esteemed imperial highness," Yskanda said with a deep bow. "Court Artist Yoli has requisitioned the best senior apprentices. This lowly assistant can get everything done if your imperial highness wishes to indicate your preferred theme, and any other instructions."

They wouldn't be alone — or as alone as Jion ever was. All right then, it was the alternate plan. Even better. Mindful of listening ears, Jion exclaimed, "But I wished to make them myself — not everything, of course. It has more meaning if I have a hand in it. Though I know you and your apprentices would do far better than I ever could."

Yskanda wondered why the prince was speaking so clearly, as if they stood at either end of a large room and not two paces from one another. Then he wondered who else was supposed to hear him — and it all slid into place then: the extra guards, the whispers. Yskanda was aware that he was used to thinking like a hostage, and he had grown up hearing the old saying that to children who have hammers the entire world looks like a peg. Even so, he was fairly certain that he was looking at another hostage. In a sense.

Intrigued, he said, "Might this unworthy assistant suggest that your imperial highness deign to enter the workroom designated for our use, as apprentices do not pollute the august environs of the inner palace?"

Jion's grin flashed, crinkling his eyes with genuine humor as he mouthed the words *august environs?*

For the first time in memory, Yskanda was severely tempted to laugh. But he bit back the impulse and bowed.

Even more intrigued, Jion decided to push against his invisible bonds. He had Imperial Father's permission to arrange the festival celebration . . . *Let's see how far we get.* He turned his head. "Whiteleaf!"

The graywing appeared at once.

"It seems the court artist has arranged my Sky Wishes plans better than I could do myself. Assistant Court Artist Afan will lead me there."

The graywing merely bowed, and Jion wondered if that as-yet unnamed ferret was busy passing a report, or maybe orders, ahead. At any rate, he walked toward the door, and Afan Yskanda fell in two paces behind him. No one stopped Jion—but he had not expected that, for it wouldn't just be him losing face. The imperial face would suffer, threatening world chaos.

"Lead the way, assistant court artist," Jion said grandly.

He got a suspicious glance out of the side of Afan Yskanda's eye at that, but the assistant court artist only bowed, and stepped up ahead and to one side of Jion as he said, "This way."

Jion was alert to the slight noises, the shift of shadows, as his nearly invisible guards moved ahead and behind him. He raised his voice slightly. "My thinking was this: the lanterns ought to be variations on the golden fish and the vase of immortal waters."

"Suanek, your imperial highness" Afan Yskanda said, then bowed.

"Speak freely," Jion said. "We're here in the garden. Though I'm sure there are at least three watchers on various roofs, no one can hear us."

You can, Yskanda thought, but of course said nothing.

Jion suspected the trend of his thoughts, and went on, "One thing I discovered while I was wandering in the outside world is that common people who like music have better manners than my—no, I probably shouldn't say that. Put it this way. Music is something most common people have to seek out. Here, it's at every banquet, noticeable for most only when they have to lift their voices to speak past it. But I plan to have music that brings back the feelings that music ought to bring, when the lanterns lift. I shall see to choosing that."

By then they had crossed the outer reaches of the garden. They then entered the narrow, clean-swept but otherwise plain warren of corridors that had once fascinated Jion.

A couple of twists, a turn or two—the servants or staff they saw either whisked themselves out of sight, or if they could not escape, they went to the ground until Jion had passed. They entered a big, airy room with tall windows down both east and west windows. A number of apprentices in gray waited, and at the sight of Jion they went to the floor. Once, Jion reflected, he had believed that was the proper way life worked.

With an inner laugh at himself, Jion said, "Rise, senior apprentices. Let that one bow do for the day, or we will never get anything done, if you have to bow every time I take a step."

They gained their feet, waiting in well-trained silence. Jion went on, knowing he was not going to hear anyone's real opinion, "I was just telling Assistant Court Artist Afan here that my thought was to divide the lanterns between golden fish and blue vases, rather than the usual random selection. I want to release them all at once, see. But beyond that, every lantern ought to be decorated differently, and of course bear different exhortations from the classics. Any questions?"

The senior apprentices eyed one another. No one spoke. Afan Yskanda bowed as he said, "May this lowly assistant ask if the lanterns are to be one size?"

"What would look best? How about all different sizes, so that once they are let go, some will rise faster than others, the only uniformity the two shapes? It seems to me if they're all exactly the same they'll be boring after the first moment."

Still no response, though they had to be thinking something. They were all artists.

Afan Yskanda said, "If your imperial highness will permit an opinion, it might be easier, and faster, to achieve if size is not required to a specific standard. And as your esteemed imperial highness observed, the effect ought to be more interesting."

Subtle nods and whispers of agreement soughed around the room.

Jion clapped his hands once, the way that Instructor Fumig had done before sending the cadets to the field. "Then let's do it."

That first day was fraught with tension. Jion was aware of eyes following him wherever he moved about the room. Elated with victory (for Whiteleaf did not show up to "invite" him back to his pavilion) he pretended not to see the tension in the apprentices, the soft whispers and surreptitious gestures meant to convey words they dared not speak.

He built two golden fish fans with his own hands, the second better than the first.

The next day was slightly easier — Afan Yskanda actually asked him a couple of questions. To both, Jion said, "I don't really know much about art. What do you think?" The apprentices watched as Afan Yskanda actually answered. And when the others saw that the imperial guards were not called in to haul away the assistant court artist for his temerity, they took their own questions to him. After all he was senior in rank. (And if there was to be blame, it would fall on him first.)

Nothing happened to him, or to them. The third day they arrived to find all their work still there, no imperial guards hovered over them, or even worse, sinister ferrets. Later that day, one of the apprentices, who was known to be somewhat absent-minded, finished painting a fish lantern and exclaimed, "Look at those frog eyes—he looks *just like* Grand Historian Bolu."

His friends chuckled—caught themselves—looked around, just in time to see the prince let out a hoot of laughter.

The atmosphere began to ease. And when one of the girls rolled her eyes and said, "Virtue," a fast exchange of looks shifted between the others until Yskanda said, quite composedly, "Perhaps his imperial highness might honor us with his views, or at least forgive our shamelessness in chattering on an assigned subject."

"Assigned?"

The youngest apprentice there, subtly encouraged by looks and one or two surreptitious elbow-digs, said, "If his highness will forgive this unworthy thing for speaking, we gain merits if we discuss the day's topic."

"Which is virtue?" Jion asked, greatly entertained, and a little suspicious.

But it turned out to be true; they really were expected to converse on academic topics.

Yskanda said, "What does Kanda write about the sensory organs?"

A tall boy in the corner, with a voice that kept breaking, said, "Our eyes, ears, and other organs are associated with physical desires, which includes art as well as music and good food. Kanda says there is nothing wrong with desires, except when they motivate us to pursue them at the cost of *ethical* motivations."

"That's right."

Jion noted that the brushes did not stop moving while the chat went on.

"I agree."

"This is an especial danger," said a short, round girl, "because our sensory desires respond naturally to their proper objects—ears to music, and so on." She blushed. "Our moral motivations are choosier, if we engage those."

Yskanda said, "You know Instructor Nar will ask me. Who can name the commentary on Kanda's statement, and the summation of ethical dispositions?"

"We *all* know *those*," spoke a lively boy, looking around at his companions.

And the group, without missing a single stroke, chanted together, "Innate ethical dispositions are benevolence, righteousness, wisdom, and propriety."

"Compassion is benevolence," a boy piped up, his voice still unbroken—and brought Ryu unexpectedly to Jion's mind.

"Disdaining evil is righteousness," stated a girl.

"The feeling of respect is propriety . . ."

Yskanda stepped up next to Jion, and under cover of the rest of the voices reciting the old lessons, he murmured, "One of the Six Principles of Painting is Spirit Resonance, which is defined here as bearing the truth of tradition. They have to know what that truth is in order to paint it."

"And you can credit them with full merit if they talk about these things?" Jion asked.

Yskanda bowed, and said, even lower, "They did not dare earlier."

Jion nodded, and Yskanda moved on—to startle as a pair of whispering boys came up to him, one raising his brush. With a quick twist of his wrist he painted a round dot of white on Yskanda's forehead, and a tiny crescent moon over it: Phoenix Moon and Ghost Moon.

As both boys bowed low, laughing, the entire room also bowed, in a ripple of laughter. Yskanda's golden skin blushed rosy as his fingers smeared the paint. "What is it?" he demanded, laughing.

"Zhao Bang, of course," the painter said, then bowed grandly, followed by the others.

Zhao Bang—the famous judge of the Yslan Dynasty, known for his virtue.

Yskanda gave them a look of acute disgust as he grabbed a rag and scrubbed the paint—which succeeded in smearing it. "Back to work, or I will report that all you discussed is who drank the most at Three Jugs and Four Winds last night."

Jion was interested to observe that they took this as an empty threat, but still the two boys scurried back to their places, and the rest of the session passed swiftly.

At the end, Jion walked around admiring the work until only Yskanda was left, then joked, "Zhao Bang, eh?"

Yskanda had forgotten the paint on his forehead. He grabbed a clean cloth and began scrubbing vigorously as Jion said, "Why the look of disgust? I didn't see abject flattery there."

"Zhao Bang," Yskanda muttered behind the cloth. "Forty-two concubines, if records can be believed. What were those families thinking, after, say, twenty?"

Jion laughed. "Have a sister, do you?"

Yskanda's thin fingers clenched on the cloth, and Jion stared at Yskanda's sudden look of horror, before his expression shuttered. It was then that Jion remembered that it was very likely Afan Yskanda had been snatched from somewhere, in some elaborate revenge plan of his father's. He winced inwardly, wishing he could cut out his tongue.

Yskanda said with that polite bow and distant tone, "A person does not have to have daughters or sisters to think that maybe that was not a good life?"

"There was a lot about the ancient days that was not a good life," Jion said, striving to recover their easy exchange. "Especially for sisters and daughters." But he knew he'd damaged it with a single thoughtless, joking remark.

He left, and in a sideways kind of atonement, headed for the archive to learn more about the Principles of Painting. After that he returned to his manor for the evening meal.

He realized as he dined alone that he was not unhappy. But still, as rain beat against the windows, he knew he was going to test himself that night. He had to because . . . because.

He spent the rest of the evening with his music, and retired. Once the distant gong indicated late Turtle watch, he rose, dressed in dark clothing, and left.

He made it to the east gate. He crouched on a roof between stone figures, gazing out at the darkened harbor beyond the sleeping city. Here and there dim lights glowed: not everyone was asleep.

He glanced down at the gate. From there, if he had to, he could knock out some hapless servant and change robes, steal his tally, and get away. If he needed to.

He stood there wet to the skin and shivering, knowing that he could do it. Right now, that was good enough: though he badly wanted to find Ryu and finish the conversation they hadn't even started, he did not want to do it as a fugitive. Especially as he had no idea where she was.

He turned and ghosted his way back to his pavilion, where he shed his wet clothes, climbed into bed, and lay staring at the ceiling until he was warm enough to sleep.

The next few days he divided between Lily — who he visited at his mother's pavilion, unhindered by his watchers — as the two of them selected appropriate poetry, and Afan Yskanda, whose manner was quite different here among the scribes.

Not that he was gabby, or loud. It was the absence of that characteristic watchful stillness, which reminded Jion of a deer when tiger is scented on the wind. Everyone was prudently afraid of the emperor. He was himself. That was part of life. But Afan Yskanda's fear seemed sharper, imperfectly hidden to the discerning eye, and untempered by the gratification at imperial notice that others displayed when the emperor smiled.

The day before the festival, Whiteleaf commandeered an army of servants to scour and polish Jion's already clean pavilion. The imperial kitchens had already detailed cooks to food preparation. On the other side of the palace, Yskanda oversaw the careful stacking of the lanterns, and dismissed all the apprentices except the five chosen to go into the imperial garden to release the lanterns on the signal. He hoped, once that was done, he would be dismissed.

No. When he reported to the court artist, Yoli said, "You'll have to supervise tomorrow."

Yskanda frowned. "You aren't recovered enough?"

"Not for sitting outside in the cold for that many hours," the court artist stated bluntly. "I can — just — manage court, as you know. But when that is over I need pain-abeyance needles. Medicine isn't strong enough for the ache in my old bones." He sighed. "Why the low face? You've done this before."

Yskanda bowed. There was nothing he could say that would make any difference.

The next morning, he waited for the five apprentices. Unknown to them, he'd been the one to choose them. Among the five were two girls, both of whom were excellent artists. Neither came from influential families. They had to make their way up the ranks by their talent, and by their ability to navigate the slights and rivalries of their fellows.

They were filled with wonder and excitement at the prospect of seeing the imperial family up close. Yskanda maintained silence as they followed the lantern-laden carts to the imperial garden, utterly unaware that his habitual tranquil silence enhanced his aura of mystery among the apprentices. He saw his silence as the prudence of a coward. He had come to terms with his own cowardice when small. First Brother was brave in defending his younger siblings. Mouse was brave in hurling herself from rooftops and climbing poles. Not everyone could be brave—there was a place in the world for the cowards whose hands made things for all.

They reached the far side of the imperial garden's lake, where Melonseed oversaw Yskanda repeating Imperial Prince Jion's instructions: instead of stacks of lanterns awaiting the vagaries of imperial hands, the golden fish and the blue orb lanterns were spaced around the lake in positions chosen by Jion, hidden behind the last flowering chrysanthemums, aster and clematis.

Once everything was ready, Yskanda said, "We can wait here in the garden. They'll come out some time after they eat dinner."

"The sun is about to set," short, buck-toothed Gar Liesi pointed out. "It's nearly lighting up time. What are we to do once the display is done?"

Yskanda said, "The graywings will bring lamps, two to each table. Judging by my past experience, you'll mostly be painting lanterns for the imperial family, rather than sketching their imperial highnesses and their august relations. The graywings know what to expect. Just do your best."

The sun sank, the graywings came out to light the lamps. The apprentices who had been standing around, most with fingers stuck into their armpits to keep them warm as the air got colder, stilled, looking at one another in excitement.

"Places," Yskanda said. "Here they come."

# THIRTEEN

THE FIRST SIGN THAT the imperial family approached was the sudden appearance of the musicians. They filed quietly to their places without paying the apprentices the least attention: their orders were to play. Whatever else happened was not their concern.

Imperial guards led the way, vigilant even in the heart of the emperor's citadel. Behind them the emperor strolled, supporting his mother, who did not see well in darkness. The three consorts followed, then their children, and after them the imperial Kui cousins who invariably were invited by the dowager empress, the two Ran cousins invited by the first consort, and half a dozen of the numerous Su cousins carefully chosen by the second imperial consort. Finally there were Yu cousins brought by the third consort, who had no intention of letting those Su brats overrun the event.

The apprentices, artists all, nearly forgot themselves at the beauty of those lamplit flowing silks, the long dancing tassels, and the wink and glitter of gems sifting through the bare branches of fruit trees and the green boughs of cedar.

But then an unseen flute player began a clear, liquid fall of sweet notes. That was their signal. As the imperial family sat down, the apprentices leaped up, blew their igniters to life, touched flame to all the waiting lamps, and up lifted the fish lamps, glowing golden in the darkness.

The imperial family was inured to music as a background for banquets, and for musical plays, but if anyone had thought to put sky lantern release to music, it had been before the Jehan Dynasty came to the throne. There was an audible intake of breath as, from across the quiet lake, which mirrored the stars, a galaxy of golden fish lamps rose toward the sky, the ruddy light beating within making them seem live.

One by one other instruments joined in: another bamboo flute, a horn, then the strings. And when the golden fish drifted high overhead, the strings shimmered a cascade of notes — echoing the larksong at the very beginning — and this time silvery blue orbs rose, the silk painted thick enough so that the lights within glowed with eerie bluish silver light.

An unseen singer's voice rose, echoing that cascading melody for the third time.

*Ascends my lamp toward the sky*
*Until it sees a thousand days ride*
*My heart rises with it*
*The winds finger its silken tail*
*Playing with my wishes*

By now the younger imperials and nobles had leaped up, running onto the zigzag walkways that extended over the water and the canals as they tried to see what was painted on the lamps. Some called out the expertly calligraphed phrases to one another, delighting in discovering hidden puns.

Then, when those had risen out of sight, Jion stood up. "Compliments belong rightly to my elder sister Lily, who helped me choose the quotes. My honored family is invited to exercise talents to better my poor display. If you'll come over here, where the apprentices have tables, I hope you will honor us by painting your own lanterns, or giving directions to the apprentices to paint them."

Second Imperial Princess Gaunon, who had of late given over dancing in favor of painting, rushed toward Yskanda, hoping for his attention as she displayed her skills. She was joined, to Yskanda's unexpressed dismay, by all the teenage female cousins.

Vaion and the older cousins went off to paint their own lanterns, smothering snickers as they competed in embedding puns in otherwise innocuous quotes from the ancients.

The dowager empress, who was chilled and wished to go inside, beckoned to the elder pair of grandchildren. Jion and Lily went at once to make their bows, and express their gratitude for her presence, after which she complimented them on the splendid exhibition. She then departed, leading a train of maids and graywings.

That left the consorts, who remained clustered around the emperor, the gems in their headdresses glimmering in the torchlight. That also left First Princess Manon, who signaled her utter disinterest in any proceedings the mutt Lily tainted, by remaining where she was, hands folded right over left, her gaze not on the golden lights winking overhead, but on the quiet waters of the lake. Not only was she furious at her own awareness of that low-born assistant court artist, she had to hide the corrosive scorn she felt at Jion's singling out Low-Born Lily for "merit" in choosing the most obvious poems and quotes. Jion had picked up a lot of very bad habits, or views, or both, while away. But would Imperial Father recognize them as bad?

She was determined not to be weak. She would also not gratify common Afan Yskanda by looking his way; the longer she consciously resisted the impulse, the more furious she was with herself.

When the lanterns had diminished to golden gleams against the silvery stars overhead, the emperor leaned over and addressed her. "I've been sitting long enough. The night is fine; First Daughter, walk with me."

Manon could be entirely justified in her inward leap of triumph at this attention from her Imperial Father, a triumph mirrored in the second imperial consort. Covertly she glanced around, delighted that none of her siblings were included in this notice from their father. She could pity Jion, Vaion, and Gaunon, but she cast a cold glance of triumph at Imperial Princess Lily, who could never be forgiven for her lack of imperial blood.

The emperor said, once they were at a distance from the others, "You must know I've received numerous requests for your hand in marriage. Six of them are worthy of consideration; the most serious is the latest, from Second Prince Er Haz of the Easterners. That is the one I consider the most important, now that First Prince Ha Nak has taken the Easterners' throne, and wants a new treaty with us—a replacement of the age-old tribute treaty with a trade treaty. Have you any thoughts?"

Manon knew all about tribute, of course—all the imperial children did. And she gloated inwardly: thanks to Great-Grandfather, she knew all about trade, specifically how the government ought to control all trade.

"I trust, if the court becomes enlightened enough to see the importance of trade coming under imperial law—which means under you as Heaven's Chosen, Imperial Father—that the Easterners will acknowledge universal order as exemplified in our laws?"

Before her father could speak, she launched into an explanation of why the government ought to restore the old governmental control. She thought she was being subtle to make no reference to her own family's place in this control, though she was edging that way when her father interrupted, saying gently enough, "I have heard the esteemed ministers on that subject; will you forgive me if I remind you that I am not in need of a repetition?"

Manon realized she had somehow made a misstep, and bowed. Then, remembering that the subject was a marriage with the Easterners—that was an interesting subject indeed—she asked, "Is there a chance the second prince will replace his brother as king, Honored Imperial Father?"

"None. And King Ha Nak is already married."

"No imperial princess could ever become a second consort, Imperial Father," Manon stated.

"Quite true. That is why the negotiations concern their second prince. I would have your eyes, ears, and your very fine mind as my eyes and ears in their palace. Also consider that you have been named specifically. Your beauty is famed as far as their islands."

Manon was very proud of her looks, but she loathed being famous chiefly for that. Young men were never praised first for their beauty. This was one of those lingering traditions that deserved eradication, and wouldn't be as long as men still held the principal ranks in the world. Nevertheless, her father's tone made it clear he expected her to be complimented.

She said, "This humble daughter of no talent is pleased to obey, though with an ardent wish to remain here and be useful to Imperial Father in the imperial court."

They took a few steps, turning west, then south, then west again, their view of the garden thus refreshing itself constantly, before the emperor observed, "It's been a long time since there was a necessity for enormous families. Our medicines, and Essence charms, have reduced child death to a rarity. And as you have learned through reading history, the smaller the imperial family, the less chance of the bloodbaths that threatened the empire of old, destroying entire dynasties."

Manon bowed her head, knowing that when an adult told you something you both already knew quite well, they were setting you up to agree to something that you wouldn't like, as an extension.

He said, "That means each of you has an importance to the empire. Each of you must marry well. I have half-promised Ze Kai and your elder sister a betrothal—"

What? Manon had not known *that!* She was so astonished she didn't even spit (if only a covert motion) at that reference to Lily being her elder sister. Manon had no elder sister.

She wrenched her mind from that to Ze Kai, a quiet, scholarly young man. He was so scholarly and hard-working one might never know he was regarded as the likeliest heir to Left Chancellor Ze, one of the wealthiest of the ministers, from a prestigious family of the first rank. Ze Kai had been part of their study group since they were small—he had been one of Manon's main rivals for first place among the scholars, and one of the very few who had not demonstrated a tendency to follow her around like a kicked puppy.

Currently Ze Kai served as one of First Censor Hoah's assistants, but everyone expected him to rise in rank by his own merit, as soon as he passed the Imperial Examination.

She had never considered him for herself. He was smart enough to help get her to the throne, but she was not certain he would be willing to do it, or would remain obedient once she was there. Now, the thought of him smiling at that spawn of a commoner, actually wanting to *marry* her, filled her with disgust. But of course it had to be the Ran family he was aiming for. That was the only motivation that made any sense. Therefore, if he were offered a better connection, surely he would take it without hesitation.

Manon considered what she could say. Imperial Father claimed to be fond of Lily, which meant everyone was supposed to profess to be fond of her. Manon could not bear the hypocrisy. The only punishments Manon had ever endured outside her own hall were consequent to her early efforts to make certain that common-fathered Lily knew her proper place.

She smiled, and forced honeyed words past her teeth, though they tasted like ash in her mouth. "This daughter begins to comprehend a small part of Honored Imperial Father's infinite wisdom and grace. But it seems to this lowly, still-learning daughter a wasted opportunity," she said, and at her father's gesture to continue, "It seems to this humble daughter that Imperial Princess Lily would be ideal for the Easterners' second prince." And when her father sent her a look of question, she regretted once more the blundering expressions of her hatred when they were all small, which had not only been useless then, but led to suspicions concerning her motivations now. Mother was right. It was *never* a good idea to reveal one's true thoughts.

She went on, determinedly smiling, "Imperial Sister Lily is so very observant. Quite the smartest of us all, I've come to believe, Honored Imperial Father. She is so modest and well-spoken, able to converse with anyone. She would be ideal in that court. Her reports would surely be equal to anything this poor daughter could write." There! That sounded fair-minded, did it not?

The emperor did not deny her, giving her hope for the space of a few steps. She added, in a wistful voice, "This foolish but loyal daughter probably ought not to say anything, but entertained a belief that uniting the Ze family to the Jehan imperial name would not only benefit us all, but might go a ways toward ending the unfortunate rivalry Ze Kai's grandfather and my great-grandfather Su inherited."

A very diplomatic way of saying that the Su clan and the Ze clan loathed and distrusted one another, almost to a man and woman.

"You thought of Ze Kai for yourself?" the emperor asked. "You've never said anything about that."

"This humble daughter is aware that to voice an unasked opinion goes against filial obedience as well as propriety. Her marriage must benefit the empire, and has tried to bow her head to necessity," she said in her most modest voice. "But in my most secret heart . . ."

The emperor hmmmed, then said, "A lot to ponder. But if you have set your face against marrying to the east, I find myself ambivalent about insisting. Your scholarship, your skills, your brains will undoubtedly be an asset to me. I expect I will have to invite that prince to visit us, to be courted and flattered into the trade treaty, if he's not to have you. Our trade with the east is far too important to risk denying him face. Too much is going on with tributes and tax troubles elsewhere."

Manon saw a natural opening to bring the discussion back to the trade plan, but hesitated. Her mother had forbidden her to bring it up on her own. And Imperial Father had already said that he had heard the main arguments. Much as Manon wished to demonstrate her awareness of court affairs, and how firmly she supported imperial law—and anything that strengthened it—she knew that if she brought it up again, and Imperial Father was not pleased, Mother would have Manon's face slapped fifty times for blundering.

During the silence in which both were thinking hard, he brought them around to the viewing area below his balcony. He said, "I am pleased with what I hear of Jion's studies. I take it you are the chief influence there."

First Imperial Princess Manon bowed modestly. "This humble daughter lives to observe the Twenty-Five Virtues to the best of her poor ability, Honored Imperial Father. Filial loyalty is a daughter's first duty, as Kanda says—"

As she hoped, her father waved off a possible long quotation. "You ought to join the others. Have a good time. Jion will appreciate it. He worked hard all this week."

Manon bowed low, and the emperor moved on in search of his son, his interest sharpening when he recognized the sublime profile of the gray-robed assistant court artist overseeing the apprentices painting what appeared to be the last of the extra sky lanterns. A cluster of teenage nephews let out expressions of awe and laughter as a luminous lantern rose, painted with a huge demon face and a toothy grin.

That was the last lantern. The cousins stood about, drinking and chattering. The emperor approached, observing their heedless joking as Afan Yskanda made a quick gesture toward the other gray-robed apprentices, who all went to the ground in a welter of gray robes.

The emperor motioned them to rise, saying, "I came here to thank you all for an excellent exhibition."

Of course that sent them to the ground again.

Jion exclaimed, "All merit goes to the artists, Imperial

Father. And to Imperial Sister Lily, who with Afan Yskanda chose the poetry."

The cousins spoke sycophantic thanks, managing to attribute all effort and talent to the emperor's grace, as they had been taught. Then, seeing no encouragement to stay, they bowed their way out of the emperor's sight, and made their escape.

"Benevolence, justice, propriety, wisdom, and fidelity," the emperor said, advancing. "From what I could see, all quotations celebrating virtue. Quite a display of knowledge, Assistant Court Artist Afan."

From the ground, Yskanda lifted his head long enough to murmur something about the greater scholarship of the imperial siblings.

The emperor, used to Yskanda's deflections, smiled as he continued to stalk his prey: "Rise, Yskanda. Who was your teacher before you came to grace us with your talents? Your teacher of scholarship, not the estimable master scribe in Imai Harbor."

Yskanda had gotten to his feet, but now he bowed again as he said, "He was a monk making his journey, your imperial majesty."

"What was his name?"

The question was framed in the mildest voice, yet Jion — looking from one to the other in this quick exchange — was aware of Yskanda going very still before he said, "We unworthy and ignorant islanders merely addressed him as Teacher, your imperial majesty."

The emperor tipped back his head, watching the last of the demon face diminishing against the stars. Awkwardly painted, it was most certainly not done by Afan Yskanda. He looked down again, to find Yskanda head bent as Jion said, "You have to be tired, Assistant Court Artist Afan. I know you were out here getting set up the moment the sun rose. Go ahead —"

The emperor had spied the five apprentices still huddled face down on the ground. He flicked a hand in their direction, expecting Bitternail to do whatever was necessary, as he said to Yskanda, "A moment."

Yskanda, perforce, stilled. Interestingly enough, Jion did as well. Probably felt responsible as organizer. There had certainly been no sign of friendship between them. Yskanda was far too reticent for that.

But a friendship between the two might be interesting.

"I have just been hearing about the virtue of propriety," the emperor said, "causing me to reflect on how often virtue aligns with desire. Any thoughts on that? Either of you?"

Yskanda deferred—of course. To fill a pause fast becoming a silence, Jion mouthed out the usual sort of answer he had given his tutor in the old days. "Propriety is the word we use when speaking of the three most important bonds of society, Imperial Father: between parent and child, between consorts, and between ruler and subject. The first two provide a peaceful home, and when the home is peaceful, it reflects in an orderly state."

"Is that," the emperor asked, "a recent conviction, derived from your . . . experiences, or merely convenience?"

Jion blushed. He had let himself get mentally sloppy, what with his sisters praising everything he said, as his tutors had when he was a boy. He ought to have remembered that Imperial Father despised the easy answer merely because it was easy.

But he was not the target after all. "What do you say, Assistant Court Artist?"

Yskanda raised his guileless, steady gaze. "If his imperial majesty requires this ignorant unworthy to speak . . ."

The emperor turned over his hand in permission.

Yskanda said, ". . . on the subject of desire, it is true that Kanda wrote that eyes, ears, and the other organs are primarily associated with sensory desires—beautiful music, art, well-cooked food, and so on."

Jion saw where he was going. "But Kanda never treated desire as problematic."

Yskanda bowed in his direction, smiling a little. But the smile was quick, almost absent. Though the air now was cold enough for their breath to come in puffs of vapor, Yskanda, in his mere two layers, laced his hands behind his back. "Kanda stated in the *Conversations* that desire can mislead by tempting us to focus on it instead of paying attention to our ethical motivations. In that way, desire can lead to wrongdoing. Especially if we pursue these desires without also engaging our ethical motivations."

Anywhere else, Jion would call this a verbal duel. Except the words really were Kanda's. And no one would be foolish enough to duel with Imperial Father.

"What if one's desire is in itself a virtue? Such as a desire for justice?" Imperial Father asked in his lightest voice.

Jion held his breath; his father's tone, if not the words, decidedly hinted at an undercurrent. His gaze flicked to Yskanda, whom he willed not to fall into the trap of arguing with an emperor over definitions of justice.

Yskanda gazed into the distance, his mind going back to Ul Keg's quiet voice as they sat cross-legged on their mats while rain hissed on the fronds overhead. How he missed that fragrance! How he missed Ul Keg's everyday guidance — how he missed the freedom of those days, a luxury beyond calculation that he had never realized he had!

He said, carefully sifting words on the topic he had discussed so easily with the apprentices, "I beg your imperial majesty to forgive this lowly subject's worthless and clumsy attempt to restate what his teacher once said, that desire can be regarded as debatable because it responds strongly to its objects, while people's moral motivations are more discerning. Kanda urges us to regard desire as a thing. Things interact with other things, and lead them along. In contrast, ethical motivation requires that our hearts engage in reflection. Does this desire lead to true harmony with the world? Or does it gratify only myself, and leave others weeping in the wilderness?"

Jion tensed — and the emperor laughed softly. "Well said, Yskanda. Testifies to your nature. Except that you are shivering, and here we stand debating the ancient truths." He then turned to Jion. "I wonder if our austere assistant court artist would remain so aloof from the world if he were to join us for the Journey to the Clouds next spring."

Yskanda's head lowered, and as he had not been directly addressed, he remained still and silent, his long, elegant hands still hidden behind his back.

Jion's gaze flicked from father to target, for he understood now that Yskanda was a target, in some sense he still could not quite define: the adherence to protocol, yet while using Yskanda's personal name, while Yskanda's every utterance must be formed around self-abnegation, reinforcing the great distance between emperor and subject. The questions like darts. The sheer attention, when ordinarily Imperial Father ignored servants as if they did not exist, except when he wanted something from them.

Well, he wanted something from Yskanda now, Jion was thinking. What?

The pause had become a silence. The emperor said, "I take it you have heard of the Journey to the Clouds, Yskanda?"

"This ignorant assistant has read much about it, your imperial majesty, understanding it to be a pleasure boat trip between certain islands during the Kraken Boat Festival."

"That," the emperor said jovially, with a flash of white teeth, "is akin to saying that the New Year's fireworks display is a quantity of gunpowder ignited with some other elements." He turned his head. "Tell him, First Son."

Jion sensed so very many undercurrents, and didn't understand a one. Whom could he ask? As if in answer, Vaion's voice echoed from recent memory: *My mother thinks Grandmother Empress believes there's some mystery.*

Promising himself to consult his grandmother, he said to Yskanda, "I've only been as a child. The imperial family does not go every year, though many nobles do, as court is of course suspended over that festival. The journey is made by sampan along a narrow passage past waterfalls, where more blooms than you can count blossom. The air is filled with their fragrances. Ancient pagodas tower above forests of aromatic trees, and along the way hidden musicians play. I am told they used to be hermits in the old days, or so I've read, but now there is a lot of competition among musicians to be chosen to play." He was going to go on about the music, then realized he was getting off the subject, and left it there.

Yskanda bowed, and Jion, to deflect his father's attention away from him however briefly, said, "Is there an occasion for our going, Imperial Father?"

The emperor smiled. "There is indeed. It seems an appropriate gesture for welcoming your sister's most august suitor, the second prince of the Easterners." He gestured. "Yskanda, you and your apprentices were excellent today. I shall speak to Court Artist Yoli on your behalf, for suitable reward." After Yskanda bowed, he added, "You may withdraw to your well-earned rest."

Yskanda bowed again, stepped back, and vanished along a side path.

"Walk with me," the emperor said to Jion, looking fondly at his son. He was highly amused by the rumors of Jion's orgies—and pleased that he had been right in his prediction about a young man of his age. "I am impressed with your scholastic industry. Perhaps, bolstered by this new endeavor, you might have thoughts to offer on the prospect of a marriage treaty with the Easterners?"

Jion lifted his head, frowned a little, then asked, "Is there trouble in the west?"

The emperor's breath hitched. Nearly the same question to Manon had elicited a long repetition of the Su clan's hope to get a stranglehold on controlling the empire's trade; Jion's first thought was strategic.

"Why do you say that?" the emperor asked.

Jion was silent, wondering how he could word his awareness of increasing trouble up in the northwest. Unfortunately most of what he'd heard was third-hand gossip at the Sky Island competition, or from other gallant wanderers. No, there was no way to bring them up without irritating his father, so he hedged, saying, "This foolish son is aware of his own ignorance, Honored Imperial Father."

The emperor gave a quiet sigh. No ambition from one, but insight; too much ambition, from the other, all focused on personal or clan power.

"Is this confession of ignorance," the emperor asked, "a sign of regret? More to the point, if I restore your privileges, is that going to cause you to return to your wild life of laundry and fish-grilling?"

Jion wanted to retort that he would like nothing better, but that would only gain him more constraints.

His father was not stupid. "What? No words about the glories of complete freedom?"

"I learned, Imperial Father," Jion said, "that there is no true freedom in the world. Everyone had some duty, even the hermit monk in the wilderness, whose chief duty is survival."

"Very well." The emperor's voice was warm with genuine pleasure. "I'm quite certain that Fai Anbai, at least, will be relieved to hear that he and his ferrets will not be required to sit on the rooftops through the coming winter nights."

A sharp pang shot through Jion: had he been seen after all? No, surely Imperial Father meant the drinking and poetry sessions on the roof . . . didn't he?

But Jion had learned that trying to convince himself of the comfort of coincidence didn't make it true. Another, harder jolt: was it possible that the imperial guards, or the ferrets, or both, had set up a little trap?

Yes. It was quite possible. Even if nothing serious would have resulted, the outcome would possibly have been painful and most certainly would have been humiliating.

The emperor slanted a glance at him and unsettled him further by making it clear his thoughts had paralleled. "I can overlook a certain number of the follies of youth. But there is a limit. Should you be tempted, remember this: if you put us to that trouble again, you will be spending the following ten or twenty years at Ice Fortress in the far north, watching for the galleys of the Westerners navigating among the ice floes, until you've learned to make wiser decisions."

Jion bowed while walking. "This unworthy son will keep the ice floes very much in mind, Imperial Father."

The emperor laughed, and as they were at his Golden Dragon Pavilion, patted Jion on the shoulder, then his fingers stole up to briefly caress his cheek. "It's best to make your mistakes when you're young," he said. "Sleep well."

He turned away, leaving Jion wondering what that was about. He gave a mental shrug, his mind returning to the close call. And to the sobering conviction that though he had learned a lot in his two years with the Redbarks, he could not outthink the ferrets.

But he came away with one small victory: for the first time, he walked back to his pavilion alone.

# FOURTEEN

JION HAD NEARLY RECOVERED the privileges he'd enjoyed when he was Gaunon's age, but it would be foolish to assume he wasn't watched. Min Ko, the big, husky ferret, was still a part of his household, and the graywings were listening, Jion was certain, to every word spoken.

Jion therefore made every word conventionally boring. That included keeping back the story of his experiences from Manon. At first, it was because of those listening ears. But that was no longer true.

His regard for her had not changed. If anything he admired her the more for her scholarship and self-discipline. He was fairly certain that her feelings for him hadn't materially changed, as she continued to visit him, bringing books and commentary on Kanda's wisdom. At least once a week she arrived with her musical instruments for duets, always something new, which invariably caused him to go into a flurry of practice.

And yet, in spite of his old habit of telling her everything — a luxury he truly missed — the urge to tell her about Redbark and Ryu had cooled. He became aware of it when, the night of his sky lanterns, he caught the scornful glance Manon sent toward Lily when he spoke of her merit in helping him plan the evening.

He considered this one morning a week later, as he mixed

dance and Redbark warmups. Vaion resented Manon for being a stickler for rules and rank, but that was so much a part of her. How could Vaion not see that she held herself to a very high standard as well?

He flipped up into a handstand—not part of Redbark—and began lowering his head to touch the ground and then raising himself to the full extent of his arms, his mind still wandering as he worked through some thirty or forty repetitions.

He simply wouldn't share that part of his life with Manon. As children, life was simple, and everything was shared without thought. As you got older, life became more complicated. He thought of Ryu, whom he had lived beside for nearly two years, but neither had shared their deepest secret: their true identities.

It wasn't being disloyal then, not to tell Manon, when he knew she would disapprove. He had plenty to share with her that she did approve of.

He did a last handstand, lowering his body until the top of his head brushed the ground. He glanced over and caught sight of a healing cut on the edge of a finger, proof of those shared interests: the cut was from restringing his guqin. He really needed to work harder on his music.

Not that Manon said anything. She didn't have to. One of her cool, steady looks acted on him worse than the loudest, longest lecture ever could. It was her disappointment that irked him. As though he had wasted his time on the wander. Well, to her, he had—and that was all the more reason not to talk about Ryu.

Ryu. Common born, completely ignorant of the manners and protocol that Manon considered necessary to life. Impatient of the privileges of rank. The only thing the two might have in common was ferocious self-discipline, but Jion could never forget Ryu's exclamation that she had nothing to say to a princess—and her recoil at the mention of the emperor, Jion's father.

He closed his eyes, hoping with all his strength that Ryu never came to the attention of his father.

As a filial grandson, he went to make his bows to his grandmother.

"My dear Jion!" She towed him into her inner room, warmed by a brazier and redolent of incense, where the portraits of her grandchildren hung.

Very impressive, he thought as he stared up at the skilled portraiture. Afan Yskanda really was a Talent. He had somehow captured familiar expressions in everyone, making each portrait true to the selves portrayed, even if the lines and the colors were highly stylized.

Knowing from old that Grandmother Empress would press him to eat, he had skipped breakfast. When he had dealt to her satisfaction with the spiced and pickled dishes, had drunk what felt like an ocean of medicinal tea, and was facing a plate of cakes, he was trying to figure out a way to compliment the portraits and lead to his question about any "mystery" involving the portraitist, when she patted his hand, then said, "What have you been doing with yourself since your return?"

"Your foolish grandson has been filling the days with study and music, mostly, Grandmother Empress," he said, certain she would be pleased.

She smiled, nodded, then said, "Who is guiding your study?"

"Elder Sister Manon."

Grandmother's gaze shifted away, then back. "I will never pretend to scholarship, but I trust that at least some of your reading is in statecraft."

"Actually, it's been entirely in ancient wisdom," he said. "With occasional visits to poetry."

Again his grandmother flicked a glance to one side, then back. "If you will permit a suggestion from an old woman whose scholarship was extremely poor, you ought to be reading statecraft. She certainly is."

"Who? Manon?" he asked. Then shrugged. "She has always been interested in court scholarship."

"She," Grandmother Empress said, "is interested in power."

"Is it not the same thing?" he asked flippantly.

"No," she said, "And on your next visit, I want you to come ready to discuss how they differ."

He set down his cup, stung. Then he laughed. Ah yes, he was truly home again—being scolded and exhorted for his own good. "What if I have no interest whatsoever in either?"

"Then you will be throwing away both your talent and the place the gods gave you, and I will grieve over the loss until I am dead," she retorted. "Begin with the records of Prince Noh during the Tan Dynasty. Both what was written about him, and what he wrote—for they copied his letters before sending them on."

"The hostage prince?" Jion said, remembering suddenly that she had sent him on a similar errand when he was much younger. He vaguely recollected a rotting old script, and a lot of nearly incomprehensible writing.

"He was an observer from the outside. His view of empire politics would be most illuminating," Grandmother Empress said. "When your father was about your age, he had occasion to be confined to his pavilion by the empress, and he was enjoined to make a study of Prince Noh. After that, his studies . . . took a different turn."

Now Jion was intrigued—but not enough to forget his original purpose. "Speaking of mysteries," he said. "I've caught some hints that there is one concerning the arrival of Afan Yskanda, the portraitist. Do you know anything about that?"

Jion's grin vanished when he saw his grandmother's eyelids flash up, then shutter, as she picked up her empty teacup and went through the motion of drinking from it. Was that tremble in her fingers old age, or something else?

"He is a Talent," his grandmother said, in a tone of finality. "That is all. Confine yourself to studies that will make your father proud."

Her tone did not invite argument—not that he would argue with an elder. Especially his grandmother, whose fingers shook. He promised to do his best, and soon took his leave, more curious than ever.

There was the great archive, which had a section that required permission, as it pertained to edicts and decrees, and court testaments in response. There were archives for each department of the inner palace, and there were archives of each department of government.

Then there was the private imperial archive, which required permission from the emperor—these were the writings of the emperors and their families. Jion had only been there once. Cold gripped the back of his neck when he recollected that experience.

Prince Noh, he remembered among the edicts and court

records. That old copy had had to be fetched, and he'd had to read it while under the direct sight of the archive graywing on duty. Afterward, his tutor had questioned him closely about it, indicating that anything he asked for in there was reported.

He could ask permission again, and be confined to old Prince Noh again — or he could take her words as a challenge, and find his way in and out on his own, which would give him a chance to look around at what else was there.

He set out to master the schedule again, discovering that little had changed. The night watch was still under the supervision of an ancient graywing named Garnet, who nodded off, especially if a pinch of night herb was put into his tea.

The best time for getting in and out was the changing of the watch, especially if something else kept the roaming guards busy at the other end of the palace. Not a fire, for then a thorough inspection would be carried out. And not mysterious theft, for that, too, would require inspection. He had learned that the best distraction was damage — what appeared to be natural damage — for the palace must be kept clean and perfect at all times.

And the only time for "natural" damage was during a storm.

The Hall of Glorious Virtue was his target — near enough to the Hall of Glorious Harmony, but not too near, requiring a deployment of imperial guards just in case. And best of all, it had been years since his last foray. No one ought to find it suspicious.

On his wanderings, he located his tree, spotted his branch, and calculated its likely trajectory in Glorious Virtue's court.

Then he had to wait for a likely day. But this time of year, with winter coming on, he did not have to wait long. Once the gong rang, he ghosted through the lashing rain to Glorious Virtue, used his weight to bring the branch down, then, with rain drumming his back, he loosened and smashed a number of tiles. He laid the branch among them where a wild draft of wind could have deposited it, and withdrew to a distance to wait for the roaming guard to set up the alarm.

It rang, and word went out, pulling guards from all over the inner palace to deal with the mess before dawn.

Jion took to the inky shadows again, and once again found himself within the dusty, still air of the inner archive. There was old Garnet, nodding off.

Jion swept his gaze along the hanging tags that indicated the dynasties, oldest to the present. He found the Tan Dynasty, and there was the old Prince Noh record, from the days of that exchange of princes. He considered himself being sent either west or east, then shook it off—he didn't know enough to be horrified or delighted at the prospect. The only constant was, life would have been different.

He put his hand on the Prince Noh book, and remembered its many critical comparisons favoring the Easterner king's court with that of the Thousand Islands. The comparisons might be interesting now that Jion was old enough to understand what he was reading, but Jion's gaze wandered along the shelves toward more modern times. *Why* did things get put here instead of out in the general archive, where each day's weather and crop and trade and tax reports were kept, and all the laws enumerated? Was it because of the criticisms of the court of the time?

He knew who made the decision—had to be the Grand Historian. Or the emperor or empress, of course. Did records ever get shifted out to the general archive where the scribe students could get them? Did they ever get destroyed, in spite of the many exhortations Kanda had left about how important it was to reflect on one's errors, that they might not be repeated? He'd memorized those lines without ever thinking about them, except to note sourly that all the wars proved people made mistakes over and over.

He turned away from Prince Noh toward the present day. Not much was there. Most of it seemed to be diplomatic exchanges, he saw at a quick glance. There was more before his father came to the throne, all from Empress Teyan, who'd had to make numerous treaties after the years of Bloody Maoyan, Jion's great-grandfather. *His* records were all in the private archive, Jion remembered, grimacing.

He was going to fetch Prince Noh and get that reading over with when his eye caught on his father's name. The label said only *Selection for First Consort Second Imperial Prince Enjai.*

That would be Jion's mother! But why would that be in here?

He pulled it out and sat down.

Yskanda had never forgotten his intent to discover what evidence he could about The Story. If that information was anywhere, surely it would be in that alcove he'd stumbled upon when he looked for records concerning past hostages.

Three times he visited the archive. All three times he had to turn away due to various challenges: the first time, roaming guards; the second, a party of scribes laboriously poring over three bamboo-slip scrolls out in the general archive, teasing out faint markings and discussing each; the third time, he nearly tripped over the frost-haired old archivist graywing slowly dusting the bags and bags of bamboo-slip scrolls in that alcove where no one was supposed to go.

The rest of the time he was too tired after very long days of labor. At last one stormy night, he was too restless to sleep, so he decided to try again. The outer doors would be locked, but the inner doors weren't, so the guards could make their rounds.

This time he nearly turned back at the outset when he heard an alarm, until he recognized the bell as the localized one indicating some kind of damage, directly opposite of where he was going. That meant the guards would be summoned in that direction. Wrapping himself in his dark gray winter cloak, he bent his head and scurried along the least-used path as the wind whipped at him, and cut around to the inner door.

When he reached the archive, he proceeded cautiously. There was old Frost Hair Garnet, his head laid on his arms. The old graywing archivist breathed the deep, even breaths of sleep.

What luck!

Yskanda heard nothing from the rows and rows of alcoves that comprised the general archive, and headed toward the alcove that he had stumbled into that day. He remembered exactly where it was.

There he halted, staring down at First Imperial Prince Jion, who sat cross-legged on the floor in a welter of silken panels, amid a moat of papers, and on his lap a sketch of . . .

Mother.

Yskanda knew her instantly, though those round, smooth, scar-free cheeks and the arched eyebrows were unfamiliar, as was the elaborate hairstyle with butterfly and phoenix pins holding it up. That straight gaze, the shape of forehead, chin, lips were his mother, at a young age—no more than sixteen.

Jion was the first to recover, Yskanda having been stunned

back into the relative mask of protocol: he dared not back up until he was dismissed.

Jion said conversationally, "Do you know what happened?"

Yskanda's thoughts scattered like moths. Training gave his mind a direction: he had been asked a question by one of the imperials, so he must answer. He swallowed in a dry throat as his eyes shifted to the papers. "If this ignorant no-talent may ask what is written there?"

"Very little," Jion replied, as he carefully folded the drawing along decades-old creases. And, as he began to reassemble everything, he went on in that soft, light, conversational voice, "I found my second mother in there, too. But my mother is not here at all, yet she's the first consort." And when Yskanda did not answer that, he went on, "I never really considered the valley of swords historians walk. They're sworn to tell the truth, but how much truth? I remember scorning the *Ancient Annals* as a boy. You've read them, yes?"

"This servant lacking in talent remembers them as the earliest written history of the empire," Yskanda said, relieved to get away from the subject of mothers. "Compiled by Mana Ta, who was regarded as the first historian."

"I struggled through the *Ancient Annals*, scorning it as a mess for its inconsistencies, with different dates for the same event scattered through it, according to this or that source, and for details about the reign of the first Bi emperor buried in the history of his grandson." Jion reached up to replace the record exactly where he'd found it, then dusted all around with the edge of his sleeve as he said, "Now I wonder if all the truth can only be written when the individuals concerned, and the witnesses, are all dead. But how much truth is there really, if there are no witnesses to corroborate it?"

Jion looked up at Afan Yskanda, whose face had drained of all color. He looked, once again, like a man expecting the headsman's axe. "That is your mother in the drawing, is it not? She was once here." His hand swept wide, taking in the imperial palace. "What exactly happened, that your mother is here and mine isn't?"

Even palace training, which had been his shield, could not force Afan Yskanda to utter anything revelatory about his family. He blinked once, then, as if released from a demon's spell, whirled around and was gone in a few swift footfalls.

And for the next stretch of days, Yskanda strove to remain calm, though he expected a summons to the west side and interrogation — execution. Every page who knocked at the door, every graywing who glided up or down some call, caused him to start violently, until Court Artist Yoli growled one morning, "Are you sickening with a fever? Do you need me to summon the physician?"

"No, Court Artist Yoli," Yskanda whispered, and bent over his work.

He had instantly recognized Yoli Jiwa's hand in the sketch of his mother, of course. That didn't mean that the court artist remembered making that sketch. As he said himself, he'd been required to do hundreds, even more, over the years. But if he did remember, he was not saying anything — because what could he say, or do? Nothing.

Yskanda took his cue from that. Everyone was talking about the New Year's Two Moons decorations and celebrations, and he buried himself in his work, the ward stone always in his clothing.

# FIFTEEN

FAR TO THE NORTHWEST, Ari discovered that winter had come
early, just as Master Ki warned.

Once it arrived there was no back-and-forth between thaw
and snow as had happened at Loyalty Fortress. Hard winter
settled in for the duration.

At first Ari was charmed by everything. She delighted in
new sets of animal tracks appearing with the low winter
sunlight in their little sheltered valley. With Master Ki's help,
she learned to identify the different footprints.

It was difficult to wake to the unending cold, but she learned to breathe Essence-warmth through her body as soon as she
woke, before she even stirred. She had discovered at Loyalty
that as long as your toes were warm before you put on stockings and boots, your feet would keep that warmth longer — but
if you tried going out with cold feet they would stay cold. She
was soon glad of the thick, warm stockings Tenar had given
her, and of the gloves Matu's third aunt had made for her.

She had to learn to cook. She'd done some preparation as
an orderly, but as part of a team. During the Redbark days,
when they were on the road, it had been Petal, with Matu's
aid, who had seen to the meals, usually while Shigan and Ari
were dancing or sparring.

With a determined will she learned which foods kept
longer, and how to make them tasty. Cooking was rather like

Essence charms all on its own.

She kept one of the little plateaus clear of snow (which sometimes meant sweeping twice a day) for her Redbark drills. Master Ki had that very old bronze sword, the handle plainly made except for a huge pearl imbedded in the top of the pommel. This sword rested on an improvised sword stand above the corner basket containing the rake, hoe, and shovel. The Ki cousins had told her that when young, before the Westerners' last invasion, Grandfather Ki had inherited that sword. It was known as Sagacious Blade, which had become his gallant wanderer name.

Master Ki didn't touch the sword, though his commentary when she did the fan form made it clear that he still had a very discerning eye. He never interfered with her Redbark drills; he often sat with the sun on his closed eyelids, doing Essence breathing. Ari assumed he was cultivating. As yet she was too young to recognize the pain of age.

One day Ari was in the middle of her sword form when she became aware of the steady chuff of footsteps in the snow. This was no animal.

She paused, glancing toward Master Ki. He stood in the doorway, his breath clouding as he smiled in expectation, his posture easy.

A man rounded the cedar tree. He was tall and rangy, with a great shock of long gray-streaked brown hair. He appeared to be in his late forties, though that was a guess as his lean face was creased with a couple of scars. He carried a staff.

"Welcome, welcome," Master Ki exclaimed. "You are in good time for breakfast."

The man raised his free hand, protected by a fingerless glove.

"Already ate," he said in a gravelly voice. "Came down to see if the youngster here wants to spar a little." And, to Ari, "Go ahead. Finish your form."

Ari had seldom felt self-conscious doing Redbark form — but she'd always tried to do it somewhere secluded. She could see by the man's wary, cat-footed walk even in ankle-high snow that he knew martial arts.

She swept back into her form, the staff whooshing and humming. Or, she tried. She had shifted from Earth to Heaven when a poke in her shoulder blade caused her to snap upright. "That's it," the man said. "Don't lean. You'll be off-balance."

She bit back an exclamation that she hadn't been leaning, then she became aware in the pressure on her toes that meant she had been. A beginner's error. How long had she been repeating that bad habit?

She returned to the proper stance, her feet squarely on the ground. Then she began again. Twice more the man's staff poked her, one smack on the side of her leg, and another on her right wrist. Both times she realized her form had slipped.

She performed Heaven and Earth slowly, concentrating on each movement, then sped up and did it again. And again. She was damp with sweat in spite of the cold air when she finally moved into Redbark, with all its emendations.

When she came to the end stance, the man gave a curt nod. "Clean. Solid. Drink some water. Catch your breath. We'll spar."

They sparred. She was outclassed, but not hopelessly so. His training was a level superior to hers, even when he did not press the advantage of his size and reach. She, for her part, did not feel the slightest inclination to use Essence against him. She was *learning*.

When they had worked so long that her entire body was awash and her muscles unstrung, he went away as quietly and as abruptly as he had come.

He was there the next morning, and the next. And so she began to look for him on all mornings barring bad weather. He never asked for her name, and because he was an elder, and a martial arts master, she did not dare presume to ask his. Even in the gallant wanderer world, there was rank—masters and elders at the top.

She said to Master Ki after about a week, "Is he the hermit?"

"He is," Master Ki said.

The next time she saw the hermit she did not ask anything, but performed the gallant wanderer bow, and said, "Your music is so very good."

The hermit had been treating her thanks for the martial training as an instructor accepting a student bow, but at this compliment about his playing, his lean cheeks flushed a mottled red, and he brought his head down in a curt nod of acknowledgment, his smile brief though genuine.

And a few days later he did not leave as usual ahead of an incoming storm, but accepted Master Ki's invitation to breakfast—and from the pack slung over his back, pulled out a bamboo flute. To Ari's surprise, Master Ki pulled from his trunk not his own flute, but a very old three-pipe hulusi, and began to play in counterpoint.

The flutes blended, sometimes speaking to one another, other times vying in playful competition. Ari knew she was profoundly ignorant about music. There had been plenty of singing in Sweetwater, but music from instruments had been rare. That, everyone said, was for rich folk.

It was clear now that music was not solely for rich folk. It served a different purpose entirely for those who lived away from others of their kind, on the high mountain. It was meditation and worship and entertainment, conversation and cultivation.

It was sublime.

The flutes embarked on a ramble through all the emotions that went unspoken, as snow fell steadily, and time seemed suspended. But hunger never sleeps, and presently Ari realized that if she cooked they would not stop playing, so she began to prepare a meal, gratified that she could do it all by herself.

The two put down their instruments when the enticing smells lured them. Once she'd dished up three bowls and passed out chopsticks, the hermit turned to her. "What can you tell me about Redbark?"

She considered that, and realized he meant exactly what he said. He didn't demand to know everything, as one who had the right. He asked what she felt she could tell.

And the answer was, very little, actually, without breaking trust with Father and Mother so far away. She found herself reluctant to lie. She sensed that this man and Father would understand one another at once, aside from the hermit's generosity in teaching her. The nonexistent Master Duin stayed in his mental shadow-puppet box, and she left the origin of the name equally unspoken. "I learned most of what you've seen as a child, but I've added some moves since I became a wanderer."

He accepted that with a slight nod. "That is the way of it. In spite of all the talk about staying strictly with tradition, styles evolve. Take double-stick defense. When I was a boy, I learned the bind-and-attack this way." Using his chopsticks, he demonstrated. "But after years, I found I had more strength and speed if I did it this way."

They talked longer about these differences, Ari feeling as if the two men treated her as an adult, not an apprentice who had not been with her new master for an entire season yet. Master Ki, whose clan had double-knife as their primary defense, added his observations, and so it went until the talk drifted to northern styles and southern styles, then to northern and southern food, and so on.

By the time the food was eaten, the bowls scoured, and everything tidied, Ari was ready for sleep. She did not want to be rude, but almost as if reading her mind, Master Ki said, "If you're sleepy, child, go ahead. When you get old, you sleep less, perhaps because you're nearer to the long sleep."

Ari bowed to the south, wishing Mother, Father, and Ul Keg well, and then spread out her sleeping things. Presently the low rumbling voices gave way once again to music. She turned over, looking at the firelight beating ruddy on the men's faces, and smoothing out the lines experience had carved.

She was not aware of drifting off into dreams: when she woke, the fire had gone out, and the hermit was gone. Master Ki lay on his narrow kang, wrapped in his quilt, his slow breathing indicating deep sleep. Ari rose, shivering, and as she set about preparing the fire, words and phrases disengaged from the fleeing scraps of her dreams. Sky Island . . . that was easy to explain: they must have been talking about the competition. Others — mostly names and places — did not stay with her. Except, she was almost sure, Yulin.

Master Ki woke to the smell of breakfast, after which they worked on Essence.

And so the winter went, the hermit coming down when weather permitted to spar with Ari. She could feel her skills tightening and her strength building — and he began using the strength he had been holding back. She fought as long as she could without using Essence, though there were times when he drove her so hard she began feeding Essence into her strikes, until thin, acrid smoke rose from the staffs.

Once she became aware of it, she stopped immediately, and confessed in a mumble, "My apologies. I used Essence."

He gave a curt nod. "I know. I felt it. Learn to use what you have — learn to control it."

And so they kept training, Ari increasingly exhilarated at her leaps in skill.

Which was lucky because she wasn't making any leaps in using Essence. She did the exercises Master Ki set her to. She could make little glows, as he called the cold lights of Essence. They were not bright unless she concentrated hard, and there was no warmth to them.

"Why?" she asked once. "If we make a fire, by whatever means, it's warm. The warmth goes into other things, like our tea." She tipped her head. "Then the warmth goes out. Why *is* that? Why can't warmth go in the way it goes out? Can Essence put the warmth back in? These glows don't seem to do much in that way."

"Essence can draw fire and shape it," Master Ki said. "But fire is as difficult to shape as water, and far more dangerous. That is a later lesson. Your instinct is to draw on Essence when angry, which is effective but as dangerous as fire."

She sighed inwardly—here were her mother's and Ul Keg's warnings all over again, though so far, anger had helped her with Essence. It had defended her and others.

But she kept silent, hoping that would get her sooner to the lessons about how to use her Essence to reach across distances. She wanted to see her mother, her father, Ul Keg, her brothers. Matu and Petal.

Shigan.

After a series of calm days of hard work, sparring, cooking, and learning to carve useful implements with a knife, Master Ki said, "I know you are eager to learn the soul wander."

"Soul wander? Isn't that something ghosts do?" As she spoke, she remembered Father's conviction that there was no such thing as ghosts. And Mother remaining silent.

"Yes, and no," Master Essence said—as usual. "You know of course that our souls have two halves. Or two natures, as the shamans of the Path say. The lower nature is our animal nature, the spark that makes us alive. It stays in the body, but the higher soul is the leader. There are some whose higher souls naturally wander, most often in dreams. Others find it easier to disengage, though it requires great control, and greater detachment from the living world. Now, we will begin with very simple exercises . . ."

They did. And she worked hard, at least as hard as she did when practicing martial arts. But no matter how hard she concentrated, she felt her own skull as limitation, and she could not reach across distances.

Finally, one dim bluish day as a blizzard howled outside, Master Ki said, "Let's work on something else. This is not a skill easy, or sometimes even available, to those whose Essence affinities are strong in either fire or metal, and you are strong in both. Some say that fire and metal come with too much attachment to the world."

Ari *hated* hearing that. Why should her attachment, which was a good thing, suddenly be a bad thing? The idea made her impatient, but above all she was impatient with her own failure, and for a few days she secretly tried harder.

Then one day, not long before New Year's Two Moons, dizziness abruptly made her unsure what was up and down. She had been standing out on her sparring space, trying to force her soul to travel, and fell on her butt in the snow. Then she gave a mighty sneeze, and blood splattered from her nose.

Master Ki spoke sharply for the first time. "That was not a suggestion, child. Anger is not a tool to depend on. At least, if you are going to be angry, you ought not to be with yourself, but with me. I ought not to have tried to teach you that."

"Anger's worked for me before," she muttered as she mopped the disgusting blood smears off her robe. "My mother used to tell me all the time never to use anger. But when I have, it worked. Maybe I'm evil as well as stupid."

Master Ki sighed. "Maybe you're sixteen, and not used to coming up against your limitations. One of your few limitations. This happens even to smart and talented people. We are not gods, so why get angry when we cannot emulate them?"

"Now I'm arrogant," she muttered, her eyes stinging. "As well as evilly angry."

Master Ki laughed aloud, his breath clouding. "Ari, my student. Anger is not evil in itself. Anger is anger. It can inspire a courageous fire, but that fire burns jade as well as rotten wood."

How she hated metaphors! But she strove to control her voice as she asked, "Jade being . . ."

"Perhaps I ought not to try to be poetic," Master Ki said with a wheezing laugh. "Let me put it another way. Anger happens, but it tends to beget anger, as fire begets fire. Furthermore, if you do not let it go, it will control you."

Well, that seemed true enough. Yulin had been angry all the time, and so had Weed. Ari's thoughts arrowed straight for that horrible emperor, and how her parents had had to hide themselves all these years. The result was righteous anger on the part of her and her two brothers, right? But they weren't angry all the time. Just when they thought about *him*.

"As I said, fire and metal do not seem to lend themselves to this skill, which is simpler for those whose affinities are air, like me, and especially for water. And wood. I had to learn that, too. We are going to work on other things. You are forbidden to attempt the soul wander until—if—you truly are ready. Not when you want to be. You do not as yet even know the difference, so put it aside. Is that understood between us?"

Ari bowed, right hand clasped over left.

"Then come inside. You'll drink a medicinal tea to clean out the accumulated poisons in your blood, and while I make it, you'll begin with simple breathing . . ."

At least, she reflected a day or two later as her staff voomed in the icy air, she had the fans and Redbark. Warmth sang through her veins and hummed in her muscles. She reveled in her strength, in the smoothness of her leaps to the crag above the waterfall and back, then again, this time with a wholly unnecessary somersault between. But it felt great. And she did *not* do it angrily!

The following day the sky dawned blue, and stayed that way, bringing the hermit down.

They fought, he with a practice sword and she with the fan. He encouraged her to touch his pressure points. It was excellent training in control for her, and he didn't mind the invisible bee sting the rare times she was able to break his defense. Then they fought with staffs, both in long form and broken into two short forms. They fought with wooden knives—Ari having carved her own—and Master Ki finally brought Sagacious Blade from its rocky stand above the gardening implements, saying, "It might be heavy for you, but that's a good thing for drill."

The hermit had brought his own blade, a fine sword with luck sutras in the ancient script on the pommel. When she asked where the sword had come from, he muttered something about his young days, and then barked, "Test your blade?"

Ari drew Sagacious, and looked down at a beautifully made bronze sword. She slowly turned it over from side to side to test its balance. A thread from the sleeve of her free hand floated in the breeze. The sword sliced through the thread cleanly. That was sharp.

Ari brought the blade up and examined it in the light. The bronze was golden-pink, worked in overlapping scales, but with a curious sheen.

Master Ki said, "I was told that a star was sent from the heavens. It was worked into the blade, which makes it very strong, but flexible. It will not shatter. The pearl is a reminder of that star, a gift from the gods."

Ari bowed; it seemed right to be formal at this moment, even if she never touched the blade again. At first Sagacious was too heavy, in a way that felt . . . odd. As if something invisible held the tip, or another hand held the handle along with hers. But gradually that feeling faded as they fought through the morning. When the low southern sun reached the height of its arc they broke to drink and eat, then fought some more as the shadows shifted eastward. Sometimes the hermit stayed to eat, and afterwards, to make music with Master Ki.

Invariably Ari fell asleep during these sessions, though she tried to stay awake, but all unawares she was doing the last of her growing, and this was the season of her life to rejoice in working hard, eating with the voracious appetite of the young, followed by deep and untroubled sleep.

Not that she always dropped off. She did try to stay awake, not only for the pleasure of the music, but because the master and the hermit sometimes fell into reminiscence, and she wanted to hear these stories. Even if most of them were Master Ki's that she had already heard.

But enough of the hermit's low, rumbling voice filtered through for her to catch images of hard fights, great daring, and most of all, the trust of a beloved companion covering one's back. The name Bi came up most often, until one morning Ari woke to snow again. The hermit was gone, but lingering in memory were names: Bi the Whirlwind, isles of silk, and . . . was that Yulin Enk, the evil tax commissioner?

Ari blinked at her tumble of blankets, stared uncomprehending at the softly falling snow, then back at Master Ki, who crouched over the low stove, stirring a pinch of sesame seeds into rice congee.

Ari blinked down at her hands, which—she realized numbly—had been fighting all this time against no less of a figure than Waoji Lion's Mane, the hero wanderer as famous nowadays as the hero Jong Siang, leader of the hundred and ten gallant outlaws of the outer islands centuries ago.

# SIXTEEN

JION TOOK A COUPLE of days to think through what he'd discovered.

Though he was now back to making his bow to his parents and grandmother early every morning, it was a formality that usually began and ended at the outer doorway, especially on court days for his father. Frequently he arrived at the same time as his siblings, and sometimes ministers' wives or sisters. He didn't mind—he greeted them all.

Getting his grandmother alone was a different matter. That happened seldom, as the consorts, and any visiting feminine relations, were inevitably waiting on her.

But on a court day, with a sleet storm hissing down, thoughtful and kindly Grandmother Empress sent her customary bad weather message excusing the family from making their morning bows. Jion went to see her, dressed in his finest court silk.

She was surprised and pleased to see him, but when he dropped down to make a formal bow, face to the floor, her smile vanished.

"Jion, what is this bow for? It makes me apprehensive, dear boy. You surely have not done anything . . ." She didn't like to imagine what he might need to be forgiven.

"Grandmother Empress, I read Prince Noh again. He was quite critical of our court at the time, both personalities and the trouble over control of all trade, and I think I understand our instructors' point about old problems becoming new ones. I looked for more written about him, and the Easterners' view, but it turns out that First Imperial Sister Manon has those."

"And the crow cries aloud that the sky is blue," the dowager empress said evenly. "Rise, my dear boy. It was a mere suggestion, not an imperial edict."

Still with his forehead to the floor, "I found something else," he said, and she remembered the subject he had brought up before, which she had done her best to deflect. "I thought of going to Imperial Father, or to Honored Second Mother, but then I thought of you."

She beckoned to him to rise. Yes, there was that determined expression in his face so like his father's. But Jion was no young fire dragon. There was still a chance to dissuade him. "Let us go inside here."

She drew him out of her receiving hall and into her own personal shrine, which contained memorial tablets to the Kui family set below a statue of the Goddess of Mercy.

She said to her maids, "I wish to be alone with my grandson. No one is to disturb us."

They withdrew and closed the doors.

"Speak," she commanded.

Jion said, "I found a drawing of a woman who is so like Afan Yskanda would look if he were a girl, they have to be related. It was made toward the end of the Fullness of Wisdom era, before father came to the throne."

The dowager empress motioned him toward one of the cushions as she ritually lit incense sticks, and the two candles. Then she knelt beside him, pressed her hands together at heart and forehead, shut her eyes, and inwardly prayed, *My honored parents, to whose goodness my present position is entirely due, please give me a sign if at any time I should not speak: if you strike me with lightning I will accept it as no more than I deserve.*

Silence, except for her soft sigh.

She turned, and there was the wince of pain in her eyes. "You are near twenty, are you not? About to come of age. And as such, what might look like a game to you will not to others. I urge you to reconsider approaching your father about subjects he does not introduce first," she said.

"Like the mystery of Afan Yskanda?"

"If you were to ask him, he might tell you what happened

that year, but he will never forgive you for asking."

"*Why?* What happened, Grandmother Empress? Does it have anything to do with why Afan Yskanda is so afraid all the time?"

The dowager empress looked away as she reached for her string of meditation pearls. "He is, yes, you are right, that is fear, much as I tried to believe it anything else." She spoke softly under her breath, her thumbs working over one, two, three pearls, then she lowered her hands to her lap. "I will tell you what I saw and know, which is very little. Most of what I learned was from Graywing Topaz, who I sent that year to be steward to your father in his new household, outside the palace. Pear Tree Garden Pavilion was a manor in my dowry, a very pretty place overlooking the bay. He wanted his own household, and the empress, and I, wished to remove him from his elder brother's sight for a time."

Jion bit down on his impatience, waiting for his grandmother to work her way to the point. She seemed to sense it, for she sighed softly once again, her thumbs still sliding over the pearls, and said, "The girl's name was Alk Hanu. She was the last of the Alks, a once prestigious and quite powerful scholarly family. They made the mistake of aligning with the wrong faction, ended up exiled, and . . ."

She lifted one hand, then said, "Oh, you can look up that history if you really need it—for there is a lesson in that, too. To resume, as I said, your father moved out of the palace when he came of age at twenty."

The dowager empress looked down at her pearls—or perhaps she saw past them into memory. "What do you know about the imperial family?"

"Not a lot beyond their names in the shrine of ancestors," Jion said. "We gleaned from one of the more garrulous Su uncles once that First Uncle Hojai tried to kill Imperial Father in my own pavilion, but never why, or what exactly happened. We were told that over and over when we asked for sword lessons that the ferrets and the guards would protect us better than we could protect ourselves. The last time I asked, Imperial Father got a little angry and said that we were not going to kill each other over the throne if we didn't know how, and I dared not ask again."

The dowager empress raised her hand. "Yes—I seem to remember telling you as well. I know I've had to remind your brother of that edict countless times."

Jion felt obliged to defend his brother. "Vaion is not blood-thirsty. He does like hero tales. Much as I did. The two of us and our Kui and Ran cousins used to secretly bash away with sticks out in the back garden when no one was looking, but we never once tried to kill each other."

The dowager empress smiled a little, but the smile immediately faded. "Empress Teyan was shrewd, as anyone would have to be to survive the previous emperor, your great-great grandfather." She shuddered. "Despite that era being called the Blessings of Peace, Maoyan was a bloody-minded war emperor. Some of that was a result of wars from both the west and the east, and some was his own character. He loved leading battles, and such was the court's fear of him that he always came back to find things exactly as he left them."

"One of my Ran great-uncles told a horrible story about the first time he didn't," Jion admitted.

"Most of that story is probably true, but I beg you not to recount it. I have enough bad memories from those days. The Empress Teyan had two consorts, by whom she had two sons and a daughter, as you know. Her first son, you'll remember, was sent to the Westerners in a hostage exchange of princes. There he married a princess and eventually died — we will probably never know the truth of what happened. According to treaty, his son was sent back to us, age five, when we sent the western prince back to his home. The little prince was renamed Hojai, and given the rank First Son."

The dowager empress gazed back in time. "Your grand-father had two consorts besides me."

Jion recollected those memorial tablets in the ancestral shrine. "Great-Aunt Liak, the first consort, had my Aunts Tianjai and Arijai."

"Correct. Tianjai, the eldest, was the empress's favorite. The one she tutored personally, and for whom she caused there to be a small throne next to the great phoenix throne, so that Tianjai could learn the ways of court. Arijai was born the week your father was. She was horse-mad, good with the sword, and a superlative archer. No one in the family could beat her, though they had frequent competitions."

Jion raised another finger. "Great-Aunt Miar had two sons, my uncles Lijai and Fujai."

"Correct again. There are two important differences

between how they were raised and how you and your generation have been raised. Tutoring included lessons in sword fighting, as you know. But as important was this: as you are aware, imperial guards are rotated in and out of duty regularly. You might learn the names of some, but it is not encouraged. Their chief never commands for longer than five years."

"I thought that was traditional," Jion said.

Grandmother Empress shook her head. "Not at all. The tradition, until your father's generation, was that the imperial children each had personal servants their own age, or perhaps a year or two older, with whom they grew up. This child's entire purpose was not only to serve, but to protect the imperial prince or princess with their life. They trained very hard with the imperial guards from a young age. Your father's bodyguard," the dowager empress said, "was named Danno. I selected him myself. He was a Spring Festival child, by one of Empress Teyan's favorite guards, so he had no family name. Thus there could be no undue influence pulling at his loyalties. Everyone felt that the placement was a lucky one. The augurs certainly thought so."

"Did he try to kill Imperial Father?"

"No, no. That is, I don't know what happened at the end — and neither does Topaz — but before then, I know for a fact that he saved your father's life at least twice. Once on the spring hunt, and another time during some sort of martial arts game stalking one another around the state buildings. Both times," the dowager empress added dryly, "Hojai was somewhere in the vicinity."

"You said that Father moved out to avoid his brother's eye. There was trouble between Imperial Father and First Uncle Hojai before the duel?"

"There was trouble between Hojai and the world. He wanted to be emperor, and conquer the rest of the world to the glory of the empire. He tormented the other imperial children constantly, especially the boys. Fujai had nightmares about him. He was the smallest, and fearful. Hojai could somehow get at him, then he'd insist that he loved his Jehan brothers, but wanted them to be tough, tougher than . . . oh, never mind that. We don't actually know how much of his wild tales about life in the west was true: he was *five* when he came to us. My point is this. He had a penchant for cruelty, and cruel as he was to Young Fu, that was actually nothing to the scorn and ridicule he poured on your father, who I believe he regarded as his real competition."

The dowager smoothed her pearls with stiff fingers. "Are you certain you want to hear all this?"

Jion could see that by bringing this subject up he had seriously discomposed her, which was not filial behavior. He forced himself to say, "If it is disturbing you, Grandmother Empress . . ."

She sighed sharply, more like a girl than a woman of years and dignity. "We've come this far. And I trust that once I finish, the subject will stay closed."

Jion bowed.

"To resume, your father moved out of the palace at twenty, for which in retrospect I can scarcely blame him, and he wanted to marry. I helped select Alk Hanu as one of the five potential princesses, so I share whatever blame there is. I don't remember much about her—in fact, I'd entirely forgotten her until I saw Afan Yskanda. He has her looks, except his jaw is very much like Danno's, and his height. He's thinner than I remember Danno being, but Hanu was slight. Short, slight, beautiful as the Morningstar God, but then all four of the other finalists were as well. Including Second Imperial Consort Su Chafar."

"She was who I was going to go to next," Jion said.

His grandmother looked away, her expression pained, then turned back to face him. "I would say you ought not to do so, but then I tried to dissuade you from asking me about this matter, and you did anyway. You will have to judge for yourself, but I will tell you three things—gods grant you will consider well. First, I don't believe she recognized Afan Yskanda. During the selection she paid scant heed to the other girls from court, and completely ignored Alk Hanu as an outlander from an obscure island. Second, she was very angry when she wasn't selected. Very angry. All her maids the following day were carried out in white cloth, including the dressmaker, whom she'd only seen twice. At least she permitted them a whole corpse in having them strangled. That was no doubt some comfort to the families." Her voice was extremely dry.

Jion grimaced. He'd heard through gossip Honored Second Mother had had maids strangled, though she'd always been kind to him, and indulgent even when he was a brat. But

one of his earliest memories of trouble between the adults was
when Imperial Father had confined her to her pavilion for half
a year after several servants had suddenly vanished from
Inspiration of Drenched Blossoms, Honored Second Mother's
pavilion. Manon had told him herself that her mother had
retired into seclusion and reflection, which meant that he
couldn't come for his dancing lesson.

"Finally, Honored Second Mother, like your father, tends
to have a long memory for certain kinds of experiences," Jion's
grandmother went on. "People in power do not like reminders
of things they consider humiliating."

Jion reflected that no one likes being reminded of humili-
ation. It's the people in power who can make you regret bringing it up. Aloud he said, "If this Danno didn't try to kill
Imperial Father, then what happened?"

"Topaz did not see everything, of course. But from what he
said, Alk Hanu was an odd girl. Quite odd." The dowager
empress tipped her head, the golden ornaments in her headdress swinging. "I liked her during the selection. She had such
modest manners. When the subject of scholarship came up, she
bloomed like a garden of flowers. We were not convinced so
unworldly a girl would make the best choice for consort, but
your father chose her of the five . . . and then she refused to
complete the marriage."

Jion had been expecting anything but this. "She did? Then
why did she come to the imperial city?"

"The call was in the nature of a summons. It was a very old
tradition, one the Sage Empress had deplored, though the
princes favored it—and so too did certain of the princesses
when it came time to find them consorts. Needless to say that
was the last time we did selections in that manner."

"Was someone else in her heart? Or did she want to become a nun?"

"Surmising is useless. The fact remains, though she was
put through the wedding ceremony, she steadfastly refused to
consummate the marriage, and I didn't know it at the time, or
I would have prevailed on the empress to step in and send her
home. Enjai could then have chosen among the other four. But
he said nothing—we did not know that Hojai must have had
his spies in his brother's house, and was taking bets and
spreading rumors among all the imperial cousins as well as the
princes. Of course everyone knew Hojai's relish for cruelty,

but he still managed to make what ought to have been a private matter between newlyweds a loss of face for Enjai among the young men of the imperial court."

The dowager empress thumbed her eyes, and Jion poured out tea for her.

She drank it, dropped her hand, and forced herself to continue. "All *we* knew was that the girl never came to court, and as there were other things far more pressing, time just slipped by without any of us paying much heed. When enough time had passed and I asked if a grandchild could be expected, Hojai gloated about the fact that Hanu was still a maiden, and attributed that to your father's lack of . . . I believe you are old enough to comprehend what sort of cruel mockeries young men are capable of."

Jion could not imagine anyone saying any such thing about his father.

"I confronted Enjai, who admitted the truth of it. I was seeking an auspicious time to request the empress to send the girl home when word came that Danno and Alk Hanu had run off together. Your father and all his personal guards chased them through the imperial city," she said, lowering her voice. "And came back empty-handed."

"Oh," Jion said.

"By then everyone was talking, until the empress put a stop to it. But for years afterward at family gatherings Hojai never ceased referring to the girl who preferred a bodyguard to a prince. This helped keep alive, I am certain, the sense of betrayal your father felt, for Danno had been the brother that cruel Hojai, and that sneaky snake Lijai, and poor silly Fujai never could. And Hojai knew it."

Jion could see the profound betrayal, then. As if Vaion— no.

Before his time as a gallant wanderer, he might have believed his father the victim here, and Danno the betrayer. "Not a *real* brother," Jion protested. "A real brother can say no. A bodyguard is forever silent unless told to speak. How is that brotherhood?"

The dowager gave a slow nod. "Of course Danno was not a real brother. He was the ideal of a brother, the one in poems and stories, who never really exists, because he has no will of his own. Danno, the perfectly trained bodyguard, never argued, always obeyed—yet he as the savior of the prince had honor equivalent to the highest minister, at least in the princes' eyes. Especially to Hojai, who'd tried very hard to lure him away from Enjai. Danno turned his back on them all when he and this girl vanished."

"This grateful grandson is beginning to see."

"But that's not all. The empress was furious. It was not just Enjai who had lost face. The imperial family lost face when the entire city saw your father riding through the city sending chickens squawking and carts overturning and every tongue clacking louder than a monk's stick on his wooden fish. Your father even got their names put on the capital list through Danno's desertion, until the empress, who usually paid scant attention to such things, discovered it and had them removed again. Your father meantime was confined to his pavilion, as I said. He was not released until the empress's death."

Jion tried to imagine his father imprisoned the way he had been.

"The other imperial children blamed him when no one else was permitted to live outside the city. Also, the empress arranged all the subsequent imperial marriages."

"Including Imperial Father's?"

"Including your father's," the dowager empress said. "You are old enough to hear these things now. Especially as your sisters' marriages are being discussed this year, and yours will come up sooner than you think."

A trapdoor seemed to open in Jion's stomach at that. He hid his reaction as she said, "Su Shafar was raised to marry an imperial prince. The Su clan had been vital back when Empress Teyan came to the throne. It was the present duke's father, and to a certain extent he, who influenced the court in her favor, for we had been on the brink of civil war."

Jion knew that much about history. Luckily Bloody Maoyan had died first.

"But that moral debt was there, and when the present duke inherited, he used that influence to begin filling ministerial positions with cronies, and he created enormous pressure on the empress for an imperial marriage. In spite of the tension between Enjai and his grandmother the empress, they were agreed that the balance of power in court would be upset if the Su clan stepped up next to the throne."

Jion nodded, fascinated by these glimpses into the elders' young lives.

"The empress arranged for your mother to marry Enjai, and as an imperial consort, not as a princess, as she was about to birth a Spring Festival child."

So that was why Jion's mother was not mentioned in that record in the archive. Jion understood what the empress had done: if his mother had married Imperial Father as a princess, Lily could have been regarded as a possible imperial heir.

"The Ran family, as you know, ranks second only to the Jehans, so the Su clan perforce had to accept not only her precedence, but Su Shafar could not have a higher rank. Therefore your father had two imperial consorts, but no princess consort. Yu Pirag, your Third Mother, came later—a month before the empress died—in an attempt to break the Su hold on court, as the Yu clan, as you know, is connected to Yulins, who had been rising, both in the military and in provincial government." She looked away again.

Jion had no interest in the Yulins. He said, "I have one more question . . ."

The dowager sighed, closing her eyes. "What happened that night? Ayah. I will tell you, then this subject is truly done."

Jion bowed his assent.

His grandmother went on in a thready, tired voice, her gaze reaching beyond the quiet spirit tablets on the altar, as she looked back at the horror of that seemingly endless night. "Though it isn't written down anywhere, we think of the night the empress died as the Night of Blood. Empress Teyan was quite ill. She knew the King of the Underworld was waiting for her. With her dying breath she wanted the imperial seal taken to Enjai before Hojai could find out."

So his father had not taken the throne. Though nothing was different, somehow that changed everything.

His grandmother went on, slowly, reluctantly, "The empress and poor Imperial Princess Tianjai agreed that the latter would never be strong enough to rein Hojai. But he had bribed at least one of the servants, and he found out almost the moment the empress breathed her last. Before we could dispatch someone to the roof to call her soul back, he went for poor Tianjai, who had been kneeling at Empress Teyan's bedside through days and nights."

She drew a deep, shuddering breath, and closed her eyes, her voice dropping. "When he saw that she did not have the seal, he killed her, then ran through the palace with his bloody sword and his favorites among the imperial guard."

She looked aside, disturbed, even ashamed. He was not alone in kinship mutilation, one of the worst sins. How could anyone expected to lead an empire with such an example? Ayah, ayah." She thumbed tears from her eyes, drew in a deep breath, and determinedly went on. "It was Arijai who managed to shoot Lijai before Hojai killed her right there before the Hall of Glorious Harmony. I'll never know how many servants and guards died—though I'm certain the ferrets know—as of course everyone had their own paid informants, as well as their faction among the guards, mostly hired through their personal bodyguards." She opened her eyes again.

"Who had the emperor's seal? Do you know?"

"Oh, yes. It was Bitternail and Melonseed who brought it to your father, though more than half of those who shielded them died."

"The *graywings* defended the palace?"

"Some. Mostly it was the ferrets, united with those imperial guards not in Hojai's faction. Chief Fai defended me and Ran Renyi against Hojai's faction among the guard."

She made a warding gesture with her hand, the pearls clattering softly. "I hate talking about that night. As for the matter of Danno and Alk Hanu, your father has never spoken about it. Even to me. But he's clearly never forgotten. It was New Year's a few years back, when one of your uncle Pan-Pan's drawings caught his eye. He said nothing. That, my dear grandson, is a warning in itself. But Topaz noticed his sudden interest. What I noticed afterward was a change in his mood, and I had a feeling something inauspicious had happened."

She sighed. "I don't know what he intends by Afan Yskanda. But I suspect before he does make a decision, he will want to make absolutely certain who Afan Yskanda is. After all, it's entirely possible he's a descendant of Alk Hanu's sister, or a cousin, or the similarities are entirely coincidence. Afan is a common name, but as far as I know, no relation to the Alks, and Danno had no family—the mother he only met once or twice died defending Tianjai the night of the empress's passing."

Grandmother Empress looked tired at this point, almost ill. Feeling profoundly guilty, Jion thanked her, then exerted himself to talk her back into a good mood by praising the portraits, and from there talking about Talents she had known, and what plays she might like to see performed for New Year's. When she was smiling again he took his leave, thinking rapidly as he walked.

The mystery was solved, or nearly. The real question was: what did he want to do with what he had learned?

Grandmother Empress had warned him against interference, but he did not need that warning. His father's silence on the subject was warning enough. He pondered that as he returned to his manor, to find Whiteleaf hovering anxiously.

"Chief Fai Anbai is waiting in the hall," the graywing said.

The ferret chief — here? Jion's heart banged against his ribs. He'd just surrendered one arm from the sleeve of his court robe into Yarrow's hands. He shrugged it back on, and proceeded swiftly through to his front hall, Whiteleaf trailing as he tried to twitch the silk back into place.

Shock was Jion's first reaction, then reason reduced panic to heart-hammering alertness: if he were seriously in trouble, then he would be hauled to the west side, where the ferrets had their lair. The ferret chief coming to him was meant to be a gesture of courtesy.

Tall, dressed entirely in black, Chief Fai Anbai did indeed wait in Jion's front hall. Previous to his capture, Jion had only seen the man once or twice, and never to speak to. "Chief Fai."

The ferret chief bowed, his expression wooden. An improvement, Jion thought, on the cold loathing he'd seen aboard the ship.

"This incompetent servitor wishes to apologize for disturbing the peace of your imperial highness — "

Jion's first impulse had been to force the ferret chief to stick with abject formality, but not ten words into that preface, it occurred to him that whatever this interview was about would take three times as long. He waved off the bow and the formality — realizing as he did so that he'd unconsciously mirrored his father's gesture. "You are here by order of his imperial majesty?"

*Surely* ferrets did not have spies at his grandmother's?

Fai Anbai's bow this time was a polite lowering of his head — a step less formal. "Not by order, but with permission, your imperial highness. I have come to request . . . to beg your imperial highness for the generosity to enlighten this incompetent by repeating what you had to report about the Shadow Panthers."

That came out a little jerky, and was spoken in a flat voice, but Jion intuited that Fai Anbai was as acutely aware as he was of the circumstances of their last conversation. Jion's first impulse (after a wash of relief through all his nerves) was to point out that this question by rights belonged to the army, correct? But that would be a verbal face slap, as surely Fai Anbai remembered very well what he had said.

Clearly circumstances had changed. And Imperial Father would be somewhere in the middle of them: the ferret chief would not dare to disturb an imperial prince without orders from the emperor. "Come inside," Jion said politely. "Whiteleaf, tea."

Jion suspected that the ferret chief wouldn't drink it, but speaking the words was an attempt to lessen the fraught atmosphere, at least on his side. "I don't know a lot," he said. "What I learned was on nights when I was summoned to play the guzheng for Screaming Hawk and his chosen followers. Screaming Hawk wasn't one to tell secrets, but he loved to brag, especially when he was drunk. Everything I learned came from drunk talk, if that helps in determining how true it is."

"Your imperial highness is gracious," Fai Anbai said stiffly. He couldn't tell if the spoiled prince was gloating or not. Ever since the rainy night one the prince sat on a rooftop gazing at the little trap they had set up, Fai Anbai and the ferrets had been on constant alert. The fact that Prince Jion had so quickly found the trap — and then stopped at the south gate — testified not only to considerable skills, but considerable self-discipline. Which they had believed completely foreign to him. They had to completely reevaluate their assumptions about him.

Fai Anbai was very aware that they wanted to think the prince was stupid. It would make everything so very much easier. "We will, of course, check the veracity of any information we are given, your imperial highness."

Jion nodded. "He bragged about his successes. I assumed that if any part of it was true, he was probably doubling or tripling numbers, or even making details up to make himself look tougher. But there were scraps of detail that caught at my attention."

"If your imperial highness would enlighten me with an example, I would be most grateful."

"He went on about taking a ship in the south last year. How they killed everyone on board and made away with the entire ship. There were details in the fight that made me think it might have been a naval ship."

Fai Anbai's brows shot upward, then met over his nose. "There was an incident, with pirates, last year. We lost a naval ship. But all the reports I received were united in insisting that the attack was carried out by pirates."

Jion opened his hands. "All I can tell you is what I heard while I was in effect a prisoner, though they called us recruits. I could not put questions. There was another one where he described the fun of taking on shipwrights."

Fai Anbai said, "There was an assault on the shipwrights at Blue Pine Island. But again, that was pirates." He looked up at the prince. "Did your imperial highness gain any sense that the Shadow Panthers ran as pirates?"

"Not that I heard." Jion shook his head. "And our drills were for land warfare—not that they were very good. But he also made it clear he was but one of Master Night's chiefs. We were told there were two others. It could be there are pirates under one of them. Oh, did I mention that a couple of things in his brag made me wonder if Master Night is noble-born?"

Jion held out his hand in invitation as Whiteleaf presented the tea. Sure enough, Fai Anbai bowed and refused with dauntingly extreme courtesy. Jion poured a cup to have something to do with his hands—and in a vain hope of lightening the atmosphere, though he suspected that the ferret chief still resented that long search.

We both do, he thought wryly before the ferret chief said, "If I may trouble your imperial highness with a further question, what kind of things?"

Jion scoured his mind, trying to recollect precise incidents. Words. "It's hard to remember specifics, there was so much brag. Drunk talk and repetition. It was more of an impression that the Master Night had plenty of wealth. No, that's not right. It's the . . . the long planning, I think. 'We have plans,' those were the words that caught my attention. Of course most of what followed was brag-promise: you'll have your own palace, you'll have a hundred dancing girls, or boys, of your own, you'll have treasure chests of gold. I can't say I know everything about gallant wanderers because I only met a few, and they're all different, but I don't remember them talking about plans for the future in quite the same way." He glanced over at that unwavering stare, and gave up with a shrug. "That's all I remember. The rest would be speculation."

Fai Anbai rose at once, and bowed as he spoke formal thanks.

Jion supposed he didn't want to remain another breath in his polluted atmosphere, but couldn't resist trying his own question. "Did Screaming Hawk tell you anything?"

Fai Anbai paused, and bowed again. "You were correct in your prediction, your imperial highness. He revealed nothing." A last bow, and ten steps took him out the door.

Jion was tempted to ask what had happened to cause this questioning, but he knew the man would not answer him unless ordered to, and Jion guessed that he'd said exactly as much as he'd been permitted to say — or was told to say — and not a word more.

He could ask his father, but to go to the emperor for answers required having a good reason for asking. *Because I was curious* would not be a good answer; meanwhile, there would be the reminder of Jion's brief life as a gallant wanderer, which everyone seemed to be pretending had never happened.

Jion went to his desk to begin his studies, but gave up after reading a single page three times without comprehending a word. He no longer wanted to consult Honored Second Mother; on other subjects, maybe, but the image of those white-wrapped bundles made him disinclined to discuss the matter with her. Or with Manon, whose bored contempt toward Afan Yskanda on the day the portraits were presented reminded Jion that she was serious about distinctions of rank. She would have no interest in Afan Yskanda's matter.

So . . . he was on his own, and though some questions had been answered, others remained. Who was it who said, *When you can't find someone in the fog, make yourself into a lamp?*

# SEVENTEEN

AT THE OTHER END of the palace, Court Artist Yoli was finishing up a lecture to the apprentices crowded into an instruction chamber, as the regular instructors lined the back.

"Colors and symbols of spring, planting, specifically rice," he said. "The ox is important to farmers, and it's the farmers whose tax contributions enable everyone else to defend and to serve the kingdom. Because the augurs say we are moving into a wood phase, which emphasizes balance, we will reflect that in colors."

A whisper serried through the throng of artists: greens of spring, browns of earth.

"I might remind you that the emperor wants the symbols and colors of peace, especially with negotiations for an imperial marriage treaty in the offing. Give important figures flywhisks and other symbols of peace and harmony. Fewer swords." He waved a dismissive hand. "That's all."

Yskanda, primed beforehand, stepped out to lead the bows, after which the apprentices all filed out.

The court artist grimaced and reached for his crutch. Yskanda sprang to his side. "Lean on me, sir."

"I wish I'd brought my cart, but no, I had to act as if I'm a spring buck and walk from court. I don't know why," the court artist muttered. "There's no bigger fool than an old one trying to pretend he's young."

Yskanda took most of the court artist's weight, which was nearly twice his own, and matched pace with his master as they headed back to their workroom. Halfway there he was glad he'd forced himself to keep up the habit of doing Heaven and Earth even after Court Artist Yoli began walking again.

They reached the workroom at last, and Yskanda helped the court artist remove his crimson court robe. He was in the process of draping it on the clothes pole for him when the little duty page popped in, eyes round, to say breathlessly, "His Imperial Highness the First Prince is coming this way!"

"Here?" Yoli asked Yskanda, who of course had no idea. "Quick, help me into my robe."

Yskanda hastily helped the court artist grunt and wince his way back into his formal robe. He'd just twitched the long sleeves and back folds into place when the rustle of silk in the open doorway caused both to turn and bow.

Prince Jion stood there, resplendent in dark blue over pale peach, his outer robe embroidered with red pomegranate flowers and lute grass patterns. The only gold he wore was in his hair clasp, and the golden silk tassel on his jade tiger-eye belt pendant. He was a striking figure, all the more in these plain surroundings; Yskanda's fingers twitched, as he suppressed the urge to grab his ink brushes.

"Your imperial highness honors these unworthy servants," Court Artist Yoli said.

Jion strolled in, hands clasped behind his back as he glanced around appreciatively. "I forgot how interesting it is in here." And to the court artist, "Glad to see you still flourishing, Court Artist Yoli."

"This insignificant dabbler is graced by your imperial highness's attention."

"Sit down. You look like you're still recovering—they tell me you suffered a fall," Jion said. "Let's be as comfortable as we were last time I saw you." He waved a hand as he came in and perched on the edge of a table, careful to keep his silk from dragging through the dish of oil waiting there to be added to the colors Yskanda was grinding.

"It is good to see that you survived during the interim, your imperial highness," the court artist observed as he grunted his way back down onto his cushion, then let out a short sigh.

"I wish I could draw." Jion smiled at the crusty old man.

"You would be very surprised by some of the things I saw."
He snapped his fan open, then described a circle, dismissing
the subject. "You know my father's birthday will be coming
along after the change of the year. I've been trying to think of
something suitable, if either of you has any ideas."

Court Artist Yoli took in the direction of the prince's gaze,
and made a guess at his true purpose. "If your imperial
highness would like to discuss ideas, my assistant would be
honored to aid you. Yskanda, please show his imperial
highness to the outer room."

Imperial Prince Jion's flashing smile made it clear that Yoli
had guessed correctly. And what more natural than to discuss
art with a Talent of his own age, especially as Yskanda had
been appointed the imperial family portraitist? Relieved to so
easily sidestep yet another interruption in a very ticklish
assignment on which he was already behind, the court artist
turned his bushy brows Yskanda's way. "You are at his
imperial highness's disposal. Send the page for tea, will you?"

Yskanda had been dreading this meeting and waiting for
it ever since the day he walked out of the archive. His sleep
had been restless as he imagined conversations—
interrogations—ranging from confused to threatening. The
latter most frequent.

At least he would no longer be wondering, he thought
wearily as he indicated the way to the seldom-used, tiny
receiving chamber down the hall from the workroom, meant
for exalted people like ministers or even higher whose sensitive noses might object to the stink of paints and varnishes.

But as soon as they reached the receiving chamber, the
prince glanced inside at the apprentice-painted silk screens
behind which pages, graywings, and anyone else might be
lurking, and waved toward the door leading outside. This time
Yskanda followed.

The prince wandered out into the cold, clear midafternoon
air, the low sun limning the rooftops of the government
buildings to the southwest. He led the way unerringly to the
Garden of Serene Contemplation, which, being primarily a
rock garden, afforded a clear view in all directions. As well
they could be seen from the inner palace wall and gate.

Jion clasped his hands behind his back again. "Think of
some kind of art for my father. No people. He likes scenery,
the more traditional the better. He also likes calligraphy. Either

one will do. And so we're going to spend this entire walk talking about it."

He slanted a mocking smile Yskanda's way.

Yskanda bowed low.

Jion said, "I've let enough time go by for you to realize that I haven't told anyone what I found." He glanced inquiringly at Yskanda, who bowed again. "Until today. I spoke with my grandmother, who remembers your mother. That *is* your mother, Alk Hanu, that you resemble so strongly, isn't it?"

Yskanda had spent too many years keeping the secret of his parents' identities to be able to speak. Especially now, here, in the midst of what to him had always been a superbly ornamental prison.

Jion glanced at his pale profile, and said reflectively, "You didn't deny it. And if I'm right, then you're probably expecting Imperial Father to strike you dead, and your family through you."

This time, Yskanda stayed silent deliberately.

"I thought so. Assistant Court Artist Afan—Yskanda—I'm going to use your name, and I wish you'd use mine. I liked having a name, no titles, when I was a gallant wanderer going wandering from island to island. Which is something the court does not know, as it happens."

Ayah, if that was even true, Yskanda had not asked for a confidence. If it was meant to force him to share his own, this was yet another form of interrogation. Perhaps not painful, but definitely pernicious.

Jion was still talking. "The problem with courtly protocol, I came finally to understand, is that it's a mask. Anything could be going on behind that mask. Some even believe the mask is all there is. I did, once. Until I got away from courtly protocol. The freedom was . . . it would be wrong to say perfect, because it could be exasperating and maddening and dangerous at times, but my grandmother reminded me today that danger is here, too."

He didn't wait for an answer, but swept right on. "My grandmother isn't going to speak to anyone. She didn't want *me* talking about it. I wonder who else knows? Probably an open secret among those over fifty who saw your mother back when she was here, and it seems that was few enough, especially after the Night of Blood. But no one knows for certain, and my father hasn't had the ferrets haul you in for one of their infamous interrogations, am I right? You don't seem to be missing any limbs."

Yskanda spoke for the first time. "True, your imperial highness."

"But. . . let me guess . . . you'd do anything to escape, had you the chance, in spite of your honored position? Which you seem to have earned. I salute you for that. You truly are a Talent."

Once again Yskanda paused on the pathway in order to bow.

"Sadly, escape is beyond us both," Jion continued, aware that Yskanda had not answered his question—but he took silence as assent. If Afan Yskanda was aghast at the very idea of throwing away his honors and running off, surely he would have said so, probably in a morass of courtly language. "I wasn't all that successful at escape myself, as you see. Though it was a very interesting time while it lasted." He glanced skyward, smiled, and added, "The result of which is, I'm probably even more closely guarded than you are."

Yskanda did not know what to think. He was nearly sick with apprehension, though he knew very well that the question of his identity was a spiderweb-thin cover behind which to hide. But he had clung to that because he had nothing else.

Jion's thoughts caromed on. "It has to be fate," he said. "My guess is, you were brought, not invited?"

"Yes, your imperial highness," Yskanda said.

"Do you know how they found you?"

A quick look revealed a little of how much Afan Yskanda had worried at that question. And had not dared to ask.

"I can tell you that much. My uncle Kui Pandan, who never sleeps twice in the same place if he can prevent it, collects beautiful faces the way nobles collect vases from the Lo Dynasty and jade ornaments and gold. He saw you somewhere and drew you. My father chanced to see the drawing, and I guess he recognized your resemblance to the mysterious Alk Hanu."

Afan Yskanda looked away, and Jion could see it was going to take some time to gain Yskanda's trust. "Fate put my uncle there, fate put you in his view, fate put that drawing in my father's sight, when he seldom looks at the hundreds my uncle makes. And yet, to think you were almost my brother!

You would have been First Prince, and Manon would have adored you had you been born a prince—you're as scholarly as she is. She would have dismissed me the way she does my rascal of a brother, though Vaion is a good brother if only she could see it. We don't seem to have a Hojai in our generation—lucky! There was one in all the previous ones. At least one."

Jion glanced at Yskanda, and saw the question that Yskanda did not dare ask. "Hojai, known to the world as Imperial First Prince, was the one who murdered most of my older relatives and dueled my father for the throne. It's why I have only one cousin on my father's side, by one of my departed uncles, and she lives with her mother's family in the Silk Islands. He tried to kill her, but only succeeded in laming her before running from my aunt with her bow, and her pack of guards."

He paused, looked, and understood from Yskanda's averted gaze that—unlike Vaion, who had a boy's lust for bloody tales—Yskanda was not enjoying this glimpse of the past.

Jion shifted the subject. "What is the difference between a feared tyrant and a rescuer of the empire? I'm wondering now if there has to be a Hojai of some sort in any dynasty in order to keep hold of the throne. Then we're all doomed, aren't we? No, there are the sages, the great emperors and empresses. Perhaps my sister Manon will be one of those. She certainly works hard enough. I wonder if each new emperor or empress sets out to become a sage . . . Say something, Afan Yskanda. Anything."

"We would never have been brothers." Yskanda heard his own voice, as if it came from far away. "Your imperial highness."

Jion stopped. He turned, long phoenix eyes of obsidian meeting almond-shaped eyes of sun-touched teak. It had been an impulse of generosity that had prompted Jion to say that, instead of something like *If your mother and my father's sworn guard hadn't decided to run off together.* But Yskanda's words were almost a slap to the spirit.

Almost, because there was no accusation in Yskanda's expression, or his tone. His gaze diffused, and his voice was mild, even detached, as he said, "My father and mother had spent every day together for almost a year. But your father was going to have her killed. And mine would have had to do it." Still detached, except this time he forgot the honorific.

Somewhere, snow fell from a branch and chuffed on the ground.

Then Jion abruptly began talking again, a quick stream of words about silk, and how brocade had become an expected tribute gift. Yskanda glanced up to find a graywing some ten paces off, coming toward them.

". . . see that it's the best silk, of course. He prefers hangings to scrolls — yes, Fennel?"

The graywing, no older than either of them, went to the ground, and when bidden to rise, said, "Whiteleaf sent this insignificant one to inform his imperial highness that her imperial highness the first princess has sent over her instrument."

Jion turned to Yskanda. "I will come and check your progress, for this present must be perfect. You may go."

# EIGHTEEN

YSKANDA BOWED AND RETREATED, unsettled by his own words, and was it a broken promise when someone already knew everything? He was also upset by how much quicker the prince had been to see danger coming. He'd thought himself alert at all times, but the prince was faster. No, that wasn't it. What bothered him was that the prince had to be alert—that this graywing had to be watched for. It suggested that the prince was surrounded by listening ears in his own home.

At least Yskanda could be alone in his room—though Juniper's clever, efficient fingers were all over everything inside that room.

What to tell the court artist? What could the court artist do that he had not done already, except be questioned?

When Yskanda got back inside, Court Artist Yoli asked, "What did his imperial highness want?"

Yskanda responded with the request for a present, and waited to see if the court artist would ask further questions.

Yoli pursed his lips, leaned back to sigh noisily, then said, "I can tell you every present I've been involved with. The emperor professes to like calligraphy, but a screen of wisdom can be dangerous unless he himself suggests the text."

Yskanda saw the pitfall then, feeling as if he'd stepped too near a cliff edge. He could very well imagine the emperor looking past the most innocuous-seeming ancient text to seek a motivation for choosing that one, and then delving for hidden messages.

Point taken: no discussing the imperials themselves. Only what they wanted from artists.

"Scenery," he said decidedly. "But what? Mt. Lir?"

The court artist shook his head. "Too frequently done. In the back archives there's an entire wall of rolled-up Lir paintings. Through all the dynasties. Lir in snow, Lir in spring, summer, autumn. Lir with smoke coming forth, fire, Lir in storms. Sacred mountain — hidden dragons — emperor, so obvious, the principle so threadbare. The old emperor might have liked it. He surrounded himself with images reflecting his power, but this emperor might be insulted at the lack of forethought, and who could blame him? It'll have to be something closer. Perhaps he'd prefer the imperial garden to Mt. Lir. Actually, come to think of it, that might be an excellent idea."

Yskanda's first reaction was relief, followed by puzzlement. "But which part of the garden? I can't do the entire garden, not without climbing to the emperor's balcony."

He said it in a tone of horror, and the court artist threw up his hands at the thought. Yskanda had only been dreading the idea of once more being in the emperor's private Golden Dragon Pavilion, but belatedly he saw what scandalized the court artist: without being ordered to paint something from that perspective, a gift from the emperor's son, looking down at the world from that precise place, might be misinterpreted to a deadly extent.

"Definitely not that," Yskanda said hastily.

"Put your mind to the problem. The prince was more thoughtful than most of them in giving you plenty of time. Consider it while we get through this list for the ministers' hall decorations. Now, about these . . ."

Yskanda discovered as New Year's Two Moons drew nearer, that when he was in the workroom he was happy. He loved grinding and mixing colors, he loved layering paint, he loved seeing what the apprentices could make of vague suggestions. He even had begun to love the process of paper-making.

The emperor's birthday gift loomed over him, but as the emperor himself did not summon him, he was able to approach it without too much trepidation. It did mean seeing Prince Jion.

The imperial garden as subject was not so simple, Yskanda had to point out. There was the limitation of size. If it was to be a silk hanging, a tree, or at most a part of a scene, incorporating as many elements as possible: sky, rock, water, the edge of a bridge, perhaps, and of course the plants.

But which scene?

They talked around and around, debating the size of the silk to be painted on, then the size of the scene to be depicted, and what should, and should not, be in it. Yskanda, Jion discovered, talked without restraint about matters of color, brushes, silk, and symbol, but the moment he strayed anywhere near the matters that brought Yskanda to the imperial palace, it was a change from spring rain to summer drought: Yskanda's face shuttered of all expression, he usually bowed, hiding it altogether, and his voice flattened into courtly subservience.

Jion was content to wait. He had nowhere else to go, and nothing else to do aside from his reading — and his sessions with his sister Manon, who never failed to bring new music, each piece more delightful than the last. And each a challenge.

Finally he said, "I know. Let's consult the chief gardener! He'll be able to give us what we need. I should have thought of that before."

He told Whiteleaf to summon Chief Gardener Nei to their next meeting. The man was there . . . and Yskanda wasn't.

And wasn't.

The hour changed with the distant gong, and though the chief gardener waited patiently, Jion could feel the moral outrage building, all the more intense for being hidden. Finally the chief gardener, in an absolute morass of self-abasement and desperate and fulsome compliments, begged to be permitted to get back to what he was doing — which was no less than overseeing a change at Honored Second Mother's pavilion.

Jion sighed, for now he'd have to go over there to apologize directly, lest poor old Nei get blamed. "I'll send for you when the assistant court artist arrives."

It was a full hour later when Yskanda turned up, breathless from a run. Now it was his turn for a morass of apologies, ending with the fact that court had gone very late.

Jion had forgotten about court. "What could keep them so long?"

"Arguing, your imperial highness," Yskanda stated.

Jion imagined those old ministers maundering on and on. What did they have to argue about?

"Over what?" Jion asked.

"Imperial granaries," Yskanda said, after a moment's inward thought, and Jion knew that Yskanda still did not trust him. Sure enough, that was followed by, "This ignorant nonentity has no awareness —"

"Understood," Jion said, hiding his impatience. "I know you have no awareness of politics, no dangerous opinions that will lead straight to Lotus Blossom Square. Tell me what you heard."

Yskanda bowed, and Jion regretted his outburst, sensing that he'd lost ground yet again.

Yskanda said, "Right Chancellor Su approves the memorial submitted by a group of ministers asking that oversight of the imperial granaries be shifted to the Minister of War's department, as the Minister of War already oversees supplying the navy and army, or to the Minister of Works. But the Left Chancellor disagrees, and somehow it all ties up with tributes, and with replacing the Minister of Revenue, who has been ill again."

"He must be well on his way to ninety," Jion commented. "He was already old when I was a small boy. Ayah, I'd forgotten the traditional factions. It's still Left Chancellor Ze against Right Chancellor Su? When I had to sit at court as a boy I wondered if the contest between them was who could be most boring." Jion paused, feeling he'd regained a little of what he'd lost when Yskanda's lips pressed in a line to suppress a smile.

But he'd learned to be careful. Friendship — the true easy give and take of the implied trust of friendship — could not be ordered, or forced. And that meant no references to Yskanda's life.

But he could talk about his own. "Through Honored Second Mother I'm related to the Right Chancellor. I've also uncles and cousins in Works and War, if things haven't changed while I was gone." He shrugged that off. "I'll call the gardener back in. At least this won't take long."

He was wrong.

Chief Gardener Nei was a beetle of a man, small, round-backed from stooping for decades, with a long drooping mustache that he fingered when disturbed.

He was fingering it now, his eyes actually tearing up as he said to Yskanda (for he dared not imply any criticism of an imperial prince), "I must have been a monster in my previous life—or I slaughtered your entire family. Why else would you insult me, for though I am a humble man of no great birth, I am a chief of my department, and your elder."

Yskanda bowed, both long, slim hands coming up in protest. "This wretched being of no talent has expressed himself badly . . ."

To cut short what promised to be a long exchange of apology and politesse, Jion said, "It was *my* idea to feature the best of the garden. This is for the emperor's birthday—I fail to see any insult here."

Both faces turned toward him.

"This incompetent perhaps begins to comprehend," Yskanda began. Even to a gardener, he was too cautious to presume to have an opinion. Servants did not think.

"This wretch might be killed for saying it, but it must be said, your estimable imperial highness, and that is, this garden is *always* beautiful," the chief gardener declared in a imploring voice. "There is no best corner, or best season. Though I and my staff are without talent, we strive with all our poor effort to make certain that in every season, wherever his imperial majesty chooses to grace with the sun of his meritorious gaze, there is never an unsightly or weak aspect. I even request the geomancers to accompany me each full moons day—"

Jion raised a hand to halt the flow. "We understand that the garden is beautiful in all seasons. I know it to be true. The piece of art," he explained slowly, "will show different parts of the garden in all four seasons. I just want to know which part of the garden ought to be matched with which season."

But this suggestion caused the tears to overflow as the chief gardener threw himself to the floor and knocked his head against it as he begged to be executed at once for neglecting his work. Jion tried to remonstrate—to explain himself—until Yskanda cast him a look that shut him up, and dropped down beside the chief gardener.

"This ignorant and lowly assistant craves forgiveness of the esteemed and illustrious chief gardener," he said softly. "And begs to be instructed." He then went on to explain that he would do a cross-section drawing from the main walkway, east to west—morning to evening—spring to winter.

At this, the chief gardener ceased wailing, and raised his head to look at Yskanda.

"The sight of the garden, and its ever-changing nature as different areas bloom, enlightens this unworthy's life better than gold or jade. All this ignorant one must learn is which plants bloom in which season," Yskanda said gently. "That's all. I can then seek drawings of those very same plants in bloom from the archive."

Chief Gardener Nei sat back on his heels, and gave them to know, very cautiously, that that might be done.

Relieved, Jion signaled the hovering Whiteleaf, who further soothed the chief gardener by taking him off, listening sympathetically to a stream of protestations, and then surrendering an embroidered bag that clinked very promisingly.

Leaving Jion and Yskanda alone.

*Because he was going to have her killed.* A very short leap from that to *Because he will have me killed.* Father had seen a picture drawn by Uncle Pandan, and then suddenly Yskanda had appeared in the imperial palace, looking as if he expected to be beheaded.

"So . . . a long horizonal painting," Jion said. "He'd like that. But won't it look strange where the seasons divide?"

Yskanda had remained kneeling on the floor, hands on his thighs, as he thought rapidly. Images flitted through his mind, then he said slowly, "Your imperial highness once said that his imperial majesty is fond of calligraphy and of pictures of nature."

"Yes."

"Then . . . why not combine both? Calligraphy at the place where spring changes to summer, with observations suitable to the reason, and so forth for each change."

Jion frowned, then got it. "And when he gets to winter, with all those bare branches and the evergreens, verses observing the changing of the year?"

Yskanda said diffidently, "I can think of a few poems that might fit—strictly concerning the seasons, your imperial highness. Though perhaps this wretch's taste cannot be trusted."

Jion laughed. "Oh, this part I have to do—borrowing heavily from the masters, of course, but Imperial Father won't expect perfect from me. He'll like the attention, and the art."

At the words "Imperial Father" Yskanda's face had lost all expression, and Jion smothered a sigh. The only other person he'd ever worked this hard to gain the trust of was Ryu.

Later, he reflected on how much he'd gained. Ordinarily he loathed winter closing in, but now he scarcely noticed, except when he went out one day after a snowfall, when the air was so icy and still the world seemed blue. He found Yskanda shivering at the west end of the garden, sketching the perfect snowfall on the ground, the arch of the bridge, and the branches of a great tree that seemed familiar. With an inward jolt, Jion recollected that it was, in fact, a redbark tree, rare on this island.

"Yskanda," he protested, loping up. "The archive is filled with hundreds of winter drawings, including that sacred tree. Can you use one of those as a model?"

Yskanda glanced up, startled, and Jion realized the Talent had been lost in some world of his own while contemplating that tree. "It has to be right, your imperial highness," he said in a voice of conviction, blowing on his fingers.

Jion turned around to retrace his steps, and told the first servant he saw to see to it hot wine was taken out to the assistant court artist. Then he retired, aware that though Yskanda still did not talk about anything personal, he at least had spoken instead of flinging himself on his face in a morass of exculpation. That was progress.

Progress toward what? As rain beat against the silk windows later that evening, he stared down at the Circle board set up between him and Sia Na the pillow maid. In the background, Alu, another pillow maid, brought fresh-baked cakes seasoned with silver milkweed to the side table, and Mimosa fanned the tiny stove under the water kettle, in order to make fresh tea.

Jion picked a cake up and ate it absently, though his mind was far from matters of intimacy. "How," he said to the sedately warring tiles on the board, "do you get someone to trust you?"

Alu and Sia Na exchanged glances, then Sia Na said, "This lacking and very confused maid desires to inquire of his imperial highness if that is a real question?"

Jion blinked. "Did I say that out loud? I did. Ayah! Do you have an answer?"

"This ignorant one has only the words of the wise Suanek,"

Sia Na said. "Trust cannot be commanded; it is an act of faith. When we trust, we give the trusted person our heart, our soul, and our mind to hold and to guard. If we have three people in our lives we truly trust, then we have more riches than a king."

Jion sighed. "Fine words telling me what it is. But not a hint of how to gain it."

The maids exchanged covert looks; they all genuinely liked the first imperial prince, but they'd noticed that sometimes he fell into moods of abstraction. Sia Na, the eldest, said, "Trust takes time."

"I know that. I ought to know that," he added, with a warmth in his voice that hinted at experience. Once again the others exchanged glances — the prince never talked about personal matters, but they all knew the tones of reminiscence, of fondness.

His next remark was about the game.

The days sped by.

The composition began to take shape. Yskanda was becoming accustomed to Jion's presence, as the prince insisted he had to be part of the entire project.

Occasionally apprentices and even a master or two wandered in looking for something, especially in the days right before the year change, which led to some conversation about choices of model. Jion became aware that artists took the slightest detail with utmost seriousness — the way Ryu had when talking about form during Redbark days.

When he was alone, his hand strayed to the ornament around his neck containing the Restoration pill. How strange it was that his memory of Redbark seemed to be eternal summer, though he knew very well there had been some tough winters.

# NINETEEN

ARI THOUGHT OF HIM, too.

She had added him to her night and morning prayer. Now she prayed for the family as she faced southwest, and Shigan as she faced southeast.

But during the days she was always busy. Ari thought about her discovery of the hermit's identity for a day or two, as an ice storm rumbled and roared through the mountains. When she woke on New Year's Two Moons, she decided that if she could not talk to her master, then who?

"The hermit," she said as she stirred the congee. "Is he Waoji Lion's Mane?"

Master Ki sent a frowning look in her direction. Not an angry look, but a considering one. He didn't speak until he brought the bowls and spoons. Then he said, "Yes, but if you bring it up, I'm sure it will be the last time you see him."

Ari sat back on her haunches. "Why?"

"Why do you think a man withdraws from the world to the mountains here?"

"I don't understand anything about hermits," she muttered.

"Try again."

She scowled at her steaming congee. "To cultivate. To live in harmony with the world without the distraction of human things. To mourn. To hide."

"What if it is all those things?" Master Ki asked.

"Mourning?"

"I believe you've heard the stories."

Ari said, "But Ul—my tutor said never to believe all you read in the hero tales."

"Good advice," Master Ki said. "Though there is often a kernel of truth in them."

"The stories said he was raised in a mysterious sect, and there was a huge battle with demons, and he was the only survivor. That's where I got the idea about Redbark," she added. "Then he was picked up by pirates, fought a duel with the evil captain and took them over, and then he trained with a band of heroes, though that part sounded a lot like the story of Jong Siang and the 110 outlaws . . ."

"Stop, stop." Master Ki laughed as he held up his hands. "I hadn't realized how many of those were circulating out there. Let us leave it at this: he has trained with many different styles, though his son is currently at Sky Mirror Island, where Lion's Mane once was a master. His most faithful partner was Bi Cassia, the woman known as Bi the Whirlwind. She was killed while saving their two children, who had been taken by an enemy. He was able to rescue the children, but the enemy, someone very powerful, escaped. No, I do not know who it is. Except it's someone with enough rank to bend the laws."

"Oh," she said, and muttered, "I *hate* that."

"So does he. And talking about it will not help him in any way."

She clasped her hands and bowed. "Understood."

"Eat up. Even though it's unlikely we will see the sky today, we will do the ritual just the same, and we'll work on soul-sensing."

Ari sat upright.

"No humans as focus," Master Ki warned. "Especially at a distance. Not that distance in the other world means anything, actually. But in your mind it still does, so we will work closer to home. Animals have simpler souls, the lower soul dominant, which is far easier for you to sense."

Ari clasped her hands and nodded uncertainly.

"This is the time of year when foraging starts becoming more difficult for the animals, and we'll see more of them right here in our valley."

She nicked a quick bow, then raced through her meal,

which was not exactly exciting, as their supplies began to thin.

Once the pot and dishes had been scoured, they sat on the rug facing one another. Ari put her hands on her knees and her tongue to roof of mouth to open her conduits, and began Essence breathing.

"Some perceive through one or another sense," Master Ki said. "Nothing is wrong. It's usual, I learned, to perceive them through sight—which means 'seeing' shapes, or lights, or something similar, behind your closed lids. Others use scent. Or hearing."

Ari nodded. "I think . . . I think that's what I'm already doing, if these little sky-lanterns are they. There's one right above us!"

"That is probably the vixen, foraging for food. She will be withdrawing to deliver her kits before long. She needs to eat as much as she can."

Soon Ari counted three tiny, wobbly sky-lanterns, which turned out to be birds. Then along glided a big, blobby one, which when she opened her eyes turned out to be a buck. Elated at having at last reached at least some success, she pushed until dizziness nearly overwhelmed her. Master Ki made her stop, breathe herself back into her body, and then quit altogether to get ready for the ritual.

Which was made transcendent by the sound of the hermit's flute floating down from the crags, in an elegiac melody that Ari had never heard before. "He only plays that song once a year," Master Ki murmured when it ended. "It's his way of sending the year's souls over the bridge to Heaven, where he trusts that Bi Cassia awaits him, that they may be reborn together."

The music stayed with Ari, bringing a tightness to her throat with its longing. But she said nothing as she distributed the day's leavings for the valley animals to find, and inside her mind, she repeated, Hermit, Hermit, Hermit, so that Lion's Mane would not accidentally slip out.

He did not reappear for days. At first she wondered if he had somehow guessed that she knew his identity. But she kept that to herself, too, and worked on her internal sky-lanterns. By the end of the week she not only could find animals close by, she could move toward them, sending calming thoughts.

Which tempted her to try once more to reach Shigan . . .

Master Ki patted her on her messy head—for she often

forgot to comb her hair for days. "Learn one thing at a time," he reminded her, and went back to carving as she went out to the garden to do Redbark.

After that, with all her chores done, she went back to Essence practice, now focused in two directions.

What Yaso had said about the terrible storm she unleashed unwittingly had kept her from experimenting with using Essence as a wind. But if she could find a way to do it without throwing Essence up into the sky and all over the place? What if she could make spears of wind?

Once again she hung shells and twigs from trees, and practiced shooting wind at them from farther and farther away. It felt like trying to shape water when she attempted *seeing* wind, the way she saw the animal souls. But when she tried using the end of her staff to "point" the wind, it became far easier.

Controlling it as well as adding power took time, but when she felt it click into place the way the two halves of her staff locked into a seamless whole, she was able to shoot a precisely shaped spear of wind across the little valley. She sensed that she might even be able to do it with fire, but that could wait for someday when she had nothing but rock around her.

The second experiment was even more exhilarating, especially when she invented the game she called Tree. She stood with her arms outstretched and her eyes shut, seeds sprinkled on her shoulders and held in both hands. Then she stretched out her mind, calling to the local birds, who flocked in, perching on her as four different types of beaks pecked up the seeds.

The birds had learned not to peck hard, but they were not really aware of pooping, so she no longer put seeds on her head. Thus she stood there, her arms and shoulders covered with birds, when the hermit's familiar step crunched and squeaked through the snow.

"Hah." His hoarse laugh filled the cold air. "Now that's not a sight often seen."

With a flapping of wings the birds took flight. Ari shook the remaining seeds onto the ground, knowing the birds would be back to find them, and happily ran to get her staff.

The wintry days passed swiftly. Though the light gradually began coming up earlier, there were some mornings when Master Ki did not waken first, so getting breakfast became Ari's duty.

Occasionally she woke to rain, and muddy spots began to appear, to vanish before fresh snow. The gray, sleety rain seemed much colder than the snow, rendering the world a dull, chill, dismal color. Sometimes, when the mornings looked especially bleak, Ari stood in the doorway looking out, and wondered if even Second Brother Yskanda would find any of these gloomy shades appealing. She hoped First Brother Muin wasn't slogging through a day like this in whatever his first command as captain was.

And what kind of day did Shigan look out on, from his palace under the threat of that emperor?

On such days they stayed inside, working on Essence.

Not long after the turn of the year, Master Ki began telling Ari to think of Essence as prayer, rather than as a pool of potential power.

The first time he said that, she looked at him in surprise, then said diffidently, "But I'm not angry when I use Essence to blow out candles, or rattle my hanging shells, truly I'm not."

Master Ki raised a hand. "I know. And in your turn, you must not misunderstand what I mean by prayer. Please do not fall into the trap of regarding it by its outward forms, for surely you understand that kneeling, the hands, the bowed head, are all aids to concentration, and that one's prayer is not always a form of supplication?"

Ari did see it—now. And she had needed such aids for Essence studies, such as touching her tongue to the roof of her mouth when she began Essence breathing.

"We are concentrating upon the higher world," he reminded her. "Which is why the temple divines talk about the holy five of prayer. What are they?"

Ari said promptly, "Entreaty and thankfulness, divination and ritual, and finally amends."

It was this last that reverberated through her like the low tone of a vast gong, more felt than heard. It was so easy to destroy and so difficult to mend. She was coming to understand what it meant that her own Essence power was aligned with fire and with metal, two of the most volatile of the elements. As Master Ki's own power was air and, to a lesser extent, water, he did not entirely understand hers. But he did his best, exhorting her to search her heart in the never-ending quest for understanding, for harmony.

She had a good heart, he believed—and discussed once or twice with the hermit, when she was deeply asleep. "What I strive to teach her, to teach them all, is that the gods grant powers along with life, but it's up to the individual to use them wisely and well."

Waoji Lion's Mane smiled grimly. "And you are reminding me because?"

Master Ki wheezed with amusement. "You have been down here more times this winter than in all the previous years since you first came up here. Let's talk about what is next for my little student. I notice that during the rains, she sniffs the air and peers southward, rather than concentrating on the world within."

"And so?"

"And so, perhaps, her fire elements draw her toward the fiery hearts of humans, and the metal toward justice, and I know that I cannot keep her lest what I see as sanctuary and freedom become a binding constraint on her, imposed by her loyalty to me."

Waoji Lion's Mane smiled. Again he said, "And so?"

Master Ki did not mention the iron band around his heart that made rising in the mornings more difficult by the day. He was already old, much older than his father or grandfather had been when as last they gave up what he had begun to think of as the worn husk of physical form. For the sake of his latest, and best, and last student, he could wish he'd live longer, or that Ari had been born earlier. But it was not fated.

"The time has come to send her out into the world again. I've taught her what I can. If we had ten years for me to understand her elements, for her to master them—but we do not. The best I can do is to tell her things that she will later understand."

"That is the most any teacher can do," the hermit said. "And I distinctly recollect learning that way myself—first the sound, and later, sometimes much later, the sense. But perhaps you have something else on your mind?"

Master Ki smiled. "It is you, my friend. I know you will also return to the world, for you also sniff the wind."

"I do," the hermit acknowledged. "But for a specific scent. There is one task I wish to do before my own life ends."

Master Ki bowed from where he sat. "I only ask that, when

you are ready, you might listen for her in that world."

The hermit bowed back in agreement, but he had a condition: "You stayed by my side when I first came up here in my wild grief and anger. I am going to remain by your side until you close your eyes last, and see to it that when your family comes up here, they will find things as they should be." Master Ki clasped his hands and this time his bow was profound.

# TWENTY

AS A CHILD IN faraway Sweetwater, the only awareness Yskanda had had of the Emperor's birthday was a line in the New Year's Two Moons ritual, acknowledging the emperor's gaining of a year a part of the world's harmony, like the turn of the seasons.

His first year in the royal palace, he'd been too sick over winter to be aware of any of the celebrations, and last year he had been too busy to notice. But this year, he became aware of the discrepancy: the emperor's birthday was still part of the New Year's ritual, yet there was another birthday weeks later. And history was full of poems and art dedicated to various emperors' birthdays, which fell in all seasons.

When he asked Court Artist Yoli about it, Yoli said, "It was the first Jehan emperor who decreed that his birthday would be part of the New Year's ritual, and in that manner."

"Why?"

"My understanding is that the emperor's true birthday happened to be in late winter, as is the present emperor's. As you know, the previous dynasty had left the empire in disarray. I get the impression from the archives that he deemed it a bad idea to stop everything again for yet another expensive celebration so soon after the traditional New Year's one."

"The emperors in this dynasty then celebrate their birthdays privately?" Yskanda asked—which explained the fact that he had not previously been aware of the emperor's true birthday.

"This particular emperor, very privately. Old Emperor Maoyan, who reigned when I was young, wanted nothing but obedience from the people. From nobles and ministers he did expect presents, and personal deference. He did not forget, or forgive, anyone who neglected to visit the imperial city with something ruinously expensive as a gift. In fact, that is when the Journey to the Cloud Empire became a court function instead of a preserve of poets. The center of it was always the emperor's birthday, and sumptuous it was. I ought to bring out my old sketches to show you—and I, being a young apprentice when he came to the throne, at first was given only the minor sights to sketch. But that changed"

"I know so little about the Journey to the Cloud Empire, save that the wealthy get in boats and see sights and write poems about them," Yskanda said.

"Ah, but what sights! I don't know what our present emperor will decide to do about the Journey to the Clouds this year. The imperials tend to go in a group or not at all. The past several years, they haven't gone." He sighed. "Where was I? Birthdays. Empress Teyan granted the staff a free day, with an enormous party, and she paraded around early in the morning, her birthday having been in early summer when the mornings were usually cool and fragrant with blossoms. We all bowed to the ground, then were free to celebrate, with a feast and a day free of labor. Our present emperor prefers to keep the day entirely in his family."

In his family.

Yskanda clutched at those words as he labored at Jion's gift. That meant, he hoped, his art would be there but he would not.

When he didn't think about the recipient, he found himself deeply absorbed in the project, which was a new style for him. Working out the perspective for each segment of the garden, while keeping it recognizable, challenged all his skills. He wasn't entirely happy with some aspects, but overall, he frequently glanced at the long roll of first-quality silk to reassure himself he could do no better.

The brushwork was largely done, then came color. The winter garden was actually the most difficult, and he covered practice paper after practice paper with the most delicate washes in order to get the right shade of palest blue, and a hint of silver, balanced by the evergreens. More than once he wished he could dip his brush in moonlight, for that was the shade he strove for.

But at last he declared that segment done—and Court Artist Yoli, after standing over it what seemed a very long time, gave his quick chin-nod and grunt of approval. That grunt meant more to Yskanda than the most effusive praise from anyone else—or it did until Jion began coming to see the progress.

Early on he'd uttered encouraging flattery, then somehow seemed to pick up that Yskanda just heard such flattery as noise. Since that time, if the imperial prince smiled and said, "It looks great," or "It's very fine," Yskanda went back to the practice sheets. The expression he wanted was the sudden widening of the prince's phoenix-shaped black eyes, the soaring of those slanted brows, and the soft exhalation of breath that escaped him when he first saw the finished winter garden.

Then, Yskanda knew it was right.

Jion muttered, "The poem I have is all wrong. No, it's worse than wrong, it's . . ." And without saying what that might be, he was gone in a ripple of silk.

Yskanda was halfway through the spring garden in the coloration phase when Jion returned with the poetry he wanted. It was the expected traditional form—five lines of five syllables each, in the musical tones mode, but the words were so well chosen that one could shut one's eyes and see that same garden, only in moonlight. In fact, New Year's Two Moons light—and with the reference to the rings of the strengthening tree, it was a salute to the emperor's official birthday, with the implication that another year meant a gain in strength and wisdom.

As truth, Yskanda reserved opinion, but as poetry, it was sublime.

Jion, in his turn, watched with his breath held as Yskanda bent over his paper to calligraph the poem in the place waiting for it. Then he stood back to survey that section, lips parted, his eyes gazing beyond the room in that way he had that meant he was seeing beyond the room, and Jion himself. Then he blinked rapidly, dove for a tiny brush, dipped it in the palest silver ink, and added minute touches to the edges of two trees.

Jion stared. It would be overstating to say that the added touches of silver transformed the whole. They changed the perspective in a way that added depth, softening the wintry light.

Jion felt as if they ought to celebrate, but a moment later the old court artist and his young assistant were discussing the next segment, plunging into a morass of spring colors and arcane references to inks, brushes, and techniques.

Time began closing in. Yskanda's portion of the workroom was covered in practice sheets of his own, and art borrowed from the archives, depicting the garden in various states during the seasons. The arduous task of choosing the most perfect representations as models, and sketching the exact shape of the actual trees and shrubs, had been done.

His progress was rapid now, and as the fine lines of the summer and autumn garden began filling with color, Jion added his poetry. This was not exactly a new mode of art — some of the earliest drawings from dynasties long gone were a mix of art and inscription — and of course the cheap storybooks to be found in every city were largely text with the block-carved illustrations. But this was a new mode of formal art fit for an emperor, and both Jion and Yskanda wanted it to be perfect, if for different reasons.

The garden reached the eastern border trees and plants, first line — leaf by leaf — then color, and Jion brought the last poem, an autumnal elegy that looked forward to the turn of the year and spring. He watched in an agony as Yskanda used his calligraphy brush to fit it into the space left for it. If the ink blobbed, or splashed —!

But Yskanda's skill was too assured for that.

The last line, the last word, and the two of them stepped back as Yskanda absently stuck the calligraphy brush through his topknot — for he did not wear his loaf in the workroom, where it might get splattered.

Then Jion watched in silent admiration as, with a slight turn of the wrist, Afan Yskanda drew a small feather in the corner.

"Give it one gong to thoroughly dry," Yskanda said, backing away, the brush in the air, "and it can be rolled up."

"Let's see," Court Artist Yoli said from behind them. He bowed in Jion's direction, then limped up to the long table.

Yskanda's hands clasped together, ink-stained as they

were — until Yoli gave his characteristic short nod and grunt. "It'll do," he said aloud, but he was thinking that none of the current artists over in the scribe wing could have done so well. Oh, certainly skillwise, but there was a sense of the whole that was difficult to characterize, and which brought the eye inward, along the zigzags and over the arched bridges, to brush up against the poetic inserts. Jion suspected that it would easily become a new and popular mode among the young nobles, especially the ones who might like an artistic background for their poetic effusions.

At last it was rolled up, and Jion, feeling something more was due, said, "I truly wish you could be there to see the effect."

"No, no, impossible." Yskanda's voice rang with sincerity. "And inappropriate." He bowed himself out, and Jion was left with the completed art, feeling a little as if he'd lost something.

# TWENTY-ONE

JION HAD JUST FINISHED dressing the evening of the emperor's birthday when a page arrived to say that the Imperial Princess had arrived.

"Lily," Jion exclaimed, going out to greet his eldest sister.

"Shall we walk together?" she asked. "Mother is already there."

Jion's brows shot up. "Alone?"

"No, they all are there." She hesitated, thinking ahead, as one must to survive in the imperial family. She knew that Jion, as did all the imperial children, had from their earliest years been at least somewhat aware of the silent competition between the consorts for the emperor's attention, on behalf of their children as well as themselves and their families.

She hoped he would now begin to see the underlying motivations. He had come back from his journeys with the same good heart he'd always had, just less impetuous. He was also, she had been glad to discover, less undiscerning, so she schooled herself to wait patiently. Fate would always have its way, and truth tended to expose itself—but habit and loyalty were strong.

She said, "It appears there was a report, or something. The navy cleared some criminals from somewhere. I came here, hoping you'd let me have a peek at your gift first. We've seen you walking the garden day upon day, and are most curious."

Jion had had his servants dig up an appropriate cedar-wood box with gilt dragons chasing around it. While she held the top of the box, he carefully lifted out the silken scroll and opened it a little ways, disclosing the beginning of the winter scene.

Her breath caught. "I know exactly where that is! It's Heaven's Path, right before it meets Fragrance Way. This is very fine, very. Was it done by the assistant court artist?"

"Yes," Jion said. "Do you recognize his style?"

"Yes—no—they're all very skilled, of course," Lily said quickly. "It might be only having sat for my portrait, but it seems to me there is something extra in the details he draws. Something that pleases the eye. No, it's more than pleases, but not quite commands. It hints at the spirit of the garden. Or the person, in the case of the portraits. The one of my mother is especially so," she added, reflecting on the hint of tender smile in her eyes, though the pose was so strict and proper.

"That's it exactly," Jion said, well pleased as he rolled the scroll back up and replaced the lid. Lily waved at her maid, standing at a discreet distance with Lily's gift, but Jion shook his head. "I'll carry it."

They set out. "I meant to tell you," she said in a casual voice, "I found my copy of Lao Sha's treatise on the sage king. In case you've decided to add it to your reading."

"Why would I want to read about sage kings?" he asked.

"To aid in discussion?" she answered. "Toward better understanding?"

He sighed. "That's Manon's area," he said. "That reminds me. She has all the archive's books on governing and statecraft, but so far, she hasn't shown any inclination to discuss the subject with me. Though that might change. What has the scholar group been discussing?"

"I can tell you what the girls have been discussing," Lily said. "The boys were separated off."

"That's right. Vaion told me. I suppose I ought to rejoin them. Though I confess, the idea of going back to recitations and strictly ordered debate on thousand-year-old conversations makes me want to sleep. It was so much better when Scholar Shan taught us."

At the mention of her father, Lily looked away, her smile pained. She was unable to regard Second Imperial Consort Su Shafar with anything but fear and dislike, but she respected

Jion's filial devotion, and would never say anything against either mother or daughter. "He liked teaching you, too," was all she permitted herself.

By then Jion had remembered Second Mother Su Shafar had somehow gotten rid of Scholar Shan, who had been replaced with the well-born, dry old whitebeard who believed that learning meant memorizing long tests and repeating them back orally, then writing them in perfect calligraphy. Always the correct sound, or appearance, never the sense. The imperial class had been forced to repeat the texts until they were perfect—which was when he began finding ways to circumvent the classes. And ended up being sent to the Silk Islands . . .

Avoiding the old, sore subject, he said, "Though I'd much rather read something exciting."

"I suspect we find different things exciting," Lily murmured, one eyebrow quirked. "Accounts of bashing and clashing swords are not exciting. They're tedious."

"Stories of duels between heroes might be," he conceded. "Though Vaion would disagree. But what about battles? Surely you don't find those boring?"

"I find them tragic," she said. "Words that inspire hearts and minds are far more interesting to me than swords and stories of fantastic Essence exploits."

"Inspiration is a welcome notion. This unworthy reprobate feels he's had enough exhortations for a lifetime," he admitted.

"As has this unworthy daughter," she said unexpectedly. "But I did not say exhortations, did I? I know the lessons you refer to that are meant to inspire, but however useful, don't. I'm interested in how one integrates the ideal with the real. What did the Sage Empress say—*There is nothing more visible than what is secret, and nothing more manifest than what is minute. Therefore superior persons are watchful over themselves, when alone as well as in company.*"

"Is this," he asked, "aimed at my benefit, elder sister?"

"It is merely a general remark. I have too many of my own needs for enlightenment to attempt to enlighten others. Which leads me to contemplate what Kanda writes about reciprocity," she said, low. "And leniency, leading toward the Golden Point of Balance. Balance is so very necessary to harmony . . . boring, it is not. At least so I find, but then I might be boring and not know it."

And without giving him a chance to respond, she turned

her head and smiled. "See who's coming! She looks like a butterfly, those shades of crimson with the blue splashes so cheering in this gray weather. Second Princess Gaunon," she greeted, bowing as Gau-Gau danced up.

The second imperial princess flicked a slight bow in return — the bow to an elder in age, modified by the difference in their rank — and inserted herself between them as she began chattering about the food to be expected.

Lily usually withdrew to the perimeter of the gathering, or to the dowager empress's side, but this day she had three purposes. The first had been her offer of the books she had made copies of herself. And her second purpose was accomplished straightaway: First Imperial Princess Manon was already there, having arrived with her mother. When she saw Jion, she smiled — then that smile hardened before smoothing into calm inscrutability when she saw Lily.

Lily did not intend to say anything. People would be themselves. But Jion had come back a young man, with a young man's awareness. What he chose to do about it was, again, his own decision.

Jion did see that contemptuous look. He had always seen Manon's supercilious glances toward those she considered neglectful of their duty, or deficient in some manner — including their birth rank. Her scorn of Lily had bothered him when they were all young, but as he told himself, rank was necessary to order and harmony, and harmony was important to Manon. But in his time away, he had ceased to believe birth rank was as inarguable a part of the world as the changing of the seasons, or water being wet. It was certainly *tradition*, which was difficult to change, but it was not *truth* in the sense of human worth.

And Manon's coldness toward Lily just seemed petty. As petty as her mother having gotten rid of their popular teacher, who even Manon had liked before she realized one day that Scholar Shan's chin was a lot like Lily's, and pointed it out to her mother.

As the family glided gracefully to their places with respect to that golden chair at the north end of the room, Jion renewed his mental vow not to tell Manon about Ryu.

Vaion rushed in, breathing hard, moments before Bitter-nail opened the doors through which the emperor emerged. At his gesture they sat at the low tables lining either side of the

room, and a stream of servants brought in plates of food and
pitchers of drink, and the musicians began playing in the
background, evaluated by Manon, and listened to by Jion.

The birthday celebration began as they all did, with the
family bowing and chanting together the ritual words wishing
him the longevity and power of Mt. Lir. He smiled as he
gestured for them to rise, and they all gauged that smile
expertly: his mood was good. They all relaxed, and their
smiles, too, were real.

The emperor insisted his mother was not to give him
gifts—instead he gave her fine things, though she always pro-
ested that she had enough, and his company, and her
grandchildren, were all the best gifts she could ever receive. So
far, things were as usual, for that happened every single year.

First Imperial Consort Ran Renyi brought forward her
present with the customary self-deprecatory comments. It was
a scroll so old it had gone an ochre color, which turned out to
be poems by the emperor's favorite, Ar Laq, with commentary
by Liad Il. She had to have been communicating with
booksellers since last year to have located that.

Second Imperial Consort Su Shafar gave him a luminously
beautiful dragon vase from the Lo Dynasty, whose porcelain
masters had kept their glazes a secret beyond the grave.

Third Imperial Consort Yu Pirag gave him a fan mounted
on thin golden sticks. Its silk had been imbued with the fresh
scent of lemon and a trace of cinnabar.

Then, when the mutual compliments and self-denial had
died away, Lily, as eldest child, stepped forward—which
never failed to irritate Manon, for as she had said to Jion when
they were young, *she* was the eldest of the emperor's *true*
children. Lily's birth was not merely unimperial, it was *low*.
But the emperor always turned to her first, and no one dared
gainsay that.

Jion was relieved to see Manon looking polite, even
gracious, as Lily came forward to make her bow, and he
reflected that he wasn't the only one who had changed over
the past four years. Then he remembered that look at his and
Lily's entrance, and wondered if that was merely old habit?

Lily brought forward her gift, which was a fire agate of
brilliant shades of color formed around a central line. When
she held the polished agate up with the line vertical, it was a
tiger-eye.

Polite exclamations of admiration susurrated around them as Lily explained in her soft, mild voice, "Created entirely by nature. It was found on Mount Lir by pilgrims to the shrine. The shaman said that it is very auspicious, a sign of longevity for Honored Father Emperor, and his long life is auspicious for the entire empire."

The emperor admired it sincerely, nodded for Melonseed to carry it within his personal chambers, and then it was Manon's turn.

She came before the low throne in a graceful rustling of silk, and as she bowed, the bird earrings she favored caught the light from the nearby candle tree in a brief reflection of fiery gold, a brilliant reflection seen by both the emperor and Jion: phoenixes.

She unrolled a scroll she had calligraphed and made herself, a history of the imperial Jehan family.

Always, the emperor thought, Manon's mind centered on thrones, and power, even in her gifts. He complimented her exquisite calligraphy, and her thoughtfulness, then turned to Jion, who presented his box to his father with a low bow.

The emperor smiled as he opened the box himself, a great concession. But it required Bitternail to gesture forth a pair of servants to unroll the scroll, which was about four paces in length, so that the emperor could see the art all at once. He leaned forward, a little frown between his eyes, then his face cleared into a broad smile. "The garden! I recognize . . . yes, there are the cedars at the west end of Fragrance Way. Ah, the pagoda. The lotuses in bloom—each in its season. Very clever, very admirable. I see your sign under the poems, but that is not your hand."

"My awkward calligraphy would have ruined it," Jion admitted. "But the verses are mine. With heavy borrowings."

"The time and thought you put into this gift pleases me," the emperor said—and Vaion groaned inwardly, regretting that once again, he'd ended up with no ideas, and pressed his mother into finding his gift.

But he faced it bravely as he handed his father a very fine bow. The emperor, who didn't expect much more of Vaion, said he would enjoy using it for target practice as glances semaphored between the second consort and her daughter: it was obvious that one of Imperial Father's imperial guard captains had had the choosing of that bow.

Gaunon was next, with the most hapless gift (which required the most praise); then they ate the elaborate meal. The conversation was, for the first time in four years, not painful — the emperor sat back, watching how Jion joked with his brother, and in turn managed to draw everyone into the conversation, as the dowager empress looked on and laughed.

The dowager empress watched her son's expression lighten. He was filial, was Enjai, and she loved him fiercely — him and his children. But, she was wise enough to be honest with herself, there were some grandchildren she favored more than others. That could include those not related to her by blood.

Seeing subtle signs of restlessness in her son, she flicked a glance toward the first imperial consort, then raised her sleeve to cover her face as she emptied her last cup of tea. "It is so very good to be with my family," she said as she set the empty cup down. "But I am old and useless, and need my bed earlier and earlier. Before I go, my dearest son and emperor, did you not say that this year, we ought to attend the Journey to the Cloud Empire on behalf of the exalted suitors to our Imperial Princess?"

The emperor glanced at his mother in mild surprise — she usually did not step forward to suggest any changes in the routine of the inner palace, much less governing. "I did."

And here was Lily's third purpose.

The first consort stood up and bowed, saying, "Your imperial majesties, please permit this unworthy consort to ease your burden by seeing to the details. Nothing would please my humble daughter and my insignificant self more than to attend to the aspects of planning that your imperial highnesses wish to deal with least." She gestured to Lily to join her.

Lily stood behind her mother's shoulder. "I join my voice to First Mother's, Honored Imperial Father — please permit this talentless daughter to . . ."

Her voice trailed off as the second consort floated up next to the first consort, draperies rippling in shades of celestial blue, gold, and palest peach, embroidered over with plum blossoms. She dropped to the floor, saying, "It is also our earnest desire . . ." But as she did, her voluminous sleeves spilled a mass of papers, which she hastily began scrambling together.

"What is this?" the dowager empress asked, before the emperor could give her a sign to desist — this was so obviously a little play set up by mother and daughter.

Sure enough, the second consort protested that the papers were nothing, mere trash — her imperial majesty ought not to trouble her mind over such insignificant waste — then added, "It is merely in hopes of pleasing her Honored Imperial Father that my foolish daughter has spent months searching and refining lists of possible music for the Journey, in case this year would be graced by his gracious imperial presence. She has been practicing with his highness First Prince Jion to just this purpose."

And then, both mother and daughter turned their heads toward Jion as Manon said in her sweet, perfectly enunciated soft voice, "First Imperial Brother Jion's taste has inspired this untalented daughter to greater efforts."

The imperial dowager sat back, suppressing a sigh; long-sighted as she was, she did not immediately see why the second consort would hasten to claim the organization of this monumental task, especially now that it seemed that Lily, and not Manon, might be destined to marry the Easterners' second prince.

But the emperor did. If he gave in, the Su clan would effectively become the hosts of the journey, which many would read as a sign of Manon's taking a step toward the throne.

And Jion, who had not known any of this, saw how he had been maneuvered into tacitly adding his contribution to Manon's effort. Which . . . yes, one look at Lily's downturned profile, had been aimed at cutting Lily out.

Nothing had changed after all. He struggled not to resent Manon for it. Or Honored Second Mother.

The first imperial consort, who could not bear even covert competition, kindly saved the emperor the need to say anything by withdrawing her offer. "Her highness the second imperial consort and First Imperial Princess Manon have worked so hard. Of course their plans would be superior to anything I or my daughter could compass."

There was nothing to be said after that. Lily resolutely blinked back tears.

But that was her fate, she reminded herself, as the emperor took in her bowed head and compressed lips. He was irritated by the Su arrogance, and yet had to acknowledge Manon's skills. She had all the makings of a crown princess — and so far seemed the only fit candidate.

The Imperial Dowager left, signaling them all to be in motion.

The emperor turned his head. "Jion. A moment."

Jion had been in the middle of his bow. He lurched up, surprised; the emperor saw the look Manon slanted backward before she and her mother withdrew along with the rest, and how her steps slowed.

But the emperor waited until she had left the room, and Melonseed shut the door. Then he turned to his son. "The Ministry of Rites predicts that the weather is expected to be fine tomorrow morning. And we have not ridden together for years."

Jion bowed, mentally tossing all his plans out the window.

# TWENTY-TWO

THE NEXT DAY, HE arrived at the Golden Dragon Pavilion at second Phoenix hour to see his father standing in the main reception room in his riding clothes and boots, which, aside from the fine fabrics, were plain, almost military in design. Imperial Father clasped his hands behind him as he regarded Yskanda's garden painting. The room, Jion saw, had been rearranged during the night, the old screens and hangings taken away. The imperial garden painting now hung in a place of prominence, covering most of a wall.

"The skillful rendering is not the whole, but suggests the whole. It captures the why of gardens," the emperor said with a glance over his shoulder, before returning his gaze to the glint of the sun on the golden roof of the painted pagoda. "You must have spent a great deal of time with this young Talent, have you not?"

Jion responded with a short bow. "This uneducated son had to return numerous times to attempt to match the poetry with each evolving scene."

"What did you talk about? Did Assistant Court Artist Afan discuss his tutors with you?" the emperor asked, his voice mild and casual, but the hairs prickled on the back of Jion's neck. "His family?"

Jion's mind flooded with everything his grandmother had said. He took a breath before speaking, and was glad at how casual his own voice came out. "Not a word. All he ever talks about is paint, ink, brushes, silk, perspective, and the Six Principles of Art. A *lot* about the Six Principles of Art."

The emperor uttered a soft laugh, and with a last glance back at the painting he led the way outside. Jion walked at his right and a step behind, the two duty guards falling in behind.

Customarily the horses were brought to the door, ready to ride. But the emperor turned toward the west, leading them along the path above the imperial garden. As they passed between Heavenly Pleasures Pavilion and the southernmost wall of Vaion's manor, he said, "You might be wondering about the result of your encounter with the Shadow Panther criminals."

Jion assented, and the emperor said, "The navy and a detachment of the Dragon Claw army obliterated the warren they discovered on the other side of the island you set afire. It was, I am told, a complete rout on dispersive ground. I can show you the report if you like."

He made a turn toward the garrison wall, beyond which Jion had never been permitted to go. There were only the two imperial guards behind, and his father was leading them well north of the House of Eternal Peace and Lotus Blossom Square, but still Jion's heartbeat quickened.

The emperor cast him a glance as imperial guards sprang to open the heavy gate midway along the garrison wall. Then they dropped to one knee, right fist at their chests. "You of course understand this term, dispersive ground, correct?" The emperor addressed Jion as he made a casual sign for the guards to rise.

Jion had stilled. Here was the interrogation he had expected weeks ago, as they headed into the military portion of the imperial palace, where he and his siblings had been strictly forbidden ever to set foot.

Under his father's direct gaze, he said, "I do, Imperial Father." And because his father seemed to be waiting, "It's one of the nine types of terrain inland of the nine types of beach. I, ah, don't know those, just that there's nine."

The emperor began walking again.

The smell of horses on the air indicated a stable nearby. Jion let out a slow breath as they turned between two neat, plain buildings of military aspect, and then entered a courtyard.

It looked exactly like the weapons court at Loyalty Fortress, except that the racks on one wall held what appeared to be real steel weapons. The racks on the other side were the wooden ones Jion had used during his time at Loyalty. Everything was new. Polished. Nothing battered and worn.

Was this his father's private weapons court? Jion had been inside his father's bedroom exactly once. His gaze had gone from the ancient, magnificent golden dragon carving behind the bed to the beautifully carved sword rack on the other side of the room, with a sword resting there, tassels hanging from the hilt. No other inhabitant of the imperial family had a personal weapon.

"But you did receive military training," the emperor said, still in that mild voice, with the slight smile that spurred everyone into vigilance. "I probably ought to have put these questions to you when we had our first conversation on your return, but I was quite disturbed then. I learned when I was about your age that decisions made in such moods are frequently regretted when one has had time to reflect."

He wasn't "disturbed" now? Jion's neck tightened.

"And so, before we begin, perhaps a demonstration. They are often so much more enlightening than mere words." The emperor waved Jion to step back, as he himself wheeled and moved away, leaving Jion standing in the middle of the courtyard, staring after his father in complete bewilderment.

He wasn't left there long. From behind came an imperial guard-in-training, sword in hand. He bowed to Jion, raised the sword, and ran at him in attack!

Shock impelled Jion straight into Redbark reaction. He whirled out of reach of that blade, and in three steps reached the weapons rack. There he hesitated. Was he allowed to defend himself? A quick glance at his father, who stood beneath the roof overhang, arms crossed.

With an internal shrug, Jion shut him out. Unless his father commanded differently, he was going to defend himself. He chose a sword to match the sword in the guard's hand, and whirled to meet a second attack. Three strokes, and he knocked the sword from the guardsman's hand.

Two imperial guards then came at him. They fought together in a tighter, harder version of the style Jion had learned at Loyalty as a first and second year cadet. Jion whirled between them, knowing exactly what was coming next, so his blade was already there, deflecting them smartly, as they cut and thrust.

He could tell immediately that they were not trying to hurt him, so he tapped the tall one lightly on the right shoulder, and the moon-faced one on the knee, then backed up, breathing hard. Despite his morning routine in his court, he had not sparred for weeks — and it showed.

But at least he wasn't spent. A third guard came out, the emperor gestured for all three to attack, and they did so. And as the imperial guardsmen saw that the prince not only knew how to fight, but understood that this was not a death match, they went to it with a will.

Jion gave and took blows, but he knew he wouldn't last long against them with this sword. He broke and ran to the racks, where he'd spotted a staff. Though he'd always like sword work best, he'd had the hardest practice with staff with Ryu over the half year before he was taken. He advanced again, and set it to humming as he warmed up his wrists. Then, with a huffed command, the three attacked once more.

Using the staff, Jion fought off the three, until the staff began to slip in his hands, and sweat stung his eyes. He longed for his old headband.

Then the emperor raised his hand for a halt. "Very impressive," he said. "Let's ride."

Jion replaced the staff and his sword in their respective racks with the absent air of one who had never had servants to tend his weapons. The training, the emperor had expected after seeing those calluses, and hearing about the fight with the Shadow Panthers. It was very clear now that Jion had not trained as a prince.

Horses stood saddled and ready outside the gate. The emperor swung easily into the saddle, noticing how, even after that vigorous sparring, his boy leaped up without touching the stirrups.

They rode in silence to the north gate. The sentries let them through, their guards falling just out of earshot behind them.

They started up the trail into the woods that Jion had not ridden in since he was fourteen. Trees had begun to leaf, and on the southern slopes grasses grew, bright green. Birds dived and called, busy about their affairs, scolding from shrub and branch at the human disturbance.

Presently the emperor said, "I thought you wandered and

played music. Where," he asked dryly, "did you get military training?"

Jion had braced for this question. If he died for willful breaking of the edict, then so be it. "I did wander and play music to earn my way. But before that I had a year and a half of army training."

"*Army* training?" the emperor repeated, his brows slanting steeply.

"Yes. I went to a spring recruit, and to my surprise I was accepted, even though I couldn't do much of anything except ride. Maybe the recruiting captain needed bodies, because they took me."

"Took you where?"

"Loyalty Fortress."

"Loyalty," the emperor repeated, and immediately had it. "Attacked by mercenaries." He cast a sharp look of question at Jion.

"That's why I left," Jion said. "I thought they might be after me and I didn't want any more people killed. Four boys died that night, and I don't know how many villagers —"

The words dried in his throat. He'd thought the emperor was angry before, but that was nothing to the white-lipped fury he saw in his father's face now. *"You were there?"*

"Guard," the emperor said, not loudly, but one of those following kicked his horse and trotted to the emperor's side, then bowed, fist to chest. Jion waited sickly to be . . . knocked off his horse? Tied up? Dragged by the scruff of his robe straight to Lotus Blossom Square?

"Summon Fai Anbai," the emperor said in the soft voice that acted on everyone in hearing like the strike of a lightning bolt. Then he turned to Jion. "Did Weken know who you were?"

"No one did, Imperial Father," Jion replied.

"How did you arrange to leave?"

"I didn't arrange it. After that attack, I walked aboard the next supply boat, following another orderly, and I guess they assumed I was a second orderly. I don't think anyone has ever run from Loyalty before, because they waved me on without a question. The supply ship took us to another island, which is where I began my career as a musician. I traveled north from there."

The emperor's horse betrayed skittishness through twitching ears and switching tail. Jion waited, his guts churning. Presently his father said, "This is the second time I've heard how very close you came to annihilation at the hands of criminal trash." He said with suppressed violence, "Do you understand how *stupid* this escapade of yours was? Why didn't you surrender yourself to the nearest garrison for safety?"

There was only one answer to be made to that. Jion halted his horse, slipped to the ground, and bowed forehead to the dirt.

"Get up, get up, get up. I'm not angry with you — yes, I am, I'm *furious*. But I . . ."

Jion had never heard his father at a loss for words before. He climbed back onto his horse, saying, "All I could think of was another attack, maybe assassins waiting for me if I went to the nearest garrison. I decided to hide in the gallant wanderer world as Shigan the Wanderer —"

"Yes, I can see that appearing to be a solution at sixteen or seventeen. I want to hear everything you saw and heard at Loyalty, but not until Fai Anbai gets here. Begin with your running from the Silk Islands. Or did you even get to White Jade?"

"I did not, Imperial Father," Jion admitted, grimacing as a muscle jumped in the emperor's jaw.

"If you did not want to go to the Silk Islands," he said softly, "you had abundant opportunity to tell me before I carefully selected a hundred people to educate and protect you."

"I didn't *not* want to go, Imperial Father," Jion said — though it was not quite true. A brief memory surfaced, a lot of wild talk about running away, a life of freedom, but he'd only shared those thoughts with his sister Manon, and she never would have told anyone. As she hadn't, or he would have had his stupid words flung in his face by now. "Leaving didn't occur to me until I met the scribe apprentice."

"What scribe apprentice?" The emperor's hand tightened on the reins, and his horse sidled nervously. "I placed no apprentices on that ship. Everyone was carefully selected for age, experience, sterling example . . ." He considered the sorry figures who had been swept up in the arrest at the governor's mansion, and said nothing more. A terrible idea was beginning to form in the emperor's mind.

"He was my age," Jion said, unaware of the trend of his

father's thoughts. "Scribe Apprentice Xia. He was funny! He brought my lunch that day, when we stopped for supplies. We started chatting while the food cooled down. He said he wished he had the luck to be born a prince, what a great life it must be, and there I was stuck in that cabin, unable to poke my nose out, and I said you can have it."

The emperor's horse sidled again.

Jion said quickly, "It was stupid brag. The words just came out, without much more meaning than I was bored, and wanted to be allowed to poke around the ship and see the sights. But no one would let me for my own safety. He admired my robe, and said he wanted to pretend to be a prince for a moment, and could we trade clothes, just so he could pretend for half the small glass, even less time —"

"I believe this, too, had better wait until Fai Anbai gets here," the emperor said.

"As you wish, Imperial Father. Then . . . might this foolish and unworthy son inquire how the substitution became known?"

"Steward Whiteleaf identified him."

"Whiteleaf?" Jion repeated. He had always liked the gentle old graywing, and had been sorry to leave him behind, but he'd been far too ill to travel. "It took him over a year to recover?"

"At least he did recover," the emperor said. "More than half who were struck down by what we thought was a disease died that spring. The imperial physicians nearly gave up on Steward Whiteleaf. And when the fever finally left him, he was too weak to rise, and he was also effectively blind. That lasted for months. I understand that his sight at a distance, and at night, is still affected."

What we thought was a disease? Jion's mind caught at that, but let it go in the face of all the other more pressing questions. He shook his head. "Whiteleaf never told me." But a graywing wouldn't, unless Jion had thought to ask directly. There was that wall of rank again, both regarding it as a part of life.

"We were just as glad you were safely out of reach," the emperor said, his voice easing slightly. "Your grandmother sent Steward Whiteleaf to be healed. He regained his sight, and when he had enough strength to walk again, he insisted on rejoining you."

Jion bowed over his horse's neck. All of this was new to

him. Whiteleaf had not hinted at any of it, all these weeks.

"He saw you, or who they thought was you. Whiteleaf went to the guard captain to report that it was not you. Because Whiteleaf had the wit to withdraw and report quietly to the garrison commander, the pretender had no warning. The guards rounded him and the graywing steward up and shipped them back here. The commander—and the ship's captain—offered to commit suicide, but I let them and the rest off with a flogging as they had never actually seen you—"

The sound of galloping horses approaching rapidly from behind caused the emperor to halt his horse and raise his hand.

Until that moment, Jion had not noticed how far they had come up the winding trail along the southmost slope of Mt. Lir. He gazed down at the imperial palace roofs below, the tiles glowing green in the fading sunlight.

Then Chief Fai trotted into view and halted his horse, bowing deeply to the emperor from the saddle, followed by a short bow to Jion, without actually looking at his face.

The emperor said, "Chief Fai, you need to hear this. First Son, tell us what happened."

Jion said, "From where should this unworthy son begin, Honored Imperial Father?"

"The beginning."

So, for the third time, Jion related the story of his encounter with Scribe Apprentice Xia. As soon as he got to Apprentice Xia's distractions over the food, Chief Fai's chin jerked up minutely, and Jion began to believe that the wild guess about poison was less possibility and more probability.

There were no interruptions as he summarized his experiences in the harbor before his recruitment, inability to hire as a musician—starving— stealing clothing—attempting gambling by winning at pitch-pot and nearly being killed for it, and then, in desperation, walking into the army testing ahead of the mob of angry gamblers. The only thing he left out was his attempt to write to his sister Manon. He did not want to implicate her, if he was in trouble, especially as his laboriously thought-out letter hadn't even gotten to her.

He gave a general description of his training time, but without naming Ryu, who would be regarded as a deserter. He sensed that all their attention was on him. Good. Keep it that way.

When he got to the mercenary attack, Fai Anbai's head

jerked as he turned to stare at Jion. His lips parted, voicelessly saying the name Shigan, and Jion knew from that a report had gone to the ferrets about him and Ryu. But for once the ferrets hadn't had time to follow up . . .

Ah, yes. Because they were chasing after a missing prince.

The wind had begun to rise, the smell of rain in the air, but the emperor did not turn back. Everyone in that cavalcade re-signed themselves to getting thoroughly wet, the guard capt-ain making the motion to disperse in the Rain Pattern, which incorporated limited vision and arrows being untrustworthy into the defense.

Jion cleared his throat, and continued. "I enjoyed the train-ing until the mercenary attack. I was so sure they were after me that I decided to desert, rather than admit who I was. It seemed like a good idea at the time. I didn't know who sent them, or why, but the way they had been searching faces, they knew who I was. That meant either orders from the imperial palace, or someone who had access." He cast a quick glance at Fai Anbai, then saw his father's tight-lipped fury, and added, "I didn't *know*."

His father said, "You thought that *I* sent them? Or that it was a ferret conspiracy?"

"No! Maybe? Ayah, I wasn't sure. It could be anyone send-ing them." Jion took a deep breath. "What I did know was, first there was that Apprentice Xia, who maybe was trying to poison me? Then the attack at Loyalty. I was a target. So I walked onto a supply ship to Te Gar. I thought I'd be safer if I went to ground." That's right, get past it fast. "It was at that harbor that I first began training with some Redbark wander-ers, and earning money as a musician. The Redbark wanderers were my age, and nobody asked questions. They invited me to attend a gallant wanderers martial arts competition the next spring, and so we took ship and traveled the islands along the way and back, earning our bread various ways — me with music."

The emperor betrayed no reaction other than that muscle jumping in his jaw. Was he thinking about dancing?

Jion went on hastily. "I was at that competition for the second time when the Shadow Panthers abducted two of us, and you know the rest. We escaped when we could, burned the place behind us, and fled to the nearest island. I was hiding from Screaming Hawk at an inn when Chief Fai appeared and swept them all up."

Not until Jion was done with his story did the emperor make the sign to halt. By now they were near the intersection with the Pilgrim Trail, which wound its way over the mountain from the temples on the back slope. This slope was regarded as the imperial preserve—no one dared venture into it except the animals and birds for whom human boundaries were as invisible as they were incomprehensible.

Jion glanced up at the white stone pagoda on the cliff far above them, the place where pilgrims climbed to find peace. A few spats of cold rain struck his cheek. Then the emperor said to the lead duty guard, "Escort his imperial highness to his residence."

The guard made hand motions to those farther down the trail. Jion watched half the honor guard move their horses to either side of the trail so that he could pass between them.

He bowed to his father and departed, relieved that, at least so far, he'd kept Ryu's name out of the account. It clearly had not occurred to either his father or Fai Anbai to equate Firebolt with the Second Ryu who had departed for Te Gar on that supply ship, as their minds were entirely on his close call. Perhaps they didn't know? Oh, they knew the name at least, or could easily find out.

But right now, Jion sensed that he was no longer the target of that anger. The Loyalty attack had shocked them. That much was clear. Who had sent those mercenaries? Jion had lived with that question ever since he left. It was all new to his father. Who really hated surprises. He tended to see them as conspiracies.

Jion was beginning to understand why.

When they were alone, the guards at a prudent distance, the emperor said to Fai Anbai, "There it is again, more evidence that there is a conspiracy. The poisonings we thought of as a scheme, and only extended to servants. But now we know that Jion was a target. Or the target. No one outside the palace could have put that young pretender on board that ship, and have him passed along *by the entire guard*."

Fai Anbai was thinking, *If everything the prince said was true.* That condition was a part of his training—he had to first prove the truth of what the prince had told them, and then go from there.

But right now he had to deal with the arrow of suspicion

pointing right at him and his ferrets, shared by suspicion aimed at the imperial guards. Because if even half the prince's words were true, someone inside the palace was a white-eyed wolf. And from the fury in the emperor's face he was very close to having them all killed.

And they still had not caught the poisoner.

Chief Fai dropped to the ground and bowed. "My first order will be an internal investigation."

Silence fell between them, as rain spattered all around them. The emperor's fury surged. He badly wanted to strike at *something*. Like the man before him, who was supposed to be the best of the best.

And he was the best of the best — he had to remember that. It might relieve his anger for a moment to watch Fai Anbai flogged to death, but after that moment, what then? His breath hissed out.

"Chief Fai. I want you to request your esteemed father to come out of retirement," the emperor said. "He is to conduct an internal investigation, on the face of it this still unsolved poisoning case. Question all the guards again. The graywings, the servants. Someone has to have seen something that was not reported at the time. Oh. And this Loyalty Fortress case. Speak plainly: where are we on that?"

Fai Anbai said neutrally, "Tek Banu asked to take that case initially, and as your imperial majesty is probably aware, she works alone. But as your imperial majesty might remember, we all laid aside our tasks to search for his highness the first imperial prince. On our return, Tek Banu departed again, but I know no more than that. She is in possession of all the latest reports — as far as they got."

The emperor hmmmed, then said, "She will send periodic status reports on the progress of her investigation, am I correct?"

She had not yet, but that was an internal affair. If Fai Anbai complained about her, they all looked bad. "Yes, your imperial majesty."

"Good. Leave all that to her, then. Put all your effort into finding out who put that impostor on my ship, the poison in his hands, and *find out who poisoned those servants*." The emperor gentled his nervous mount, apparently impervious to the rain dripping down his face. He wheeled the horse and they started back down the trail as the rain began to increase.

The emperor spoke again, in a musing voice, "Of course my first thought goes to the Su clan. Who else has such over-weening ambition? Who else has the wherewithal to insert people into the palace, under my nose? But the old duke wouldn't be that stupid. He'd have to know the first suspicion would point right at him. Second Imperial Consort Su Shafar as well."

Fai Anbai drew a breath at this last; he had long known of the emperor's cold and unrelenting loathing for his second consort, all the more unsettling for the fact that there was never the least sign of it. According to his carefully placed spies among the second imperial consort's maids, she had no idea of it—she still believed she could become empress.

He bowed over his horse's neck as he said, "I can go over the reports from that spring, but I remember we were able to account for the movements of every one of the Su clan before his imperial highness departed for the Silk Islands. Where each went. Who they spoke to."

"*Someone* tried to kill Jion. That someone is in the dark, while we are toiling in the light. I want that reversed," the emperor said.

"Yes, your imperial majesty." Fai Anbai's heart thundered.

The emperor's voice eased no more than a hair's breadth. "I understand now why Jion worked so hard to remain undiscovered. Two assassination attempts, one by mercenary attack! At his age, I don't know that I would have done any better."

"Yes, your imperial majesty." Fai Anbai had already realized that he was going to have to reevaluate the prince yet again.

The rain began in earnest, but the emperor paid no heed. "Before this matter came up, I took my son to my private training court, and set one of the imperial guard trainees at him. Then two, then three. Granted, they were being very careful not to harm Jion, but even so, he was able to disarm them using only a staff. Detail someone to discover more about this sect, what was it called? Redguard? Red something."

"Redbark. Same as the sacred tree," Fai Anbai supplied, thinking that he *really* needed to reevaluate his assumptions about Prince Jion. "It will be done."

# TWENTY-THREE

JION'S PRIMARY DESIRE, AS he rode down Mt. Lir, was to confront Whiteleaf.

He was escorted directly to his manor, where Yarrow took one look and sent Fennel and the other younger graywings scurrying to make a bath. Warm and dry again, Jion said to Yarrow, "Where is Steward Whiteleaf—"

Whiteleaf walked in at that moment, bearing fresh tea. Jion looked up into Whiteleaf's long-familiar face, aware for the first time of the graywing's slight squint, now that he knew the cause. He should have noticed on board Fai Anbai's flagship, except he'd been too busy feeling sorry for himself. He then should have noticed on his return to the palace, once he'd found out that he wasn't to be the next item on the block at Lotus Blossom Square.

Time to test the boundaries. "I want to speak to Steward Whiteleaf alone," he said.

Yarrow gestured to the two other servants, and they all bowed themselves out. The door was shut, and Jion faced Whiteleaf, who stood with hands folded, eyes downcast.

"How good is the privacy?" he asked. "Probably not very." He held his hand up to cup his ear as he tipped his head toward the door.

"This unworthy shall check, if it pleases his imperial highness."

"Do," Jion invited cordially.

Whiteleaf betrayed no sign of surprise, or anything else, as he glided across the room, then slid the door open enough for Jion to see that the space was empty beyond. No servants fell inward.

Jion suppressed the grin that wanted to erupt at the vivid image. Of course, Whiteleaf's duty was no doubt to report this conversation to either the emperor or the chief ferret or both, but Jion shrugged that off. It wasn't as if anything he was going to say would be new to their ears.

"Steward Whiteleaf, what exactly happened when you got to the Silk Islands and discovered that I wasn't there? Please speak plainly."

Whiteleaf's expression did not change as he poured out the tea for Jion. He spoke in report mode. "I traveled on the courier ship, your imperial highness. When I reached the governor's palace, the false prince was just returning from riding. At first I thought he might be a visitor, but everyone gave him the correct bow, so I retreated to the guard captain, who was on duty, and asked where the true prince was. He said you had just returned from riding. I pointed out that I had never seen that individual before, but it was definitely not your imperial highness, First Imperial Prince Jion. And, because I had seniority over the graywing who had replaced me as steward, I asked for him to be summoned."

"Who was it?" Jion asked. "Anyone I know?"

Whiteleaf hesitated, thinking back, then said, "He was never a part of the inner palace staff, your imperial highness. He had served mostly in the imperial kitchens, first as an assistant to the tea master, and then he was promoted to delivery. I was too ill to be a part of the selection process, but someone put his name forward as my replacement at the last moment. I understand they were in a hurry to get your imperial highness safely away lest your imperial highness catch the supposed illness, and so the process by which his name was put forward was blurred."

"Supposed?" Jion pounced on the word, recollecting the words his father had spoken about what Jion had always thought was an illness going around. "Did you know that Apprentice Xia, or whatever his name was, tried to poison me on board the ship? It seems. Chief Fai seemed to think so when I was telling him and my father about it. I could see it."

Whiteleaf paused as Jion drank down his tea, then said, "There are two conversational paths at present, your imperial highness. Which should this incompetent address first?"

Jion waved a hand as he leaned forward, forearms on knees. "The apprentice. And the steward in charge, who had to know him. Someone put that tray in his hands!"

"The steward's name was Baycloud, your imperial highness."

"One of the tea generation," Jion said. "I definitely did not know him."

"He insisted to the very last that he had never seen you before he boarded the ship, and that he believed the pretender to be you. And yet, when I asked for him to be summoned, it is very possible that word reached him first that I had arrived on the courier ship, for he attempted to run. He was caught by the guard trying to get through the gate."

"What about Scribe Apprentice Xia?"

Whiteleaf said, "If your imperial highness wishes a full report, I believe that Chief Fai might be requested to provide one."

"All I want to know is if he really tried to poison me. If he knew what he was doing. I mean, I believe he was trying to poison me, but perhaps he'd never done it before. He was so clumsy in trying to distract me. It seems, in retrospect, he carried the tray past the guards and either forgot to put the poison in the food or didn't get a chance to, and was trying to do it while I was sitting right there. Did anyone defend him from the scribe wing?"

"No one knew who he was, your imperial highness. That was another fact against Graywing Baycloud: it is believed that he smuggled the pretender onto the ship when it stopped for supplies, and had the proper clothing waiting among his own effects. At any rate, when the rest of the ship's guards were questioned later, no one actually remembered seeing a scribe that day."

"They probably wouldn't notice a familiar robe if they were in the middle of getting supplies in, and sending reports out," Jion guessed.

"Your imperial highness is correct," Whiteleaf said.

"And so I take it they brought the two back here, and turned them over to the ferrets' tender mercies?"

"Your imperial highness is again correct," Whiteleaf

stated. "It was believed that Graywing Baycloud was going to speak—they had summoned this lowly incompetent to wait in case corroborative detail was needed, but then he, the pretender, and the guards, turned up dead by poison."

"Poison again!" Jion exclaimed. "Right here! When everyone knows that even having it in the same room with you is an instant death sentence, no questions asked. Even for us." He flicked his hand at his embroidered robe.

"Again, correct. All those concerned with bringing food to the prisoners were executed, though every one of them went to their deaths insisting they knew nothing about poison."

His voice had hardened slightly. Jion, listening closely, said, "Did you know them? Did you believe them?"

"I knew one, Graywing Lushan. He and I had shared a room during a portion of our training, and many classes. He had been reassigned to delivery on the west side that day, though later no one could find the order. But he was executed just the same."

Jion said slowly, "They—I don't know if it's the same they, or another they—tried to kill me when I was at Loyalty Fortress. That makes two assassination attempts." He shook himself, remembering his father's fury. No doubt every single ferret was busy investigating. And the guard would be doubled again.

Who was investigating the ferrets?

He forced his mind away from matters he had no control over whatsoever, and looked up at Whiteleaf. "But you said supposed illness. Which means the poisoning started before I even left. How did you find out it wasn't an illness, Steward Whiteleaf?"

"His imperial majesty's servants assumed it was an illness, as you will remember, your imperial highness. So many among the staff honored to wait upon the imperial family struck down at once, the way illnesses spread. This unworthy servant was, by the grace of her imperial highness the dowager empress, sent to a healing temple. The shaman there uses a number of dogs, who, she says, are trained to detect by scent certain things in patients. She told me I was suffering not from illness but from the effects of poison, which attacked nerves, mainly in my head."

"I was told you were blinded by it."

"This unworthy servant was indeed blind for a time. Once

the poison was driven out of your servant's system, and a great deal of medicine was taken, most sight was restored."

"Whiteleaf, you don't have to be so formal. This is just me and you, and for the four years I was gone, I never once had to listen to people refer to themselves as unworthy servants and lowly worms and the like. I miss that, badly."

Whiteleaf bowed.

"Please continue," Jion said.

"Thank you, your imperial highness. I reported what the shaman said, but then I was told not to share that with the rest of the staff until I was given permission. It was felt that there would be far more alarm if that illness was to identified as poisoning, and the culprit not found. I believe that order does not extend to your imperial highness, especially given the information with which your imperial highness just now honored me."

"Poison," Jion repeated. "Someone tried to kill us both, and was never caught."

"Yes, your imperial highness."

"Someone still out there! No, *here*. It has to be someone inside the palace, or who knows its ways. Or, was. Nothing like it has happened since I first left, is that correct?"

"It is, your imperial highness."

Jion frowned, eyeing the snacks that Whiteleaf had brought. "That effectively kills my appetite."

Steward Whiteleaf bowed again, and hiding a spurt of amusement, said, "Perhaps it will ease your imperial highness's mind to be informed that tasting all food that comes into this manor is the function of Min Ko." Naming the big servant who Jion had recognized as a ferret the moment he laid eyes on him.

Jion leaned back in surprise. "I thought he was here to spy on me, and report every sneeze and fart to the ferrets."

Steward Whiteleaf bowed a third time. "Would his imperial highness care for more tea?"

Jion laughed aloud at this wryly adroit response. They both knew the inner palace—no doubt Fai Anbai would be summoning Whiteleaf for a repeat of this very conversation.

There was a knock at the door, and Fennel's soft voice: "Her imperial highness First Imperial Princess Manon has sent over her instrument."

"Manon!" Jion leaped up. "Look at my hands. Ayah, I

actually have blisters forming. Too long without practice . . .
Yarrow!"

A short time later, First Imperial Princess Manon was
bowed in. Jion charged in at the same time through the back
door, exclaiming, "Elder Sister! You honor me." He made a full
bow, playfully mocking, and she rewarded him with a smile
as he said, "You can send for me now. Imperial Father lifted
the restriction."

Manon said with that same smile, "You are so thoughtful,
Younger Brother. But truth to tell, I enjoy getting out of
Inspiration of Drenched Blossoms Pavilion now and then."

Jion accepted that, saying as he accompanied Manon to his
best parlor, "I didn't think I'd see you at all anymore, now that
you have what you wanted: congratulations, and
commiserations, on being awarded a mountain of work to
organize the Journey. Unless you like that sort of thing?"

"If it pleases Imperial Father, it will be well worth the
efforts of this unworthy daughter," Manon said, her knee
dipping in a graceful bow.

Jion made a face of acute nausea. "Do not give me that
unworthy daughter talk. You certainly have to feel quite
worthy, or you wouldn't have booted Lily out of what she
obviously really wanted a chance to do. Especially as they're
trying to work out her marriage treaty."

Manon looked down modestly, her forehead so smooth
Jion could not tell at all what she was thinking as she said, "But
hers is not the only marriage treaty being discussed."

"You too?" Jion grimaced as he reached for his guzheng.
"That's right, they sometimes marry girls off sooner than they
do us. Probably not a compliment to us," he added wryly. "But
I really hate the thought of you going away. I'd miss you."

Manon's cheeks glowed with color and her head tipped
forward as she lowered her gaze, her long golden phoenix
earrings swinging against her smooth cheeks. "Mother wishes
me to contribute to easing Imperial Father's burden, and there
is little my poor efforts are capable of as yet. But organizing
the spring journey—Honored Mother feels I will not
disappoint him too badly."

Jion had been about to approach the subject of Lily, but at
the mention of Manon's mother, he said instead, "All those
papers Honored Second Mother dropped when bowing—
those were plans?"

Manon said, "They are copied from old records. Traditions from past Journeys. She thought we ought to combine the best of them for this year's."

Jion understood now. He still did not know how to think about Second Imperial Mother, after what Grandmother Empress had told him. She had always been so kind to him, and yet this same person had destroyed the lives of her maids as if they were nothing.

But Manon had not murdered anyone. He might not trust Second Mother anymore, but he would not extend that distrust to Manon. "I see! She really does have her heart set on you organizing the Journey. Filial obedience leaves you little choice," he added, with extra meaning, but then observed, "I wish that the matter had been less painful for Lily." He began a warmup chord.

Manon did not question his shift in tone. "You know Honored Mother admires your taste in music. And so I have the first of a range of choices for us to consider for the first leg of the Journey. I hoped you might go over them with me, and honor me with the benefit of your opinion."

He answered by finishing his finger warm-ups with a flourish. "What shall we attempt first?"

They played through all four of the songs she brought at least twice, and then paused for tea and snacks. After this was brought in, he said, "I can promise none of it is poisoned."

She looked up, startled, and nearly dropped her cup. "Poison?" She caught the cup, but had gone pale.

"Sorry, sorry," he said. "Some surprising things I learned today. I shouldn't make a joke of it."

"It seems you have developed some regrettable habits," she said severely, but with a quick, concerned glance from black eyes so much like his own. "I was going to ask if you could discuss your ride with Imperial Father, for I understand that was where you were earlier, when I first came to find you. But if the subject he discussed was poison, I don't think I want to hear about it." She ran her hands up her arms in a quick gesture.

"Maybe you ought to," he responded, and began to pluck out a melody, to make it more difficult for any listeners at the door. "This is not for the staff to hear — might spread panic. But I was nearly poisoned. No, not today! It's the main reason I left the ship taking me to the Silk Islands."

"Jion!"

"Oh, but I am not finished yet. That sickness going around when I left? Poison as well. They haven't caught the poisoner yet, which is probably why nothing has been said. They might be waiting to see if it makes a reappearance. I would," he added. "And then trace it to the source while the trail is hot."

She held her arms close against her sides. "Should we be afraid?"

"Well, I've now got a poison taster that the ferrets assigned me." He waved a hand toward the far door—and as he did, the Restoration Pill in its locket bumped against his chest. But he was not going to talk about Ryu, yet. "You might have a poison taster in your household as well. In fact, I'm sure of it. All of the imperial family."

Manon laid aside her pipa and wrapped her hands around a fresh cup of tea. "And I was going to ask if Imperial Father lectured you about resuming studies with the scholars."

"Oh, I'm sure that will be next," Jion predicted gloomily, and won a smile. "Come! Let us try to forget poisons and assassins, and go through these songs once more."

Several days of delving and questioning and reviewing passed before Fai Anbai stood with his father outside the ferret archives. They let themselves in, and Fai Anbai engaged all the Essence wards as Grandfather Fai checked every door and window.

They sat down in the tiny cubby that constituted the ferret chief's office—it was basically an archive with a desk large enough for an inkstone, a lamp, and the Essence-imbued paper the chief ferrets used. As had become usual, Fai Anbai and Grandfather Fai each gave the other a precise report of everything they had done that day.

At the end, Grandfather Fai let out a long sigh. "I confess I do not know whether to be relieved or disturbed that what we assumed was youthful rebellion by Prince Jion was actually reaction to two assassination attempts."

Fai Anbai, always precise, said, "One for certain. The prince was not certain about the poison, so his leaving the ship was in some measure youthful rebellion."

Grandfather Fai shook his head. "It might have been

instinct rather than deliberate decision to escape, but the two events together paint an altogether different picture than what we had assumed about his motivations for his disappearance."

"That," said Fai Anbai, "is true. This entire case needs investigation, but whom can we send? This was Tek Banu's case!"

"She might be investigating now," Grandfather Fai reminded his son. "We don't actually know for certain."

Fai Anbai accepted that with a nod, still staring down at the paper with a troubled expression. "So much left undone. The fact that we knew the name his imperial highness gave to the army, and did not put 'Shigan Fin' together with the 'Shigan' among the criminals, is a serious reflection on us, even if there was a year between the Loyalty Fortress report and our discovery of name Shigan up north."

Grandfather Fai said slowly, "Again, it's Tek Banu's failure—and so I will inform his imperial majesty if he asks."

What that meant was, Tek Banu had all the reports. All the ferret office had was the summary of each report. They both looked down at the words *Shigan Fin: Deserted*. Fai Anbai had a vague and troubling recollection of himself dismissing that name.

His eye strayed to the name above. "Second Ryu. We never followed up with that, either. He would be a senior cadet at Te Gar now, wouldn't he?"

Grandfather Fai waved a dismissive hand. "One of the many twigs on the Ryu tree. The most important point is that there has been no subsequent report of amazing Essence displays since?"

Fai Anbai shook his head. "None."

"Then it's most likely that the youth possessed some sort of Essence artifact, which he used against the mercenaries. And, being a boy, could not resist letting Commander Weken assume he fought with godlike skills."

They both looked at the summary, which stated *A flash of light that exploded outward, knocking down the attacking force.*

Grandfather Fai tapped the paper. "The leap from the wall might be a part of the Essence artifact." He gave the shrug of experience. "If we have not heard subsequent stories about this cadet's skills from Te Gar, we can assume the amazing ability is the hyperbole of battle. For instance, what is taken as extraordinary skill, one against many, could be no more than the mercenaries running from the one who held the Essence charm that felled their advance line. This attack occurred late at night, in a rainstorm. No one at Loyalty is experienced at warfare. We all know how extreme emotions distort memory."

Fai Anbai accepted all that as reasonable, until proven otherwise. The problem was, he did not have agents enough to travel out to Loyalty to investigate what amounted to a one-time miracle that happened almost three years ago. He also had yet to send someone to investigate Redbark, which — as it apparently comprised fewer than five youths — seemed little to no threat.

Far more urgent was tracking those mercenaries — and who sent them. "Then we can leave the matter of Second Ryu for now. At least we know where he is. Aside from the mercenaries and the poisonings Tek Banu is my primary worry. She would be the best at burrowing for clues, but where is she? She did not send me the required six-month report, as I believe you know. I thought she might be reporting directly to the emperor, but I didn't get the sense that he has heard from her either, when the subject of the Loyalty investigation came up."

"That's not like her," Grandfather Fai said. "But that has happened before, usually to agents far from our relays, running a hard hunt. She might be gathering evidence and keeping it tight, especially if she intends to force you out of the position of chief. We have until she reappears to resolve this case." He looked around, and then added meaningfully, "And to prepare in here."

# TWENTY-FOUR

WE MUST RETURN TO First Brother Afan Muinkanda, who was about to finish at his first post.

"Ryu. You're wanted at the south gate."

"Ten-Blade! Summons from the stone throne."

Afan Muinkanda, known in the army as Ryu Muin, heard at least three similar messages as he made his way from the garrison stable up the stairs and along the sentry walk to the front gate. The wording of these messages invariably fell into two distinct categories: straightforward summons from Commander Wei's longtime staff, and the reference to the throne from his own company under Captain Falik Tan, words never heard by Commander Wei's people. Much less their private name for him, which was Old Turtle, for the way the commander seemed to like wearing full armor all the time. Wagers had been spirited over whether he slept in armor (for various definitions of "slept").

Muin slowed when he sighted Old Turtle standing in his favorite spot, directly over the front gate of the garrison, from which he could look down upon the road leading off toward the town, and Milky Springs Harbor. Dusty as Muin was, he took up a position behind Falik, his face arranged in the stolid expression of endurance perfected after nearly a year of listening to Old Turtle's nasal drone.

Something had displeased Old Turtle, that much was clear

to Muin. Old Turtle was well embarked into his When I Was a Young Captain speech, which was one of his longer ones — if he was to be believed, he had shown the most promise of anyone in his year, never straying from orders or rules. And yet here he was, at fifty years old still a sixth rank garrison commander, while Falik, not much over twenty, was a seventh rank captain-of-company.

Falik stood impassively under the verbal barrage, as he always did, though Muin knew that he'd been stuck once again with supervising the night sentries during what his fellows termed the Ghost Watch in the middle of the night till early morning — after which he'd had to attend Old Turtle on the morning's inspection when everyone else on night watch got to go to bed.

Old Turtle loved inspections. They had been told by Falik's first commanding officer that once a week was usually sufficient, but they had discovered that Old Turtle wasn't satisfied with once a day. There were frequently two, the second usually during some hellish hour, and always when the commander was in a peevish mood.

Dun and Muin, as commoners, had expected nothing better. Neither was surprised when Old Turtle utterly ignored them, after detailing them to supervise supply unloading, cleaning details, and horse training. Lots of horse training. Muin figured he was an expert now, though ten years ago he had never even seen a horse.

What surprised them was Old Turtle's outright abuse of Falik — all strictly within the law. Old Turtle, apparently, loathed Falik's famous father with the focused hatred born of envy.

"... needless to say your promotion commences when you step into your new post. Until such time, I expect you will conduct yourselves in an orderly manner, as befits a company under my command," Old Turtle was saying heavily, his voice sharp with annoyance.

What was this? Muin blinked, paying attention. Promotion? Could there possibly be orders at last? This "temporary" post had dragged on for most of a year.

"You will carry out your normal duties until your departure," Old Turtle finished up, his mouth crimped with irritability. "Dismissed."

They saluted, then wheeled to withdraw. Muin shot Falik

an interrogative look, to get back a flicked glance toward his shoulder: wait.

Orders? At last?

After Falik's successful Imperial Military Examination, they'd had one glorious month under Detachment Commander Huek, before the latter was ordered to command an expedition somewhere to the north, and Old Turtle had temporarily replaced him, bringing his three captains and their companies with him.

"Please say we've orders," Muin breathed without moving his lips. "Either him going, or us."

Falik's upper lip quirked, and that was all Muin needed. He waited until they reached their cramped quarters over the stable. Falik gave Pigear a single glance, which sent the orderly scouting around to make sure there were no listeners, before taking up a station before the door to Falik's box of a room.

Falik dropped onto the narrow kang, elbows on knees, as Muin perched on Falik's trunk. Falik's serious face lightened in what passed for a grin for him as he said, "We're off to Green Jade Island in the morning. And we become a true company."

"You mean," Muin said with growing delight, "you're a panther now?"

"Captain Falik, with two new silver seahorse lieutenant captains under me. You and Dun." Falik smiled broadly.

"Green Jade?" Muin said, still dazed. "That's directly south of us!"

He'd begun to regard the map of the empire as a series of interlocking rings of fortresses: Imai, where he'd been born, in the extreme southwest of the empire, its garrison considered part of the western border demarcation; the Inner Islands were the large ones centered around the imperial island; the Silk Islands, southeast of the imperial island, made up the eastern part of the Inner Islands, and had their own inner and outer islands, all garrisoned.

This stronghold he stood in lay directly north of Green Jade. Table Hills Island was small and mostly rock. It served as a supply post for army and navy at this end, and a naval training center on the other side. Below the fortress, along the natural curve of the harbor, thrived Milky Springs Harbor, a trade town catering largely to merchants traveling to the Silk Islands; higher up the mountain a monastery perched near the origin of the mineral-heavy spring, that many regarded as healing waters.

"This is probably why we're the ones going," Falik said. "We're the closest company."

He didn't mention Old Turtle and his three companies, any of which could have been ordered south. Nor did he mention that he might have been asked for by the governor of Green Jade.

"Who's commanding there?" Muin asked, mentally already escaping the tedious, fault-finding mediocrity of Old Turtle. "Oh! I know, it's Blue Hawk Han —"

"I am," Falik said, lowering his voice even more. "That is, I'll have command of the garrison. The governor has his own private army, of course. I expect that's why only one company is going —"

"A garrison full of peacocks," Muin muttered.

Falik rarely used the epithets common to everybody else, but he didn't deny it. Certain high-ranking nobles had their own armies, due to hard-won treaties of the past. The Silk Islands were prominent among them. Muin stared at Falik. "Company commander, not just a captain!"

"I'll still be a panther, but I'll be a very temporary garrison commander," Falik reminded him. "Commander Han will not be there when we arrive, I expect. He has an excellent record, and I wish he would be on hand to ease us in, but I'm told he's going north."

"Going north?" Muin repeated.

"I was not told where or why," Falik said scrupulously (of course Old Turtle wouldn't tell him, Muin thought sourly), "but a look at the map, and the moons, makes it very likely that the imperial court is once again making the Journey to the Cloud Empire."

"Which is . . ."

"It's a nobles expedition on sampans," Falik said. "I don't know much more than that, except that both army and navy are called out as escort, especially when the entire imperial court, including the emperor and his family, travel."

Muin grinned, relieved to escape *that* duty. He never wanted to have to bash his face in again in order to avoid the emperor's evil eye.

Falik said, "That means temporary duty for all the escort, until the emperor is safely back on the imperial island. If I'm right, Commander Han must already have set sail. I just hope he leaves me notes on how best to integrate with Duke Yulin's private guards—"

"Yulin!" Muin exclaimed. "Please tell me he's not related to Yulin Pel. I'll serve you for my next five lifetimes if—"

Falik waved that off. "Yulin Pel's father was disgraced years ago," he reminded Muin, and looked aside, which Muin knew by now meant there was more to be said, but Falik was not going to say it. "Governor Duke Yulin Laq is old, an affable fellow. I was there a couple times with my father before I was sent to Loyalty, and I liked him very much."

Falik sighed at Muin's inquiring glance, and relented, though he usually avoided gossip. But these were well-known facts. "The Yulin duke some generations ago, ah, had numerous consorts besides his first consort, who was a princess."

To Muin's secret delight, modest and abstemious Falik actually blushed.

"He ended up with equally numerous sons by these consorts, few of whom had noble connections, especially in his later years. Families of rank were not inclined to send young daughters to someone with close to twenty consorts, even a duke."

"Twenty!"

"Yes. It's in the records. Governor Yulin is a direct descendant of that duke, the head of a very prestigious and respectable family. But there is the matter of all those sons from ever younger and ever more ambitious consorts from poor backgrounds. The first generation or so did well—the heir, of course, was a son of the princess. He was very generous to his brothers. But after that generation, the proliferation of cousins was given less by the main branch of the family, until they were finally sent from the Yulin manor altogether, and told to make their own way in the world. Most went into the military, but I'm told that many of them ended up fighting each other. The Yulin we knew came from one of these side branches of the family."

Falik stopped there. "Enough of that. Right now, I want all my company's liberties cancelled. Everyone is to return to quarters and prepare for inspection. We'll be called out to one as sure as the moons rise. Probably between Turtle and Tiger watch, and Commander Wei will be sniffing for any possible reason for demotion or even a flogging, which he will call a last training exercise."

The first on the list to get a flogging would no doubt be Falik — they both knew it.

Muin slapped his hands to his knees. "I'm off."

He got up, but Falik held up a hand. "Ryu."

Muin paused.

"Trickle has liberty, since he had night duty in the kitchen. Don't send a runner. You had better talk to him yourself."

Muin grimaced. Trickle was an excellent orderly, as loyal as they came. He and Dun were the best logistics stewards they had — Trickle especially could scrounge anything — but he still never took anything seriously.

"Catch him before word begins to spread," Falik said earnestly. "You know he won't be able to resist sticking a straw up the tiger's nose."

Muin threw a salute and ran down the stairs three at a time. He hoped for the best. After Old Turtle came, Trickle had taken two bad floggings for "insubordination," which at least had made him a little more wary, if not more circumspect. Dun was on duty, so Muin had to be the one to try to talk some sense into Trickle.

And he knew right where to find him.

As soon as he walked into the perfumed atmosphere of the Dancing Fan, he heard Trickle's laugh rising above the giggles of women.

". . . and our company will be the garrison," Trickle was saying as he leaned back, thumb in the front fold of his riding robe.

How had he heard so fast? Muin wondered, exasperated but not really surprised. Word had obviously spread in the short time he and Falik had been talking.

"Oh! You're sooooo *young*," a familiar high-voiced woman cooed, hanging on Trickle's arm. "Have you won a lot of battles?" Pink Plum was always downstairs when the garrison got liberty, flirting and flattering. She reminded Muin of over-ripe mangos. He preferred the quiet girls.

Trickle opened his mouth, saw Muin, and grinned ruefully. "Of course we have! Ayah, not really *battle*, more of a mercenary attack," Trickle admitted. "But our company captain was the best at our training fortress! Though we'll just be a company, we're better than a regiment — "

"Liberty cancelled," Muin said loudly, before the insult to

Old Turtle and his beloved captains could be spoken—and inevitably passed along as swiftly as word had reached Trickle. "Report to barracks. Now."

Trickle sighed. "I guess this is it, my pretty Pink Plum." He passed out kisses instead of the boaters he did not have, and disentangled his arms from the caressing fingers, Pink Plum's bangles clashing sweetly.

With Trickle safely stationed at the door, Muin made a fast round of the place, chased out four liberty warriors, and started back, Trickle in tow. "You blab way too much," he said.

Trickle's cheeks were flushed—of course he had been drinking. "What? Do you think the girls're a bunch of spies for the Easterners?"

Muin sighed. "Of course not. What Falik is worried about are your duck-headed quackings that might very well net you twenty before we board that ship—and Falik fifty for not training you properly."

At that, Trickle looked abashed.

Muin went on grimly, "There's sure to be an inspection, probably midway through the night. Falik wants us perfect."

Trickle's mobile face brightened to a knowing grin. "I should have thought of that—I've never known someone more expert at scolding the dog to chastise the tiger than Old Turtle." He ran off to make a competition of cleaning, polishing, and sweeping.

No man in Falik's company got a wink of sleep that night, and none of Commander Wei's officers, who had to make the inspection.

The two companies were so busy, one preparing for inspection and the other carrying it out, that no one ever noticed the single-sail craft that left with the fishers on the dawn tide. This craft was sailed by a soberly dressed young woman named Pa Jan, almost unrecognizable from the painted, bangle-clashing, silk-tasseled Pink Plum who had listened so wide-eyed to Trickle's brag.

Pa Jan sailed off undisturbed as in the garrison, Trickle's diligence in getting his fellow drudges to expend their best efforts paid off. Look as he would, Commander Wei could not fault them for a speck of dust anywhere, an unpolished weapon, an unrepaired bit of horse harness—even the ones obviously left in storage since their fathers were boys.

They were too young to understand the bitterness of a fifty-year-old man who prides himself on his strict obedience to the rules, yet has been continually passed over for promotion while forced to stand by while yet another young sprig launches like fireworks into the sky.

But as he completed his round, and realized that he was not going to find anything, he decided that he had had a salutary effect on this latest young sprig. Falik would of course go away remembering how tough a commander Wei had been, how fine his adherence to military law. And by the time he settled to sleep, he had talked himself into believing that the fear and awe he inspired was a satisfying recompense for the blind stupidity of the higher command.

He contrived one last face-slap after all: a reason to keep half Falik's company for himself. After all, Han down south at Blue Jade had a full company. That tiny island certainly did not need two companies, even for a short time, whereas he could use the men.

Having been up all night inspecting, he saw no reason to see Falik and his company off. He wrote out the order for splitting the company — and keeping their ten support staff — leaving it for his senior captain to carry out.

Falik woke to that, stung bitterly. But at least the somewhat abashed senior captain permitted Falik to choose the ninety men he was allowed to keep. He kept his own twenty-five cavalry, and Dun and Muin and their twenty-five apiece. Trickle was summarily broken back to orderly, which permitted Falik to keep him, along with Pigear, and Muin's orderly.

Despite this last nasty blow on Old Turtle's part, a general atmosphere of liberty reigned over the exhausted, diminished, but exhilarated company as they tramped aboard the transport ship the next morning.

Falik kindly dismissed them all to rest as they could for the half-day's journey south. He and Muin stood at the rail, watching with equal satisfaction as Table Hills Island sank beyond the horizon, putting them safely out of Old Turtle's reach.

Presently Falik said, "I apologize for ten months of horse training."

Muin lifted a shoulder. "What could you do? Anyway, I'd much rather be around horses than Old Turtle." They're smarter, he added to himself.

Falik nodded seriously, big hands resting on the rail as he asked, "Have you stayed with your drills?"

"Yes," Muin said. That lesson he'd learned from little Mouse, whose actions the night of the mercenary attack still threaded his dreams. "Every day. Even if it was in my own cubicle, or out at the far end of the horse paddock. Dun was usually with me, if we weren't assigned to opposite watches."

Falik gave a short nod. To him, Old Turtle was a thing of the past. His mind was on the future. "Green Jade is peaceful. It's the eastern islands in the group that have been attacked the most. The way I see it is, we can use this post to get our company back into fighting shape, and when we get reinforcements, which I'm sure Commander Han will arrange, you can take over training so that when Commander Han goes to escort duty, we'll be in excellent shape.

Muin assented, then said, "I hear the governor there has a defense force. Are we responsible for them?"

"No. The governor's guards have their own traditions. We will not presume to interfere without orders from our own chain of command. But should we be needed, I want our entire company fighting as well as you do."

Tired as he was, for he'd been up through two nights, Muin chuckled with anticipation. "Yes, sir," he said, and ran off, wondering if the reinforcements would include new seahorses from the training fortresses. Wasn't Mouse supposed to be promoted this year? Wouldn't it be fun if her company was assigned to Blue Jade, which after all, was small and peaceful—a perfect place to get some seasoning, and nothing like Old Turtle to endure.

# TWENTY-FIVE

MOUSE, AS WE KNOW, had outgrown that name almost as soon as she left Loyalty Fortress. Training with Master Ki, she was trying to accustom herself to a new identity as Ari of Master Ki's Valley. How long would she live here for cultivation? She had learned so much, so very much, but there was still a long way to go. Probably years. Maybe she ought to build a new room, so she wouldn't have to sleep on the uneven stone floor for all those years.

Thinking about her family, and Shigan, and Matu and Petal, she found herself sniffing the air for scents from down the mountain . . .

One morning the hermit appeared in Master Ki's valley, a staff at his side. "The path to the lake is clear," he said to Ari and Master Ki after they exchanged greetings.

"And in good time," Master Ki said genially. "Ari, my student, here is your opportunity for your next level of endeavor."

Ari paused in the act of tying on her headband and gazed from one to the other.

The hermit said, "I'll show you the way."

Ari looked bewildered. "But . . ." She glanced toward the top of the path, aware of severely mixed feelings.

Master Ki said, "You have learned well over winter. Much more than I expected — more than I did at an older age than you are now."

Ari had begun, "But I . . ."

The words *at an older age than you are now* stopped her.

"The planting is done, and everything is ready for another spring. There's just enough food left here for one person until things grow enough to harvest." He did not mention that they were mostly down to bamboo shoots and rice, which they had been eating every day. "This valley can be left to the earth, the rain, and to me. It is time for you to venture into the world, and to use your lessons as you gain experience, in order to make lessons into knowledge."

"But . . . I thought . . . I would study for years," she said in a small voice. "Is it because I wasn't able to learn to send my higher soul out?"

Master Ki took her hands. "Child, must I repeat that many never learn that over a lifetime? It is seldom that those with affinity for fire and metal are able to command Essence in that way. Perhaps you will waken one day and there it will be, as if it was always there. I was wrong to try to give you that lesson. If Essence talent shows up in my clan, it tends to be with water or air affinities, which find that particular skill easier to master. Perhaps you will find a teacher whose elements match yours, but you won't know until you look."

All she could do was bow in acceptance.

He said, "You are as gallant as you are talented. I believe you will do well in the world."

She ducked her head, swallowing in a tight throat.

His gnarled, callused hands let go of hers and he walked to the door to peer out. "A fine day. And you have been sniffing the air of late. It is time."

The lump in her throat seemed to be the size of a cannon ball. "But I can return? If I need to, if I don't . . . even if it's in a week?"

He smiled. "Of course. You will always have a home here. Even after I'm gone. The animals know you. But this old sinner believes that your heart is divided, and that might be another reason the higher soul lessons are elusive at present. Go. Find the people who are important to you. Know that they are safe — or do what must be done to see to their safety." He turned and lifted Sagacious Blade from its resting place above the basket with the rake and hoe, and with both hands held it out to her. "Take Sagacious with you. She might decide to speak to you—"

"She?" Ari exclaimed, then blushed and ducked her head at her rude interruption.

But Master Ki only smiled. "There is a . . . soul attached to this blade. I don't know the story myself. As you can see, the handle is very worn, but it is a strong, true blade for all that. I believe she needs to be out in the world again. At least, she does no one any good sitting there with a rake and a hoe as company. Take her along on your quest."

As soon as he said the word *quest*, Ari sensed a shifting inside, as if she had been off-balance, but was no longer. *Find the people who are important to you.* She had followed First Brother Muin onto the recruiting ship without a second thought when she was ten years old. She would be seventeen come harvest time, and even if her parents figured she had gone with her brother, surely they must be wondering where she was now.

Then there was Shigan.

It hurt to think about him—to think of him at a distance, far beyond all the conversations she wished so very hard that they could have, and they did have in her imagination. But he was somewhere on the imperial island, surrounded by the emperor's sinister spies and guards. He might need rescuing. Or, he might not want to leave. She could not know. That was a large part of the hurt, not knowing.

She accepted the blade in both hands and bowed formally. He handed her the harness. They adjusted it together, until she was comfortable with the sword slung across her back. She discovered that the harness contained two loops for extra weapons. She could put both halves of the staff there when she needed her hands free.

She packed up her few things, and took leave of Master Ki, bowing once more to the ground. She meant to be back soon, but somehow it felt correct to take her leave with full formality. As if a bow, even a formal one, could possibly convey all her gratitude.

He laughed a little huskily, raised her up, then said, "Give my greetings and love to my family. Tell them I will be remaining up here this year."

Ari's eyes stung. "I will." Her hands came together, another bow, and she forced herself to turn her back and join the hermit, who waited patiently a little ways down the trail.

The journey was largely done in silence, both lost in their

thoughts. When they stopped, invariably they ate a meal, then unlimbered their staffs to do some sparring. It felt good – even when they'd been walking all day.

The descent was considerably faster than the climb. Each day was warmer, and finally they began to see the deep blue of the lake between slopes. The glimpses got wider and longer, and at last they wound down to the shoreline. Here they found not only Master Ki's boat right where they'd left it, turned upside down up high on the shore, but a carefully wrapped package resting on it. This disclosed a sealed letter.

"Is that for Master Ki?" she asked.

The hermit held the note. "This is for me. From my son. The Kis probably rowed it over."

"Oh."

The hermit said, "The Ki clan will be looking for the boat. Tell them Master Ki is spending this year up in the valley. They'll bring supplies from time to time, which I fetch for him."

Ari clasped her hands and bowed. "I will."

Together they carried the boat to the water, and she bowed again. "Thank you for everything."

"We will see one another again, no doubt," he replied easily. "You were a good student. He is very proud of you."

She bowed again, and climbed into the boat. He gave it a shove, and she plied the wooden oars, noting that it was a lot easier than it had been coming out three seasons ago. It seemed she'd had one last growth spurt, for not only had her warm weather clothes turned out to be short in the wrists and ankles, but her arms seemed longer when she plied the oars. And she definitely had more strength. Augmented with Essence, her rowing sent the boat skimming over the placid water, her wake arrowing out behind in ever-widening ripples, as birds wheeled and dived all around her.

When she pulled up onto the opposite shore, a patrol of young Kis raced to help her drag the boat up onto the rocky shingle.

When they saw Sagacious's handle jutting beyond her shoulder their eyes rounded, but they said nothing about the sword as they welcomed her back. Instead they pelted her with questions about Grandfather Ki and her time with him as fast as they could speak, scarcely listening for answers, until they were assured that Grandfather Ki was well, but no, he would not come down this spring.

"Second Uncle will send over baskets of good things," one of the cousins foretold, and then the subject switched to the Sky Alliance Prize Competition, and was she going? Had she practiced at all, or was life on the mountain all sitting around and memorizing affinities and Essence jabber?

"There's a letter for you," the youngest cousin confided, when he could edge a word in. "From all the way south. It's from Cousin Matu."

Matu! Curiosity warred with residual regret.

When they got to the house, the adults not busy about work came out to greet her. All eyes went to Sagacious Blade, but no one said anything as one of the aunts shooed the patrollers back to duty, and settled Ari down with fresh tea and a meal that was not comprised of plain rice eked out with bamboo shoots and increasingly withered scraps scraped from the bottom of the autumn stores. Matu's aunt watched with complete understanding as Ari inhaled the early peas and the fish grilled in sesame sauce with tiny cobs of corn.

First Uncle came in as she finished, and said, "We kept the ship from sailing in case you and Grandfather Ki came down the mountain. I see that Sagacious Blade decided to come with you."

That was a strange way to put it, but Ari remembered what Grandfather Ki had said about a soul. "I . . . think he loaned it to me. I plan to bring it back to him," she added quickly.

First Uncle's smile was a little sad. "Grandfather is very old, much older than you think. He had a rough life when he was young. He was there defending the islands when the Westerners invaded, and then there was Bloody Maoyan — but he can tell you those stories, or not. I don't know them all myself."

He indicated the blade. "He always said she would choose whom she would go to, and it might not be family. He inherited Sagacious from a teacher, not from his ancestors. We hoped she might be passed to one of us, but never expected it."

"This grateful student will regard it as a loan," she confided. "Does it — she — really have a soul?"

"I don't know that story either. Grandfather said so."

Ari said doubtfully," I've heard stories about swords with charms, or wards. That can . . . fly."

She said the word tentatively, expecting a laugh the way

her father had, when he gave her her first lesson in Heaven and Earth.

But First Uncle didn't laugh. He said, "I know the tales are full of martial artists who are trained in the lightness skill using their swords to guide their bodies through the air. I don't know how many are true. I do know that there are charmed swords in the world, and that these tend to be very old. It could be there was more Essence back then, when dragons were often seen in the sky."

She said, "I met a charmed sword. That was the time when Matu and Shigan and Petal were with me . . ." Her voice faltered when she mentioned Shigan's name. "That Sunset Harbor pirate captain had a sword that craved blood. I could feel it."

"That is the one you shattered, am I correct?" First Uncle said.

"Yes."

"Did you ever stop to consider how difficult it is to break or shatter a blade?"

Ari's lips parted. She was about to say that it had been easy, then she hesitated. "Oh. Are you saying there was some . . . Essence matter, or even . . . a god present?"

His smile widened. "I don't know. I was not there. All I can say is that Grandfather Ki must have heard, or sensed, or something. Sagacious Blade chose you. So. I would like to be able to offer you a spring of training and rest, which might yet come, but the Sky Alliance Prize competition is very soon, and the ship is waiting. Would you like to compete? You did drill, did you not?" he added, in question.

"I — there was a hermit," Ari said, then stopped when First Uncle's brows shot upward toward his hairline. She said diffidently, "Ought I to go? I don't really care about competing for a prize."

First Uncle laughed. "The 'prize' is of course the purse made up of contributions by all the sects, but really it's fame, which translates out to the fact that you'd be courted by every sect there. The Shadow Panthers will not be competing, by the way. The alliance agreed to a treaty, forbidding them to step on that island."

"Good riddance," Ari muttered.

His smile widened. "To resume, prizes also mean being offered work as a master, and passage on ships if you agree to defend."

Ari brought her chin down. "Then I'll definitely compete. I spent all I had coming north last year. I don't think I have five tinnies left in my pouch."

First Uncle was very pleased with Ari's assent and went away to let the rest of the family know. He and Second Uncle assembled them for a last drill before nightfall, after announcing that they'd depart before dawn to get down the mountain to the ship.

Ari knew the drill was for her sake. She longed for a real bath, after having washed out of a basin for months, but it could wait. Her letter also, as it had already waited months.

She took Sagacious out to the shoreline, not quite sure why she did, but then set the sword aside when the others picked up wooden blades. They could see that in her time on the mountain she had gotten a little taller, and her style had altered in a way difficult to define—except to those who knew Lion's Mane.

And then, like a wind, she blew through all the family. With Second Uncle she fought to a draw, but they all sensed that she could have won. She knew she could have won if she had brought up Essence.

But then they drilled with two knives, for in the Ki clan, sword work was mostly warmup. Second Uncle beat her, after a fight that left her wringing with sweat.

She bowed and thanked him gratefully for the lesson, he bowed back, and the youngsters were dismissed to get ready for the evening meal. They ran off, chattering with happy expectation. Ari, being with the Ki clan, was sure to bring them glory.

Second Uncle, Second Aunt and a couple others had lingered. "Did Grandfather teach you the fan?" Second Uncle asked.

Ari bowed. "I learned the poke, but I was just beginning the throw."

"Throw is much harder than the poke," Second Uncle said. "To be used only when you are very sure of your skill."

Second Aunt came forward, and offered her a fan. It was plain, heavier than a regular fan. The sticks had somewhat rounded protuberances at the top. They sparred one on one instead of sending her against a target. This was a first. All that Ari had been taught snapped into place: sorrow swooped through Ari when it struck her that Grandfather Ki hadn't sparred with her because he no longer could.

They fought until each had tapped the other lightly on various acupoints.

Then Second Uncle and Second Aunt snapped their way through the advanced form, which ended with hurling the fan in a horizontal line as it whipped around in a circle and came back to their hands. The fans looked like blurred circles, which lent the form its name, Ghost Moon within Phoenix Moon. Other Kis held up strips of paper, which both fans cut through—and then whirled back to the martial artists' hands.

Ari worked at the form. She could snap the fan with speed, but her circles wobbled and came back several paces from her hand—if they didn't crash into a tree or ground first. Again and again they worked, Ari with that exhilaration that came of learning something new. She managed to get her fan to tear a piece of paper, though it was sadly jagged, and not the clean slice of the elders.

Second Aunt told her a few things to refine her practice, and then the brassy sound of the gong called them all back to the house. Ari carried Sagacious back again, unused.

Her first true bath since late fall, when ice began floating down the stream from above, felt delicious. While she soaked, she read Matu's letter. It was very short, little more than hoping that she and his family were well. The interesting part was covered in two sentences: Petal was now the owner of the Blue Hibiscus Inn, her stepmother having been bonded for life for a list of crimes that Ari knew came directly out of greed and cruelty. Sometimes, the law worked.

Ari laid her head back against the wooden rim, her hair floating all around her.

She knew what she wanted to do first, after the competition. Matu said Petal had specifically asked him to invite her to visit—they were establishing themselves as an inn for gallant wanderers, and already they'd had two beg to be taught Redbark sword. At the bottom of the letter Petal had painstakingly written *Please come.*

Ari would, but there was something to be done first. She'd have to be careful how she went about gathering information. She expected the elders would go silent, after three people had vanished on this quest.

The next day they rose, ate a sumptuous breakfast, and took ship for the competition. During the short journey Ari couldn't help but think about all that had changed since she last set eyes on the laughing Fox God — and when they got there, and her eyes swept the familiar strutting figure, she felt a sense of welcome. But it was not home.

They each lit an incense stick, made their bows, and headed up toward the north end of camp where they usually set up their tent. The area had been left empty for them, a sign, Ari understood now, of the respect the others held for the Ki clan.

Ari kept looking about her. There was the spot where she and Shigan had not-quite-argued. And there was the grassy area where she'd confronted Matu. She looked away quickly. How did others flirt so easily? She was a failure at that. Maybe she was meant to be unlucky in love.

To shake those thoughts, she pitched in to help raise the tent, and turned her hand to whatever task presented itself. The Ki clan, pleased at how cooperative and modest their somewhat famous guest was, kept leaning over to pile the choicest bits from the banquet into her bowl, until it was heaping, and she had to bow and wave them off.

The next day, with a sense of relief, Ari felt all her worries fade like fog before the sun when she stood before her first duelist. Her stance, to those with the sight to see it, promised skill; everyone else saw a teenage girl standing with a staff, in preference to using the old-fashioned sword she wore across her back.

Those who recognized her, or that sword handle with the pearl on the pommel, gathered in expectation.

She did not disappoint them.

Her first bout was with a burly swordsman who grinned at her from above his braided beard. A whiff of burnt orange and a trace of brownish pink distracted her. She blinked, willing her focus to sharpen.

"A staff against a sword, young gallant?" he said, not unfriendly. "My steel will chew up that nice wood."

Ari waited.

He tried again. "I see you have a blade there. Is it just for decoration?"

"I prefer to use my staff, elder gallant," Ari said politely.

"On your head then, youngster," the man retorted, charged — and in the next breath found himself flat on his back, his ankle twinging, and his sword lying somewhere outside the circle, where it had flown when she struck it out of his hand.

"Two moves!"

"No, that counts as one—she just brought the other end around. . ."

"Two or one, that was . . ."

The crowd roared, loving it. Ari bowed to her former combatant, who was dusting himself off, and walked out of the circle.

She alternated between using her staff and double knives. Sagacious Blade remained in its sheath.

Ari faced three women, all excellent. One glowed green with Essence until Ari blinked away the distracting glimmer. Ari found herself sweating hard in that match. The woman's sudden grin made it clear that she sensed Ari's using Essence as well, and the two of them dueled with the wooden knives for quite a while, gathering a huge crowd before Ari was able to use her opponent's heel slipping on a rock to get her further off balance and tap her blade against the woman's breastbone.

"Thank you!" Ari's opponent gasped, her head still surrounded by glowing spring green, bringing a whiff of fresh cedar as she wiped her arm on her sleeve. "Best bout I've had in five years. You're not Waoji Lion's Mane's daughter, are you? Isn't she a sailor?"

Ari blushed to the ears. "No, I'm not. I'm Ari—"

"That's Firebolt, wearing girl braids," a scrawny teenager yelled, his voice cracking. "Why are you disguised as a girl, Firebolt? Are the imperials after you?"

"Ayah!" someone else called. "I hear after you burned down that Shadow Panther lair, the imperials chased Redbark and obliterated you."

"I *am* a girl," Ari said to the circle. "I was living as a boy. And the imperials . . ." She did not know what to say about Shigan, so she shook her head. "Redbark dispersed for a time."

People accepted that, agreeing in low voices. *Good idea — let the imperials chase someone else — go to ground.* And, of course, *Redbark* whispered from lips to ears.

Ari looked around, realized that she was still in the competition circle, and that everyone was waiting. Respect-fully waiting, but that somehow made it worse. "Sorry," she said with a general bow, and hastened out of the circle.

# TWENTY-SIX

THE YOUNG WOMAN FOLLOWED her, and the next two competitors replaced them in the circle.

Ari was distracted by the colors she occasionally saw around people. This woman had glowed that pleasing green before the bout and after she'd lost. Were the colors and the scent-that-was-not-scent related to emotions? Ari didn't understand what these false senses might mean, only that whichever emotions the woman had felt before and after the bout hadn't altered much, even though she'd lost.

"What was your name?"

"I'm Ari of Redbark. You trained in Essence?"

"Lie Tenek. And only in fighting. I have little talent. It spends itself fast, but at least I can hold my own in a fight with anyone of any size. I could tell that you far outmatch me there."

Lie Tenek was taller than Ari, similar in build — lean and panther-like in musculature. She seemed to be about ten years older than Ari, mid-twenties. She was paler than bronze-skinned Ari, with faint freckles across her nose. Some ancestor had been a Easterner — probably more recently than the Easterner in Ari's own family history.

"I don't belong to any sect, right now. I wouldn't be averse, if I found the right one." Lie Tenek shrugged, and added with her quick, one-sided grin, "Back when Reckless and Feckless were pups, I trained some with them. Before Bi the Whirlwind was killed." Her smile vanished. "And Feckless — she stopped using that name — went to sea. Your style really reminds me of them in some ways."

To avoid the implied question, Ari asked how she met Waoji Lion's Mane's two children.

"I was at Sky Island for a while when they first arrived." Lie Tenek told a few typical stories of young training, then added, "Reckless should be somewhere about. He's one of the judges now, being a master."

"Ari of Redbark," someone bawled — it was time for her next bout.

At the end of the day, Ari was among those who had not lost a bout. She repaired to the Ki tent to see if they needed hands, and was waved off firmly but respectfully. Someone among them seemed to have decided that a potential winner ought not to be burdened with homely tasks like cutting up vegetables or scouring dishes.

Ari turned away from the tent with a sigh — and nearly ran into a young man of maybe twenty-five, tall and rangy, with a wild shock of hair escaping from its clasp, framing a face with a familiar jutting brow and hawk nose that she had been seeing all winter.

He had to be related to Lion's Mane.

He bowed over clasped hands. "Waoji Reckless." And when she had introduced herself, he said, "Did you by any chance just come from Ten Leopards?"

'Yes," she said.

"Were you cultivating with old Grandfather Ki?"

"I was."

"Ah," he said, smiling broadly.

Ari looked her question. Waoji Reckless (who, unlike his sister, had gotten his nickname because as a small boy he was painstakingly careful about everything he did, from tying his shirt ties to practicing his forms), glanced round, saw that they were out of earshot, and said, low-voiced, "My father's style. Certain moves of yours show it. You don't have to say anthing. It's just that I can tell he's recovering well if he's training people again. Do you happen to know if he got my letter?"

"He did. I was there when he found it."

Reckless's smile broadened. "Trust the Kis!"

For the first time, Ari realized that gallant wanderers had to be wary of using the post that the rest of the empire used. That meant trusting messages to others to carry.

Reckless went on, "I notice you have Sagacious Blade. Is that permanent?"

"I don't dare assume so. Grandfather Ki handed the blade to me directly as I left." She still had trouble calling a sword by a human pronoun.

Waoji Reckless gave a short nod. "But you must have worked with it."

"Nearly every day," Ari admitted.

"But then someone told you that blade possesses a soul. And now you're, what, afraid? Not you. Not if you've done half the things I've heard. Unsettled?"

"I don't know," she admitted. "My fa . . ." She cleared her throat, decided it was safe enough to say "father" to another gallant wanderer, and stated firmly, "My father told me once that weapons are just weapons. He wasn't even sure he believed in Essence wards on them. He said that weapons cannot have personalities, or desires. Their wielder might imagine so, after a lifetime spent with one's sword in reach."

"And yet you use Essence."

"Yes," she admitted. "I was being tutored in the affinities by one parent, while the other didn't believe in them. Most of them. I accept what I experience, except if a master tells me a thing that I don't know yet. I think . . . I think I can believe that. Because I already know I don't know everything."

"That's fair enough. We have to rely on our good sense — but be aware of our limitations."

"I don't always know how to tell the difference," Ari admitted as Waoji had led the way to the pavilion. Others there withdrew, leaving the two space to talk, which Ari found disconcerting. As if she'd spent thirty years instead of not quite one in cultivating. They were treating her as if she were an elder. Or . . . a master.

"My grandfather once scorned a shaman summoned by my first aunt on my mother's side. This shaman was to treat my cousin, who had headaches. The shaman made my cousin eat walnuts while he chanted in circles around the bed. Later he explained that the shape of walnut halves resembles the shape of the human brain — an affinity. My cousin had to ingest the walnuts' Essence, which the shaman sent to banish the imps causing the headache. This was to bring about the cure."

"Did it?" Ari asked.

"He got up, said he felt great, and for a few days he said he had no headache. But as soon as he resumed lessons, there it was again. There was a nun teaching the girls. A Phoenix Moon nun. She said his eyes were weak from seeing small things close to his face, and that he was straining over the letters in reading and writing. My aunt said he was just lazy since he never got anything right."

"What was the result?" Ari asked.

"I don't know what happened exactly after that. We took ship, then . . . other things happened." He looked away, his friendly profile severe for a heartbeat or two. "I saw my cousin again a couple years ago, and he's fine, but I noticed he doesn't do any reading if he can help it."

Ari nodded. "I was taught there are true affinities, that we cannot perceive all the ways the world is connected, each bee and butterfly connected to krakens a week's sailing away, and everything is connected to the stars in the Heavens. This is what augurs spend their lives studying. It cannot all be false."

"No."

"I was also taught that the false augurs are mostly found around the rich. They and false healers gouge people of their coinage. My father once said that augurs are *all* frauds, telling the powerful what they want to hear, or they lose their lives. But if they always lie, would they not lose their lives anyway?"

"Certainly if a lie is caught. But if they use words that can be interpreted several ways, so that they are never completely wrong, if never completely right . . ." He shrugged.

Ari thought immediately of the phoenix feather. "But aren't omens and portents sometimes genuinely difficult to interpret?"

"That is true enough," he said. "Life is full of surprises, and portents are among them. The powerful as well as the powerless would like to know what will happen tomorrow, and so we need — or think we need — people to explain them." He laughed. "But whatever type of prediction we hear, or don't hear, we still must wait to find out the truth."

"My mother, a healer, said that sometimes nothing she can do will help, but she doesn't say so, for that would take away hope. Mother said that belief can be a powerful healer in itself."

"Very true. Ayah! Given our discussion here, what do you believe about Sagacious Blade, especially if you trained with that sword before you were told of its history?"

"It," Ari repeated. "Not she. You don't believe the sword has a soul?"

"I don't know. I haven't handled it, or faced it in battle. Would you like to hear my suggestion?"

"Please." Ari bowed. "I would be honored."

"Don't use it if you face Argan Bei of the Five Bulls Sect. Beat him with that staff. Much as I want to see him lose, I suspect he'll be vindictive if he loses to yon sword. Especially against someone who is not in his sect, or close to his size."

Ari already knew who he was. She had heard his loud, arrogant voice from two competition circles away, and when she'd turned to look, she got a whiff of burnt rust amid a swirl of sour yellow shot through with blood, almost like veins. She'd avoided him after that glimpse. "I will do my best." She bowed again, as someone behind Ari caught his notice.

"Ayee! I apologize for my rude interruption, Reckless, but we must set up for the meal now."

"I want to wash my hands," Ari admitted.

They parted, she noticing what a relief it was to be able to go off to the privy the women used. She stopped at the stream to wash her hands and face, thinking about how friendly Lion's Mane's son had been. She still was not accustomed to being social—the closest she had come was during her orderly and cadet days, and she and her hut mates had always been under orders. When she had liberty, she was invariably alone. Later, she'd found the cheerful chaos of the Ki household nearly overwhelming.

She had no idea that that casual conversation had revealed a great deal to Waoji Reckless, who found a chance to speak to a couple of trusted elders. "Ari of Redbark was definitely with my father. He must be doing well. Also, the fact that he chose to train her speaks well for her."

"As do her actions," the eldest said approvingly. "Modest, as friendly to losers as to winners, not that she's had to deal with someone beating her yet." And then, addressing the question they were all thinking, "Can you beat her?"

Waoji Reckless pursed his lips. "I don't actually know. Without Essence I'd say we might be even with the staff. Maybe even with the sword. Her strength probably would not match mine, but I believe she's faster. Her fundamental training is superior to ours. That plus the Essence makes her truly a Talent—if she used it on me I expect she could lay me flat in ten moves. I need to learn more about Redbark."

"We could make no use of Essence a condition," said another.

"Not this year," Waoji Reckless said firmly. "Essence-skill is so rare, and interfering with it is too much like fishing in muddy waters. In any case I don't believe she needs to be taught a lesson in humility."

"Nor do I," one of the other masters said. "Let her win with or without Essence, if it's her fate."

"It will be interesting to see what she does next," the eldest commented thoughtfully.

"It'll be interesting to see what you do with Argan Bei," Lie Tenek said to Ari after the evening banquet, as musicians played in the background.

Ordinarily Ari would have stayed to listen, but the flute, guqin, and pipa together reminded her of Shigan. It was strange, how beautiful music could hurt. No, it wasn't the music. It was the feelings the music brought up.

When Lie Tenek suggested a walk in the balmy spring air, Ari agreed.

"I'd rather have a bout with you," Ari said. "You'd surely beat me next time."

Lie Tenek flashed her grin. "I don't think so! And that's not false modesty. I have a pretty good sense of my strengths, and I was going my hardest against you yesterday. But I don't think you were going your hardest against me. I was going to ask if you still did Redbark drills in the early mornings. Oh, yes, I know about those. Heard all about them over winter." She peered at Ari, then her voice altered. "Ayah! I'm sorry."

Ari did not know how her face had changed. She looked away, then back. "We dispersed. It seemed a good idea."

"I'd go to ground, too, if I was chased by Shadow Panthers *and* imperials," Lie Tenek said.

Ari spoke quickly. "But if you'd like to do martial arts drills in the morning, I'd like it, too."

The two met before the sun rimmed the eastern ridge beyond the pavilion, and went behind the Ki tent. There, as peachy light picked out the contours of Ari's form, Lie Tenek watched Redbark Sword form.

She remained silent until the end, noting that Ari had fin-ished in the exact spot she had begun without once looking down. Superlative footing, always her worst problem. "That," she said, "is what I call art. I am honored to have been permit-ted to see it." She clasped her hands and bowed. "Please teach this seeker?"

Ari sheathed Sagacious Blade, and bowed back. "Sure. But you're going to have to start over. I mean, you are an excellent fighter. But your footing . . ."

"Is all over the place. I know. I was never trained to do anything with my feet other than the horse stance."

"All right. Let's set aside our weapons and just work on that," Ari suggested, and used Sagacious in the sheath to draw out the circle with the S curve within, representing light and dark. Then the six smaller circles around the circumference, each half inside the circle and half outside. "You are going to be stepping from one circle to the next . . ."

Lie Tenek got it fast. By that time Ari had decided against teaching her Heaven and Earth. If Lie Tenek wanted to learn more, they'd use some of the Ki forms, which were perfectly good. Ari was *not* going to start Redbark again. It seemed always to lead to disaster.

After breakfast it was time for the final competitions in all areas. Ari did not compete with the horses — she hadn't ridden one since that first competition. She was one of the top five in sword, double knives, and staff.

With each bout, she found herself distracted by the colors and scents-that-were-not-scents. Since it was happening, she tried letting it happen instead of ignoring it. The most surprising one was the bout with Argan Bei of the Five Bulls Sect. She'd already fought two from that sect, one swordsman and a man who fought with a spear against her staff. She had learned through these two bouts that Five Bulls selected for size and strength, and their martial artists shared a similar strategy — coming on fast and hard.

But Father had reminded Ari that long ago day when he first demonstrated Heaven and Earth that a finger can deflect a boulder, and that the slow, deceptively mild style called Eel depended on balance, not brute force, yet it was one of the most effective styles in martial arts. She deflected all that rushing, pushing strength, and before they recovered, turned it back on them. These fights ended the quickest, every time.

She found fast, observant fighters much tougher to defeat, especially when they knew how to retreat, how to deflect. Then she had to rely entirely on speed and skill.

Her fight against Argan Bei was nigh, and when she stood in the ring considering the way he gripped his weapon, breathing hard, she sensed beneath the roiling orange and yellow a deep line of . . . fear? No. Not fear. That is, not fear of pain, or even death. Losing face?

No. That was not it. Quite. He charged, and she had it: this strength, this weapon was in his view all he had. To lose was to lose himself.

Remembering what Reckless had said, she left Sagacious in the sheath, and readied her staff, though she already knew she was going to win. The Five Bulls martial art was too limited. But she decided that, unlike her bouts with the spearman and the swordsman — neither of whom had been objectionable persons — she was going to let this bout spin out.

And so she did, retreating twice to the edge of the circle, then leaping aside and twirling her staff until it hummed. It was not at all a real fight. It reminded her of Old Rock a bit, but she saw the colors around Argan Bei blur and realign. Still orange and yellow, but brighter, though he was tiring. Big men tended to tire faster.

A last flurry of flashy moves, and she got her staff behind his knee. He went down.

She stood next to him, leaning on her staff. "Good fight," she said.

He rolled to his knees and got up with a grunt, giving her a look hard to interpret. Then gave a nod. "Good fight," he said.

After the midday meal she lost her first bout, against Mountain Walking Ki, otherwise known at First Uncle, a soft-spoken man whose formidable martial arts she had seen in action at the Shadow Panther beach. He had saved many lives that night. She remembered that he traveled back and forth between Eagle Island to teach there, and Ten Leopards, which was one reason why Second Uncle did most of the teaching to the Ki youth.

She could have forced a win with a surge of Essence, but it would have drained her. His skills were superior — and she saw where she needed work.

She bowed, hands clasped. "Thank you for the lesson," she said. "For it was one. I really need to work on my weaker hand."

"It was a pleasure to spar with you," First Uncle replied. "You would be welcome to come to Eagle Island for further training whenever you wish."

She bowed again, aware that this was a rare, and earned, compliment.

First Uncle and the winner of the last bout — crescent blade against forked spear — then faced one another, knives against the forked spear. Walking Mountain Ki's knives flickered almost too fast to see, and he won in a dozen moves.

That was it for the fighting competition. Ari had come in third. The gallant wanderers cheered the top three winners, and then everyone went off to watch the last of the archery competition, both on horseback and long shooting.

At the banquet, people came up to Ari to congratulate her, and ask what she intended to do next. There were numerous invitations to come to various sects, as Reckless had promised. She turned away invitations with smiles and asked her own questions, careful not to hold any of these conversations within earshot of the Ki clan.

At the end of the evening, as many swayed off to bed, full of good wine, Lie Tenek emerged out of the darkness. "Well done," she said.

"Thanks." Ari clasped her hands together and bowed. "I'm not going to say that I lost to First Uncle Ki because of this, but I don't like how my braids wrap around my throat or bang against my back when I'm really active. How do women stand it? Is it something you get used to?" She sighed. "I'd cut mine off if it wasn't unfilial."

Lie Tenek gave her a sympathetic nod. "Your braid is really thick. I could show you a way to do it so you don't have that heavy rope strangling you. And it looks far better than a topknot."

Ari was going to say that she didn't care, but this was a kind offer. And she was trying to learn how to be a girl. "I would like that," she said. "Does it really stay out of the way?"

Lie Tenek grinned. "Trust me."

They met in the morning early, before people began packing up and moving toward breakfast. Lie Tenek had Ari sit on the ground, and she began brushing out Ari's hair. "This is good hair. Curly, which I know isn't the fashion. Thick, but not too long. It'll make a perfect Serpent Ring."

Ari found having someone else's fingers in her hair odd; she remembered Shigan's hands wrapping it up for her once, and shivered.

"Cold?"

"No. Go on."

"I need to brush out these tangles, then . . . here goes. What you're going to do is part it into three, like a braid, can you feel it?"

"Yes," Ari said.

"But you're going to be braiding it right next to your scalp, starting over one ear and going around your head."

Lie Tenek demonstrated, pausing every now and then so that Ari could feel it, and then try a few strands herself. When she had a tight braid all the way around her head in a coronet, Lie Tenek secured it with the tiger-eye hair stick, which also served as a hairpin. "There. Now, that will stay right like that through the toughest fight. But it looks good. Yes, that style flatters your face." When Ari gave her a comical look, Lie Tenek laughed. "I know, like me, you're no beauty, but you have a nicely shaped head. And you've got nicely shaped eyes under those formidable brows."

"I like my brows," Ari protested. "My first brother has them, too. We got them from our father." It felt so good to refer to family members! "Thank you!" Ari patted the coronet around her head, liking how secure it felt.

Lie Tenek sat back, her knees drawn up to her chin, her arms crossed over them. "You're welcome. Now, in trade, you tell me why you were so cagey, asking questions about Benevolent Winds Island, but never around your hosts."

Ari looked up. "Did they notice?"

"They were too busy being proud on Mountain Walking Ki's behalf. But I noticed, because everyone kept saying you hadn't accepted anyone's invitation. What's going on?"

"A rescue," Ari said, after a long moment. "A rescue that's already had two failures. Someone important got snatched by imperials and forced into mines. If I told the Ki clan what I want to do, they would all try to talk me out of it."

Lie Tenek grinned. "A hopeless rescue! Permit me to join you." She clasped her hands and bowed.

# TWENTY-SEVEN

IN THE BEAUTIFULLY DECORATED, hidden world of the Shadow Panthers' main headquarters, a young woman was passed from guard to guard, after enduring close questioning at each ring of perimeter.

At the last, a messenger came to inform Master Night that Pa Jan, one of his pairs of eyes, had a report that only the master could hear.

Pa Jan was passed right on.

Master Night regarded her narrow-eyed. "Your report that my perimeter chiefs could not hear?"

Pa Jan glanced at the listeners behind the chief, but complied. If Master Night wanted them there, there they would stay. At least she'd come this far—and no one could claim this nugget of news as theirs. "Commander Han was taken from Green Jade to head the defense fleet for the imperial court doing Journey to the Clouds," Pa Jan said.

The gods were smiling at last; Master Night hid his surge of elation and eyed her. Sometimes these spies of his got a little too ambitious. "And what, I'm going to attack the entire imperial court?" he asked acidly.

She stood straighter, her arsenal of false cooing and flirting as Pink Plum utterly suppressed. She'd heard what happened to anyone who tried to seduce Master Night for their own ends—there was nothing worse, he said, than spies trying their skills on the Master. "Commander Han was replaced by a single company, headed by a new commander. With new captains. Two are ghost seahorses."

Master Night smiled. "All right, that was worth hearing. Are you certain no one else was sent in support?"

"Not that I heard," Pa Jan said, her gaze shifting.

"Do we know this young, untried commander?"

"General Falik's son."

"Heh," Master Night barked. "Hah! I wonder if he has half the brains of his father."

In the background lounged one of his chiefs, who was very bored. "Shall I give the order to muster to attack Green Jade?"

Master Night pursed his lips. "We could, if we wanted to test our people by letting them destroy this company." (No one considered the governor's own force worth mentioning.) "But the Journey to the Clouds only lasts a few days. When Han is sent back, we would have a difficult time holding it," Master Night said. "And my goal is to hold it—and expand," he reminded them.

The other two waited in silence as Master Night stared at the priceless porcelain he had taken from a manor before he'd had all the inhabitants killed, and razed it to the ground. Then he drank from a tiny cup whose previous owner had been given the Thousand Cuts by Master Night's own blade.

Fate. It was fate! But he must move carefully. He set the cup down. "Escort duty for the imperial court's outing . . . there is a very good chance that the Minister of War is preparing to promote Han. In which case he's the most likely candidate to go east, if the marriage treaty does happen. Practice escort here, and if all goes well, escort to the Easterners, and then he'll come back a general. If that happens, if—I say if—Young Falik is left alone on Green Jade, where nothing ever happens . . ." He turned his head and motioned lazily to his clerk. "Give our pair of eyes here a reward for worthwhile news And you." He turned to Pa Jan. "Find a position on that island. In fact." He turned back to the clerk. "Give her pigeons, and a trainer. If Han does go east . . . and this young sprig is not reinforced—and we might help that along, yes, we shall. Falcon! You and your boys go ahead and run a raid on the winter stores up north . . . here. We can always use more stores as our numbers increase." He tapped his map. "That ought to keep the navy busy for a time. As

Kanda says, justice comes to those who wait."

In the silken, sunlit world of the imperial court, the principal topic of conversation was anticipation of the elegant, serene pleasure of the Journey to the Clouds. Especially among those on the select list of invitees.

Much less spoken of were personal goals, few of which had to do with wind and flower, snow and moons. The foremost subject not spoken of was the order of the boats. Whoever was placed closest to the emperor gained the highest honor; the farthest boat might as well be home, except no one invited ever refused. It was better to bear being last with becoming modesty, and for the rest of the year, brag about the Journey to all who could not go.

Much heartburning was expended upon conjecture of the order of the boats, as boat rank did not necessarily reflect court rank. Though what happened at the Journey inevitably influenced court maneuverings for some time to come afterward. No one dared to assume anything — out loud.

Whoever organized the Journey must submit a list to the emperor, who either set his seal in approval or else reordered it with a stroke of the brush. After which the planner would smile, bow, and have to reorganize everything to reflect the emperor's wishes.

This year, Emperor Guiyan judiciously plied his brush. First Imperial Princess Manon, who had worked hard during the intervening weeks, had placed herself directly after the consorts' boats, as eldest of the imperial children, and leader of the social events planned for the Journey. Having been told that Lily was to have her own boat for the first time, Manon had listed her after Vaion's boat — his first time with his own. Gau-Gau of course was still too young for her own boat, and she sailed with her mother, the third imperial consort, third in line after Manon's boat. Thus Lily was ranked least of the imperial party, farthest from the emperor's boat, site of the best entertainments.

But when Manon's chief steward brought back the red-stamped paper that Imperial Father used for personal messages, she got an unpleasant surprise: Lily's boat had been moved all the way up behind the emperor's. Manon regarded the slashing ink mark, nearly unable to contain her fury.

Control had been instilled in her since early childhood. She took it to her mother, perhaps hoping there might be some way to change it, to be met with her mother's inscrutable face.

"Before we discuss this matter, I am thinking only of you when I observe that I do not like hearing that you have continued to go to Jion's manor. If you must continue your ruse with music, you ought to be summoning him to you. Unreflective observers might assume you are giving him the precedence."

"I considered that, Honored Mother. But if I go to him when it is convenient to me, I am better able to discover how he is filling his days. Since his return he no longer tells me everything in his head, and if I visit him, I will better be able to descry what he might be planning. You were the one who honored this grateful daughter by pointing out how pleased Imperial Father was when the rumor went out that Jion had collected a harem of pillow maids. That could be perceived as a step toward the throne — it is very male thinking, according to your lessons." Here Manon bowed. "I need to know what else he is doing that he does not talk about, and I cannot find out as well if he comes to us."

The second imperial consort hummed, then acknowledged her daughter's point by changing the subject. "You did not expect your honored father to alter your plans, Daughter? You ought to have. You gave up the Easterner betrothal negotiation in that mutt Lily's favor. His imperial majesty, in his wisdom, not surprisingly put her next in the boat line because the Easterner prince will be your father's guest. But this can still be a triumph for you, and for the Su clan, if every detail is perfect. Everyone will ask whose mind was behind the arrangements, and the answer will be your name."

The second imperial consort eyed her daughter for a protracted moment, then, satisfied with Manon's perfect mask of control, added, "Remember, this year your Aunt Siar will be sailing with the Su boat." And then she betrayed how she set the clan interests above Manon's by adding, "I expect you to make certain she is paired with Jion as often as possible."

Manon considered her words carefully. If Su Siar — daughter of Manon's grandfather, a year younger than Manon — married Jion, she had a very good chance of becoming empress one day — assuming Manon did not secure the throne instead of Jion. Su Siar would be working very hard to achieve exactly that. Manon had absolutely no doubt that her clever aunt could bind easily-led Jion in a ribbon of lust, judging by how quickly he'd gathered a harem in his once-decorous manor. Either way Mother got the Su clan what they wanted. Ah, but *she* would not be raised to empress or empress dowager.

Did Mother have her own plans for deflecting Su Siar?

Manon's gaze lifted to her mother's narrowed eyes. Her fingers tightened in her skirt, but her expression was smooth, under her control. She would face such maneuverings when she ruled the court, she reminded herself. Learning now how to use every weapon at her command was excellent practice for when at last she wore the empress's crown.

Only two persons in the imperial palace were utterly indifferent to the prospect of the Journey to the Clouds.

One was Afan Yskanda, who hoped to remain behind with the majority of the servants. But the emperor did not intend to permit Yskanda far from his sight until Tek Banu returned with his father — whoever he was.

Yskanda was told that he would accompany the court artist.

At least, Yskanda discovered, he was not to be housed with Court Artist Yoli on the enormous floating city that constituted the emperor's sampan. Instead, he was to ride on First Imperial Prince Jion's boat.

"This means," Yoli said, "you'll be expected to sketch the events involving the young generation."

"And you will have the ministers and the ceremonials to sketch?" Yskanda asked.

"Exactly. If a betrothal treaty is negotiated, we will both be there to combine our efforts," Yoli added. "I ought to warn you. You might think that your room in the palace is small."

At this, Yskanda hid a smile: the room he'd shared with First Brother and Mouse had been half its size.

"The rooms we will be in are scarcely worthy of the word. More like trunks that you can stand up in, with no window, and barely enough space to unroll your bedding. Pack very, very lightly: two outfits only, and all the rest will be your inks and brushes."

"No windows?"

"The walls are mere lattices and silk, open under the roof.

There is no privacy. You'll hear every sneeze, but you'll be so tired you'll sleep anyway. There are fewer servants, so longer duties. The servants are housed in a narrow row in the middle of the boat, where they can be instantly summoned, and remain otherwise hidden from view behind long decorative screens. You will like those. As well, because you won't see anything else except when on duty," he warned.

Yskanda bowed. As long as he could avoid the emperor's personal boat, he would gratefully sleep in an actual trunk.

The second one indifferent to the Journey was Jion.

He wasn't thinking of it at all. His mind was still on finding a way to earn more freedom within the palace. He was ostensibly doing what was required, at least the outward forms. He and his harem on some nights simply drank together, playing various games. He even taught them pitch-pot, which his room was just large enough to accommodate. He had to use fine porcelain vases for the pots, but those could be replaced.

What pleased him was that he could do (or not do) what he liked, the women took no harm, and he had the reputation of enthusiastic obedience to his elders' dynastic wishes: once they married him off, surely grandchildren would promptly appear, securing the Jehan line.

The next and most difficult task he had left to the last.

One morning Vaion came to invite him to go riding. Along the way, very reluctantly, Jion asked, "Where and when do the scholars meet?"

Vaion's flash of surprise had a very strong element of misery shared. "We're still at Heavenly Pleasures," Vaion said with a heavy sigh. "Last hour of Phoenix all through Horse. First and third days."

Jion exclaimed, "Right when Manon's been coming to my manor. But of course the girls would be meeting in Heavenly Harmony over on the women's side of the palace, second and fourth days."

Vaion was about to repeat gossip he'd overheard between his mother and First Mother—that Manon was deliberately preventing Jion from resuming his studies—but he knew Jion would scoff. And he didn't even know if that was true. After all, if Jion really wanted to fight boredom at Heavenly Pleasures, all he had to do is send a polite note to Manon saying that he would be attending school with the scholars.

Sure enough, Jion said, "I'll have to remember to send

Fennel with an apology to Manon."

For the rest of their ride, except when they raced down the last stretch, their guards pounding determined behind, Vaion entertained himself with a lot of warnings about tedium, boredom, and dullness—as if Jion had forgotten how tiresome Master Zao's lessons were.

And it was exactly as dreary as he'd remembered.

Having sent Fennel to Manon with an apology, and a gift of a very pretty pair of pearl earrings, Jion attended the very next day. Master Zao droned on, making each scholar repeat the ancient lines with perfect enunciation, without allowing any discussion of meaning. He told them what each line meant and expected them to write his words down, and memorize those, too.

But after the stultifying session, toward the end of which he fought yawn after yawn, his reward was a genuine welcome from his cousins. Su Ysek—who used to break the tedium by running cricket races behind his inkstone and brush stand—insisted on sitting by him, though he no longer pulled pranks. The scholars had all grown, and many had begun low-level positions in the bureaucracy, though they still studied because they expected to take the next Imperial Examination. Even their families would not loft them to ministerial positions if they did not pass.

Once Old Zao departed, the scholars surrounded Jion to welcome him back. All exclaimed variations on how glad they were to see him alive, but he noticed that no one asked where he'd been, a lack that seemed more significant the more he thought about it. One or two not asking, he could understand. But everyone? In the past they had all been curious about the outer world. He wondered what warning they had been given, as if his time away were a disgrace.

The next day, Manon sent a maid with a message:

*Dare I ask how you like attending class once again?*

He sat down and scribbled an answer:

*You may dare. And I will dare an answer: it's exactly as tedious as it ever was. At least I understand what we are parroting back, or mostly. But we still are told what the ancients thought, instead of being able to discuss the meaning ourselves.*

To his surprise, Manon replied.

*If you wish to do that, as it happens, I planned to hold discussions during the Journey to the Cloud Empire — but with rewards. Since we do have to continue our studies. It is not solely a pleasure journey. How does that sound?*

He wrote back:

*I have one question. Is Master Zao to lead us? If so, I will run away again.*

But of course he did no such thing; the classes, he decided, were exercises in self-discipline. If his cousins and younger brother could endure it, he could. And did.

The result after a series of days in which he did not miss a lesson was an Imperial Edict, delivered by no less an august figure than Melonseed.

Jion had just finished breakfast, but on Fennel's spotting Melonseed on the way, the young graywing scudded into Jion's room to warn him. Jion called for a court robe, which Yarrow brought on the run. Jion was neatly robed and waiting in his formal hall when Melonseed entered and announced in a hieratic voice that he came to speak with the Emperor's Voice.

Jion knelt, his entire household behind him. He was fairly certain he wasn't in trouble — was he? — did someone see that ridiculous message he wrote to Manon about running away?

"Because his imperial majesty is pleased with the diligence of First Imperial Prince Jion, he has decreed that if his imperial highness desires to recommence his martial exercises, the west court will be open to him daily, any time during Phoenix watch. So it is decreed." Then the elderly graywing betrayed himself by a smile, his eyes crinkled kindly.

Jion made a forehead-to-the-floor bow, uttering his thanks to his gracious majesty, echoed by the household. At a glance from Whiteleaf, the graywing steward bowed to Melonseed and offered him a pouch of golden boaters kept for this express purpose. Melonseed departed, and Jion kept the court robe on, deciding he may as well get his morning bows made.

He went first to his father to thank him, then to his mother's and his grandmother's. Between these manors he gloated to himself. It wasn't perfect. That would be finding Redbark again, and facing Ryu every morning. How he had witlessly taken that for granted!

He was in the west court before the sun rose the very next morning. His heart pounded at the idea that his father might be there and watching, but he soon learned that the emperor never went there during the mornings, a fact that Jion found a relief and also curiously disappointing, for he wondered what sort of training his father had had.

He decided it was prudent not to ask—he did not want to risk anything changing his father's mind, especially since his grandmother had revealed why the emperor had spoken the edict that forbade the imperial children from even touching weapons. This was already an astounding break from that edict. He relished having sword in hand again, even if it was only wooden.

Enjoying the bigger court, and the feel of a sword in his grip, he swung into Redbark. The early morning hour, the sword and the space around him, brought Ryu so vividly to mind he closed his eyes, and imagined her next to him, matching movement to movement.

His reverie was so absorbing he was unaware of being watched narrowly by a gray-haired, barrel-chested sword-master from the balcony overlooking the court. Presently a few young, low-level imperial guards entered the court, all with strict instructions ringing in their ears: no matter how hard the prince hit, they could not harm him, on pain of death.

Jion sensed it almost immediately in their stances, their grim, set faces. He said nothing. He knew that in scrapping, action would be more convincing than words. As the hour went on, he saw in the covertly exchanged glances, and the slightly relaxed faces their discovery that he had both the will and the control to pull his blows so that no one walked out of that court with any more than a smart tap.

At the end of the hour, he did not drop his sweaty-handled weapons on the ground and expect the others to tend them, but headed unconsciously, as one with the habit, to the wipe cloths and then to the rack to store them neatly. "Army trained," someone whispered, and that passed from lips to ears as fast as the wind.

# TWENTY-EIGHT

THE SECOND DAY WAS the same, though they came at him harder, at his repeated plea. And again with the third.

Once word went through the guards that the prince knew what he was doing, but he was not using them as target practice, what had at first seemed an unwanted duty became popular; everyone wanted to see his singular warmup drill, and they especially wanted to see the first imperial prince make the staff hum.

Jion found it difficult to separate himself off from his Redbark habits, which meant a lot freer behavior than was normal between the imperial family and those who served them. He even began to learn the names of some of the guards.

A few days before the court was to depart on the Journey to the Clouds, the swordmaster was called to report to the emperor. "The swordmasters who had the training of him were skilled, your imperial majesty," he said — and though he was an unimaginative and honest man, decades of survival in the imperial palace caused him to add, "His imperial highness the first prince clearly learned good habits in his time in the army, however short. What's more, his time among the criminals did not spoil those habits."

The emperor knew immediately why the swordmaster had amended his words, but let it pass. It might even be true. He turned his mind to what was far more interesting: "How can you tell there was more than one instructor? How many?"

"At least three, your imperial highness." And at a sign to continue, he said, "When his imperial highness is paired with one or more, he uses our current methods of fighting in line. This old incompetent of no talent might be wrong in seeing some of Old Fumig there — now he's Instructor Fumig, out at Loyalty. We served together early on." Seeing impatience in the emperor's forehead, he passed over the reminiscence he would have shared at length with anyone else. "But there's the *old* drill in there, too. During the days when your imperial majesty and their imperial highnesses each had one body-guard," he explained. "That training took longer, your imperial majesty — much longer — well, you know. Goes right down to the bone. It's the style you favor, if you catch my meaning."

The emperor looked up sharply at that. "Do you by chance know the name of this instructor?"

"Not for certain, but his imperial highness did not learn that in the army. It might be a result of his experiences in Redbark Sect. We suspect that the swordmaster in the criminal world was once one of ours before he joined the Redbark Sect."

"What was his name?"

The swordmaster blinked in surprise at the sharpness of the question.

"I believe the ferrets have reported that, your imperial majesty. Leastways, they did to me. Man's name was Duin."

"Duin," the emperor repeated. "But he died the Night of Blood, defending my mother. I distinctly remember that."

"Could be another Duin, your imperial majesty. Common enough name. In any case, this Duin is also dead. His imperial highness, and Chief Fai, both say that the swordmaster of this Redbark Sect that his imperial highness briefly traveled with was dead before his imperial majesty joined what was left of said sect. Which was all of one or two boys."

"Ah." The emperor sat back, clearly losing interest.

The swordmaster finished his report, and left, puzzled.

He was still puzzling over it later that night, when he met his wife in their snug little bedroom in the building off the imperial guards' main training court. They invariably retired early, as both had to be on duty before the sun rose.

She, a seamstress under the Imperial Household, put away her embroidery tambour and studied her mate of twenty-five years, whose frown between his brows meant he had something on his mind. "What troubles you, Husband?"

The swordmaster had been thinking back over the conversation with the emperor, and then considering what he'd seen in the first imperial prince. "There's something in the prince's fighting style. And in parts of his drill. Reminds me of that bodyguard back in the old days, the one who used to shadow the emperor, who was a prince then. What was his name?"

"Danno," his wife said. "Ayah, he was so handsome — why do you think the maids used to come watch the competitions? It was to see him win. And if we were really lucky, his robe would stick to his ribs. Very fine ribs. And all the rest, too."

She smiled reminiscently as the swordmaster choked on a breath, and gasped out, "Wife!"

"Ayah, who is around to hear me except for you?" she scolded fondly.

He blinked. "Of course, of course. I find myself surprise-ed . . . I thought you attended to see excellence in skill . . . I did not think young maids had thoughts like that."

"Why should we be any different than you boys, who used to make extra trips to the laundry, just to catch the comeliest maids in their wet clothes as they stamped and scrubbed sheets? We just were not as loud — except among ourselves. You boys, always fighting day and night, what did you know about girls?"

The swordmaster had to acknowledge the truth of this observation, but it did not give him much comfort. He reverted firmly to the previous subject. "In any case, he was the one. There's something in the prince's style that brings him to mind. The emperor was asking about it, earlier, but I couldn't recollect his name, and then I got distracted by the details of Chief Fai's report about the dead swordmaster Duin." He repeated the conversation, then turned to her. "Ought I to write a memo, and bring Danno up?"

"No," she said emphatically. "No. That name was forbidden for years, and then forgotten. Let it stay forgotten. No good can possibly come of bringing it up again, especially as there isn't the least scrap of evidence your mystery swordmasters have anything to do with Danno, who surely is long dead. You said yourself, how one swordmaster influences another, and they pick up styles and moves from one another, much the same way we pick up a new stitch, or an exceptionally clever design."

"True, true," he observed, still troubled that he might have inadvertently misled his emperor. To reassure himself, he said, "Patterns from our imperial training are bound to show up among the criminals in one form or another, until those who ran the Night of Blood are either killed or die of old age."

It was his wife's turn for discomfort. She shivered under her warm quilt, hating to recollect the terror of that night, and how she had hidden among the dye vats for what felt like an eternity that was broken only by screams and shouted threats. "Does anyone know how many of us died that night, and how many fled?"

The swordmaster sighed. "Not that Old Fai has ever said to me. So many chases going clear out to the bay, this faction against that faction. Terrible. Up in the imperial hunting preserve behind the palace, Old Fai told me once, every year or two another set of bones turns up there, usually after snowmelt. You're right." He leaned over to blow out the candle. "Bringing up an inauspicious name is like expecting good luck when a hen starts crowing."

His wife settled next to him, then chuckled in the dark. "Oh, the heartburnings when Danno ran off with that bride the very day that terrible storm struck the island, and caused the river to flood. And the storybooks that circulated hand to hand after! My favorite was the one that said the two weren't drowned, but were rescued by Blessed Suanek, and taken away over the eastern sea to a land among the clouds."

At the same moment, Fai Anbai was reporting to the emperor as the later glanced through a sheaf of depositions. ". . . and rumors are going through the imperial guard that his imperial highness First Prince Jion spent time while away under cover at an army training fortress to evaluate the training."

The emperor looked up at that. "Really? Who originated it, do you know? And has this fortress been named?"

"No, and no, your imperial majesty. But we suspect it's speculation that by the third or fourth set of ears has been accepted as imperial decree, in the way rumors often evolve."

"Interesting," the emperor said. "And yet there is still the matter of someone having tried to assassinate him. Twice."

Fai Anbai bowed.

"But . . . do not impede spread of that rumor," the emperor added. "It might sharpen up the training. Never a bad thing."

And lend a veneer of respectability to the prince's missing years: this went unspoken.

Fai Anbai was dismissed about the same time that Jion was preparing to receive Sia Na, her tea master friend, and a pillow maid who had a talent at baking. These women were just bringing in a handsome feast when a little maid scudded in the servants' entrance to tell Whiteleaf that her imperial highness First Princess Manon was coming this way!

From Whiteleaf to Yarrow to Jion, who exchanged a startled glance with Sia Na. He said, "Everyone, stay in here." He swept his hand around his bedroom.

He pulled on a day robe, and went to his formal room to meet his sister.

She entered wearing dark clothes and a veiled hat.

Jion hurried forward to greet her. "Are you well? Is there something wrong?"

With one gesture Manon ripped the hat off her head, and tossed it aside, revealing eyes so wide they reflecting the lamplight in twin flames. "Tell me," she said, low and urgent, "you are not truly fighting over in the imperial guards' court."

Jion drew her to a sofa, and sat down next to her. He couldn't smother a soft laugh, but at an injured look, and a sheen of tears in her eyes, he said, "Imperial Father handed down an edict. Even if I did not want to go, I had to. But I do."

"Why? It is so dangerous!"

"Who told you that?" Jion retorted. "Manon, it's not the least dangerous. We do warmups, and then play around with scrapping. Wooden swords, wooden everything. And all the weapons stay right there in the courtyard. I don't even own a knife." He held out a hand as if inviting her to search.

She compressed her lips, and it occurred to him that she demonstrated no surprise about the edict. Presumably she would know all that. Why then was she here? "Manon?" he repeated.

She looked away, then back. "I realize that Imperial Father approves . . . but . . ." She lowered her voice, and leaned toward him. "Have you considered that he is still angry about your four years away from the family? He might not *intend* to put you in the way of danger . . ."

"And what, cause an accident that kills me in the court-yard?" Did Manon really think that would frighten him? He shook his head, trying not to laugh. "If Imperial Father wanted

me dead, I probably would have vanished over the side of the
ship after the ferrets caught up with me. And a suitable story
concocted thereafter. Or I could have died in Lotus Blossom
Square if he wanted to give the rest of you a demonstration. It
could have—and still could—happen so many ways. But I
really don't think he would permit the first year guards to
crack my skull for me. Think how much face the imperial
family would lose!"

Her mother had been furious when they found out that
Jion was being permitted weapons training. To the second imperial consort, that was an extremely dangerous precedent,
Jion being granted a special privilege not offered to the other
imperial children. Manon agreed, and found it the more objectionable in that it was something father and son shared—and
she did not.

In the past, Jion had always sought her approval. He still
loved her, she knew. It was time to exert herself, and recover
what she had lost.

Lost! Her eyes burned with tears. "Beloved brother, I see
you being pushed in a direction you never wanted to go, and
I grieve," she said, low. "The weapons court. The scholars.
And you watch. Next it will be your wedding they are going
to negotiate."

He flinched, as she suspected he would—what boy wants
a wife when he can have as many lovers as he wants? Then he
said said, "You're older. Yours probably will come first."

He saw that impact her, and took her hands. "That did not
sound right. Honored Elder Sister Manon, your worries on my
behalf are diamonds and jade to the spirit. But I'm doing all
right—Father has repeatedly said he's pleased with me."

"And it's destroying the life you wanted, a step at a time,"
she said. "Oh, how I miss the days when you came to Drenched Blossoms and we danced together. Then you danced the
ancient sword and shield for me. Don't you want to continue
the lessons? You said you wished to master the Leap dances."

Jion flashed a grin. "The Leap dances are even more
dangerous than my playing around in the weapons court with
the imperial guards, who all know I will never have to defend
myself. It's all just play, Manon. I'll never be in the front line
of any battle."

"Really?"

"Emperor Father would have their heads if any of them

put me in the slightest danger."

Manon gave a quiet sigh of relief. Then she began fervently, "When I—" She stopped there, but they both heard the obvious follow-on, *When I inherit the throne*. It would be inauspicious, and unfilial, at the very least to finish those words.

She pressed her lips together, then said, "What I wish for
is you to have a happy life, a carefree one. As you always
wanted. Protected by those who care most for you."

"I enjoy my life now, Honored Elder Sister. And a lot of
that I owe to you. Is there anything else? Will Honored Second
Mother be looking for you?"

There was that in the quirk of his eye and the curve of his
lips that reminded her he was now a young man, and young
men were seldom alone at night. "I forgot your pillow maid
harem," she said crisply. "I ought to go—I have taken up your
time to no purpose."

"You don't have to go," he said, but he rose with her, still
holding her hand. "It means so much to me that you have
always been my most steadfast friend even after I returned in
total disgrace. And I try to be as much a friend to you. We are
living proof that the Dragon Throne does not poison every
imperial family."

Her gaze slid away as he laughed again. "Aside from that,
I hope you enjoy yourself *once* in a while. You can't always
study." He rolled his eyes in the direction of his bedroom.

"The elders are still very traditional," she said. "We princesses have to be discreet."

Everyone had to be discreet, he could have countered, and
princesses had pretty much the same freedoms, and
constraints, as princes. But he was not about to argue over
what she clearly considered to be a distasteful matter.

His intuition was right. Or nearly right. She took a step
toward the door, wanting that subject left behind, for it was a
subject that still troubled her; she knew the feelings. Fought
the feelings. What she saw in rare glimpses of the elders'
passions was that surrender meant a loss of control, which led
directly to a loss of power.

She would do *nothing* that might lose power. Her goal was
to gain it.

He leaned down to kiss her cheek. She picked up her hat,
and joined the maid waiting obediently out in the hall. The
maid picked up her lantern, and they vanished into the night.

# TWENTY-NINE

ARI HAD NOT WANTED to go southward into the heart of the empire, where the great imperial capital crouched like a dragon preparing to leap. But Benevolent Winds Island lay to the south, just above Ran at the west end of the Inner Islands.

At least it was the opposite end of the Inner Islands from the imperial island.

Over that first week after leaving Sky Island, she and Lie Tenek had sailed with a gallant wanderer trader going to Tortor Island. Ari and Lie Tenek left the ship on the last stop before, knowing that it was difficult to get on and off that reef and rock-protected island.

They found a tiny inn and sat cross-legged on the floor of their equally tiny room. Both stared down at the collection of coins before them: strings of bronze cash, a dozen boaters, and three gold pieces.

"What do you think?" Ari said finally. "It looks like wealth to me, but five tinnies is wealth where I come from. I'm no good at calculations."

Lie Tenek had been rapidly figuring on a mental abacus.

Ari said, "What I want to know is, how long will it last?"

Lie Tenek thumbed her chin thoughtfully. "It depends on how you mean to live. If you are your usual frugal self, this will get you easily through the rest of the year. If you live high, it could be gone in a month. You're certain you don't want to slip into the capital?" She made a sign warding bad luck. "Flame-in-Ice. What a name for a city. It sounds inauspicious."

Ari shrugged. "It sounds pretty. Or, did. I pictured icicles with the sun catching in them. I saw that, the years I was at the fortress. But I learned that the name comes from strange blue flame burning there, in or near the mine. It's supposed to be a fine sight from a distance."

Lie Tenek didn't care about blue flames. "I'm reasonably good at drifting into places. No one pays much attention to plainly dressed girls. It's the boys they give the wolf-eye. Especially places where gunpowder is either stored or made. Even fireworks."

Ari shook her head decisively. "Maybe that's why I've heard that at Benevolent Winds, there's no slipping in. It's an imperial island. They hate gallant wanderers. I'm quite sure that Matu's mother entered modestly. The grandparents probably did as well, counting on their plain dress and gray heads to enable them to look around. None of the three sounded like they were foolish, or brazen. And they weren't inexperienced! And yet all three vanished along with the father. I'll wager they were spotted as gallant wanderers—and if the rumors I heard at the Sky Island competition are right, they were probably arrested as soon as they got off the boat, on some pretext or other."

"Are you changing your mind, then?" Lie Tenek asked, chin in hand.

"No. Perhaps we need to go to Benevolent Winds as the opposite of gallant wanderers. Disguised as rich people. Not one of those rumors said anything about snatching the rich off the streets."

"Rich what? Nobles? *They* certainly would be safe enough from being snatched off the street and shoved into mines. But what would be our purpose? I've never heard that it's an island where rich nobles go, unless they have family or trade in brimstone."

"We can't go as nobles," Ari said. "One thing I learned being around one—"

"The mysterious Shigan I kept hearing so much about?"

"Yes."

"Who got taken by the imperials while they left you behind. Why?"

"That is his story to tell, as my old tutor used to say. And I only know a little of it. The important thing is, I learned that nobles get trained to think, and talk, and even walk a certain way from the time they are babies. I can't fake it. Can you?"

"I doubt it," Lie Tenek admitted. "I see them from a distance strutting about, and I can make fun of the little steps the women make, but you and I did not spend days and days walking back and forth across the inner court, up the stairs and down again, with teacups on our shoulders and our heads. If we're pretending to be newly-wealthy merchant girls? That I can do. But again, why would we go there? We'll have to have a likely story."

"Looking for work, which lets us ask questions. My first thought was to pose as dancers, but what if they want us to dance?" Ari said, sighing.

Lie Tenek shook her head. "I can't dance, not well enough to pose as an expert. Anything we do, if we pose as experts we have to be convincing. So . . . how about businesswomen? We want to start an entertainment house."

Ari's eyes widened. "Can you sound like an expert?"

Lie Tenek made a face. "I know how my aunt ran hers. But most of her custom was farmers at harvest time, New Year's Two Moons, and Spring Festival. She got enough custom from caravans to stay in business, but she wasn't wealthy."

"I think we need to be wealthy," Ari stated. "Everyone smiles at wealth."

Lie Tenek looked down at the coinage and went back to stroking her chin, this time with three fingers.

Ari said, "There's one possibility. I looked on the navigator's chart. It's not a straight line from here to Benevolent Winds Island. It's pretty much a triangle whichever way we go. But a small one. It might be worth it to go a little out of our way to consult Madam Nightingale. She did invite Redbark back . . ."

Lie Tenek had heard of Madam Nightingale. She gave Ari a skeptical glance. "She invited Redbark, or the handsome and mysterious Shigan?"

"Ayah, yes," Ari admitted. "They called him Comet, but yes. It was he they invited back. However, if I promise her that if he turns up again he comes to her first, perhaps she might help us . . ."

The ship journey was short and uneventful.

An hour after they clambered down the ramp, they were conducted in Madam Nightingale's elegant office, which was painted a soft peach, the furniture edged with pearl.

She regarded the two new arrivals, and sighed. "Before you try making any promises you can't keep, you ought to know that my sister wrote to me over winter. She doesn't pretend to completely understand the scholar tongues, but she knew enough to surmise that the imperials were not going to let your Shigan go willingly. I don't know if he robbed some duke or led a rebellion, and I don't want to know. With the imperials, it's always better to know nothing they can drag out of you. But dangling the name Comet to get entrance to my office . . ."

Ari was genuinely affronted. "I apologize sincerely, Madam Nightingale, but I didn't dangle his name, I only used it so you could identify me. When I was here before, I was dressed as Ryu."

"And now you're a girl," Madam commented dryly. "Are *you* by any chance in trouble with the imperials?"

"No," Ari promised. "Surely Madam Swan told you in her letter, they questioned us and let us go. My partner here and I aren't even planning to stay. We just need some advice."

"Advice," Madam repeated, not unpleased — few dislike being asked for advice. But she was a businesswoman, aware that time was the great enemy to women in her work. Every coin she put by now would be a comfort during the winters of old age. "My experience does not come without a price." She didn't miss how the girl and the young woman before her exchanged glances, before the one-time Ryu said grittily, "We'll pay."

"What is it you want to know?"

"How to present ourselves as first rank entertainment house proprietors," Ari said. "We want to start a business in a wealthy town."

"First, what town?" At Ari's habitual hesitation, she added, "I believe you are already familiar with my sister's and my discretion. I don't pretend to know everything about every town, for customs vary widely, as I am certain you are aware. But that goes for custom among merchants, even those under the same emperor. A great deal depends on the local governor and officials, to give one example."

"Flame-in-Ice, the capital of Benevolent Winds."

Madam's brows lifted. "Benevolent Winds," she repeated slowly, in a musing tone. "What do you wish to do there?"

"Rescue someone from a mine," Ari said.

"Ah-h-h-h," Madam sighed. She spoke in a reflective voice after a short pause. "This changes everything. Yes. I'll help you. And you needn't worry about charges."

"Do you have someone who needs rescuing from one of the mines?" Ari asked, thinking: *four* people?

"No. I know nothing about the mines, except that they are widely regarded as miserable places, to which the imperials retort that they only send murderers there, rebels, and other hardened criminals, when sentenced to labor for Imperial Works."

"The people I mean to rescue are not any of those things," Ari said in protest.

"The imperials find it convenient to regard gallant wanderers as such. Until they need them as go-betweens and the like. Never mind that. Let us say that I have a specific grudge against the governing family in particular, and I would very much like to see them thwarted, even in such a small way as removing some of the poor victims they force through those gates to Hell." *If your friends are still alive*, she added to herself, but could not say it to Ari's hopeful, honest gaze.

She cleared her throat. "First, the appropriate clothing . . ."

Two days of shopping at too many stores to count passed.

Thoroughly bewildered, Ari sat in Madam Nightingale's office as Madam served fine tea in cobalt and gilt porcelain. "Now that you are adequately accoutered, you will need two maids, at the very least. No one will believe you are wealthy girls born to the merchant class without maids."

Ari and Lie Tenek accepted this stricture with sober attention.

"I've considered carefully, and though there are several of my girls who're willing to go along with you, I've narrowed it down to two, Oriole and Rosefinch. What I'm about to tell you stays between these walls."

Ari and Lie Tenek murmured assent.

"Oriole was raised as a thief, until her father was caught and had his hands chopped off. He didn't last long after that. Her mother abandoned her, and she ended up with me. She doesn't steal from me or my custom, unless I ask her to, and she won't steal from you," Madam said bluntly. "She is very popular with men. They brag to her to get her attention, and she learns things without ever having to ask a question. As for Rosefinch, when someone made up the saying 'five aunts and ten grandmothers,' they might have been thinking of Rosefinch. She's incurably interested in everyone's business. But she knows that, and she will accept being told no. I want to send her along because you won't find anyone better at noticing things. Hearing things on the street, from counter tenders in shops, even from the servants loitering outside an establishment as they wait for master or mistress to conclude their business. What you will get is someone to tend your new wardrobes and carry your parcels."

Ari clasped her hands and bowed. "I do not wish to insult you, or them, but how much do they expect to be paid? I ask because I have a certain amount, and how long I'm able to stay there depends on how fast that goes."

"I already thought of that," Madam returned, unperturbed. "Oriole will make certain they come out very well. And she will not interfere with your concerns."

"Oh." Ari thought of the newly purchased trunk of fabric, ribbons, shoes, fans, and headdresses in the room she shared with Lie Tenek, and was relieved. A trunk! She was used to carrying all her worldly belongings easily slung over one shoulder.

"Now. You have the clothes, you have the maids," Madam Nightingale said. "I've put out feelers about the right type of ship for you to hire. It's time to work on the two of you. You cannot think or act like martial artists and remain convincing. A martial artist is going to immediately recognize that cat-walk of yours as a martial artist's walk."

"Cat walk?" Ari repeated, looking down at her feet.

Madam's smile was crooked. "You know martial artists by the way they move, correct?"

"Yes, but—"

"They will know you the same way."

"Oh."

"Your first lesson is one that women have honed over centuries in order to survive: men come to entertainment houses for all the usual reasons, but under it all they come to be made to feel important. The more demure you act, the more demands you can make. If you are barely able to pick up a fan, you'll have every man in the room competing to pick it up for you. And when the inevitable search comes through after you take away your miners, no one will think twice about delicate flowers barely able to lift a golden spoon. Let's begin with your walk. The simplest way to change it is to put pebbles in your shoes, but I do not believe you need go that far . . ."

They practiced while Madam's trusted contacts made inquiries about hiring a ship.

Living at the edge of the empire and the gallant wanderer world, there was a great deal of business talk at tea houses during the afternoons warming in the spring sun, and dance emporia at night. Someone knew someone else, who had a brother, who was married to the daughter of . . . and so on, until they found a cheerful man of about thirty-five, his consort acting as his navigator. Their two children were part of the sailing crew. This family earned their living by renting out the beautiful little ship he had inherited from his grandfather, which he couldn't bring himself to sell. It was built as a pleasure boat for a low-ranking noble family who had subsequently fallen afoul of someone higher up. It was largely useless for carrying goods, but oh, it was so fast!

All Ari's ship journeys so far had been a slow negotiation between wood, wind, and water. But this ship was designed a lot like the navy couriers, and the wind seemed to curl around it, glimmering with Essence promise. Ari thought about her brothers occasionally, but the first day on that ship reminded her somehow of Yskanda, who always used to look so wistfully at the sea, his eye catching on the more graceful boats as they slanted against the wind.

"What's amiss?" Rosefinch stepped up beside her. "You look seasick."

"Do you see her heaving over the side?" Lie Tenek asked. "That's not seasick."

"Oh. Forlorn? Did you leave a lover behind?" Rosefinch asked, her unremarkable face intently interested.

Madam was right, Rosefinch was incurably nosy.

Acutely embarrassed, Ari mumbled, "Nothing."

Oriole appeared, catching her long hair with one hand, and winding it around her wrist. "Rosefinch, let be."

Rosefinch sighed, but turned away without any sign of resentment.

Ari gratefully bobbed a bow toward Oriole, who put a finger to her lips and dropped a merchant's bow, hands clasped in sleeves, bending slightly from the waist. Ari bowed correctly, and they all resumed walking about the deck.

She spent most of the following journey on deck, exhilarated at the sails piercing the flying clouds, the bow breaking the waves that foamed along the sides and rippled behind in a widening V through the vast, restless sea. Some-day, she thought as she gazed toward the clouds scudding high above them, I will ride across the sky.

Her entire body prickled with possibility as she stood on her toes, so buoyant she felt as if she could float away.

# THIRTY

BENEVOLENT WINDS EMERGED ON the horizon two days before Ari expected to see it.

Many of the islands she had been to so far had been small, a size that seemed natural to her. Most were dominated by a single mountain. The western end of the empire was dotted with these, the greater proportion of which were uninhabitable rocks jutting up like broken teeth. This was the area, and the type of island, that made up most of gallant wanderer territory.

When she got a closer look at Benevolent Winds, she began to perceive why the imperials seldom troubled themselves over those small jutting rock islands. It took two days and nights to sail along the shoreline of the island, along the middle of which rose a series of mountains, like the bumps along the spine of a great beast. At last they reached the harbor, also the capital, which like most imperial harbors faced the southeast.

At this end of the island, the mountains were smallest, the land the most fertile, fed by a river that gathered all the inland streams. The south side of the city was built along a gentle slope that angled down toward the river. This bank, with its fine year-round western breezes, was where the wealthy had their homes and shops. As the ship drifted in on the tide, they could see beautiful roofs with upturned eaves sporting at least one or two guardian spirit statues. The whole was dominated by the governor's palace with its double roof, and seven guardians on the eaves. Everything but the roofs was obscured by high walls, and flowering trees in extensive gardens.

On the north side of the river, the houses were crowded in a jumble. This side of the city, Ari and Lie Tenek shortly would discover, lay just out of reach of the clean western winds, blocked by jutting palisades along which the garrison was built. The north side was where the occasional pungencies from the brimstone that furnished the island's main trade item formed a miasma, especially in summer.

The north side had also by far the largest population — the common folk.

Scarcely the time it took to burn a single incense stick, and already Ari hated whoever governed the island, though she knew that the city had existed in this state for centuries. She was very aware of the stares along the dock from the gorgeous ship with its painted scarlet sails with the gilded slats, and its many banners and flags. She stared back, dismayed by what seemed to be a swarm of blue and brown: the imperial army.

"There are so many of them," she murmured to Lie Tenek from behind her fan. Both stood at the rail, dressed in fluttering silks. "Is there a war?"

"War! Ayah! This is a very rich island," Lie Tenek responded. "Pirates and the like would love to get hold of all the brimstone brought out of here. I'm sure these warships're all guards for the cargo ships carrying brimstone. Oh, and they might be on liberty for Kraken Boat Festival."

Kraken Boat Festival. How could Ari forget that? She hoped that the inns wouldn't be charging far higher prices because of it.

As a breeze toyed with the ends of the ribbon hanging down from her high-piled hair, she brushed them back impatiently. She disliked these flimsy clothes with the many panels and the long floating sleeves, which caught on everything she passed if she wasn't careful. But the robes did force her to a slower, more demure walk.

The ship drifted up to a wharf, which Ari had learned was going to cost her one of those gold pieces. Whatever happened, she wanted the fastest retreat possible, just in case.

As if to underscore her tension, the sound of drums signaling the hour reverberated from the garrison on its palisade overlooking the bay. The drum towers, and the tiger-eye dynasty banners rippling in the wind, were forcible reminders that they were back within the reach of the imperials. Very few gallant wanderer or independent towns could keep a city guard, much less pay for timekeepers or fast couriers — or the warren of scribes to register and administer a city.

Oriole hungrily eyed the bright banners with the extra-long streamers, representing the kraken's tentacles. Lie Tenek leaned against the rail, studying the warships out of the corner of her eye. Rosefinch's gaze darted everywhere, taking it all in. She and Oriole exchanged nods: the fine decorations promised a wealthy town — at least on the south side.

Dock workers sprang to help the sailors settle and secure the ramp, hoping for largesse from this wealthy-looking vessel. Ari had prepared an embroidered pouch for the purpose, and readied herself to descend. It seemed like everyone in the entire harbor was staring, including all those warriors.

"Flirt," Lie Tenek breathed, smiling coyly.

It was all very well, Ari thought, to teach her five or six poses typical of successful entertainment house women. But when it came time to put all this new knowledge into practice, she likened it to teaching a scholar or a baker five or six martial arts moves and a week later putting the baker or scholar into a duel with a master.

In other words, though it all had sounded reasonable, and practicing in Madam's room had been easy, when it came to remembering it all she was a centipede trying to remember which foot to move first.

Luckily, Lie Tenek did not feel the same way. "I'm going to be my mother-cousin," she confided to Ari as they approached the ramp. "Just copy me."

Lie Tenek turned from an easy-walking, practical person into someone who tripped along with tiny steps, her fan raised to hide half her face, her free hand delicately held out so that the embroidered butterflies on her knee-length sleeve caught the breeze.

Ari handed the embroidered pouch to Oriole — rich people did not sully their hands by doing transactions themselves — and stepped behind Lie Tenek, trying to shorten her strides.

Scouts for the finest inns, having seen the fine ship drift up on the tide, approached, and Lie Tenek took over. Ari hung back, her tongue completely tied, as, with elaborate politeness, it was determined that yes, they needed an inn, no, they did not belong to any great clan, yes, they were merchants here to mix business with pleasure. A scout—a young woman—detached herself from the crowd, and led them up a street thronged with people, but all Ari noticed were the sword-tasseled captains and the neat rows of half-armored army foot warriors. With a certain amount of dread she searched the faces among these, but none were former hut-mates from Loyalty Fortress.

Lie Tenek paid them no heed, twirling slowly. Ari assessed the defenses of the harbor as quickly as Oriole evaluated the young men in bright silks, their hair half bound with ribbons and flowing down their backs: wealthy scholars on holiday, looking for fun. She could work with that.

Ari glanced back, reassured to see Oriole and Rosefinch, the first tallish and thin, the second shorter than Ari and round as an apple. Lie Tenek haughtily directed a dock worker, who had put their trunks on a cart, as Oriole and Rosefinch followed meekly.

The inn Lie Tenek selected was midway up the street. It was named for Lu Frei's Owl in the folk tale. Lie Tenek hired a suite, and the four gathered in the central chamber. Ari counted up the costs that had been laid out so far, and to the three waiting faces, said, "Looks to me as if we've five days here. Six if we're careful."

Five days to break into mines, find Matu's family, and get them safely away.

"Disperse for information?" Oriole turned her gaze between Ari and Lie Tenek, the latter her own age. She had trouble believing a sixteen-year-old could be the chief of a group.

Lie Tenek turned to Ari, who said, "Let's eat first."

Rosefinch brightened at this. "I love Kraken Boat food!"

"Everybody does," Oriole said tolerantly.

They went out walking. Vendors caroled their wares everywhere: sticks of fried vegetables, pickled carrot strips curled into kraken tentacles, every type of noodle dish were most commonly seen. While traveling, Ari had thought it would be so simple: mention the word "mines" and angry or disgusted or betrayed people would willingly pour out information. But those blurred faces in her daydreams were not at all like the thin, square, pear-shaped, pale, ruddy, dark faces she looked into now. The only commonality shared by all these faces was intent on some important matter at hand. Not a one seemed to be talking about mines.

By the time they'd eaten a delicious meal of hot, spicy mussels made with noodles and savory-sour purple cabbage, the sun had vanished behind the western hill and businesses were closing up for the day—street vendors first, then stores.

When dark had fallen, music drifted on the sea breeze: the entertainment establishments were opening up. "Time to become peacocks," Oriole said. "People talk to peacocks."

Lie Tenek dressed in fashionable silks of shades of silver, peach, and spring green, her hair done up with golden hairpins decorated with pearls. Oriole and Rosefinch walked modestly behind her, dressed in brown and gray. They forayed downstairs, through the common room and out into the brightly decorated street.

Ari changed into one of her new outfits, and set out, mentally reviewing all Madam Nightingale's lessons. How hard could this be?

# THIRTY-ONE

THE ELITE OF THE imperial court was not celebrating Kraken Boat Festival—the departure day for the Journey to the Cloud Empire (also known as Journey to the Clouds) arrived.

The first leg of the journey involved travel by ship for a day and a night. Yskanda, safely housed in cramped quarters with the rest of the servants and thus out of the emperor's eye, found conditional enjoyment in being on the sea; on learning that the front of the ship was reserved to the imperial family, he stood shivering at the back for hour after hour, gazing down into the water in hopes of glimpsing the life there.

One gloomy morning he was almost knocked down by Second Imperial Prince Vaion, who was running the entire length of the ship just for something to do.

Vaion staggered to a halt and flushed. "Assistant Court Artist Afan! I did not see you there."

Yskanda bowed, apologizing for getting into the prince's way, even though they both knew he wasn't.

Vaion waved off the words. He knew that Jion liked talking to this assistant court artist at least as much as he used to talk to crusty old Court Artist Yoli. The court artists, like the loaf-wearing scribes, were not servants, but not a part of court. That made this assistant court artist—alone on the deck aside from sailors— someone Vaion could talk to. And he liked to talk. "Are you excited? I am! I get my own boat for the first time, instead of being stuffed in with my mother and Sesame Oil." His upper lip crimped with disgust.

"Sesame Oil, your imperial highness?"

"My mother's favorite," Vaion uttered with loathing, then eyed Yskanda, whose expression had altered from politeness to something Vaion couldn't read, but which reminded him of Jion's expression from time to time. Always accompanied by silence.

"What?" Vaion demanded impetuously.

Yskanda bowed. "This clumsy servant of no worth apologizes for any expression that might offend his imperial highness's eyes."

Vaion heaved a sigh. Jion thought highly of this assistant court artist, who wore that same sort of expression Jion had recently begun wearing when uttering words that, however polite, meant the same as a closing door. It was the court face, as impermeable as wood. It meant the subject was closed. However, Assistant Court Artist Afan was not a part of court, so Vaion tried again. "He's oily. One time I ran into my mother's room and found him painting her toenails, as if he was a maid."

Yskanda bowed. "This ignorant one wishes to know how large these boats will be."

Vaion mentally shrugged—that was definitely the door slamming, but at least he was polite. And Vaion didn't care about the subject enough to pursue it if he didn't get instant agreement, or at least sympathy.

He launched into an enthusiastic description of his sampan, on which he apparently expected to host many parties featuring hot wine and fun games. "Scholar Shan won't mind," he finished. "At least it's not Old Zao—I might as well be stuffed in with my sister and my mother and Sesame Oil if *that* were to happen."

"If this ignorant servant is permitted to ask his imperial highness a question, what can one expect to see in this famous passage?"

"It's a tricky one, full of rocks and waterfalls and flowers. But they all say that's what makes it interesting to look at."

Yskanda looked down at the water again. "May this ignorant one ask if there is swimming, your imperial highness?"

"Swimming!" Vaion exclaimed in the tone one might use

for *Execution!* "Seawater is dangerous!"

It was Yskanda's turn to sigh—the same words he'd been hearing all his life.

Vaion gave up on the assistant court artist. He continued his run. Yskanda continued to watch the water.

The next day, they arrived off the rocky peninsula of a jagged volcanic island that was dominated by a garrison outpost. On the north side of the peninsula lay a narrow bay, where a row of luxury sampans awaited the imperial party. These were decorated with banners from all twelve Houses of the Stars, and over all, the Tiger-Eye of the imperial Jehans.

After the emperor and his family boarded, the rest of the nobles followed, unaware of—uninterested in—the hundreds of people involved in protecting and serving them. Many nobles sent covert glances back and forth to see who had been invited, and where in the line they were placed. An army of imperial guards was stationed out of sight all along the route. Out in the waters surrounding the island patrolled warships in line of sight.

First Imperial Princess Manon watched the last of the transfer to make sure her orders had been carried out. As she swept her gaze over the servants crowded in the last boats, most clutching baskets and parcels, her eye caught the outline of a straight shoulder and the curve of a dark head above the palace service gray-blue. Her breath caught.

It was *him*.

For months, every single time she paid her morning visit to Grandmother Empress, her eyes had gone straight to that portrait of herself and Gaunon on the wall. It was easy to mentally edit out Gaunon, but impossible not to study her own features minutely, wondering what Afan Yskanda had been thinking as he painted each perfect detail. But she had not seen him until now. Her fingers trembled as she watched, her breath bated as she waited for him to turn, to search for a glimpse of her.

But he did not turn. She wrenched her gaze away—to recognize the vulgar spade chin of that common-born Scholar Shan, boarding her younger half-brother's boat. Between one heartbeat and the next, her conflicted emotions boiled to cold rage.

She knew instantly what had happened: a conspiracy

between the first consort and the third, ostensibly to oversee Vaion's studies. But of course Scholar Shan would want to intrude himself into Lily's marriage negotiations. Her fingers tightened on a fold of her robe. She longed to send her steward to toss him into the ocean to be eaten by sharks — but such a change in her plans could only have been approved by Imperial Father. She turned away again, catching a last glimpse of Afan Yskanda.

Completely unaware of this scrutiny, Yskanda was rowed to the imperial prince's craft, where kindly Steward Whiteleaf was on hand to point the way to his tiny cubby. It took the space of a heartbeat to put his scant belongings inside; then he withdrew to figure out what he was supposed to be doing.

Jion spotted Yskanda, delighted that his father had thought to put the assistant court artist with him, instead of squashed among the servants and old folks on the great dragon sampan. Jion anticipated seeing the Journey through Yskanda's eyes. "There you are! Let me introduce you to—"

"Cousin Jion!" The call came from smiling young man dressed in shades of yellow and green, leaning over the rail of a small flat boat being poled alongside the great sampans.

"Cousin Ysek! You escaped the dust piles of Registry?"

The young man whirled his fan in the air. "It was Great-Grandfather Su whose charms sprang the lock. Listen, cousin, no one has said a thing, so it seems this wearying, meddlesome cousin is left to ask: Where were you all those years? You must tell us everything!"

The prince uttered a laugh instead of an answer, and turned to greet another cousin. The prince was dressed very formally, the front part of his hair drawn up into a golden, pearl-encrusted clasp, the back part hanging loose except for three braids fastened with golden bands. He wore a kingfisher-blue over-robe, whose long sleeves nearly brushed the deck of the sampan. The gaps in the sleeves, and the slits up the side of the robe gave glimpses of the layers of silver, peach, and pale green, embroidered with golden dragonflies amid longan and peach blossoms. From the jade-studded belt round his narrow waist hung an elaborately carved ornament, with a tassel so long it reached the top of his knee, swinging and dancing at every step.

Yskanda comprehended at last that this was not a pleasure journey so much as a formal court event. That impression intensified as another boatload of elegantly dressed guests turned up, poled up by another slim craft with decorated awnings. He was surprised when Jion turned to him with a quick, apologetic smile before he was surrounded by a bewildering number of imperial relations and ministers' sons and daughters swarming the prince's craft, fans deployed with grace as they exchanged bows and greetings in the melodious courtly speech, amid a graceful dance of deference in which each seemed to know when, and how, to advance or retreat.

But where was Yskanda supposed to be? In a place like this his position seemed anomalous—his job was to record the journey, which meant being in the presence of the court and company, and not hidden behind the screens until summoned like the rest of the servants.

The scenery distracted him. The slanting ochre rays of the sun dimmed to a ruddy glow as the last bit sank beyond a jutting clifftop. The air abruptly turned plum-blue—and then the entire company fell silent, gathered in rank order, facing toward the emperor's sampan.

Whiteleaf gestured to Yskanda, pulling him toward the back of the vessel.

A gong reverberated, the echoes bounding between the striated, rocky cliffs to either side. Darkness gathered quickly, strengthened by clouds sailing overhead, blanketing the pure color of twilight. From up front echoed scraps of a ritual, a waft of incense drifting on the breeze. Then lamps were lit, first on the emperor's boat, making it look like a vessel of golden stars floating between dark water and equally dark night.

Next Imperial Princess Lily's sampan lit up, followed by the consorts' and then Manon's. Whiteleaf nodded to Fennel and Yarrow, who lit the lanterns hanging to either side—and light sprang into being around Yskanda.

Suddenly, from both sides of the rugged cliffs, hundreds of lanterns began floating skyward. All sizes and shapes, painted with dragons and phoenixes.

As they rose skyward, creating an arch of golden luminescence, from the front an elegant craft began to move down the line: the emperor was coming to greet his guests.

Lanterns hung along the canopy, the emperor's golden hair clasp effulgent in the glow. At his right stood the visiting prince from the east, a tall figure in deep green, the elaborate golden embroidery on his robe almost drawing attention from his prominent teeth and slightly receding chin. At least his hair was not the garish rust-colored frizz so commonly seen in many Easterners; it was dull mouse brown, barely visible beneath his elaborate headdress. At the emperor's left, straight as a wand, stood the Imperial Princess, and a step away First Imperial Princess Manon, who knew herself the most imperial-looking of the younger generation.

She needed the satisfaction, for she was very aware that the double-luck characters on the lanterns—while perfectly acceptable symbols for spring—were usually brought out for marriages. Imperial Father had, with this one alteration, completely changed her theme of dragons, statecraft and wisdom, to one of courtship.

She took it as a challenge.

They drew even with Jion's sampan. The young people gathered there bowed low; a flash of bright silk caught Manon's eye, and there was another unpleasant surprise: Su Siar—who was clearly starting her campaign to marry Jion. And make him emperor if she could.

The emperor gestured for them to rise, freeing them to utter greetings back and forth.

"Dear Niece," Su Siar called in her fluting voice. "The lanterns! That was an inspired gesture. I'm minded of a poem:

*The quiet waters flow,*
*spangled with ten thousand rising suns.*
*They take the music to the sky.*

You must have been thinking of Ar Laq at the river when you devised so beautiful a welcome."

The company applauded lightly, then Vaion's voice reached them from the next boat. "The lanterns rising were as fine as we saw them on Sky Wishes Day, when Elder Brother introduced this delightful style. He let them go like fireworks from around the imperial garden lake to the sound of that opera about the ghost lakes of Yinyong Island. I wish you had been there to enjoy it with us!"

Su Siar, midway along Jion's boat, cast a smile and a flirt of her fan back to Vaion. She turned the subject adroitly. "Your kind wishes give me almost as much pleasure as the deed." She then faced Jion. "Such a sight is better than a thousand phoenixes dancing and a hundred dragons flying—though I admit that I would like to hear again the Lament to the Ghosts at the Gate of Heaven."

Her voice carried over the quiet waters, and although Imperial Father was exchanging greetings, Manon knew he had heard. Further, he would hear beneath the compliment a reminder that she had merely copied Jion. Future rulers do not copy those they strive to transcend.

Everyone else might hear Su Siar's words as a graceful compliment, but Manon seethed, knowing them as a deft strike in their duel for the phoenix throne. Siar was going to use Jion as her weapon if she could.

Unless Manon could deflect that.

Manon composed herself, for the ministers were next. But she was aware of Jion's guests crowding around Su Siar, full of flattery and their own quotations about lanterns, stars, and reflections in water.

The only one detached enough to observe the whole was Yskanda, who noted a quiet, melancholy smile from the gentle Imperial Princess Lily. Yskanda turned to see whom she gazed at, and observed a glance of resignation in the countenance of a tall, high-browed young man.

The emperor's boat moved on down the line. Yskanda caught a last glimpse of the two princesses standing side by side, one less beautiful with an expression of calm acceptance, the other very beautiful indeed, but so full of frost.

Then they passed out of sight, and on Jion's boat, everyone was in motion now that the emperor was safely past. Vaion climbed precariously onto the rail of his sampan, heedless of his fabulously expensive clothes. He stood poised, arms raised, then he leaped to Jion's.

Yskanda, feeling awkwardly misplaced again—ought he to hide behind the screens or not?—jumped out of the way.

Vaion's long sleeves flapped like the wings of a graceless bird, then he tumbled onto the deck of Jion's boat, which was so heavy the shudder of his impact was scarcely perceptible. "Ayah, the deck is already wet," he muttered, standing up and brushing at his robe, which only succeeded in smearing the dampness farther over the fabric.

He noted Yskanda standing uncertainly, and flashed a rueful grin startlingly like Jion's. "Enjoying yourself?"

Whether Yskanda was or not, there was only one answer to be made, and after his bow of assent, Vaion asked, "Did Jion tell you who everyone is?"

"This ignorant servant suspects that his imperial highness meant to, but there was a sudden flood of arrivals, and then the sun set."

Vaion clapped him on the shoulder. "They're glad to see him with his own boat, and away from the tedium of Master Zao at last. Do you need anyone explained?" Vaion preened, very ready to show off. "I know everyone, of course."

Yskanda was grateful—now perhaps he could learn who he ought to be sketching among all these beautifully dressed people. "This unworthy one would be honored if his imperial highness might inform him who the one in blue with the popinjay butterflies on her robe is? She was addressed as Aunt. But she seems very young for that title."

"You did." Vaion chuckled, relishing the memory of Manon's stone face. "Great-Grandfather Su has a lot of consorts, so the generations are spread over years. A *lot* of consorts. Though Su Siar is only a year older than I am, she's Manon's aunt. Mine, too, by way of Second Mother," he said. "But she calls Gaunon and Jion and me Cousin, as we're not really related. She used to do school with us, until Manon got her sent home. Sometimes she uses her generation rank when Manon is especially nasty. I wish she'd use it more."

Yskanda glanced along the rail and mentally sketched the outlines of Su Siar's diminutive figure. She had the heart-shaped face of a warm russet shade so praised by the poets, with well-spaced eyes the color of cedar, dimples at either side of her red mouth, and a tiny star-shaped mole at the edge of her left eye, which was everywhere regarded as the Kiss of the Morningstar God.

Vaion added, "She just had a birthday, and with Jion back, I expect Second Mother will invite her more often to palace celebrations. The Su clan wants her to marry Jion, so my mother tells me. Manon hates that, and hates her. They once got in a fight, hair-pulling and kicking, until Manon threw Cousin Siar into the lake." He laughed at the memory. "I'd just started school with them. But sadly, it was never that exciting again. Anyone else?"

"The one with the high forehead, if your imperial highness would honor me with his identity. He's dressed in shades of amber and brown, with the crimson jujube patterns embroidered on his robe?" Yskanda blinked, becoming aware that the haloes around the lamps were not exhaustion, but drifts of fog.

"That's Ze Kai, our school sage," Vaion said. "Elder brother of my old friend Ze Bai." He then went on to point out his own Kui cousins and his particular friends until Jion emerged out of the gleaming silks, a whiff of hot wine trailing him.

"There you are, Vaion. Yskanda! Are you cold?"

At that moment, a moist surge of warm steam blew in their faces, smelling of damp rock. Jion laughed, then said, "We all ought to get some rest. We're entering into the fog, which means our silks are going to be clinging, damp, and squeaky—"

"That rice has already cooked," Vaion muttered, squeaking his armpit.

"Tomorrow will no doubt be a long one, beginning early for the cascades—and Manon has something prepared for school."

"Sure as rats bite," Vaion muttered—Yskanda was not alone in having seen that silent pain in Lily's and Ze Kai's faces. Or Manon's icy demeanor when Su Siar spoke.

"Cheer up," Jion said low-voiced to his brother. "At least we're free of Old Zao for a few days." And to Yskanda, "Do you think using a stick to whack scholars actually makes one learn better? What kind of tutor did you have?"

Both brothers looked inquisitively at Yskanda, who took refuge in protocol before saying. "This incompetent studied under a wandering monk, your imperial highnesses. If there is nothing needed of him, he will retire." Yskanda bowed himself out.

He returned to his cramped quarters, reflecting on the danger of discovering that he actually liked the two princes. And it was a danger. First Imperial Princess Manon was far easier to guard against: she behaved as he expected an imperial to behave, which kept him vigilant as well as disinclined to speak. The princes asked questions whose answers they seemed to genuinely want to hear—which was a bridge of knives.

As he settled as best he could in his cubby, which was already stuffy from the breathings of the servants all around him, he reflected that whether or not the emperor had assigned Yskanda to his sampan so that Jion could elicit information about his family, Yskanda had to remain firmly in the background. He knew enough history to be aware that imperial family life was inextricable from high politics. Emperors could, and had, executed their own blood relations in the name of treason, and Jion had to know as well. If the emperor summoned his son to find out what he'd learned from Yskanda, of course Jion would have to answer.

Silence was not just prudent, it was a shield.

Out on the balcony of the sampan, alone with Jion, Vaion stared after Yskanda for a time, until Jion said, "Why do you wear that expression, younger brother?"

"Oh, something that happened earlier. He reminds me a little of you!"

"Oh, how so?"

"Or I could be wrong. Mother says I ought to be learning to observe what is implied when it is not said. But my favorite cousins and my friends all say what they think, and nothing terrible happens." He scowled. "Is that because what we think doesn't matter? Take Sesame Oil, who I would get rid of if my opinion mattered. I said something about that, and I wondered if Afan Yskanda was saying something by silence, the way Grandmother does, and you've started doing." He repeated his earlier conversation, then said plaintively, "Don't you find Sesame Oil disgusting?"

"I have never seen him," Jion said.

"That's right, it was after you left that he started showing up more often. Then Imperial Father gave mother permission to make him a favorite, and we've never been rid of him since."

Jion looked amused. "Is that the worst you can say of him, that he paints your mother's nails?"

Vaion swung around to stare at him. "Then . . . the assistant court artist thinks I'm a prig?"

"Did he say so?"

"No—he wouldn't dare," Vaion muttered, and glared at his brother, and yes, there it was again. Jion's expression was just like Yskanda's. A very unpleasant thought struck him. "*You* think I'm a prig! That I sound like Manon!"

"Ayah, don't you?"

"That's not it at all! I just can't stand him. And what if they have a child! Mother is still young enough—they can have children at thirty-six, can't they?"

"So I'm told." Jion smothered a laugh, but then he gave

Vaion a pained glance. "If they do, I admit I'll feel sorry for that child. I can just hear you joining Manon in calling him a mutt. Consider what it would be like, to grow up in the palace the way Lily did, with one common parent. Given his common birth, might that be what Yskanda was thinking?"

Vaion's face tightened, and for the first time he resembled their father. Then his gaze dropped. "I see that, I suppose. The court doesn't say what they think because it's dangerous, so mother tells me. Servants don't say what they think because it's forbidden. The assistant court artist, who isn't a noble or a servant, doesn't say what he thinks because . . ."

"Because he's kind?" Jion asked. "And because he might have his own dangers, of which you are unaware?" He patted his brother's shoulder. "If you want opinions, go seek out Old Yoli. He will give you plenty of opinion."

Vaion shrugged. "What I want is someone to tell me I'm right. At least I have my own manor now."

Jion laughed. "Hop back to your floating manor. Tomorrow will be a long one."

# THIRTY-TWO

"IT TURNS OUT," ROSEFINCH said to Ari, Oriole, and Lie Tenek over breakfast the next morning, "a lot of the army captains in our inn are here for a wedding."

Lie Tenek nodded. "The wedding's in three days. That's all anyone was talking about. The bride is the governor's daughter, so all the locals are expecting parades and fireworks."

Oriole added wryly, "From what I overheard, it seems the governor's family isn't quite important enough to be invited to the Journey to the Clouds, so they've decided that holding a wedding on the festival day is auspicious. The wedding procession will follow after the Kraken Parade."

"I heard that, too. But the interesting thing is," Rosefinch said, "there's to be a party going to the mines to see the blue flames at sundown, for those who don't want to watch the kraken boat races this afternoon."

"They're going to more than one mine? How many are there?" Ari asked.

"They mentioned an old mine, underground, and a new one on the surface not far from the old one. It wasn't really clear."

Ari sighed. "All I found out was that there are two big barns, both owned by the government, or the governor. I don't know the difference. I don't care what it is. I can't get a horse."

At both these barns, the stable hands seemed to take

pleasure in informing her that, whether buying them outright or trying to hire horses, no one got anywhere without what amounted to a judicial interrogation as to the purpose of the ride. *You can't even hire a chicken,* one stable hand declared, spitting on the ground. *Horses, cows, medicine shops, it's all owned by the governor's family. The only hire is the river and canal boats. Everything in this city is carried on water.*

"*Nobody goes inland*? she'd asked.

The man's eyebrows shot skyward. *Inland,* he'd exclaimed, as if she'd asked to see the governor's bedroom. *Who would go there? Nothing grows inland but biting insects and snakes and other demon creatures, each worse than the last. And the mines. And no one goes near there. Unless under guard, and a yoke for criminals.*

"Can you find out when that touring party is leaving, and from where?" Ari asked.

"Already did," Rosefinch declared cheerfully.

Ari sighed again. She'd only had the two conversations in an entire day of trying to find things out. At the end of the second the stable hand had stared at her as if she were a stench bug just crawled out of his steamed bun, and added, *Why do you want to know where the mine is?* She'd mumbled something about wanting to avoid it, and slunk away. But Rosefinch and Oriole seemed to have effortlessly gained a wealth of information.

"They're going in carriages," Rosefinch warned Ari. "Every seat spoken for. I don't see how you can get in, not being known to anyone in the governor's party."

"That's all right," Ari said. "They won't see me."

Everyone dispersed to do more scouting, agreeing to meet again in the afternoon. Ari, left alone in the huge room, used the opportunity to work through Redbark a few times. She went out and roamed the streets, doing no more than practicing her walk. If she didn't pay attention, her strides lengthened to Ryu's gait. Learning how to walk like a girl was hard work.

By afternoon they had gathered again. Rosefinch and Lie Tenek had no startling news to offer; Oriole was silent about where she had been.

It was nearly time for the mine visit.

Ari dressed in her comfortable, sober-hued gallant wanderer clothes, then sketched the warding sign on her body. Before the others' surprised gazes, she climbed out the window and vanished to the roof.

Now that, Rosefinch thought in delight, was promising.

Ari leaped from wall to rooftop until she dropped soundlessly to the ground behind a cluster of servants lugging baskets and jugs to the last and plainest carriage in the row lined up before the west gate.

For her own purposes, Rosefinch had decided to follow Ari. At first she was dismayed when she realized Ari really had gone to the roof, but she knew where Ari was going, so she ran along the streets, and arrived panting . . . to discover no sign of Ari.

Rosefinch frowned, scrutinizing the square where the carriages awaited the guests. A flicker caught her attention — and there was Ari. How could she have missed her?

Then Rosefinch was distracted by the guests climbing into the carriages, and the servants loading baskets and food boxes into the last carriage. Rosefinch concentrated — and watched, fascinated, as Ari drifted along, barely visible, apparently completely unnoticed by the big party and their servants.

The sentries at the gate checked the tally held by the caravan leader, and then the captain of the sentries motioned for the gatekeepers to open the heavy gate.

Rosefinch kept her gaze on Ari, or she meant to. The big gates graunched open — Rosefinch took her eyes to the gate for a heartbeat — but when she looked back, Ari had vanished.

The carriages then started through, and Rosefinch turned away, both disappointed and intrigued. It seemed possible that Ari really was Firebolt . . .

Unaware of her, Ari jogged behind the last carriage, trusting to the warding sign, until they were well through the gate. When the road rounded a clump of dove trees, putting them out of sight of the wall, she took a few running steps and leaped to the roof of the last carriage, landing lightly as the conveyance jolted over the uneven ground.

She settled herself cross-legged and looked around. Plantain trees! A reminder that she hadn't been this far south since she and Muin left Imai Island. How long ago that seemed! She folded her arms over her middle, struck with a sudden, intense longing to go home. To see her parents. To explain everything that had happened to her, and — she hoped — see approval in their eyes. Only then would she know for certain she had found her path.

The forest cleared after a time, revealing tiers and tiers of farming following the contours of the low hills. The road wound among these, playing chase with the river, then bending westward to run alongside one of the many streams that fed the great river.

They passed farmers stooping over rows of plants, using the last of the day's sunlight. She renewed the wards on herself and stayed still, trusting the curious to be staring at the finer carriages up front, with the characters for *Su* painted on the lamps at either side of the driver.

As the sun dropped toward the distant mountains, the terrain began to change. The road wound upward, the horses slowing. What had been a pleasant spring day rapidly warmed, and the greenery gave way to eddies of black rock below striated cliffs. Every so often the restless winds carried a tinge of smoke. The sun, a fiery red ball, touched the western mountains as they climbed the last distance toward the top of the rise. The smoky stink increased, with a throat-cloying stench below it, like very rotten egg.

The horses were blowing hard when at last they crested the ridge. Faces pressed to the windows in the carriages, as the guests gazed out in the fading sunlight at what seemed to be another world. They looked down at a vast, shallow dish — a crater or caldera of glittering sand and black stretches of rock solidified in swirls and ripples. In the distance ooze veined with glowing red slowly boiled.

Around the caldera's rim there appeared to be frozen foam of a nasty shade of bright yellow that reminded Ari forcibly of her days as an orderly, cleaning up after one of the boys had sicked up somewhere. Black dots trudged slowly around this yellow, like ants struggling through invisible mud. Every so often a flame shot skyward from the ooze, glowing an eerie blue.

The drivers slowed the carriages, and brought them to a halt beneath an archway of rock. Servants had earlier hauled up great barrels of water for the animals, as there was no water anywhere in sight. The guests got out to stretch their legs and wander and exclaim, some of the women (and three of the men) making play with embroidered silk handkerchiefs to hold over their noses as they marveled over the vast, desolate sight.

Ari remained where she was, trusting to her wards. As long as she didn't move, she wouldn't catch the corner of anyone's eye and cause them to look more closely. The horses already knew she was there, having smelled her at the outset, so they wouldn't give away her presence.

She scanned the caldera and began to pick out details.

First, those ants out there had two legs instead of six. She strained her eyes, trying to make sense of what she saw. The bent-over figures seemed to be gathering the yellow stuff. Was that brimstone? She had seen it in powder form at Loyalty Fortress, but not in its natural form.

To the east, marking the caldera's ridge on the far side, there lay a dark crack. A cave? Figures trickled in and out. Then she understood what she was seeing. The crack, or cave, led to the old mine. The new mine lay farther around the disc of the caldera, probably much harder to get at, so the digging was going more slowly.

Closer by, a sudden hot gust of wind hit Ari and the wedding guests with a chest-burning surge of the brimstone stench. That must be the air off the blue flame gouts, she realized, as another gout rose skyward, causing the wedding guests to sigh, "Ah-h-h-h!" as if it were fireworks. Except they covered their noses and mouths.

The servants had by now set up lamps and unpacked the food and drink they'd brought in the last carriage. The wedding guests sat in the shadow of the archway, talking, pointing and laughing, as way across a landscape that ought rightly to belong to the King of Hell, those slow figures ended their day in heat, stench, and misery.

The darker it got, the brighter the blue flames. Each time, the watchers cooed and laughed, and after each rolled another wave of stench. The cooing gradually lessened. Ari was thirsty, and she knew it would get worse before it got better. How often did those miners get drinks of water? She would wager not as often as the horses did.

Another, worse miasma of stench reached the guests—the wind off the most recent blue flame, a very bright gout—and they began coughing and complaining. Now all of them held cloth to their faces, and the meal was hurriedly packed up and removed to the last carriage.

Between the servants' trips, Ari leaped down, reached through the window, and hooked one of the jugs. She sprang back up a heartbeat before someone rounded the corner with a laden basket. She was going to drink whatever was in the jug, but she hoped it was not rice wine.

She waited until the animals were hitched up again, and the lamps at the front of each carriage lit. Everyone was inside the carriages for the return trip before she dared to move again. She unstoppered the jug and smelled lukewarm tea. She drained it all, as the carriages began the much easier descent. All the way down she kept trying to grapple with the enormity of what she'd seen, making and remaking plans in a furious heat.

Phoenix Moon was setting and rising Ghost Moon being overtaken by thick clouds when they spotted the torchlit walls of the city. Ari sat on the roof, head bowed over her empty jug. Palanquins and handsome, decorated carts awaited the guests. Ari waited until the last of the servants piled the leftovers into a cart and began tiredly trudging alongside it.

When she got to the inn, the others were all there, anxious because she'd been gone so long. "Where did you go? Did you find them?" Lie Tenek asked.

"Them?" Ari repeated in a light, tired voice. "Oh, yes. I found *them*."

Nobody missed the emphasis on the word.

"I have to get them *all*," she said, her voice husky.

Three different voices rang out, "What?"

"All of them." And she told them what she'd seen. "That was from a distance," she finished up. "It has to be so very much worse right up close."

"But . . . but . . ." Rosefinch had listened with wonder and delight. This was just the sort of thing Firebolt would do!

Only it was *dangerous*. She looked uncertainly at Oriole.

Who said evenly, "The judicials will tell you that there are murderers in there, who deserve such punishment."

Rosefinch's gaze darted from her to Lie Tenek, who said sourly, "There's murder and there's self-defense. And there is . . . what do you even call it when a noble of the first rank has her maid beaten to death for dropping a dish, and nothing happens, whereas a laundry woman stabbing that noble for killing her daughter is considered a hardened criminal?"

"I'm not saying it's right," Oriole stated. "I'm pointing out what they'll be saying if we're caught. Those people do not feel the least sorry for the miners. They believe they're getting what they deserve."

Lie Tenek looked down at her hands, her ire dying. "Ayah! I care nothing for what they think. I'm in. And if there's fighting, I'll fight."

Rosefinch said in a small voice, "I don't know how to fight."

Ari shook her head. "You don't have to. Look, I've thought it all out. What I need is a . . . distraction, or diversion. Something to draw the garrison in one direction, so I can . . . at least give those people a fighting chance. I can do that part, if I can have a diversion here. I have to try. Or I'm going to have nightmares for the rest of my life."

Lie Tenek chewed her thumb, trying to think of what possibly would distract a street patrol, much less a garrison.

Oriole rapped lightly on the nearby table with her knuckles, then gave the other three a very strange smile. "It is quite possible this lowly one might be able to arrange a distraction."

"I'll help," Lie Tenek said — on a rising note of question.

Rosefinch looked wide-eyed. "I will, too. If I don't have to fight."

Oriole nodded at them. "No fighting," Her smile curled upward on one side. "They'll be too busy for that."

Ari got to her feet, itchy from the dust, the heat, and the horrible air of the mine. But she was far too restless for a bath. "It's a cloudy night, ink-black out there. I'm going to go on the roof and do martial arts exercises. I've been sitting too long, and I need to think . . . I still have the horse problem . . ."

She dug through her trunk to the bottom, where her staff lay in sections next to Sagacious Blade, both wrapped in cloth. Her fingers brushed the staff, then strayed to the sword. Maybe doing sword form with an actual sword might feel good.

She took out Sagacious, and soon was on the roof in her bare feet, so that no one below would hear her moving about. The tiles were the usual curved ones, but she was used to those. She liked the smooth feel of them under her feet — she could grip them with her toes.

Slowly, deliberately, she began the warmup and then swung into Heaven and Earth, instead of Redbark. Heaven and Earth felt right at this moment. It was a pure form, exactly the way Father had taught her. She was ten again when she did Heaven and Earth. She could see Father's face so clearly —

how he'd listen with his eyes narrowed. He never talked much, but when he gave his short nod of approval, you knew he meant it.

Father would say the problem was simple: she had to protect those who could not protect themselves. A faint whiff of brimstone from her clothes brought the horror of that boiling caldera vividly back to mind, and the flimsy shelter of childhood memory was gone.

She had a task. A proper one. She struggled against a surge of anger as hot and acrid as one of those distant blue flames. Even Mother would be angry at the thought of Matu's grandparents forced into a situation like that.

I even know how to get in there, she silently told her parents. It's getting there in the first place that is the problem. That, and getting everyone out and away.

The sword swung and glinted in her hand as she switched from Earth, Redbark's ground defense, to Heaven, defense against mounted. Her blood sang, and as she sweated away the grit blown over her from that horrible caldera, her skin cooled. The movement, the flow of Essence ignited the inner heat, and she watched the glints and sparks along the sword as she —

Glint?

She stopped and looked around. All she saw were the golden lights of the upper stories of a few manors, high on the hill, too far away to cast such a bright reflection. She looked up at the low blanket of clouds. No moonslight or starlight at all.

Anyway, reflected lamplight would be gold, not blue-white . . .

She held Sagacious up. The sword was curiously light in her hand — she hadn't even realized it, she had moved so easily. She smiled and leaped, performing a frontal attack and a backhand swing, the sword vooming in the air as she came down slowly on her toes.

Very slowly.

She looked down at her feet, blinking as if she'd discovered someone else's feet attached to her legs. There were her familiar feet. She wiggled her toes to reassure herself. Everything was as it should be. It was just strange, how *light* she felt.

She brought the sword close, right hand gripping the handle, the tip resting on the first two fingers of her left hand. The blade glinted, blue light glimmering along the edge, and . . . sparked?

Essence brimmed inside her, as if in answer.

She lowered the sword, gazing out toward the west, and that vast, unseen caldera. She could feel it out there. No, not the caldera. What she felt was the pool of liquid fire beneath it, seething with evil Essence. No, not evil.

*Essence is what it is. Good and evil are what we make of it.*

That hellish landscape was hell because humans made it so for other humans. The creatures that lived out there surely did not find it evil. It was home to them.

She shut her eyes, reaching with her senses toward that whiff of brimstone. That was not evil. Again, brimstone was itself. True, it was an important part of gunpowder, which did terrible damage—but gunpowder also made beautiful fireworks, which harmed no one. Brimstone became an evil or a good through the actions of the humans using it.

She turned west again.

The Essence was there, a vast pool of fire. Her element. All she had to do was . . . *reach.*

The sword glowed softly in her hand. She sensed . . . movement? Readiness for movement? It was so light. *She* was so light. Which had happened before, beginning with the night of the mercenary attack at Loyalty, when she had leaped from the wall and landed as lightly as—

Was it *possible* she could . . .

Wonder flooded her soul, a sudden bloom, which promptly withered with doubt. Cautiously she bent to lay the sword on the roof tiles. Then, very carefully, she stepped on it.

Nothing happened.

A sharp pang of disappointment—then a snap, as if something, or someone, flicked her inside her forehead: Wake up.

She stood very still.

Begin with the first step.

She went back to Yaso's breathing exercise, focusing on the familiar pool of Essence inside her. Steadied by the sense of immanent power, she considered all her lessons with Master Ki, whose natural elements were air and water. His teaching metaphors had therefore been related to his elements.

She consciously imagined Essence as a great fire, lifting sparks high into the air, and herself rising with it.

And Sagacious began to rise.

For a moment Ari wobbled, the sword sidling wildly. She

clutched desperately at it—and it skidded sideways, half-spinning. She fell off with a thud that knocked her breath out.

She stilled. Had anyone below heard that? She waited, heart beating in her throat. No reaction. Maybe there was an empty attic beneath.

She set the sword down, and despite shaky limbs, stepped carefully on it again. She knew how to balance! But . . . on something stationary.

She knelt on the blade in the military bow to the emperor, right knee down, left foot in front of it. Only instead of pressing her right fist to the ground, she wrapped her fingers around the handle. And folded her other hand over that one. Then she put her chin on her left knee. That felt sturdy. Steady.

She set her sight firmly on the ridgepole—and the sword lifted lightly to the ridgepole, then hovered there.

Oh, was that it, she had to see where it was to go?

She turned her head, sighted on the curving edge of the roof—and the sword moved straight to that edge. She wobbled a little, then clenched every muscle, determined to stay on.

She didn't fall.

She looked over at the roof across the street. The sword glided away from the roof, out over the street.

*Don't look down.* How many times had she done exactly this in dreams? Always, in the dreams, if she looked down, she would swoop downward, or even fall. But if she lifted her eyes to the horizon and looked—

*Out.*

Slowly at first, then gaining speed, the sword cut through the air.

It was not a dream. For one thing, the air buffeted her face, and hurt her eyes unless she squinted. Her clothes flapped absurdly, pulling at her. But she kept her focus on that caldera, whose presence she felt; the powerful fire Essence emanating upward buoyed her in the air.

High and then higher, she sped over the spring-full treetops, and skimmed green-fuzzed hills. Traveling by horse had seemed rapid, until now. She zipped through the air like a comet. The scents of growth and soil gave way, overpowered by the stink of brimstone. By the time she topped the rise she had crooked her elbow over her nose. There below lay the beating glow of the lake of burning rock beneath its crust of half-cooled stones. The blue gouts were as brilliant as lightning in the darkness.

She turned her eyes away. She had learned while a cadet that a sentry who stares at a fire won't see an enemy creeping up behind in the darkness. She needed to see that cave, if it was a cave. She held her breath and sketched the ward charm over herself as she swooped across the expanse of the caldera, the air hot and acrid.

Yes, there was the cave, with armed guards who all wore some sort of kerchief over the lower part of their faces. She could see Essence glow to those kerchiefs, and knew that someone had figured out a charm for warding the brimstone in the air. As she huffed out a breath and sucked in another, forcing herself not to cough, she wondered if anyone had bothered to pass those kerchiefs out to the prisoners.

She was not going to risk entering that cave, not now. She did not trust flying inside what might be a narrow space. Even more urgent, she could feel fatigue curling low in her stomach and pulling at her limbs. She had to return. And soon.

But how to get all those people safely away? It would take them *weeks* to walk all the way to the coast — assuming there was food, and no pursuit.

Wait. Think. How could they get the brimstone back to the city to send out? They certainly didn't use that path the carriages had followed.

She lifted her gaze to the broken ridge behind the cave entrance, and soon rode above it. Ah. Sure enough. On the other side of the mountain, the river hugged the curve of the slope. Barges waited to be loaded, all under guard. A camp with tents lay along the opposite riverbank. These had to be where the guards lived — moved when one cave was emptied, and another opened.

She'd seen enough to plan.

Ari turned her face eastward again. She was breathing hard when the welcome sight of the city lights appeared below.

She found her open window, and climbed heavily inside. Sagacious's glow had died out, leaving a length of lifeless, heavy metal in her hand. She sheathed the blade, drank down an entire pitcher of water, then fell into bed.

# THIRTY-THREE

FIRST I MUST OFFER you a little background about the Journey to the Cloud Empire.

How it was conducted had not changed in essentials for centuries. The navigators and pole attendants were all descendants of previous navigators of the great sampans. They knew every rock in the twisted passage, and how the currents flowed. They knew how to manage the unwieldy boats in all weathers — when to slow them, so that come morning, the first glimpse would be the famous cataracts.

Their brethren were trained at a young age to manage the smaller boats that drifted along the great sampans, bringing supplies and visitors back and forth, and then returning them. And all knew how to slow through the great fog, when the sampans would gently ease around a sharp turn, unfelt by those slumbering in their silken cocoons after imbibing quantities of hot rice wine.

Yskanda never remembered falling asleep. It seemed moments later that a whisper clawed through his dreams. "Assistant court artist!"

Yskanda became aware that the words had been repeated several times. He murmured, "Awake."

"I was sent to warn you to be on duty before sunrise. This is the only time you will get to eat." It was Fennel, who slid in a basin of hot water and a tiny cup of tea to rinse his mouth.

Yskanda whispered his thanks, and tried not to make any noise as he washed up as best he could in the chill, stuffy air, dressed, then picked up his art tools and the basin and cup.

When he stepped out of the close atmosphere, he almost wanted to return to it, for at least it was relatively warm. The back door, which opened to the rear of the sampan, let in cold, damp air. He had never minded dampness, but the cold made him shiver as he dumped his wash water over the side, and stacked the basin in the pile. In the mist-haloed light of a single lamp he found silhouettes huddled together, their shadows painting the deck and halfway up the wall behind him.

He ventured toward them, to discover servants from Jion's household, sharing out tea and pancakes. The sampan guides stood at their posts, imperturbable and immoveable except for their long poles. Yskanda's artistic eye evaluated the shadows as he accepted the hot pancake Yarrow handed him, and a covered cup of tea.

"Quick," Whiteleaf said to Yskanda, ruddy lamplight beating over his round face, and glittering in his eyes. "When the servant boat comes along to collect you, you must go."

Yskanda obediently forced down the scalding tea, which at least warmed him from the inside. He was still finishing his pancake when a glance forward revealed the shadow-black shape of a rocky mountain looming ahead. Startled, Yskanda glanced at the polers, but no one seemed to be alarmed by the imminence of a collision.

As the mountain towered overhead, he discovered that they were passing into a tunnel. Cold, dank air enveloped them, but he was scarcely aware of it, for over the hushing sound of water lapping at the stones to either side rose a single voice in song.

He recognized the melody, and then the words as the echo from the stone of the tunnel amplified both with heartrending purity: an old sutra greeting the sun god. The singer had begun as soon as the emperor's sampan entered the tunnel, and would repeat the song as long as the line of sampans lasted.

This signaled the start of the Journey's planned delights.

As soon as Prince Jion's sampan emerged from the tunnel, a boat that was little more than a raft glided alongside, crowded with people in gray. Servants.

Yskanda had forgotten the pancake in his hand while he listened to that ethereal voice. He shoved the rest of the pancake into his mouth, picked up his bag, and stepped across to the raft-boat.

The trip was only to the next sampan up, belonging to First Imperial Princess Manon, but in that short journey he learned that they were expected to gain their assigned spots and remain there until dismissed. Which might be all day. From the terse words, the bracing shoulders and stiff hands, he gathered that no one expected any relief for the servants during what was certain to be a long day, the servants silently and smoothly making food appear and its remains vanish, and Yskanda recording the imperials and their noble guests with brush and ink.

The fog was so thick that the princess's sampan was barely visible except as a bulky shape until they drew next to it.

Swiftly the servants boarded, bearing their supplies. The princess's steward was there to point out where each should go. Yskanda was sent forward to a corner partially blocked by decorative plants, from which he could see the spacious setting for the morning's activity. A plain desk had been placed there, and a mat woven of hemp. A lumpy mat, he discovered; Sweetwater's mats had been far better made.

He sensed the sun rising behind his shoulder, which would furnish excellent light, but he was below a moon window open to the air, which meant a steady flow of cold, dank air down his neck. Also, he discovered, he had to peer around the solid pot holding the plant. Totally lacking a capacity for spite, he did not recognize the deliberation in the wretched mat or the pot being placed there: he only knew that he was as screened off as was possible, which was a state of affairs he was used to from court. Servants existed to serve, not to be seen.

The darkness began to lift to the dull gray of dense fog as the guests began to arrive.

One of the last was Jion, who readied himself in his spacious cabin, smiling with expectation: it was still foggy out — they were past the great steam vents now — and chilly, which meant they would soon clear the mist. And then to find out what interesting things Manon had arranged for them. He knew the music would be excellent!

Vaion was on the decorated boat that pulled alongside. They scarcely had time to exchange morning greetings when they reached Manon's sampan. They stepped across to the prow, which had a broad deck offering a perfect view to front and sides. Desks and embroidered silk cushions had been arranged in a square facing inward, the same as school, but they soon discovered they were not seated in merit order. It was rank order. Vaion sighed. He didn't mind sitting with his brother, but he'd been counting on being at the back with his particular friends, so that they could exchange notes and covert comments.

He had Jion on one side, and his most serious elder Ran cousin on the other. He sat back, resigning himself to a morning of tedium, as Jion looked at the beautiful jade ornaments hanging from the canopy support beam above. Long tassels swayed gently with the almost imperceptible movement of the sampan.

Manon came around to greet each of them, superb as always in severe blue, black, and rose, with golden phoenixes cavorting among lotus blossoms embroidered on her over-robe.

"I like these ornaments as decoration," he told her.

She smiled at him, finger to her lips — she had other plans for the decorations.

She made certain everyone sat where she had placed them — her steward could be trusted for that. The only one who did not appear was Scribe Shan, whom she had relegated to the back with the lower servants should he have polluted her boat with his presence.

With impeccable timing, she waited until the first lancing shaft of morning sunlight heralded the clearing of the fog, and they emerged into pearlescent light, spangles dancing on the quiet waters.

Jion glanced around, and spotted Yskanda stuck in a corner behind one of the pots. This ought to appeal to an artist — and his reaction was everything Jion expected. Yskanda's eyes widened. His jaw dropped. Wonder limned his face, his body, as he took in the cascades on either side of the passage. Two great waterfalls, one close, one far, each surrounded by short falls, broad falls, thundering and roaring. Rainbow after rainbow glimmered in the mists rising from the frothing waters, and then — just as they reached the midpoint between the two great falls, another cascade, this time of sound. Hidden somewhere in the greenery above, a single flute player trilled a waterfall of melody, entrancing as birdsong.

Jion smiled, thrown back to autumn when he and Manon argued amicably over this very piece. He watched Yskanda, whose eyes glistened with moisture. Jion had not known until then that Yskanda was also sensitive to music. When did he get to hear any?

When they passed the last cascade, and the music faded behind them, Manon stepped to the center. "This morning's challenge," she said as she swept her gaze around the group, "is taken from the Sage Empress's first Journey to the Clouds, when she was a mere princess. We will hold a competition in poetry, upon the topic of the filial virtues. You see twenty-five jade ornaments here, one for each filial virtue. The poem that best represents each will gain its writer a jade piece, and the poem will be ornamented by the court artist's assistant."

Yskanda's head came up sharply at that. He had not known he was to make twenty-four illustrations in addition to his regular duty of recording the imperials at their activities. But of course his time was the imperial family's to dispose of; as he began grinding ink, he reflected that until the first imperial princess spoke, he had not considered the gulf between the title *Assistant Court Artist* and a mere noun, *court artist's assistant.* It was plain that the first imperial princess regarded him as the latter.

He was busy preparing ink and brushes, so he didn't see Jion's slight wince on his behalf. On the other side—safely out of conversational range—Su Siar hid her face behind her fan when she heard Cousin Manon's dismissive reference to the beautiful young man everybody said was a Talent.

Manon shot Yskanda a look under her lashes. Instead of looking properly chastised, he seemed to be preoccupied with his inks. Her gaze moved to Ze Kai, who gazed back unblinking, his expression shuttered.

Her heart gave a jolt, and she lifted her chin. Let him remember who would sit on the throne, should they marry. But first she must be sure of him. Which was in itself a challenge; usually, one glance was all it took from her, and the boys followed her like overgrown puppies. She did not even know how to behave in that disgusting way everyone called flirting.

But she did know how to flatter—in a suitable, dignified, *imperial* way: she had learned that from watching the interactions between Imperial Father and Great-Grandfather Su.

She waited until most of the brushes had been laid down,

and the papers on each desk filled with five lines of five characters each.

She said, "I have fortune sticks in this vase, as you see.
Someone choose one, and the possessor of its number will
be the first to read their poem."

Half the boys rose from their little desks and
crowded around to choose the first stick. She took care to
smile around her before turning to offer it to Ze Kai—who
was not among them. He knelt still at his desk, one arm,
clad in cloud-and-wave woven silk in shades of silver,
leaning on the desk so that his long sleeve flowed like water
as he bent his head toward Jion. She caught the words, ". . .
wild mustard," before the ins-istent boys around her began
trying to get to the fortune sticks.

She held the vase out, and a younger Su cousin was
the fastest. She smiled on him graciously, aware of being
well posed. If that assistant court artist was paying
attention, this pose would do: look, admire, but you will
never touch. She then turned her mind to the poems. She
already knew who would win, but she must have an
adroit answer ready to support her judgments, one that
complemented her thinking as well as whatever the
students wrote in their poems.

At first Yskanda was afraid he could not do justice to two
separate jobs, but he discovered that he could work on
the group illustration while they wrote their next poem. As
for ill-ustrating the winning poem—that was easy, too. The
poems were very traditional and predictable. "Glorious
cassia" showed up twice, and "wild plum blossom" no
fewer than four times, "chrysanthemum" three—all common
symbols of familial virtues. The princess appeared to favor
the poems that emulated the masters the closest, which
made it very easy to illustrate them with standard images.

He was content, for his expectation of being treated
with respect was low.

Jion's was not. As he half-listened to the poetry, most
not worth remembering, he became increasingly restless.
He could see the wall of politeness that Ze Kai put up, which
influenced his followers among the young scholars, future
ministers all. Did Manon not see it? Perhaps she did. She
might even favor that blank politeness. He had begun to
realize that during the time he was away he had lost
something crucial in their relationship, and he no longer

understood her. Until he did, he was reluctant to bring the subject up.

No, he decided after Ze Kai was given his third jade ornament for a poem so rigidly influenced by Ar Laq it might as well have been copied outright. He watched Manon's smiling, graceful speech, and then he had it. Of course she was under orders from her mother! He'd nearly forgotten the marriage negotiations going on aboard Imperial Father's sampan. But that did not explain why she treated Afan Yskanda so disdainfully, especially as he was sure he had seen her watching him once, with unblinking intensity. Or even desire, though he was not certain how that would look on his cool, controlled sister.

Jion remained quiet, watching from under his eyelids as Manon, who had been walking about, neared Yskanda and bent to look at the drawing under his hands. Then she moved on as if she had never stopped, a satisfied lift to her chin betraying some emotion that she smoothed before Jion could be sure of it.

Shortly after the last poem, Manon said, "We will arrive at Heavenly Scents soon. I invite everyone to remain for the midday meal."

Covert glances exchanged, then Jion rose, and crossed behind to glance down at Yskanda's drawing of the group. As expected, it was beautifully rendered, quite properly centered around Manon. But each person there was caught in a characteristic manner—Cousin Su Siar with her sideways, laughing glance; Lu Fan's expressive hands. Vaion mock-solemn, a hint of grin in his narrowed eyes, as though the next moment would bring out a laugh. It was excellent, and Manon had betrayed herself in a way that showed she knew it was excellent, but she had not said so much as a word in acknowledgment.

Jion turned away. Manon either did not see that Afan Yskanda was a prisoner staked out as bait, or did not care. There was nothing Jion could do about Imperial Father's personal feud—except to watch over the innocent victim as much as he could. The way Ryu would. "Assistant Court Artist Afan, there's something I wish to show you, if you are finished."

Here was Vaion, like a colt escaping its pen. "Let me see!" Lu Fan was at his heels until all that were left were Manon's Su cousins and a few of their followers.

Jion perforce had to invite everyone who crowded around him. But at least morning school was over, that was understood. He sought Fennel, who hovered along the rail out of the way, and signaled with his eyes. Fennel turned to wave down the transport boat: though Jion would love to jump up on the rail and leap to his own sampan, it would not do.

Yskanda rose and began putting together his tools — then halted when Cousin Su Siar drifted up.

The boys parted like grass in a wind, as she put out a small, dainty hand to halt Yskanda. He bowed; she gave him a dimpled smile before bending over the drawing of the group. "Ayah," she exclaimed softly. "It is very good. Very!"

"This beginner without talent is graced by the kindness of the noble lady," Yskanda said in his soft voice.

Siar looked up into his face. He was even more beautiful up close. She did not understand Manon's rudeness, unless he was also arrogant, or insinuating. "Tell me where you studied," she asked, smiling. "I know I have never seen you before."

"He's a Talent. From one of the southern islands," Vaion spoke up, to forestall the humble speech appropriate to the situation. Then, pointing to the loaf that all could plainly see on Yskanda's head, "He even passed the Imperial Examination."

"This assistant with little talent was at the end of the list, and lucky," Yskanda murmured, gaze downcast.

"Here's our boat." Jion gestured, long sleeve swinging. "Anyone who wishes to join us is most welcome. Assistant Court Artist Afan, that includes you."

Yskanda bowed acquiescence, and excused himself to Siar with soft formality. Not a hint of arrogance, much less presumption.

Manon had ordered a repast prepared for the entire group on the assumption that naturally they would wish to remain around her. She gazed after Jion's disappearing back as he led the others aboard the princes' little craft, Afan Yskanda last. She ought to have said something to keep Jion — she had forgotten that the others would find him interesting, after his time away. Now they were all following him, like lambs after a sheep.

Very well. She could adapt her plans, as soon as she got rid of these unimportant sycophants. Though it was too early for the marriage treaty negotiations to be anywhere near completion, she could benefit from being seen aboard the imperial sampan, paying attention to state affairs. Perhaps she might even find a way to offer a well-considered opinion —

A rustle and a waft of scent caused her to turn her head. Annoyance sparked when she recognized her "cousin" Siar, who said, "You don't like that pretty assistant court artist, dear niece?"

"There is no matter of liking or disliking a servant, honored aunt," Manon replied, forced to use the formal familial title as Siar was senior in rank, though *not* the elder, and had used hers first.

Su Siar flicked a laughing glance at Manon over her fan. "He's very polite, very humble, and very talented. Has he insulted you?"

Manon kept forgetting how quick Siar was, quick and elusive as a butterfly. She said with all the indifference at her command, "Even if he dared. If a dog bites, do you bite it back?"

Siar's brows lifted. "Did you really want to use that saying?" — reminding them both that the rest of it was, *you beat it to death.* The humor had vanished from Siar's face, except for a little moue of her lips signifying her distaste.

Manon could see that she had erred. Her own ambivalence was so strong that she moved away, as if she could leave her error behind. She gazed unseeing up at the snow-covered cliff tops, where an eagle drifted wing-still high in the air. She gazed at it without really seeing it until she had perfect control, before she forced a smile, and a slight curtsey, niece to aunt. "My morning duties being complete, I must leave first, to pay my respects to Imperial Father. Would you honor me with your company?"

"Thank you, dear niece, but no. I dare not go unless I am summoned. And I have not had time to reacquaint myself with darling Cousin Jion."

She moved away, leaving behind a drift of peach blossom fragrance. Manon turned her back, summoned her boat, and had herself taken to Imperial Father's sampan, where the musicians were still playing, music drifting over the water.

When she bowed herself into her father's presence, prudently staying at the back, she discovered that the visiting prince was playing some kind of metal flute along with the musicians. Lily sat next to him, playing a counterpoint on a wooden flute. Manon had not even known she played. Half a song later, Manon suspected that the playing was new; she had been far superior when she was that silly rabbit Gaunon's age.

The song ended, and Imperial Father gestured to invite her to join them. She might have refused, but she decided to make a gesture so that this prince would comprehend the true quality of the empire, to which he could never hope to aspire.

She motioned the guzheng player aside, and knelt in the approved manner. The musicians, all of whom had been chosen by her, awaited her signal. As she swept into a song it occurred to her that manners required her to let the guest lead—but *she* did not have to flatter the chinless prince. Right now she had a point to make, and she made it, exhibiting her usual excellence won through hard discipline.

At song's end, the visitors applauded and spoke compliments. As soon as they were done, she said with her gaze cast down and a modest tone that her mother had schooled into her before her sixth birthday, "It was nothing. This incompetent daughter thanks the august visitors for their kindness and forbearance—and hopes to wish, if it is permitted, that you might hear my first imperial brother play. He is excellent, I promise."

The prince's uncle bowed. "Surely there can be no one as adept as your imperial highness."

Manon inclined her head. "Oh, but this envious incompetent assures you. Many is the time I tried to match his skill, but was called away by my tutors to my studies of history and statecraft, and my tears flowed as I heard my brother's exquisite music drifting behind me."

There! That was sufficiently modest, and also gently reminded Imperial Father—who prized family amity—that she and Jion were close.

She rose to excuse herself, but Imperial Father turned her way. "First Daughter, shall we have your instrument fetched? While we wait to round the corner into Heavenly Scent, why don't the three of you refresh our spirits?"

There was only one answer to be made to that.

# THIRTY-FOUR

JION WAS SURPRISED AT how the atmosphere lightened in the short time it took for the pole-men to get them from Manon's boat to his.

The reason, or a reason, was soon evident. Lu Fan nudged Cousin Zuinan, Vaion whispered and shrugged, then Lu Fan said, "Your imperial highness, you have to know that all kinds of rumors have been circulating about where you were. Now's the time to give us the story. Where were you?"

"Traveling," Jion said. "I saw a great deal of the empire. Very instructive, I assure you. And hot and dusty at times. The memory brings back the thirst." Jion lifted his head—and there was Whiteleaf with trays of snacks and fresh tea. By the time everyone had been settled in Jion's spacious viewing room, and he had commented on types of tea he had encountered, the subject had turned to others' journeys and what new teas, and new treats, they had discovered.

He kept that going with interested questions until he caught the first drifting scent of the next surprise on the air. He looked around for Yskanda, who had been set up in the corner with his ever-present desk, but with a pile of cushions, and an unimpeded view. Trust. He suspected that Yskanda still did not trust him. Perhaps could not trust him. They might not be able to talk to one another with the freedom of the gallant wanderers, but that didn't mean Jion couldn't try to ease Yskanda's way if he could. "Here we come to the Heavenly Scents," he announced.

The sampan began its gentle turn, as ahead, Manon's boat slid past Old Pagoda Cliff. And then, little by little, they emerged into an astonishing sight: a world of orchids, dotted here and there by other brave, tenacious plants.

Yskanda's breath hissed in, his eyes widening as he gazed at the wild variety of hues. He breathed in the heady combined perfumes as his mind flooded with images of nature at its most graceful, and his fingers closed hard on the ward stone in his sleeve. Some of the confusing shimmer of image cleared away, enabling him to focus more clearly on the detailed glories of a stunning variety or orchards.

He blinked twice, his fingers groping for his brushes. With impressive speed he plied his brush until he covered several sheets with sketches of the orchids. Music drifted from high above: in a tiny pagoda, five musicians plied their stringed instruments.

Jion smiled at his sister's excellent choice. Too excellent. As often happened with superlative music in the right setting, the urge to dance twitched at his muscles. He turned away to distract himself.

A few steps away his brother—unmoved by lots of flo-wers—bent over Yskanda's shoulder. "How do you paint them to look like they're floating in the air?" Vaion asked.

Yskanda jolted as if startled, laid down the brush, and rose to bow before answering, "This student of no talent thanks his royal highness, and wishes to explain that the technique is called dry brush."

"Oh."

Yskanda sat down again, picked up his brush, dipped it, wiped it, and—

"That brush isn't really dry," Vaion observed. "It's more like you got rid of half the ink. My tutor would have made me rewrite it a hundred times if I drew any letters with those wispy strokes, but it's perfect when you make orchids."

Down went the brush, up came Yskanda, who bowed and uttered a properly self-disparaging preface to thanking Vaion for his kindness.

After a brief silence, Yskanda sat, cast a longing glance at the orchids, which were nearly all behind them now, dipped the brush—

"I never really watched you painting when you did my portrait," Vaion said. "Ayah, of course I could not, for I had to sit still. That I remember—that and I had the worst itch on my—"

Down went the brush, up came Yskanda.

But before he could bow and launch into his deflection, Jion lounged up to them. "Yskanda, sit down. Ignore my magpie of a brother. Vaion, if you don't sit and keep quiet, I will have to assassinate you with this bowl of hot wine, which is the only weapon in reach."

"But I just wanted to say how much I like what he's doing," Vaion protested.

Jion reached out, and for the first time, laid his hand on Yskanda's shoulder. He pushed Yskanda back into his seat before he could rise to thank the younger prince as he turned a mock scowl at Vaion.

Vaion mumbled, "I didn't know he could make drawings of things besides us. I don't know why, but I find flowers actually boring, but pictures of them, pictures like this one, I really like. I'd very much like to have those."

Jion promptly put his hand back down on Yskanda's shoulder, said, "Keep painting!" and to his brother, "You'll get more of them to choose from if you don't make him bob up and down like a chicken on a fence in order to keep apologizing for his incompetence and thanking you for your great forbearance and measureless grace."

Vaion sighed. "Every time I try to lay aside the honorifics, I get into trouble." He sent a sour glance in the direction of Manon's sampan.

Jion noted a variety of bemused and surprised glances from the scholars. His father would be displeased if he extolled the easy exchanges he'd enjoyed while he was gone, but he could come at it another way. "I must confess, I miss the freedom of our converse when we were all boys and Master Zao wasn't looming like a thunder god. I wish to invite anyone who also misses those days to speak freely while on this boat." He turned to regard Yskanda. "That includes you, Assistant Court Artist. What goes through the mind of a Talent when first beholding the Heavenly Scents?"

Yskanda reddened, his head bowed over his painting, his brush still. Jion instantly lifted his hand, after noting how bony Yskanda's shoulder was—but there was surprisingly defined muscle beneath. They let the scribes and apprentice artists get some kind of exercise besides painting?

Yskanda said, "If your imperial highness truly wishes an answer—"

"My imperial highness most certainly does."

"—this ignorant student wondered how so many orchids grew in one place. In the south, orchids grew aplenty, but never like this." Yskanda was painting again, with quick, sure strokes.

"I don't know," Jion admitted.

"I can answer that," Ze Kai said—thereby breaking the hitherto unassailable wall between servers and served, for in no sense was Ze Kai issuing an order, which was supposed to be the only time one noticed anyone but fellow courtiers.

With one glance at Ze Kai's high-domed forehead and his lifted chin, Jion sensed that Ze Kai, the most scrupulous of their generation, had done it deliberately. "My mother takes a great interest in the growing of flowers at our manor. I was told that several centuries ago imperial orders were issued to bring rare orchids from all the islands, to be fitted in where their coloration was most pleasing to the eye. This stretch of the passage, between the great cascades, apparently has a great deal of water in the air, which she says is necessary for the growth of orchids. The ones that survived transplanting are longer-lived than a man. Like trees. Also, we come at midday, during the coolness of early spring, for the scent of so many orchids combined is very intense at sunrise, and sunset, and in summer. It can be overpowering, I was told."

Yskanda laid his brush down to get to his feet, but Jion's hand kept him in place as he said over Yskanda's head, "Ze Kai. I take it you will not feel obligated to order his death for not rising to utter the customary abjurations and thanks?"

They had never been friends—Ze Kai had been too dedicated, and too competitive, a scholar back when they were young. Jion chiefly recollected his disgust and derision at Jion's evasions of the grinding boredom of repetition. But at these words, a very brief flash of humor narrowed Ze Kai's eyes as his lips pressed against a smile. Then he said, "It appears to me the assistant court artist is doing his utmost to comply with the ritual responses. Which we can forgo, if he will keep painting."

Jion turned to Yskanda, hand still on his shoulder. "You

are permitted to paint from nature, are you not?—ayah, of course I remember the Imperial Garden, I was very much a part of that," he said to his brother, who had been about to protest. "I mean on this journey; I trust your orders are not confined to painting us?"

Yskanda bowed from his seat as he took refuge in the classics. "When outlining this unworthy student's duties, your imperial highness and honored scholars, Court Artist Yoli quoted Kanda, who said, what Heaven confers is termed Nature. Harmony with Nature is termed the Path. Cultivating the Path is termed education, and so the education of such as myself extends to Nature's art."

Ze Kai nodded thoughtfully, clearly approving.

The scholars then began talking among themselves, permitting Yskanda to paint in peace, until the sun slid behind one of the towering rocks, casting all in shadow. As Yskanda hastily finished, mostly from memory, Ze Kai lifted his face, his eyes closed.

> *"I have seen three cranes riding the wind*
>
> *Pale grace against pale Ghost Moon.*
>
> *The master teaches that men only weep twice: once when entering the world*
>
> *And again when understanding why.*
>
> *I raise my glass as crane calls to crane . . .*
>
> *Orchid fragrance*
>
> *Crowned with three-petaled iris."*

It was then that Jion remembered that was Lily's favorite poem.

# THIRTY-FIVE

WE RETURN TO BENEVOLENT Winds, which was not all that far from the Journey to the Cloud Empire.

That same morning, Ari wound her hair into the old topknot, which would keep it firmly out of her way. She skewered it with Shigan's tiger-eye hairpin, then she put on her old, familiar Redbark clothes.

Daylight was barely lifting the darkness over the water in the harbor when she climbed out the window, knelt on Sagacious Blade, and sped up into the fleeing night.

She was gone when the others rose a short time later, and dressed soberly.

Over breakfast Oriole shared with Lie Tenek and Rose-finch her plan for the diversion—and why she was doing it.

"In my experience," Madam Nightingale had said as the two of them sat on the balcony and watched the locals practice the kraken dance in the square, "the most evil people are those who believe there's a perfectly good reason for what they do. It's fate, it's expected, or, in the case of Su Suanek, it's the game, played against cousins within the family for rank, for family merit. They hand off a trunk of golden boaters to build a fine temple, where monks or nuns can pray to the nobles' ancestors on their behalf, and believe themselves firmly on the path to righteousness. And they name their children for great leaders as reminders of their own greatness. Like Su Suanek," she had added. "Who was as unlike Goddess Suanek as a person could possibly be. You'd think she'd have a tiny sense of shame, forcing a sixth-generation medicine store into selling for a tenth of its worth merely so that she could own all Flame-in-Ice's medicine stores?"

"Su Medicine Stores. I've heard of them," Oriole had said.

"Who hasn't heard of them?" Madam Nightingale said, lifting her teacup to her lips. "They start by charging mere tinnies for expensive medicines until the other healers are forced out of business, and then raise the prices so that only the wealthy can afford them. They clearly want to own every medicine store in the world. As for high prices . . . My own family charged high prices, but our herbs were the best. And charging more to those who could afford it meant that at night, we could see to those who could not afford any medicine. Everyone on the north side of the river came to us at night."

Oriole had nodded. In the wandering world there were many of those old shops, redolent with pungent herbs, filled with entire walls of jars and tiny boxes handed down through the generations. They dispensed medicine, charms, even needle treatments, to those who could never afford to consult a physician, but had something to trade, even if it was sweeping the walkway. Everyone benefitted, not solely the shop.

Madam went on, "My sister and I began practicing on those night visitors, with Grandmother and Grandfather looking on. The poor knew we were learning, but they were getting their medicine for free, so they were patient with clumsy fingers and uncertain diagnoses until Grandfather would correct us. Then he'd make us write out the prescription ten times to get it into memory."

"I didn't know you trained as a healer," Oriole had exclaimed.

"Only began, only began," Madam Nightingale said. "Why do you think I know so much about cosmetics and fragrances and how to treat dancers' feet? My sister and I were just girls. We had scarcely begun practicing on actual patients when Su Suanek showed up, a girl close to our age, wearing pearls and jade and silk, smelling of magnolia. She ignored us and addressed Grandmother as if she were the lowest of her servants as she said she would do us a favor and buy the store for half what it was worth. Grandfather came out and refused—and she said, 'You'll be begging for that price by year's end, but you won't get it.' She smiled, the smirk of the Circle player who knows she always wins. And she won," Madam said, setting the teacup down.

"We were eating once a day, and heating our hands over candles, by Sky Wishes Day. Then Grandmother got sick from the cold, and . . . ayah! When the nest is overturned, no eggs remain whole. Father had answered the conscription call two years before, and never returned. Mother's mind broke when Grandmother died. She's at the Crane God temple behind my sister's hill. Grandfather did not long outlast Grandmother. That tenth sale price barely covered the doctor's fees, and no one would hire us. Inauspicious, they said. Our bad luck would spread to others. We knew the Su family was spreading the rumors about us. Everyone was afraid of them."

Madam then said, "I don't usually talk about the past, and I would appreciate your keeping this sorry tale confined to the four of you. If you can aid Firebolt in his, ah, *her* attempt at freeing her gallant wanderers in the mine, it would please me very much to see the Su family thwarted, even a little. Nothing else ever seems to touch them."

Oriole finished relating this conversation, and regarded Lie Tenek and Rosefinch. "Madam Nightingale was good to me when she did not need to be, and gained nothing by it. She will always have my loyalty. I meant to deal this Su Suanek a blow on my own, risking only myself. I have a plan that can give Firebolt her diversion, and give Su Suanek a stunning face slap at the same time. But it is very risky."

"I'm already in," Lie Tenek stated.

Rosefinch, more of a coward, looked from one to the other. "I don't know anything about fighting. Except with my ink brush."

Oriole raised a hand. "I can think of ways for you to help that have the least risk. But only if you are willing."

Rosefinch's voice quivered, but she tightened her hands into fists, vowing, "I am."

"Then I shall scout quickly, while you get ready. Wear your most sober clothing, and you'll wait in the street while I scout."

The sun was just coming up, but already the south side of the city was awake, as an army of servants began the last preparations for the wedding.

A robe snatched off a drying line, an under-robe from a

mending pile, and Oriole was able to join the new servants, who were all bond-workers, standing with bowed heads as the governor's house stewards lectured them. One group had already been dispatched to set out pots of fragrant blossoms to brighten the streets along which the wedding procession would proceed.

Oriole bowed submissively, listening to the scolding directions of a governor's house upper maid, while she memorized the faces of new servants and old. It was these latter she had to avoid. She and several thin, beaten-down women in new servant robes were put to work arranging flowers in more pots.

Oriole's fingers quickly twitched and shaped bouquets of fragrant sweat peas, lilies of the valley, and peonies, as her mind ranged over her plans. Madam Nightingale had no idea that it was Su Suanek herself who was marrying today. Su Suanek and not the governor had chosen the man, who according to the gossip whispered on all sides, was expected to rise fast in the military — some even said to generalship, though he was barely thirty, five years younger than his bride — and very handsome, as well as being the third son of the younger brother to a marquis.

Oriole would not interfere with the wedding ritual. That would be a sin, and even a thief heeded some rules. But once that ritual was completed . . .

Oriole's quick fingers and her pose of submissive obedience were rewarded when the scolding chief maid pointed to her as part of the group to proceed to the house that the governor had built for the bride and groom. The garden was too new to look its best, though at night it would be impressive enough with painted lanterns hung everywhere, hiding the empty places where plants were too small yet.

The house itself was so magnificent no one would look anywhere else anyway. Oriole and her team were ordered to hang lanterns around the new terrace, and on the eaves of the overhanging roof.

As the morning wore on, the stewards became more frantic to get everything done, and Oriole was able to slip away, pick up a basket, and move through the house to learn where everything was, before she slipped out to the street.

Lie Tenek and Rosefinch sat at a table outside a tea house, waiting for her. She bustled up, having organized everything in her mind.

"Here is what we will do," she began.

A brief but heavy rain cleared out the brimstone odor long enough to bring in the scents of wildflowers and the heady sweetness of budding plantain trees, a familiar scent that burrowed into Ari's heart as she flew high overhead. She was a lot faster that morning, surer of herself on the sword, though she still knelt. The only other weapon she took was her Ki fan.

When she cleared the ridge that rimmed the caldera, Ari paused long enough to refresh the deflection ward over herself. Then she crossed the caldera as fast as she could, breathing lightly. Staying high, she was soon deep inside the cave of the older mine, as carts of brimstone were brought up from caverns below. Hot as it had been outside, it was far hotter inside. The miners, all unrecognizable with grime-darkened faces, had not even been given prison clothing. They wore whatever they had been arrested in. Some of those clothes had been reduced to rags, covered with bloodstains and filth so that the original dye was impossible to make out.

Men, women, even children worked grimly, hopelessly, driven by the clubs of guards whose contempt was made manifest by the idle blows to anyone not moving fast enough for them. At first Ari trembled with tension, but in that noisome murk, the miners walked bent, heads bowed; some of the men wore wooden yokes, which slowed them even more. No one ever thought to look up. It seemed they could not even straighten up as they dragged carts filled with bright yellow stone. The guards watched their prisoners, some desultorily, a few others with cruel intent, hawks eyeing mice.

After one fast circuit to assess the territory, she decided to land. She did not want to tire herself out too soon.

Hot as it was, she was glad she had put on her stockings and boots, as the ground was covered by a poisonous powder, judging by the horrible sores on the feet of all those who wore only sandals. Many had removed stockings to cover their hands as much as they could.

Ari's assessment included the guard patterns. On her second round through the cave, she was fairly certain she had spotted leaders among the prisoners. Elders all. She had thought that out on the flight: she did not believe anyone would pay attention to a teenager, which meant finding someone they *would* listen to. Like the big man with the deep voice. He was a prisoner, but the other miners gave him respectful berth, and when he barked an order, the rest obeyed without question.

That was her man.

When she emerged from the cave entrance, she was shocked by how far the sun had jumped across the sky. She made a swift flight to the site of the new mine, from which prisoners dragged away carts full of chunks of virulently yellow rock. She flew upward to breathe air not poisoned by the acrid stench of brimstone.

The wedding, Oriole had said, would begin when Horse gave way to Dragon, the most auspicious hour for a soon-to-be-general and the heir to the Benevolent Winds holdings. She had better get started . . .

The hundred-person kraken parade danced through the main streets of the city, the tentacles before and behind weaving and unweaving in pleasing patterns as others in fish costumes danced in and out, twirling and leaping.

In the kraken's wake, the groom appeared at the head of a long line of servants and musicians. He rode a prancing white horse decorated in red and gold, and began his procession to the bride's house to fetch her to their new home, cheered by the enormous crowd. He paused every now and then to toss golden coins out, provided by the governor—unaware, or uninterested (for the money was not his), in how many of the supposedly impressed and grateful recipients were north-sider children carefully dressed up, and running ahead to rejoin the crowd in order to snatch the largesse out of the air.

Servants began lighting red lanterns everywhere, which cast a festively ruddy glow. At the new mansion, the last of the red bunting was twitched into place by hasty fingers.

Presently the happy roar of wedding guests following the procession rose over the banging of the gongs and the loud screel of horns. The servants had finished preparations, and those not under orders crowded down to the street to see the arrival of the wedding party, and perhaps to catch a glimpse of the ceremony, as the two families gathered in the hall.

Oriole gestured to Lie Tenek and Rosefinch, who had been lurking in the garden, pretending to straighten lamps and bunting. "Now," she said, and the two dispersed—Lie Tenek to make her way along with Oriole through the house, Rosefinch detailed to guard a handcart, and wait in the street.

Rosefinch pounced on a cart that some servants had just lifted wine jugs from, and stationed herself across from the new guardian statues flanking the south-facing door. Once or twice harried servants tried to commandeer her cart, but she turned them away, claiming the steward had ordered her to wait there. Everyone was still too busy to argue—there was now the banquet about to be served.

How was Rosefinch going to get inside the gate? Oriole had said very mysteriously, "You'll know when."

That would sound good in a tale, Rosefinch thought nervously. But what exactly did that mean? She tried to calm her galloping heart by reminding herself that if everything worked, she stood a chance of making her fortune at last.

At the older mine, a single gong rang the watch change to Dragon.

The new mine had been closed up, the prisoners marched over and herded in to sleep at the old mine. One group of guards went off duty, replaced by the night guard. Ari followed the retiring guards down the steep hill to the riverside camp. Torchlight burned here and there, sometimes flashing blue as the miasma of brimstone fought the cleaner airs over the river.

Ari picked her first guard, a picket on the far side of the camp. He was alone, pacing back and forth the length of the camp, looking bored.

Ari stilled Sagacious from clattering against her back, and brought up her fan. The sentry did not notice her until she was within arm's length.

"Here, you—" He never got farther as the rounded point of the fan stick jabbed lightly into his Gateway acupoint, midway between his collarbones and the point where the ribs joined.

He stilled, then blinked once. She jabbed him again,

increasing the force, and this time he stilled completely. She reached for a thick wrist to check his pulse: yes. The slow, steady lum-dump of a person in deep sleep. First Aunt had said that this, the Sleep Strike, would paralyze the target for some breaths, but if she added a charm, it would last longer. Ari traced a charm over his chest, pouring Essence into it, bound to the rising sun.

Ari now had a full night to act. She sped away to the next outer guard.

This one also took two tries — he was so much thinner than the first, and she did not want to hit anyone so hard she stopped their heart.

By the third guard, she knew exactly how hard to strike, and she moved swiftly around the perimeter, leaving the two cooks for last, a big, burly man with a sour, morose face, and a short, solid woman with iron-gray hair hanging in a long braid down her back. No one made a sound, as no one expected her. More than half of those she tapped had been in their tents, asleep.

The hardest was the circle around the fire. They sat in a row on a log, hunched over their bowls of rice with freshwater fish and peppers. As she crept behind them, considering where to begin, she got close enough to hear the gist of their low-voiced mutterings.

". . . stupid enough to answer back. You're lucky you didn't find yourself up there in the mine."

"He wouldn't dare. My uncle didn't blink when I was transferred here. He's always hated me. But the old dragon would thunder if they insulted his house by putting the bond neck-yoke on the nephew of a count. How long are *you* in for?"

"Six more months in this hell," said another. "Six months of keeping my mouth shut. I advise you to do the same, Count's Nephew."

She sprang at them, moving fast before they could overcome surprise. Then she went back and worked the bowls gently from the fingers of those holding them. She wasn't sure what the effect would be on muscles holding a bowl of food through the night watches, so she tried to ease her victims into postures that would not place undue strain on limbs.

Last she checked the fire under the great cauldron of fish soup. It was a very low fire, set the way she had been taught as an orderly. It would burn out before too long. There was no danger of it spreading to the tents, to burn helpless guards.

She pulled out Sagacious, took a moment to breathe in the river air as she counted the barges waiting for morning's cargo, then reached for the vast pool of Essence and sped up the steep, barren sides of the caldera to the cave.

Here, she waited at the mouth of the cave for the guards to emerge on their circuit, and one by one took them out. Nothing would ever be so easy again, she thought grimly. Surprise was her greatest weapon, but that could only work once. Second strongest was that evil air, hard for guards and miners alike to breathe.

Now she had to get the leader to take the miners to freedom.

# THIRTY-SIX

THE WEDDING WAS COMPLETE, and the bride escorted to the new bedroom suite, where she sat decorously on the edge of the bed, her veil covering her face. So very different from her first marriage when she was scarcely seventeen and her husband not quite two years older. At least that had happened on another island, well forgotten here. What a brute he'd been! But he'd managed to kill himself horseracing while drunk, and after the mourning period she had told the family that she had done her duty. If she married again, she wanted to be able to choose the man.

So she had. She smiled, pleased with this turn in her life, but what was taking him so long? Those male toasts should not be lasting all night.

Bored, she sent the waiting line of maids away, just to get rid of them. It never occurred to her that they had been standing on their feet for hours.

Oriole had joined the line, and her feet ached as well. But as the others filed noiselessly out, she took a sidestep behind a spirit screen, so she was there when Su Suanek threw back her veil and lay down, heaving a huge sigh.

The loud voices of men echoed up the front stair: the bridegroom was on his way.

He entered in a sweep of crimson and gold, then shut the door firmly on his followers, who were still shouting bawdy jokes, amid laughter.

Ah, Oriole thought. Was that a whiff of smoke? Too many candles. It was already hot enough.

"There you are," Su Suanek said, sitting upright.

"My sweet, sweet consort," he exclaimed, too loud.

Su Suanek sighed sharply, not really surprised that he was drunk. Best to begin civilized — at least one of them. As she'd remind him when he was sober. "I'll pour you some tea, honored consort," she said, pointing to the table with the ceremonial offerings, everything either gold or pure moon porcelain.

"I don't want tea," he slurred. "Come here . . ."

Oriole groaned inwardly at the sound of fabric rustling and sloppy kisses. What was Lie Tenek *doing* out there —

A frantic rap at the door was followed by a high, nervous voice. "This miserable wretch begs forgiveness — "

The sounds of scrambling. "I'll slap her face off," Su Suanek muttered.

"Send her away . . ."

". . . fire!"

Sudden silence inside.

"Please, madam, did you hear me? His grace the governor sent this lowly servant to warn you, and to come away — "

Behind the spirit screen, Oriole smiled.

"Fire?" Su Suanek's voice was sharp. "The augur said today was auspicious!"

"My house," the man exclaimed, then, louder, angry, "My *house!*"

Su Suanek had risen, but she paused, snapping around so suddenly that her bridal robe swirled, sending the candles flickering and streaming. "*Your* house?"

He was too drunk to consider his words. "I never had my own house." Then an incoherent, aggrieved mumble that she didn't even try to understand. "Third son . . . chance to make general . . ."

"Please, madam!"

"We're coming!"

Oriole dared a peek, watching Su Suanek haul her new husband to his feet, her mouth a thin line. A pulse of sympathy surprised Oriole for the woman who had just married a man whose first thought in danger was not of her. Had she known that in marrying her, he was a carp leaping over the Kraken's Gate?

"Come," the bride said to her husband. "Let's get you into the garden. I'd better make sure those wretched servants aren't running off and abandoning us."

They started to the door, then he stopped, swaying. "Your father's gift! The gold!"

"It's gold," Su Suanek replied, as Oriole peeked around the edge of the screen, trusting to the shadows. "Even if the fire gets this far, gold will just melt. Father will get them to reshape it. Or replace it. Come, come. We have to stand over those lazy, worthless wretches and make sure they put the fire out instead of running out on us!"

A drift of smoke sent them scurrying out and down the stairs.

Oriole leaped out, threw the bar to the door, and got to work. First, she flung open carved box after carved box, until she found jewels. She set those on the table—the gold was beneath that box, in a huge chest.

A double rap at the door stopped her: the arranged signal. Lie Tenek stood there, a servant robe covering her other clothes, arms clasped around a chamber pot. Oriole dove for the one near the bed—newly made, never used. She pointed, and the two loaded in jewels and gold, testing every so often to make sure the receptacles were not too heavy. When each hit her limit, Lie Tenek said, "I left the side stairway clear, but it's filling with smoke."

Oriole nodded. She upended a jar of lamp oil around the room, tossed a candle onto the bed, another candle onto the pool of oil on the floor, then she picked up the chamber pot. With a wince of regret for all the work that went into the carvings and paintings and embroidery in that exquisite room, she followed Lie Tenek out.

The smoke was bad. They struggled down the back stairs, which had not yet caught fire—Oriole had been careful about that when she poured oil earlier. Still, their lungs were seared, and sweat poured down their faces by the time they reached a back exit only used by servants.

More fumbling about, and they reached the street. Here Rosefinch waited, cart at hand, a third receptacle in it. From the smell, either she or Lie Tenek had located the stinkiest chamber pot on the street.

People ran past them as they started down the street. Once they had to pause as what seemed to be the entire garrison ran past, buckets clanking. "There's your diversion, Firebolt," Oriole thought, as the three pushed their cart downhill, passers-by taking one sniff and giving them wide berth. "Good luck."

Ari found her leader easier than she had expected because the miners apparently slept where they sat down. He was not far from where she had first spotted him. He had what might be considered an almost comfortable spot on some rotting hemp sacks, no one crowding near. It was so hot in that mine that no one was ever going to get chilled, though none had a blanket.

She touched his arm. He reacted so violently she jumped back. A lantern on the wall revealed a flat, angry gaze below the forehead tattoo CRIMINAL. "Who *are* you?" he demanded.

"Here to get you out. But we have to move fast."

"What?" He looked around quickly for the guards.

"They're asleep until dawn."

"They never sleep."

"They are now," she said. "Charmed —"

The man showed his teeth, then said savagely, "Give me that sword. I'll kill them all."

Ari's stomach churned sickly. "We have to get the people out of here. I came to you because I thought you are a leader."

"I *am* a leader," he retorted. "I was, am, the Chief of the Green Eel Fleet, the fastest ships in the east. No one tells me what to do!" The man's muscles bunched as he swept that rage-filled gaze over her. She stepped out of his reach a heartbeat before he lunged. Then he fell to his knees, coughing hoarsely.

Ari stared down at him, sick at heart. So much for her entirely sensible plan of finding a responsible leader.

But she was not going to give up. If she could get *one* miner to go with her, maybe the others might follow? Raising her voice, she shouted, "If you want to escape, wake up!"

Heads popped up, and people slowly sat, all looking around fearfully, surreptitiously, suspiciously.

"If you form a line, it'll be faster —"

As she had feared—for she had seen what panicking people did when Screaming Hawk had come on the attack right before Shigan was taken—the biggest and strongest lunged up and shoved others aside.

*Of course* they wouldn't pay attention to a short teenager girl who stood there alone.

Furious, she ripped Sagacious from the harness. Summoning up a surge of Essence from the pool beneath her feet, she struck the rock at her back with the blade. White light splashed out as the blade rang reverberations through the stone chamber. Everyone jumped at the sound, as grit and dust sifted down from overhead.

The shovers stumbled to a halt, and now they all looked at her in fear. At least they were listening. She filled her lungs, pulled up Essence from deep within, and shouted in a voice that startled even her with its volume: "Line up! Now. No one will escape if you're *all fighting each other*. Get down to the barges—you know the way. I'll see you there!"

It took an effort she was beginning to find tougher each time, but she banged the sword again, and once again bronze rang on rock like a temple bell, when it ought to have been a clank. Sagacious, she thought as people scrambled into a ragged line and began shuffling toward the entrance as fast as they could go, almost seemed to approve of what she was doing; it was easy to see how someone might think it was alive.

She kept moving deeper into the mine and waking clusters of people. Fast as she was, word somehow spread faster. Which was good: the line up front pulled everyone else behind, and more swiftly than she'd let herself expect, the miners began streaming upward toward the mouth of the cave. Presently she reached the end. No one was left.

She whirled about and ran up the ragged, shuffling line, hand on her sword, every so often stopping to say, "Is anyone here from the Ki clan of Ten Leopards?" But all she got were blank looks or averted faces.

When she reached the mouth of the cave, she glimpsed the frozen guards still standing, wide open gazes fixed on infinity. She was just in time to see the Green Eel chief pick up a heavy rock, and bash it into the unresisting head of the nearest guard.

"Stop!" She used the Essence voice, her throat raw from all her yelling in this horrible air.

She brandished her sword, which glowed with Essence.

The chief of the Green Eels snarled, turning to face her. "I'll kill them all!"

Frightened, sober looks sidled toward him, then her, and many stopped moving. They crowded around in a circle, some whispering.

She sensed they were on the verge of attacking those frozen guards, until now avoided. But the one who had fallen lay helpless. That seemed to give them courage, as a few edged closer. A man bent to pick up a rock. A teenage girl picked up another.

"Think," Ari said desperately. "If this doesn't work and the garrison rounds you up again, *because of all the time you are wasting*, they will put you right back to work, won't they? Especially if you blame it all on me," she added recklessly — after all, there was no hiding what she'd done. "They call me Firebolt."

Two or three reacted to that: no more than widened eyes, and a startled exclamation, then whispers serried through them.

Speaking louder, she said, "Whereas if the garrison comes up here and finds all their guards dead, what do you think is going to happen to you when they catch up? Especially if they are on their way right now, while you stand around wasting time smashing people who cannot fight back?"

With a furious oath, the Chief of the Green Eels flung away his bloody rock and stumped off toward the road leading to the notch between the hills, which led down to the river.

The big man dropped his rock, and retreated. The teenage girl flung hers away, and rushed to the side of a frail woman. They, too, trudged up the path, as the rest began shuffling as fast as they could.

Ari flung herself down beside the guard with the bleeding head. A touch of his neck disclosed a faint, fluttering pulse. She hesitated, reminded of Brother Banig. Though he had been about to kill her. This man had just been standing there. She did not know if he relished his power over these prisoners, or if he was like the Count's Nephew and forced to be up here, or if he wavered between. She only knew that she could not walk away and let him die.

Sighing, she dropped to her knees and yanked out the Restoration Pills she had been wearing. She mentally resigned Yskanda's pill to this person. Being a scribe, way back in peaceful Imai, he was least likely to ever need one. The last pill could go to Muin.

She shoved a pill between the guard's chapped lips, then worked his throat the way Mother had done to her patients back in Sweetwater, until he swallowed. She held her breath, then let it out when the man glowed with Essence. His faint breathing strengthened, and even in the uneven torchlight she could see color in his face again. The wound on his head stopped bleeding. His eyes opened, and his gaze met hers.

"Choose a better life," she said—though she had little hope he'd listen to her. But that was what she had learned from the monks, from dear Grandfather Ki, from Petal, who got away from that terrible stepmother, though she did not know where she was going or the people she was going with. But scarred as she was, Petal had bravely come to believe that as long as you were alive, you could choose to lead a better life.

There was nothing more Ari could do here. She rose and glanced after the shambling line, some of whose bare feet left bloody footprints.

A deep disgust rose in her at the way these people had been treated. She backed away, gazing up at a sheer wall of rock. She raised Sagacious, pointed it, and brought up . . . fire.

Then, pointing the tip at the rock, she burned the characters for the word SHAME into the rock, each stroke the height of a tall man. When that was done, she sped to the site of the new mine, which was empty of life. She shut her eyes, feeling with her inner sense the way Master Ki had taught her. Not even so much as a lizard around.

For the first time, she smiled.

She circled slowly until she spotted a gaping hole full of the nasty yellow, pulled up a gout of flame, and sent it into the center of the hole. Fire splashed about, blue and eerie. The hairs on her neck rose—something was about to happen. Instinct caused her to speed away. She had nearly reached the old mine when a blast nearly knocked her from the sword. The ground below heaved, and the world around Ari lit up like a new sun.

Little blue fires licked everywhere . . . and as she halted, blinking the dust from her eyelids, a crack, a warning rumble, then a deep FOOM issued from the old mine. The entry belched a cloud of dust and small debris all over the forest of frozen guards as the inside of the old mine collapsed.

She steadied herself on Sagacious and rose into the air to begin the downward trip toward the river. Another demonstration might be due, lest there be a fight for the barges, the strong pushing aside the weak.

She was so tired she could not hover in the air without sinking. Pulling Essence became more of an effort; she flew above the road until she spotted the end of the long line, then lit on a cliff above them to rest a bit. Then she got an idea. She scrawled the charm that removed the deflection ward on her, and not five breaths later a young teen spotted her — someone not yet bowed down, like the adults around him. Word passed swift as wildfire.

She'd hoped to catch their attention, without any idea of the effect of her appearance perched there on the cliff moments after that enormous fireball and he ground-shaking rumble. All she noticed were upturned faces, pale in starlight.

She lifted her voice. "On the riverbank you will find some clothes. And some fish soup. If you go into the river to wash off the grime, you will be dry by the time you get to the estuary."

Her heart lifted a little when she saw comprehension in those tired faces, and a renewed vigor in their steps.

She stepped back out of sight, sketched the deflection on herself, and flew down the line until she found a good perch above another segment of the line. She repeated the message, and then flew, perched, and shouted a third time.

By then she spotted the river below. She sailed over the water to the camp again, then went through all the tents, helping herself to the guards' clothing. It took several trips to lug the stacks of clothing to the riverbank. She hoped that a bath, clothes for those who needed them, and the food might keep them from trying to kill the helpless guards.

By the time she had emptied the cauldron into a number of water buckets, and carried the baskets of steamed bread along with the soup down to the riverbank, she could feel exhaustion tugging at her limbs, and flickering at the sides of her vision.

Oh. She'd forgotten to eat and drink.

As the first of the line of prisoners stumbled down the last stretch of road toward the river, she gobbled down some lukewarm soup, and drank stale tea straight from the spout of a teapot. She felt less drained by the time the miners reached the riverbank. Most plunged straight into the water. Some dove for the food — they were all too thin, obviously fed the minimum to keep them going.

The big Green Eel chief, flanked by several other men, approached her warily. They seemed to be bemused by how fast she had gotten ahead of them, and she wasn't about to tell them how.

"We want justice," the pirate chief said. "These demons have been killing us off."

"The more time you waste, the less time you have to get away from the pursuit," she retorted. "You should be on the first barge *now*."

The big man spat on the ground. At least it wasn't on her dusty feet. He turned away, and she let a pent-up breath go.

Splash! The first barge pushed away, bearing a group of people slumped together.

Splash, splash! Exhausted and frightened people crowded onto the other barges, many after having grabbed food and clothes. Ari waited on the riverbank. When the last barge reached the water, she had to do Essence breathing. Her strength was waning.

She concentrated on letting Essence flow through her, then took to the air, aware that balancing on the sword was getting to be easier. She rose above the line of barges, then sped ahead, following the river as it widened, joined with streams, and then made its way toward the sea.

Once she circled back, though she was tiring rapidly now that she was moving away from the caldera and its vast pool of Essence. She tried to remind herself that distance was not a measure with meaning for Essence. But it was getting difficult to convince herself.

Her intent was to go from barge to barge to seek once more for Matu's family, but where would she perch? Instinct warned her against letting them know she could fly: once word got around, the imperials would surely hear, and they would always be looking upward.

Besides, she discovered as she flew unnoticed high overhead, more than half the barges had vanished from the river. Shock lent her strength. She soared upward, and spied the ink-black curving lines of the river branching off. Ayah! Those barges had taken river branches. Some were heading for the great marshland north of the city. They would have a difficult time in the marsh, unless they knew how to move in treacherous ground — but they would be that much harder to track down.

By the time she reached the city again, the sun was nearly rising. How long before the fan-frozen guards would stir, and waken, and then send up the alarm? She wanted to check on the miners . . . she wanted to find Matu's parents and grandparents . . .

Maybe after she rested, she promised herself. Her hand was heavy as she sketched the sight-warding charm over herself. She could feel the effort it took to bring Essence up through the sword to keep her aloft, with less and less effect.

She made it to her window.

She managed to shuck her clothes, and sink them into a basin of water to soak away the telltale stench of brimstone.

She washed as best as she could with what was left in the jug of water, fell into bed . . . and knew no more.

# THIRTY-SEVEN

THE JOURNEY HAD REACHED its halfway point when the line of sampans glided into the Sea of Heaven's Peace, a body of water fed by the greatest cascade in the empire. This mighty half-circle of thundering waters created white clouds of frosty vapors, above which thrust snowy peaks. The mist below the cataract resulted in the name Cloud Mountains Island. It was long believed the gods lodged in these, the highest mountains in the empire, a north- and south-running range regarded as the spine of the empire's dragon.

When the sun rose, the sampans began the slow circle that gave them a morning-long view of the spectacular cascades on the right-hand side, and on the left, the little island in the middle of the Sea of Heaven's Peace, on which long ago had been constructed one of the most beautiful of the empire's rare nine-roofed pagodas. Those interested in such things marveled at how so beautiful a structure could have been built on such precariously vertical rock faces, below which lay the monastery that served it. The monks and nuns (rare in the empire except for the Crane God's shamans, both sexes were permitted to join, keeping silence except to sing the ritual prayers) maintained the pagoda in perfect condition, climbing the rocky spires with ropes and picks in order to do so.

First Imperial Princess Manon had given the musicians a rest that morning, knowing that the sampans would be passing near enough to the small island to hear the combined sacred choirs singing the morning sutras, with the steady hiss and thunder of the falls in the background. She could not impose a schedule upon the emperor or his consorts or ministers, but in case Imperial Father took this opportunity to once again visit all the boats in the line, she had arranged another scholarly competition for her peers, with jade rings as prizes. The subject: the virtues of harmony.

The jade rings were expertly carved, the topic one sure to earn approval from the elders, the scenery beautiful, and Manon had chosen to wear robes of silver and blue, touched with gold, which she was confident set her off well against the mighty cataract as a background.

But luck, or fate, was as wayward as a butterfly: in spite of her efforts, the poetry competition went very quickly — too quickly. Jion, sitting silently on his cushion listening, suspected that others beside himself had guessed the drift of Manon's competitions and prepared with standard poems learned in childhood, which could be adapted with a word or two.

Jion lifted his gaze to the others, and caught Vaion and their Kui cousins fighting yawn after yawn. The only people who did not look slack-jawed from boredom were Manon's particular followers, led by Ze Kai's younger sister Nolu, who gazed on Manon as if she were the Morningstar God. Especially when, after years of being ignored, Ze Nolu found herself winning not one, but two jade rings. Pride and gratification turned her moon face and jug handle ears red, and Jion found himself feeling sorry for both Ze Nolu, whose poetry was awkward at best, and Manon, who seemed to think it her duty as host to praise bad poetry, as the wearying morning dragged on. The only one whose composure seemed unimpaired was Afan Yskanda, who illustrated indifferent poetry with fine art.

That was the problem — the poetry *was* indifferent. Good poetry excited everyone. Moved them. But Manon either could not discern good poetry from bad, or was unwilling to — unlike music. They both had hated bad music since they were small. Should he say anything? No! Not unless they were alone, and only if she asked.

Ah, was that the last jade ring?

Before Manon could speak, Vaion rose, bowed to Manon and then to the company with his very best manners — which meant he was up to mischief — then begged to be excused for an errand, which everyone took to be a trip to the necessary. But instead of going through the canvas door behind the potted plant, he walked down the length of the boat, crimson sleeves swinging.

Then Lu Fan, on what obviously had been a signal, rose, bowed to Manon first and then the rest of the company, and also excused himself.

Cousin Zuinan scarcely let him finish before he, too, begged to leave. At that point Su Siar bowed, her fan held before her face, and followed, sky-blue silks a flutter. With her departure, most of the scholars followed — including Ze Kai.

Jion saw Vaion loitering along the rail, just out of Manon's sight. Vaion beckoned to him, grinning. As soon as Jion neared, Vaion said, "We're going to your boat because it's larger than mine."

Morning school was the tradition, but that was over. Tradition freed them, though Manon had clearly planned for them to stay. Jion went to Manon, who turned on him her coldest face. Aware of other eyes, he fell back on formal mode as he thanked her for the morning's instruction, and excused himself first.

It saddened him a little that he felt he ought to be formal with her. And yet this was the way the adults spoke to one another. He knew that if she did move into the Pavilion of Sun's grace as heir, formality would replace the old, easy ways, as she was generally a very formal person.

He started away, then stopped when he spotted Afan Yskanda still sitting in his corner, his hands still. Yskanda was not a house servant, but Manon treated him as one. In the old days, he would have asked her about it — no, he realized, he would have shrugged it off. He had grown up with her firm division between ranks; it was only since his return that he had become conscious of it. Even so, in other matters, he had spoken his mind without giving much thought to it. That impulse . . . was gone. He was not sure why, but right now it did not matter. Suspecting that if he left the assistant court artist there Manon would forget about him, leaving him all day in that corner without anything to eat or drink, he gestured for Yskanda to follow.

Manon watched them go, so furious with Vaion that she scarcely noted the assistant court artist beyond his meekly following Jion. At least he was obedient. But that little beast

Vaion! He was growing to be more unmannerly than Jion had been before he left. Or was captured. She still did not know what had happened; she had strenuously avoided the subject on his return, and he had never brought it up since. Which was surprising, as hitherto Jion had told her everything.

She pushed away the subject from habit: he was back again, that was what mattered. As for her own plans, now that she was free . . . Go where the power is, her mother always said. If Imperial Father was not visiting, then that meant someone important was visiting him, and a future imperial crown princess ought to be there listening, with something intelligent to say.

We will leave her to it.

Scholar Shan Rou deserves his own chapters.

Because those chapters would have little to do with the phoenix feather, I make reference to countless tragic ballads centering around a low-born scholar studying for the Imperial Examination, who meets and falls in love with a high-born princess in disguise. The unhappy story of the romance between Scholar Shan Rou and Princess Ran Renyi is like those ballads.

His life the spring he turned twenty soared with the eagles seeking the sun when he won the coveted first place in the Examination. While he waited to see which branch of the ministry would get him, he and his beloved celebrated Spring Festival by dancing all night, as they say.

But however high they fly, eagles never catch the sun. Ran Renyi had to confess her identity when she turned up pregnant, though both had been careful to drink silver milkweed. There was no chance of crimson and gold wedding clothes for the daughter of a prince and the son of a tailor.

The empress — who knew she was dying — acted fast, and the week after a healthy daughter was born, Ran Renyi became first consort to the then Second Imperial Prince Enjai.

Though it caused the ruin of his life, Shan Rou could not let her go. He petitioned and begged first to marry her, then to see her; he lost his exalted position in the Registry, then the fine manor that went with it. Nobody in court would risk displeasing the gods (either in Heaven or in court) hiring him after that.

His steadfast loyalty, however, did not go unseen — and in

his despair he did not know it, but the empress, and Ran Renyi's new mother-in-law, had hearts to see it. The newly married imperial consort could not speak to Scholar Shan Rou herself, but the empress gave orders to see to it that he could visit his little daughter, and after the empress's death, and Second Imperial Prince Enjai succeeded to the throne as Emperor Guiyan, the new Dowager Empress Kui Jin had Scholar Shan brought into the palace as a tutor.

Life settled into a semblance of peace until the Second Imperial Consort, angry over being denied the primacy she had believed her right, discovered Shan Rou's background, and succeeded in having him removed from contact with the imperial children.

Shan Rou set up a school for the poor on the outskirts of the capital city, funded by First Imperial Consort Renyi, with tacit approval of the dowager empress — and the emperor. There, Scholar Shan Rou was able to see the Imperial Princess once a month, when she accompanied her governess to the Ghost Moon Temple. This benevolent tradition was carried on until Jion's disappearance, and resumed in the month before the Journey to the Clouds — a visit whose importance should not be forgotten.

In the meantime, the once-lovers' ardor cooled to friendship, first on her side, then on his. He saw his princess's ardor transfer to the emperor, and accepted it as fate, the reward being a tranquil friendship that the emperor tolerated, for he appreciated the scholar's persistent love for his daughter.

On this journey, the first and third consorts had conspired to include Scholar Shan once again in his capacity of tutor, approved of by the emperor, for Lily was soon to be forever removed to live among the Easterners.

Being a dedicated scholar, Shan Rou was determined to tutor Second Imperial Prince Vaion to the best of his ability. He also had another goal, as we shall see.

Scholar Shan received word that morning school had broken early, and his charge, Second Imperial Prince Vaion, was moving to his brother's boat. Scholar Shan went over. He took in Vaion's mutinous face and the restlessness of the others, as Jion's servants brought out tea and snacks.

At the sight of him, Vaion bowed, but issued a long sigh. "Please, Scholar Shan. No more poetry!"

Scholar Shan said, "I believe the Twenty-five Virtues are

your topic for the day, is it not so? And harmony is one of the Virtues. Tell me, is nature harmonious?"

Mock-solemn, he used one of the synonyms for nature that included human nature. Vaion, suspecting that his scowl lay behind the Scholar's question, blushed.

Jion suppressed a laugh. He had always liked Scholar Shan, who had guided his first characters. Suspecting what the scholar was about, he said, "For two days I've been hearing the rest of our study group recite the lessons we all shared together, under the guise of writing our own poems. Which were all borrowed from ancients who can't answer back."

"Ayah," Cousin Zuinan protested. "*I* wrote mine!"

"You wrote half yours," Su Siar murmured, disposing her fluttering silks daintily as she took a place in the midst of them. "Unless you were Yul Shao in a previous life, for I recognized half of his 'Dancing with My Shadow around the Star-filled Pool.' As for the other half, I must confess if you are Yul Shao reborn, you must have been a lot more wicked than we knew to end up with the poetic ear of a water buffalo."

Cousin Zuinan bowed elaborately at the insult—banter between the two of them nothing new.

Scholar Shan tucked his hands into his sleeves. "I suggest a return to Kanda, always a very good place to begin. Let us discuss what 'good' actually means."

With the ease of years of teaching, he guided them past the usual virtues of benevolence, righteousness, propriety, and wisdom, so often preached to scholars but not often enough seen in courtly life.

"What other virtues are there?" he asked.

"Mana Ta says that other virtues are mainly manifestations of the great ones," one of the more serious boys stated primly.

"Such as?"

After a brief silence, "There's courage," Scholar Shan pointed out, and noted who sat up a little straighter. "What can you tell me about courage?"

He looked right at Jion, who said, "According to Mana Ta, there's the courage of daring behavior, assaulting anyone who insults you. And in fearlessness. And in a commitment to righteousness."

Ze Kai spoke up. "That, according to Kanda, is the highest form."

"Correct," Scholar Shan said, and Jion wondered if he was

imagining it, or was the scholar directing this discussion his way? "Courage based on righteousness will lead to fearless opposition to wrongdoing, but also self-effacing acceptance when one finds oneself in the wrong. Or when one discovers that someone once admired is in the wrong."

Ze Kai said:

*"Mt. Lir often tricks our eyes,*

*A lonely hill seen from the sea,*

*From the drums of the imperial city a
towering crest.*

*The true portrait is always hidden*

*As we can only know someone from
within."*

"Em Sien," Scholar Shan said approvingly. "Interesting choice. What is another form of courage?"

"Strength," Vaion stated, and held up his arm, flexing it.

His friends snickered, whispering insults.

Scholar Shan just smiled, then said, "It takes strength to permit others to disagree. It takes strength to convince, to persuade. The opposite of coercion."

Lu Fan had been playing with the tassel on his waist ornament, but at that he looked up. "I've had to write that one a hundred times. Ten hundred times! 'Merit accumulates through good character and acts of kindness and generosity. Kanda says that children willingly follow the teachings and actions of a kind and generous father' —"

"And a mother," put in Su Siar. "According to the Sage Empress."

"The earliest writings are from Suanek the Blessed," added Ze Nolu self-importantly.

Lu Fan bowed her way, and corrected himself, " —a parent with Virtue, without the need for coercion."

Ze Kai finished the quotation. "'The wise parent uses ritual as a model for ethical behavior; the wise parent demonstrates through daily actions and decisions the importance of the family, and of ethical cultivation through education.'"

Bi Kandatai leaned forward. He was a small round ball of a boy, and would be a big boulder of a man. The others, inured

to the earnest and painstaking scholarship of the Minister of
Justice's son, braced for a long speech. "Substitute noble for
parent, which is Kanda's entire point, and we come to this: In
our earliest, more savage days, a lord was a leader, a warrior,
who led his defenders into battle to protect the community.
The lord was known primarily for his prowess and courage.
'When his war horns blare from hill to hill,' in the old song, it
meant safety for the people under a good lord, and danger
from a bad one. As enlightenment spread civilization, a
virtuous lord was known not only for courage and prowess
but for benevolence and wisdom."

Now that the subject was their own rank, of course the
young scholars would defend it. Scholar Shan let them talk,
while a few paces away, Yskanda stood at the rail with his
paper and brush, distracted as he gazed down and down into
the deep waters as sunlight spangled the rills rolling slowly
behind the sampans. *How* he wished to dive in. But if he did,
he would be hauled out again, after putting the guards to
considerable trouble. And then would the kindly imperial
princes be punished for not preventing him?

That recollected him to his duty. He swiftly sketched out
the shape of the circle, listening with part of his attention as
the noble youths assured each other that the wise lord's desires
for wealth and companionship were not problematic in
themselves, unless pursuing them in a manner that ignores the
benevolence that directs the noble to share joys with subjects.

"Which means not losing the lives of subjects through war
or privation, but allowing them to live fruitful lives, eating
well and having families," stated the earnest scholar.

"Is that all that makes a good lord? Benevolence?" Scholar
Shan asked.

"Order," stated Bi Kandatai.

"Merit," said the elder Ran twin, tranquil in the
expectation that when he was old enough, he would slide right
into a suitably high post, where he would serve the empire
blamelessly.

Bi Kandatai spoke up again. "Then we must look at history, specifically the early laws of Shinek Win, who before the
empire was united in peace and harmony, advocated promotion through merit. Nobles, who did the work of government,
and contributed warriors for defense, were exempt from the
laws—"

" —except when they rebelled —" Jion murmured.

"And lost," Su Siar said softly, sending him a long glance from under her lashes.

"And lost," Jion acknowledged without seeing that glance, "which was treason. And so all members of the family were executed, to the ninth generation. Which became an ominous tradition."

Once again Jion heard Yskanda's quiet voice: *We never would have been brothers. Your father was going to have my mother killed. And my father would have to do it.* That was the problem with such ideas as treason. Too often, history proved that the palace, and power, made a battlefield of the human heart.

Jion could not say that—not now. Without explaining, he knew would be misunderstood. At least he could do something simple for the innocent result of one of those private battles. As always, there had been a boat before dawn, bringing baskets of fresh fruit as well as other supplies. He looked down at the peach he had been peeling. He was not even that hungry, but he'd picked it up because it was a beautiful peach.

He set a spray of grapes on the plate next to the peach slices, and flicked a glance at Fennel, who came at once and knelt by his cushion. "Eat something. Split this with Yskanda," he murmured, under cover of Bi Kandatai's voice droning on in a long description of King Shinek Win's laws.

Fennel bowed, suppressing a smile—he had been looking at that fruit longingly. He went over to Yskanda, and gave him the plate, after taking his half on his palm.

# THIRTY-EIGHT

SCHOLAR SHAN TOOK IN the assistant court artist's startled reaction. He had heard from the first imperial consort that there was some mystery about this young man, and he could see that for whatever reason, the first imperial prince valued him enough to make what he thought was a kind gesture.

Scholar Shan suspected that the assistant court artist was reluctant to break the invisible wall of protocol before the entire group, so he drew attention away from Yskanda by saying, "Before we go farther, perhaps I ought to relent. You have worked hard today. Those wishing to play Circle, there are boards set up over there, as you can see. Those who wish to continue the debate, we can resume with a smaller group."

He could have predicted who would go and who would stay. There were some exchanges of glances, then Vaion and his particular friends fled. By the time the last of them had settled around the various game tables, Yskanda had abandoned his half-finished sketch, swiftly downed the plate of fruit, then spread a fresh sheet of paper to capture this new group.

Master Shan looked around at the small set—all future ministers, or would be married to ministers. Except for First Imperial Prince Jion.

"We can resume with harmony again, from the perspective of education," he said, willing Jion to listen—to truly look below the surface. "Knowledge. These revolve around two questions: the harmony of the universe, and the harmony of society."

"Uniting the two in ritual," Bi Kandatai said slowly. "Ritual is important."

Ze Kai gave a slight bow in his direction. "If the vital energies, man and woman, light and dark, are in balance, then the universe is in harmony. Unity."

No one disagreed with that, though Jion wondered what the real point was; when people stated the obvious, there often was a negation of some sort right behind. Unless the person was a pompous pedant. Though he had only seen Ze Kai at morning studies over the past month, and not for those several years before, he didn't think he'd turned into a pedant. Serious, yes. But Ze Kai's steady gaze was too watchful for pedantry.

Ze Kai went on, "The enlightened person emulates the highest ideal of the unity of humanity and Heaven. Then it becomes natural to serve the public good. As the parents govern the family, so the emperor governs the empire."

The word "emperor" dropped into a silence, ringing out in rustles of shifting positions and covert looks.

Where was he going with this? Jion wondered. Of course. The heirship. Wasn't Ze Kai supposed to marry Manon? Yes. Scholar Shan had some point, but it was clear the rest were reluctant now that the shadow of the dragon had passed overhead.

Scholar Shan said gently, "What we debate here are ideas rooted in the Five Classics, the very fundament of our traditions. When we debate the words of writers of thousands of years ago, how can that possibly refer to any one person now? This is a hypothetical emperor, and our context the Great Five, each a different and necessary vision. What are these?"

"Poetic," Su Siar said, with a flirt of her fan.

"Social," Ran Ysmin added.

"Historical," his twin brother said quickly — the third of the safe ones.

"Political," Jion stated. "A subject I am completely ignorant about," he added, with a mocking glance Ze Kai's way.

After the laugh died down, Scholar Shan said, "And metaphysical, which is at least as important as these others. Five times more difficult to understand. It might be fruitful to leave interpretation of celestial signs to those studying augury, for now. Politics seems to be a volatile word," he added, observing the little signs of remaining uneasiness in the Ran twins, and Bi Kandatai's frown of concentration. No one wanted to speak words that surely would be repeated, and perhaps misinterpreted. "It should not be, in a circle such as this, its goal enlightenment. Your imperial highness, can you give us a definetion?"

Jion had heard Manon on this subject — it was, in fact, her favorite quote. "Politics is said to be the tension between interpretations of principle and doctrine. Without strong leadership, that tension becomes conflict."

"That is one definition," the scholar said. "Do you agree?"

Jion had never really cared. But as he spoke the words, he actually listened to them. "It's a justification for central power — some say, for the emperor to be above the law, Heaven's Chosen in perfect virtue. He in turn leads the court in perfect virtue, which leads to order, harmony, and peace for virtuous subjects."

Ze Kai sat back, arms crossed. Jion's easygoing Ran cousins eyed him with an attitude of question, and he suspected that he'd backed himself into another one of those invisible walls with the words "perfect virtue." That was the highest ideal for a ruler — though some believed that the concept was embodied in the ruler. Therefore — as Manon believed — whatever the ruler did was . . . perfect.

And nobody was going down that path.

"We know what personal virtue is," the scholar said into the silence. "We have been discussing that. But what is virtue in government?"

Jion appreciated how the scholar neatly sidestepped the emperor, without seeming to. Anyone who would be a part of government in future could discuss its ideals.

Whiteleaf appeared with fresh tea, and Jion held out his cup. "Kanda distrusted laws, that much I remember. He said that virtue and ritual need no laws."

"While Mana Ta believed that law was virtuous if even the king of his day obeys it," Bi Kandatai commented. "Implying that the ancient kings were not above the law. My father says that while the Twenty-Five Virtues are absolutes, we have to remember that Kanda was born in a period of constant war, with bad kings rising like tigers on every island, and claiming to rule the whole. Every ship on the horizon scared the people because it probably contained an army, not aid. Kanda insisted that if people behaved righteously there would be no need for kings."

"No need for kings!" Ze Nolu repeated, aghast.

"That's a mere metaphor. He didn't actually say we ought to have no kings," Bi Kandatai said quickly, as unsettled as so phlegmatic a young man ever could be.

"Of course he would not—that's treason . . ."

". . . was a plea for people to act righteously, from beggar to . . ."

". . . the question was, what is righteous? How do you know when Heaven decides an action to be righteous?"

"That's why we have ritual and divination, to understand what Heaven wants . . ."

"Peace, peace," Scholar Shan said. "When everyone speaks at once, no one can hear."

Then Ze Kai said to Jion with a slight bow, "If your imperial highness would honor us by completing your thought."

"This lazy person is not certain it's worth hearing," Jion said, bowing back. "We are used to speaking to one another, as I said. But I learned only last season that we are not the only ones who debate. Assistant Court Artist Afan here led debates among the apprentices while everyone was painting."

Yskanda, working at his little table by the rail as usual, had frozen, brush in the air as he gazed down into the water, which was so much clearer than most sea water. Even with all that fresh water mixed in it would still be too brackish to drink, but shafts of light reached down, revealing the graceful undulations of tall plants, and beautiful sea life darting and gliding among them. He longed to fall over the rail and dive down so that he could *see* . . .

"Assistant Court Artist Afan Yskanda?"

Hearing his name, he looked up, startled.

"Nature and harmony?" Jion asked, smiling. "You are an artist. What is your observation on human nature?"

Yskanda recollected what Court Artist Yoli had said: no good could ever come of a court artist voicing an opinion on court affairs. Except that the question was no longer on court affairs.

He set down his brush, stood, and bowed, and because he had in a sense received an order, said slowly, "If this ignorant and talentless one is unsure, it is better to begin at the beginning, with the words generations of scholars recited as small children." His soft voice shifted to the singsong of recitation mode: "At the beginning of life, our natures are good. Humans when born are alike in nature, though custom and habit make them different. To retain the good, nurture must be good."

"You are on very solid ground with Kanda," Scholar Shan said with a smile in his eyes. "But?"

Yskanda flushed. "This foolish novice would never presume to contradict the master. It is only that . . . in his ignorance, this unworthy of no talent risks annoying this esteemed gathering by adding an observation from experience. Which emphasizes Kanda's point about custom and habit." He looked up — to see Jion as well as Scholar Shan indicate permission for him to venture into first person in speech as well as experience. He bowed, then said, "It was my old master's habit to send us out to draw the people we saw on the streets, whatever degree — "

"Where was that?" Ran Ysmin asked.

Yskanda looked down, wretched at how he had exposed himself — but then he hadn't, truly. His island was known to the emperor, so it didn't matter who else heard it. He took comfort in Ul Keg's whispered words that blessed day in the temple. "This lowly student passed early apprenticeship on an island called Imai, honored scholar," he said.

"Never heard of it," Ran Ysmin commented, not unkindly. "I thought you might have come straight from a famous school of artists."

Yskanda bowed again, and Scholar Shan indicated for him to finish his thought.

"It was observed," Yskanda said, "your imperial highness and honored scholars, that in any group, each would react differently to any event, such as a clap of thunder. One might be afraid, another bored, a third angry, and a fourth full of glee. The point, which is probably not worth hearing, is that commoners do not all share one thought and one emotion."

"They seem to in crowds," Ran Hamin said slowly.

Yskanda bowed to him, suspecting that sons of princes probably only encountered commoners in cheering crowds. Or jeering crowds, in the case of executions.

"Crowds do seem to share one emotion while they exist as a crowd, honored scholar. But in the experience of this worthless novice, they are much like a thunderstorm, appearing swiftly, making a great noise, then dispersing as individuals."

Scholar Shan nodded. "Can you bring that to our point about rulers as stewards?"

Yskanda hesitated. It seemed to him he'd already said too much.

"Tell us," Jion encouraged. "I've heard you speak among your artist apprentices."

Yskanda reddened, but complied with another low bow. "This ignorant novice's unworthy attempt at understanding, your imperial highness," he said slowly, "is that all relationships should be beneficial, but each has its own principle. Stewards," he said — for he could not bring himself to say *rulers*. "Stewards must act benevolently before they can expect reciprocation from the people. So Kanda says," he added.

The son of Minister of Justice Bi fixed earnest eyes on Yskanda. "And rulers *are* stewards. Although Kanda admired rulers who were able to establish peace, Mana Ta seemed to think that peace would only come after clarifying the proper hierarchy of human society."

"Correct," Scholar Shan said approvingly. "And Assistant Court Artist Afan is correct. Although rulers have a higher status than commoners, they can in a sense be regarded as subordinate to the commons in that they must guarantee harmony and succor in disaster. According to Mana Ta, whose three rules of government are carved there on the stone monument above the capital city, first in importance is reporting disasters, that the emperor might alleviate the suffering subjects. Second, sending and receiving documents, which includes registry and taxes as well as news. And third, investigating crime and overseeing punishment, that the subjects may live in harmony and peace."

*Assistant Court Artist Afan is correct.* Coming down the side of the boat, First Imperial Princess Manon heard the hated voice of that common Scholar Shan Rou. Did that mean the assistant court artist was actually speaking before his betters?

The first imperial princess had had a very trying day so far. First the lack of success with the carefully planned, and very expensive morning. She had begun the day not seeing any of the fine jade ornaments she had awarded Ze Kai hanging from his belt. The poetry was uninspired, and when she went to her father's great sampan, it was to discover that he and his purple robe ministers had closeted themselves with the Easterners. She ordered Bitternail to send her name in, to be told that the emperor would join his family later in the day. "His family." Relegating her to a group with fools like Gaunon and Vaion, and not acknowledging her leadership of this entire journey!

She had gone straight to her mother's boat, where the second consort had greeted her with a wry, "Closed out as well? At least that disgusting common pleasure boy of Ran Renyi's is not in there with her, Lily, and the Easterner prince." She added acidly, "Ayah! One chinless, the other too much chin. It's surely fate. What is that saying? Shave the top off a mountain to fill in the ditch, and at least you get a flat road."

Manon perforce heard her mother out. While the excoriation of the first imperial consort and Imperial Princess Lily were sentiments Manon shared, they were familiar — words her mother had repeated for years. Manon took her leave as soon as she could, her plan to join Jion, and reestablish her seniority. Prove her leadership. Surely Imperial Father would be visiting the boats again, after a dull morning with Prince Chinless. She could not fool around with a sword over in the guard court, but she could be seen leading future court leaders in intelligent discourse.

But what did she hear first thing? That disgusting Scholar Shan Rou talking, and apparently letting a servant presume to speak in company?

The question was answered immediately. Afan Yskanda's soft voice reached Manon, "It is this ignorant one's understanding, honored scholars, that Kanda believed the state must not exist for its own sake, or what transpires is the state of constant war Kanda lived in, never having a permanent home."

"You are correct." Was that *Ze Kai* speaking? He ought to be punishing the servant for presuming to raise his voice in the company of his superiors. But Ze Kai said, "Kanda spent his life seeking a safe environment, and thus valued the subjects being able to bring their own ideas, and experiences, to enlightened debate. That's the passage the Sage Empress expanded on when she stated that Heaven sees as the people see· Heaven hears as the people hear. If the ruler does not act ɨ accordance with the kingly way, the people are justified correction." Ze Kai had not said so much in the entire two ɾ

Manon had conducted the morning studies!

Resentment rose in Manon as Bi Kandatai's monotonous voice droned on, blathering stupid, no treasonous ideas. Why didn't Jion slap him hard? Because Jion was lazy, and sometimes stupid himself — and her life would be so much simpler if he stayed that way.

"... Kanda also writes that no human is devoid of a heart sensitive to the suffering of others. Such a heart must be possessed by the righteous ruler. Only then can the righteous ruler cultivate the four cardinal virtues: humanity, justice, ritual, and wisdom."

Manon would not criticize Jion, for a number of reasons, but she did not have to put up with treasonous blather fouling the air from mere ministers' sons and her bumptious Aunt Siar. It was time to restore her leadership.

Straightening her back and modulating her voice, she passed by the wind screen, swept her gaze around the little group, and said, "You are forgetting that the world is not benevolent, or wise, or there would be no need for an emperor, just as a child needs a parent. There are problems that require the use of force, such as controlling an ignorant populace, which riots first thing when there are disasters."

She looked around for challenge, but no one disagreed. She moved to the center. "As the dragon on the mountain can see all, so the ruler sees all, therefore must be above the law."

"Imperial sister," Jion said, imploring her inwardly to return to their once-equal free exchange. "Is there no room for debate?"

Manon turned to him, determined that whichever words were carried away about her would reflect her strength, her respect for Imperial Father, and her worth as his successor. "Why debate the truth, Honored Brother?" She turned her back squarely to the servants, of course, which included Shan Rou and the assistant court artist. "The empire is a permanent structure or else it will not function to shelter the subjects, just as a fortress must have a strong and lasting ceiling, walls, and floor."

As she went on to lecture on the necessity for a strong emperor, Jion realized Manon really did not perceive how her entry had deadened the discourse. It wasn't because she was stupid, or oblivious. Her tone made it clear that she regarded them as receivers of wisdom, not sharers.

Further, he realized she had always been this way. What kind of an empress would she make?

She was not done yet.

". . . I trust future discussions will be confined to those who will need such wisdom?" And then, after a gesture toward Yskanda, still standing, head bowed, near the back rail, she chided gently, "Have you not considered — when you expect a parrot to write poetry, is it not cruel to the parrot?"

Jion raised a hand. He'd thought so, too, once. At least he'd been raised that way. Thinking back to those pleasant days in the airy workroom as Yskanda gently led his apprentices in talk and work, he said, "Imperial Elder Sister, perhaps you did not know that the scribes debate and discuss many of the same topics so familiar to us. They have to, to understand where their art serves court life. Do you know the Six Principles of Painting?"

"My tutor discoursed on these," Cousin Siar spoke up unexpectedly. "There is Bone Method, which I understand is the skills of the brush; Suitability to Type, which has to do with proper use of colors; Division and Planning, which means arrangement on the page. Then there is Correspondence to the Object, which has to do with shape and line, and Transmission of Copying, which this person of little talent assumes is clear as said. And the most interesting, according to our shared cousins who study the art, is Spirit Resonance, which refers to the flow of Essence that includes theme, work, and artist. Nie Benno, the great artist, says that without Spirit Resonance, there was no need to look further at any piece of art."

Through all this Manon waited politely, and at the end, she still waited, her attention on Ze Kai, implying that he was worth listening to, should he care to speak.

But Ze Kai seemed preoccupied with peeling a peach.

Bi Kandatai cleared his throat, then addressed Jion. "I understand, your imperial highness. What you are saying is that artists have to understand not just history, but divination. The arts we use in governing. In order to reflect them properly in their art."

Jion turned his head. "Assistant Court Artist Afan, what does the painter in you say to that?"

Yskanda bowed. "This lowly one has only one answer, of doubtful worth, as I can see the tiger, but I cannot paint its bones. In like manner I can see people, but cannot paint their hearts." The deliberate cruelty of the first imperial princess's words had shocked him. He bowed again, then sat down and resumed his sketch as he tried with all his might to be invisible to her icily derisive gaze.

Ze Kai rose then, bowed to the company, and said softly, "No one can paint what does not exist." He signaled to his waiting boatmen to pole him back to the Ze sampan.

Jion stared after. Though Ze Kai's tone had been even, his face calm, Jion had sensed a flash of the hatred he tried to hide. Cold pooled inside him as he turned to his sister, to find her calmly, even complacently helping herself to the fruit. Had she not understood Ze Kai — or had Jion himself completely misunderstood?

# THIRTY-NINE

ARI WOKE LATE TO light glowing in the paper between the window lattices. She winced, feeling as if she wore several suits of heavy armor.

She had to do Essence breathing before she could rise. Her breath smelled of brimstone. She forced herself out of bed, drank fresh water, and almost immediately felt somewhat better. Hearing the light murmur of women's voices, she remembered the others, and readied herself quickly.

All three were gathered in the outer suite, the windows wide open to the soft morning air. From below came the cadenced ring of boot heels reverberating up the walls.

"Searches," Lie Tenek said succinctly.

"They've already been through here twice," Oriole commented over a cup of tea held in both hands.

A sense of alarm blossomed in Ari, then died when Oriole added, "I'm surprised you slept through it." Two searches, come and gone: no one suspected two rich merchants and their maids.

Ari drank a cup of tea, ate half of a stuffed bun, then stumbled back to her room and fell into bed.

When she woke next, the window was dark, as was her room, except for a small lamp someone had put on the table along with a fresh water pitcher. She lifted her hand and tightened her innards to make an Essence fire, then discovered she hadn't enough strength to do even that.

She rolled heavily out of bed, knee-walked to the table, and helped herself to the water pitcher. Then she used the lamp to light a candelabra.

The suite door opened, and Rosefinch came in. "I saw the light change," she said, pointing to the lattices in the sliding door. "Are you sick? You slept all day."

Ari was about to say that she wasn't sick, but she remembered the thinness of the walls. "Caught a cold," she said. Her voice came out a little hoarse. Her throat was still sore, though not much. "I just need to sleep."

Lie Tenek came in behind her, and slid the inner door shut. The two joined Ari at her low table, Rosefinch plopping down cross-legged, and Lie Tenek kneeling like a martial artist, ready to spring to her feet.

Low-voiced, Lie Tenek said, "The little girl brought dinner. Oriole will keep her busy."

"I must have smelled it in my sleep," Ari said. "I'm starving. What happened with you?"

Lie Tenek said, "Oriole's plan was to burn Su Suanek's house to the ground. After robbing her. They're still searching for the gold and jewels."

Ari gave her a dubious look. "Why? Is that going to bring trouble on us?"

Lie Tenek said, "I don't think so. Anyway, she did it for Madam Nightingale, not for us. I suspect that's why Madam helped us."

"Oh."

Lie Tenek went on, "At first, all the local talk was about the fire. Then, after the fire was put out, the horns and drums raised the alarm all over again—that was this morning—and the garrison emptied out. There was one more search, then nothing until just now. The little girl who brings the food also brings whatever gossip she overhears. Right before you came in, we were hearing wild tales about bond-miners vanishing by demon magic and lightning bolts thrown about by the demons who attacked the mine." She cleared her throat. "A fireball was seen by the governor's messengers half a day's ride away. Everyone is talking about an army of demons led by Firebolt of Redbark."

"Don't forget the cliff with the threat blasted into the rock, bigger than the biggest castle," Rosefinch said. "The demon-leader Firebolt used gunpowder to say that he was going to kill the governor and all his officials."

Ari rolled her eyes. "It was the word 'shame'. And the characters were no taller than that wall. Threat, ayah."

Lie Tenek smiled as Rosefinch clapped her hand to her mouth. "Even if you would have put 'happy birthday', the governor would see it as a threat."

Ari shrugged, still too tired to care what the governor thought.

Rosefinch said, "I can bring you some dinner."

"Thank you," Ari said.

Rosefinch sped out, whispering to herself, "*Firebolt and the Mine of Shame.*"

Completely unaware of Rosefinch's plans for her tale of the gallant wanderers, Ari found enough strength to eat a bowl of rice with crispy fish and vegetables. Then she lay down again, closed her eyes . . .

She woke to morning again.

This time all three had come into her room. "Breakfast," Lie Tenek said, bearing a tray.

"What exactly happened at that mine?" Oriole asked.

"It was terrible. You can't imagine how terrible," Ari said, her mouth dry. "I got them *all* out. I take it there are more rumors. About the miners?"

"Yes and no," Oriole said. "A group of former pirates who wore the tattoos of life sentences attacked one of the trade ships in the harbor. They hadn't a hope of escaping, of course. But apparently before they blew themselves up, they maintained that they drowned all the rest of the escaped miners. However, there is no word of bodies floating in the river, though there were empty barges. It's whispered among the servants and the water-boat polers and the cooks that the former prisoners who didn't escape into the marshes melted back into the north side of town, which a lot of them came from. But though the garrison has sent through searchers in huge parties, they haven't found a one."

"Tell her the other rumor," Rosefinch urged.

Lie Tenek's grin was lopsided. "It seems that there's a rumor that Firebolt wields a sword made of lightning. Then was taken away from the mountaintops by the Ghost Moon God, after getting everyone out."

Ari drank tea, hot as it was. "Oh, I needed that. Goddess of

Mercy grant they didn't really drown! I did go back once, and saw that half the barges *had* vanished into the marshes. I hope they can stay away from the pursuit."

"If there are locals among them, or people who know how to navigate marshes, they will," Oriole said. "You need to be seen, or the innkeeper will start wondering about serious disease, and offer to summon physicians."

Ari said, "Out of bed it is. I feel fine. Really," she added to the dubious glances. And to get away from those glances, "No more chamber pots for me. I want to go to the privy."

"I'll go with you," Lie Tenek said.

It seemed everyone staying in that inn was either holed up in their rooms or out in the streets gleaning the latest gossip, as the place seemed empty. The two were alone in the privy.

"There have been two more searches," Lie Tenek murmured. "Four all told. I'm surprised you didn't waken. You didn't find them?"

"Them?" Ari repeated blankly. "The Ki father and grandparents? No."

"No? You emptied *an entire mine* of prisoners?" Lie Tenek gave her a skeptical glance. "You are most definitely 'the other family's child' who is always so much more outstanding than one's own. I'm beginning to wonder if you are even human."

Ari snorted. "You're sitting right next to me, listening to me pee, and you have to ask that?"

Lie Tenek burst out laughing.

"You really robbed that governor's family?" Ari asked.

"Oriole insisted. Apparently Madam Nightingale gave orders of her own."

Ari sighed. "As soon as we can leave, let's do it."

Lie Tenek said, "We can't until the search is lifted. What we need to do is sit here and play tiles all day, then flirt at night, and talk about the entertainment house we'll start, so that nobody puts us together with any part of what happened."

"I don't know how to flirt," Ari said. "I'll stay here and sleep."

Lie Tenek gave her another of those skeptical looks as they washed their hands in the brass basin left for guests. "Raised by nuns? Or are you promised to someone?"

"There was someone," Ari admitted shyly. "I was very stupid about it." Her mind leaped straight from Matu to Shigan, but she said nothing more. There *was* nothing to say, was there? The whole subject was too much like singing opera without any rules.

"Did the two of you exchange any vows? Any promises for the future?"

"No," Ari said. "I don't think he could — "

"Say no more," Lie Tenek stated, her expression pained. "Do not tell me you are wasting your young years waiting for someone who has probably forgotten your name."

Ari surreptitiously fingered her tiger-eye hairpin. "I don't think he'd forget — "

"If he made no promises, he got on with his life," Lie Tenek assured Ari. "You are young, and strong, and you owe it to yourself to look about you. Find someone new to flirt with. Drink your silver milkweed and dance with wind and flower, snow and moon, if you are in the mood. And don't look back."

"Don't look back," Ari repeated.

Two watches later, she repeated it again to herself, as she stood in a group around a pair of men, one wearing a naval captain's hat, and the other in silk that proclaimed his noble birth, as they played a high-stakes game of Circle.

Ari already knew that the captain was going to win, probably in fifteen moves. She wandered toward the window to look down at the lamps outside. People strolled back and forth in the summery air, laughing, talking.

"Bored?"

She glanced up, into the face of a young man with a thin mustache. He smiled at her from wideset eyes. "Want to take a walk?"

She did, but not with someone who would ask questions she didn't want to answer. "I'm fine here," she said, and thanked him.

"I can bring you another cup of wine," he offered.

She had scarcely drunk any of the one in her hand. It smelled too sharp. "I was just thinking I want tea," she said.

His smile widened. "I know of a little room, right off the landing there, where tea can be delivered. And anything else you like." As he spoke, he stepped close, his hand gliding lightly over her shoulder and down her back.

She stiffened, and when the light fingers began to trace the curve of her backside, she shifted her stance, right hand coming up and —

"Oh *there* you are, Cousin," Oriole trilled. "No drinking and no flirting, with you getting married next Phoenix Moon — *your father the general* will be very displeased!"

The man lifted his hand as if burned and backed away, muttering politenesses before he vanished in the crowd.

Oriole sighed. "Just in time."

"He had his hand on my butt," Ari muttered, her face aflame.

"I know. I saw. And instead of pushing him away, or using your fan, you were about to throw him through the window. *That* wouldn't call attention to us."

"Oh. Uh." Ari blushed even deeper.

Oriole guided her away. "There are plenty of perfectly decent men here, but once they get a drink or two into them, twenty generations of grandfathers assure them that they can take whatever they want. Come. I'm going to teach you how to handle men."

"All right. Wait. I don't actually want to turn into a . . . an expert flirt."

Oriole crossed her arms and tipped her head to one side. "If I ask for sword lessons, and you give me a day of stances and poses, will that make me an expert duelist?"

"No." Ari smothered a laugh.

"It's the same with the dance of courtship," Oriole said. "What you'll get is a little understanding, and a trick or two that saves everybody's face. A couple days of practice, and the four of us will sail away, no one remembering us a day after we're gone. Which will *not* happen if you toss through the roof some grabby boy with too much rice wine in him."

Ari nodded humbly.

# FORTY

DURING THOSE DAYS, THE Journey to the Clouds continued, though the atmosphere had changed, a tension seeping through the mist-wreathed, beautiful line of floating boats.

The imperial family sensed it first, about the same time as word of disaster filtered through the various member of the Su clan.

When First Imperial Princess Manon went early to greet her mother, to her surprise, the second consort made certain the flimsy doors were shut, beckoned her daughter close, and whispered, "Whatever you do today, make certain it is excellent. Traditional. And when you see your father, you will be as polite, as filial, as you have ever been."

Manon thought back to the day the news went through the family that Jion was missing—but she had nothing to worry about, she reminded herself. "I always do, Mother, but thank you for instruction," she said with a hair too much irony as she bowed.

The second consort slapped her across the face. Then, as deliberately, she slapped Manon on the other side so the red marks would match. "You had better be more filial than that," she said. "My Second Uncle's mines were blown up. That will touch Honored Imperial Father's interests."

Manon gasped, pain forgotten for the moment. "What? Who would dare?"

"I don't know. Rebels — pirates — something or other about the criminal wanderers. Until I hear from my own family sources, I wouldn't trust too much to the details of these rumors, except that *something* happened, and anything to do with gunpowder gets your father's attention. There were boats going back and forth all night, and the air was full of pigeons' wings."

"Today's schedule begins with the Easterners' poetry reading before the ministers, then there will be the play to commemorate the betrothal treaty —"

"Don't waste your breath telling me. Go make sure every detail is *perfect*," the second consort ordered, and Manon fled.

She busied herself checking everything, which succeeded in only getting into everyone's way, and she carried such an aura of tension that her presence, as well as the whispered rumors about ferrets coming and going all night, created an atmosphere that was the very opposite of peace and harmony.

The morning passed with excruciating slowness, everyone painfully correct.

The emperor did not visit any boats.

The next two days passed in superficial peace, everyone still in their best clothes, and on their best behavior. Only the music continued — on the surface, everything serene.

There were no more extemporaneous debates, and no more unplanned visits back and forth. Vaion stayed on his boat, having been ordered to remain there by his prudent mother; Scholar Shan stayed with him, dutifully supervising lessons, though his gaze often strayed to his daughter's boat when the sampans rounded a curve.

Jion sat with his mother most of the first day, as they talked over what little they knew of the Easterners' land. Lily remained on the emperor's boat, speaking with her betrothed — actually, she was doing her best to learn his language, and to understand something of the land she was to live in.

The eastern prince, to his credit, tried his best to present his homeland favorably, so that she would find it welcoming, without raising unreal expectations. But she scarcely heard a word. The hypothetical had become real, and she barely took in the superficial details: two main islands, both large — the inside of the largest mostly uninhabitable desert — great traders, some said swift pirates — new treaty, valued silk over gold. They even traded in bolts of silk, as did many in the empire.

Jion could see that his mother was far less worried over whatever alarm had gone up than over the prospect of her daughter sailing away, perhaps forever. But it didn't do to say so. They stayed firmly on the subject of the freshly signed betrothal treaty, and so the emperor found them when he abruptly walked in that second morning. The sight of his eldest son with his mother, both bent over a map of the Eastern islands, soothed the irritated emperor somewhat.

The three of them breakfasted together, and then the emperor was told that Fai Anbai awaited him on his boat, and he vanished as abruptly as he had come.

After that, Jion returned to his own boat, and there he stayed. Except for Vaion jumping back and forth between his boat and Jion's whenever he could escape lessons, he had no other company beyond those already there—which meant Yskanda. Jion was content with that, for Yskanda still interested him.

He discovered that Yskanda, for all his dreaminess, played a slippery game of Circle. Furthermore, the parity of sitting on either side of the Circle board got past Yskanda's vigilance in a way that pleading never had, and to Jion's satisfaction, they continued the debate about human nature and the virtues, which led to their respective reading, and that led to almost every subject under Heaven—except personal matters. But Jion had not expected anything different.

The hours fled by. Jion exulted whenever he could make Yskanda laugh. It was somehow a familiar laugh. Not the sound, but the way his head lifted, and his delight flashed freely, so very different from the studied courtly titter. He could not identify that sense of familiarity. He certainly had never met anyone who resembled Afan Yskanda—that he would have remembered.

As for Yskanda, he no longer felt a jolt of shock at Jion's first appearance, or thought of him as a younger version of the emperor. Instead he found himself identifying the subtleties that differentiated the first imperial prince from his father— the humorous quirk of eye, the mirth in his flashing smile, the attitude of hands. At night, before he slept, he liked sketching these individual characteristics in his mind.

That was the only privacy he got in that stuffy cubby. He

had long learned the trick of memorizing details for later drawing, though he wondered at the variety of expressions Prince Jion exhibited, going in moments from a wicked humor to a sobriety that seemed older than his years; he'd lose all those years, and more, when he gazed up at the spectacular cataract, but in the next moment, the resemblance to his father would come thundering back. Yskanda marked those moments, which he took as an excellent reminder to mind his words.

There was plenty to paint in his surroundings, in soft light and strong, even at night, as Ghost Moon waxed. And so, they arrived back at last to the glowing vents, which added vapors to the thick, swirling fog that the polers always took them through at night.

The quality of that fog was different, with Ghost Moon full beyond it. Yskanda longed for a method by which he could dip his brush in that moonlight, to paint the world shrouded in silvery mystery. Though the boats remained in their precise order, it was easy to imagine each isolated from the others.

As the fog curled gently around them, Jion sat forward in his boat, alone with his guzheng. If Manon, in her boat immediately forward, heard Jion's music, she chose not to come join him in a duet, though he'd hoped to inspire music to drift out of the mists. Jion played on through watches. Occasionally he sang, which Yskanda had not heard before.

Then late one night music drifted along the steep canyons from the sampans ahead, poignantly beautiful. Jion was again alone, Yskanda having gone to mix up a fresh set of colors. Jion assumed it would take all night, which meant no Circle game or even conversation. As well—it would be terrible to waste such music . . .

But Yskanda had heeded Court Artist Yoli's advice to mix as much as he could ahead, so he was soon done. Hearing music, he wandered forward with his habitual soundless step. Thus he came on a sight that shocked him still: Jion, alone, lit by only moonlight, dancing to the faint strains from musicians unseen.

The sight took his breath away. At one moment, Jion seemed to float in a fabulous leap, his silk rippling and swirling about him. He was the epitome of vigor, grace, and strength, the angles of shoulder to hip, knee to chin, shifting in compelling patterns as he moved through the ancient fan

dance known as Sword and Shield. The fan sometimes pointed, or jabbed, mimicking a sword's thrust, then unfurled with
a snap, becoming a shield. It was an essentially masculine
dance in every way; Yskanda, dazzled, reached for a brush
that was not there—then caught himself. He had not been
invited to this private, this intimate moment. He was staring.
He withdrew, one step, two, and retreated to his airless cubby
where he lay gazing upward until his heart slowed its race.
The thought occurred to him that politeness, though a necessary part of the ritual of society, masked the truths of the heart,
whereas music inspired it.

The next morning there was no mention of dancing.

Jion, unaware he'd had an audience (and he would not
have cared if he'd known Yskanda was there) was in a good
mood. It had been far too long since he'd felt the urge to dance
and was actually able to do it. Others wrote poetry, or chanted
sutras, when in that sort of mood. He expressed those
emotions through movement.

Yskanda struggled to behave as if nothing had happened,
though he felt oddly unbalanced, as if his life until yesterday
had reached the end of a scroll, and a new one was yet to begin.

The next day was quiet, undisturbed by anyone as the fog
drifted along the decorated roof of the sampan and softened
its contours to mystery. Whiteleaf and Fennel oversaw the
appearance of meals and the disappearance of dirty dishes.
Jion and Yskanda sat on the prow through most of it in
companionable silence, Jion reading, or napping. Yskanda
busied himself while the intermittent light was good, painting
the quick glimpses of towering spires and lonely waterfalls, as
drifts of song wound through the sampan.

*" . . . the spring-new lute-flowers. . .*

*. . . upon the nests of herons in the
moonslight . . .*

*Cloud-banners fly as the dragon-king rides
the whirlwind . . ."*

The shadows began to meld, and Jion went into his cabin
to change his clothes before going to his brother's sampan for

hot wine. Night had fallen, the rocky passage on both sides hidden. Yskanda turned away. There would be no more drawing this night. The moisture in the air was already curling his papers. Time to put them away.

He scurried inside the narrow corridor at the back. The air was heavy with the sense of others slumbering; it had become late without his being aware. He felt his way down the row and found his cubby. The door was no more than a canvas flap; because it was dark as ink inside, he tripped over his bag, which he had left sitting inside the door slightly out of place.

He fell to his knees on the bedding, clutching his paper and brushes and ink to his chest lest they fall and clatter and clink, waking everyone around him. Two soft thumps were the only sound—his knees and then the warding stone falling out of his sleeve.

He felt around until he oriented himself, then carefully laid his materials and tools neatly where they belonged. Then he stood uncertainly. He had not been dismissed—but Jion had relaxed formalities. He knew he would not be scolded if he went to bed, except he was not tired. He was, if anything, restless, and that stuffy little cubby seemed more than usually intolerable.

He smoothed the bedding for his return. All he'd have to do is crawl in, shed his clothes, and roll up.

He straightened, back to the canvas door, remembered the warding stone still on the floor, then shrugged inwardly. He knew exactly where it was. There was no company to be vigilant around—First Imperial Prince Jion had gone to his brother's boat, and most of the servants had been dismissed for the night. The fog made an effective wall around the boat; surely he could forgo having the thing knocking against his side for a little while.

He slipped out, and made his way down the dark, silent corridor toward the light at the front of the boat.

"Ah, back again?" Jion asked, startling him.

Yskanda was thinking the same thing, but of course kept silent.

Jion had found Vaion already drunk out of sheer boredom. He'd ordered him to bed and returned, restless and bored himself. He toasted Yskanda with his wine cup, and as Yskanda bowed himself into retreat, Jion said, "Don't go." It was meant as an invitation, but of course Yskanda heard it as an order.

Jion went on, "I remember the first time I came on the Journey, the fog was so thick that I couldn't see the back of my father's boat. I kept hoping that I'd walk into the fog and end up somewhere else in the world." His voice was full of rueful humor.

Yskanda did not have to see his expression to know the slant of his expressive brows, the sardonic curve of his mouth. The prince sat alone on a pile of cushions with his guzheng on a little table before him. Yskanda turned away from the golden light pouring out of the cabin behind them, and gazed ahead, to recover his night vision. It came quickly as he watched the drifts of vapor half-obscuring ink-black rock spires, facets winking and glittering in the starlight glowing between drifting clouds. They were beginning to come out of the fog at last.

A warm breath of air on his right cheek brought his gaze in that direction, to see steam billowing up from a vent in the rock. It glowed a deep ruby red.

The smell of the steam was pungent—a grounding, clean-soil scent that helped to steady Yskanda's head, for as he gazed about him and above him in wordless delight, his head throbbed a little. Not painfully. He was not ill, the way he had been that first New Year's. But the heady sensation, as if the sides of his skull had dissolved, freed his thoughts to encompass the clouds, making him almost unsteady on his feet. Almost. For he felt oddly light as well.

He breathed in slowly, reveling in all forms of water present: the sea below, the steam at his right shoulder, the drifting fog off the as-yet unseen waterfalls to the left, and above . . .

Yes. He raised his hands, though his eyes had closed, for his fingertips tingled with memory of the cold bite of snow on the great heights. His chest thrummed with the thunder of the fresh water drumming just ahead. And below his feet he sensed the vastness of the ocean deep, brimming with life.

He was beyond question; he had not the words for the glimmering, glowing lights drifting, darting, diving below. Around him, too. Both sides of the rocky precipices sheltered softly gleaming lights. Different from the diamond sharpness of the stars overhead: these were living, breathing beings, all.

One of the drifting clouds passed between full Ghost Moon and the waters below, sending down a brief shower.

Jion scrambled to his feet and ducked under the awning. Then he gazed in surprise at Yskanda standing at the prow, oblivious to the drenching rain. Wreathed with fog, Yskanda was barely visible in his blue-gray robe, his hair a shadow against the rocky spires . . . until he began to shimmer with an eerie glow.

Jion rubbed his eyes, hard. He wished he had not drunk so much wine himself; on Vaion's boat he'd drunk to blot out the patient sadness in Scholar Shan's gaze.

He blinked. He had only seen that glow twice in his life, at Loyalty Fortress and while on the wander. Somehow it seemed utterly impossible that it could happen here, surrounded by his family and the imperial court.

He started forward, but halted as rain spattered in his face, shocking him with cold. The mild muzzy warmth left by the rice wine vanished like smoke, leaving him staring uncertainly at Yskanda's back.

Yskanda looked, and was, oblivious to the rain. The cold. His body felt light as that steam rising from the vent, as if he could step out onto the water, the better to see the beguiling forms of life below the surface.

Jion pushed past his amazement, his uncertainty, concern for Yskanda foremost. "Come back under the awning, Yskanda," he said, chuckling at the assistant court artist's typical cloud-mindedness. "You needn't get so wet." He glanced skyward; the shower was passing, though rain still poured down.

Yskanda turned his head, and yes, he really was glowing, though Ghost Moon was still hidden. This was no reflected glow from the moon. This truly was the same glow Jion had seen from Ryu twice, and never before or since.

"Did you know there are people among these rocks?" Yskanda asked conversationally — no titles, no disparagement.

Jion was not about to call attention to it. He said with grim humor, "There ought to be. Gods grant they give extra pay to the imperial guards shivering out there."

Yskanda was distracted by another drift of fog. He breathed it in. And when he turned his head the other way, he sensed a familiar presence, though neither could see the other. "Chief Fai Anbai," he murmured. "Why is he here?"

"Do you see him?" Jion asked, his voice low as he stared into the blank fog.

"No," Yskanda said — puzzling Jion exceedingly.

Jion said carefully, as though addressing someone younger than Vaion, "The ferrets, and the imperial guards, are out there, but under orders to remain unseen from our vantage . . ." His voice suspended when he saw that Yskanda leaned over the rail. The waters, usually a deep indigo at this time of night, were fast turning black as if ink poured down from one of the fog-shrouded cataracts.

Instinctively Jion caught Yskanda's wrist, meaning to keep him from falling overboard.

He froze, nerves flashing icy and hot at the same time, and his breath stuttered as the world changed.

The water shimmered, then glowed with a roiling surge, though his ears detected no sound of water, and the boat was steady below his feet. But before his eyes a tentacle rose, glimmering with blue light, and thick as a man's body. It rose and rose, looping impossibly high. Then another tentacle rose on the other side of the boat.

Numb with shock, his thought seemed to come from far off. He had no weapon — and even if he did, how could he fight so measureless a creature that seemed to be here and not here? Then the end of the first tentacle lifted free of the water, and lowered toward Jion and Yskanda. Jion still gripped Yskanda's arm, and he tried to draw him back, away from that glimmering tentacle, but Yskanda stood rock-still, and reached up with his free hand, palm cupped.

Yskanda was not aware of Jion at all. He stood there in the grip of a dream-not-dream as a deep voice thrummed through his bones, far too deep and vast to be heard through his ears. He could not catch the sense of it, and felt a little as if his fragile, too-small skull was about to fly apart.

Then the sucker at the very end of the tentacle touched his hand, as delicately as a butterfly lands on a petal.

The nearest emotions he could descry were wonder, and a wash of curiosity, followed by a stream of sensations Yskanda's human self was ill-equipped to comprehend. He did his best — wordlessly he questioned — after which he was answered.

Of course his mind attempted to force what he heard into human words, the sense of which was *The great one hears you*. But it was not right. For one thing, the "you" had wider reach than Yskanda standing on that boat — and Jion, still holding onto his wrist.

As if this attempt at communication were as wearing for the ghostly form of the kraken as it was for him, the tentacle lifted, and vanished beneath the water without a splash.

The inky darkness rippled away in the water, and was gone.

Swathed in fog, the sampan continued to glide quietly, as the water rilled around it. There was no sign of the kraken—if it had even been there. All that had happened within a dozen heartbeats. Jion drew a shuddering breath, realized his fingers were still crushing Yskanda's wrist, and he let go. Yskanda staggered against the rail.

Jion said, "Are you hurt?" And, "What *was* that?"

"No," Yskanda said, almost too softly to hear. "I'm so tired."

"Go . . . rest?" Jion said, dissolving into helpless laughter. The word seemed so inadequate after what had just happened.

Yskanda walked away, leaving Jion full of question: what exactly *had* happened? If that kraken had been real, the boat should have upended. Probably Manon's and Vaion's as well. Maybe five or six of them. But it *seemed* so real! Then he frowned at the inadequacy of the two choices, real and unreal. That was something altogether different, not a waking dream, and certainly not an augury. Already he distrusted it— distrusted his fumbling attempt at interpretation. The kraken that was no kraken, the sense of familiarity—all that was surely his mind playing tricks.

He made his way to his spacious cabin, where Yarrow, half-dozing, sat waiting to aid him in readying for bed. Jion looked into that sleepy face by the light of the single candle and knew that the graywing could not possibly have seen a kraken and remained so drowsy.

He tried to sleep, but tossed restlessly in his fine bed, while fifty steps away, Yskanda sat in the darkness, fists tight on his knees, willing that entire experience to be nothing but fanciful dreaming. Not madness.

But he was thrown back in memory to when he was very small and village aunties whispered about demons and madness. He no longer remembered what he had said, except that he wanted to paint the beautiful things he saw that others did not seem to see. It was *not* madness, which he associated with anger and loud voices. When he was left alone with his experiments in making paint, life was quiet and good. It made sense.

Until one stormy night, when he could not sleep, though Mouse and First Brother slumbered. Mother was there, talking to Ul Keg while they peeled lychee nuts. Demons . . . gods . . . the Alk Gift . . . the burden Mother's sister carried. . . He did not remember finally lying down and sinking down and down into memory and dreams of deep water voices; he woke with a start when someone moved past his canvas door. He remembered everything — including Jion being there.

The prince was going to ask questions. Of course he would — Yskanda had his own questions. He remembered everything with pitiless clarity. Something had happened, because he had left the ward stone behind. And Prince Jion had seen it.

What to say? What even *was* it? Madness — or augury? Court Artist Yoli's warning repeated in his inner ear: no good ever came to augurs. Instinct insisted it was something altogether different, that had nothing to do with foretelling the future, or even of reading signs for affinities in order to interpret Heaven's will. But he could not say what it *had* been.

If Prince Jion spoke to the emperor, there was nothing Yskanda could do, and his life was already balanced over a river of knives.

When he emerged with his paper and brushes and inks, he was ready. He soon saw Jion, who was in company with his brother and several cousins, chatting back and forth as they stared into the swirling fog.

Jion sent Yskanda a strange look, full of question, to which Yskanda responded with . . . nothing. The question turned to doubt.

"What was that?" he asked abruptly.

"May this ignorant servant inquire what was what?" Yskanda asked, bowing.

"Don't hide behind protocol," Jion retorted, exasperated. "That kraken. I swear I saw it, but the boat never moved. How is that possible?"

Yskanda bowed his head and addressed the deck. "That the boat never moved suggests to this ignorant one that his imperial highness labored in the grip of a dream. There was an empty bottle on the table, I noted."

Jion stared. Yskanda seemed utterly calm. Which no one

who had actually been touched by a glowing tentacle as long as a five-roof pagoda could be. Had he truly been dreaming? He definitely had been drinking. In the light of day, that seemed the likeliest explanation.

A mountain loomed out of the thinning mist, and they glided into the tunnel. Another voice, this one a boy, sang a farewell song from the sutras to the Goddess of Mercy, his voice echoing as if falling from Heaven.

The Journey to the Cloud Empire had ended.

# FORTY-ONE

ARI DID AS SHE was told, listened to what she was taught, but her internal sense of danger turned to urgency between one day and the next.

That third morning after she woke, she said to the others, "If we don't leave now, we might not be able to. The local searchers seem to be done, but if more were being sent from the imperial city, wouldn't they be getting here soon?"

Oriole set down her teacup. She had been enjoying herself immensely, but she had come to trust Ari's tactical sense, young as she was. "From the imperial city? We have a few days."

Ari shook her head slowly; there was something about the lack of search the previous day, the sheer quiet, that disturbed her. "I want to go. I can do that on my own if you'd rather stay."

Oriole knew that Madam would be disappointed. Bowing to the inevitable, she turned to Rosefinch. "You settle up. I'll make it clear to the right talkers that we are going back to get more money and plan to return with our grandmother to make a final selection, so that it doesn't look like we're running away."

All went as planned.

By midday they stood on the deck of their luxury ship, fans plying as they waited for the tide to turn and carry them out.

The crew chatted, trying to look unconcerned. But everyone was thinking about all that stolen gold in its reeking containers below as they watched the last of the incoming ships doing their best to get into the harbor.

Or nearly everyone was thinking about it. Ari seemed the calmest as she watched the boats in the harbor. "It seems as if the gold is no more than sand to her," the captain's teenage daughter grumped — for the sailing family had been promised their share, should the gold remain undiscovered by the searchers. (As it had. The flies buzzing around the chamber pots as well as the stench had guaranteed that.)

"It *is* almost sand to her," Lie Tenek said, hiding a smile.

"She's a runaway noble?" the daughter asked, eyes huge.

"No, no, no, no," Oriole assured her, with a slight frown as if the daughter had accused Ari of being a child-stealer. "Ari was so poor I don't think gold is quite real to her. She hates to part with a single tinnie. I've seen beggars less careful with their cash."

Lie Tenek wiped her damp palms down her thighs as she glared at the choppy waters, wondering if the demon-cursed tide would ever turn again in the history of the world. "To us, gold is power. To Ari, Essence is power."

"Oh-h-h-h," the daughter said. "One of *those*. She might as well be a hermit! Or a nun in some faraway sect, learning how to quiet the dragons under the earth!"

Lie Tenek turned away, smothering a laugh. Oriole kept her eyes out for the harbor guard's boats — it was too easy to imagine a surprise fourth search.

Oblivious to them all, Ari learned on the rail as a breeze toyed with the ribbons binding up half her hair. The Circle board was still being set up, the first moves in the opening. Alertness tightened through her when she spied a knife-like small ship — a courier ship — sailing in from the sea on the very last lap of the inflowing tide.

Her gaze caught on a tall, lean figure dressed in black, standing on the foredeck as he scanned the harbor. Every line of his body was expressive of hard training. He stood still, balanced, capable of exploding in any direction; Ari suspected those clothes concealed any number of weapons, though he chose not to wear any in sight.

This man was dangerous; further, his outline was famili- ar . . . then she had it: the man in charge of the search for Shigan.

An imperial ferret.

She knew immediately that if he caught her watching, his interest would sharpen. Though it took every bit of will, she turned her back, ignoring how her shoulder blades crawled with the urgent need to turn again, to watch him the way the hiding prey watches the stalking predator.

"Who is that?" Oriole appeared at Ari's side. She leaned negligently, one hand toying with a long lock of hair, but her gaze was sharp and unblinking.

Ari turned slightly, keeping the back end of the courier ship in view as she said, "That's the imperial ferret who closed off the entire harbor before capturing Screaming Hawk and the rest of those Shadow Panthers chasing us." *And Shigan.*

"Imperial ferret! That's bad." Oriole breathed the words, looking as unsettled as Ari had ever seen her, but then she smiled and toyed with her embroidered sleeve. "It *is* bad, isn't it? Should we throw the gold overboard?"

"Gold?" Ari repeated blankly, and Oriole thought that Lie Tenek had it right.

"Ayah! He's looking this way!" Then Oriole, being long-practiced, reached over and took a lock of Ari's hair. She began braiding it as she said, "Stay still. We're two rich girls . . ."

Ari didn't need the warning. Though she was certain it was probably fancy — she had had no success with learning to hear others' thoughts the way Grandfather Ki had described — every instinct, every nerve, was alight inside her. She could feel that assessing gaze sweeping over their ship, with its fine carving, the beautiful red-lacquered sails, the crew in their matching clothes, Oriole. Herself, leaning against the rail as Oriole played with her hair . . .

And moved on to Rosefinch on the bow, toying with a jade bracelet on her wrist as she smiled across the water at a couple of young naval sailors on the ship following the ferret's sharp-prowed courier.

Then away.

"We're safe," Oriole breathed a moment later.

"Not yet," Ari said, trying to remember what Instructor Shaz had said so long ago. "If he carries the emperor's tally, he can take over the island. And send the navy after us. Though that would be the worst sort of insult to the governor."

"True," Oriole said. "I wish I could see it happen."

Whether or not it happened, Ari did not want to be there

to see it, still less to be the anomaly that caused the ferret to lock down the island and its bay for a thorough, and professional, search. She went on—talking was better than worrying—"There are two kinds of searches. Overt, which is taking over and using the garrison guards and the navy to search everyone on land and sea. Or covert, which means he sends searchers you might not even be aware are searchers. We want to be well out of sight for either."

Oriole turned, shaking her glossy hair back, and letting the brimstone-acrid wind toy with her ribbons. "It seems the tide is on the turn at last."

While she spoke, their ship had subtly come alive, and it began to move toward the sea along with the miscellany waiting around them. Slowly they sailed in the wake of a wallowing trader, gliding between two watchful naval ships. Lie Tenek and Rosefinch flirted openly with grinning sailors as they passed.

No shouts. No horns.

Outside the harbor they caught the true wind as it veered around the island. This strong wind no longer stank of brimstone. They began to put distance between them and Benevolent Winds Island.

Ari remained where she was until they had sunk the island behind them. Then everyone but the crew at the helm and tending the sails went below to celebrate their escape. The owner family described the three searches they had endured, and how none of the governor's finely dressed guards, or the disgruntled garrison guards, had gone anywhere near those fly-buzzing articles. Everyone laughed in pent-up relief.

Ari's mind was on that ferret.

But nothing occurred to mar the last of Ari's journey to Madam Nightingale's. Rosefinch was still writing madly, glad she'd had the foresight to purchase a complete scroll of paper. The other three thoroughly enjoyed their luxury journey the more for knowing it would soon end.

Before they reached the island, they got those chamber pots dunked into the ocean until the smell went away. After the gold got a thorough washing, Oriole divided their loot fairly, paid off the ship, with an extra contribution from each, and hired a cart at the harbor to take their trunks to the inn.

Madam Nightingale was given her share, Rosefinch vanished at once to a bookseller she knew who dealt with gallant wanderers as well as with imperials, with what she confidently expected would be a very popular book, and Oriole sat with the proprietor describing, in detail, the disaster of Su Suanek's wedding.

"It's not justice," Madam said grimly at the end. "My mother is still broken, our family legacy ruined, and that governor will shrug off the jewels and the burned house. He has plenty more. But at least it thoroughly ruined Su Suanek's wedding. My sister will enjoy that."

She paused when her chief assistant told her that Ari wished to speak to her.

Oriole got up to go, and so she passes from our view, not knowing that she, too, would reach fame as a result of Rosefinch's story book, though of course under another guise.

Ari was escorted onto Madam's private balcony overlooking the square. She said, "I think I'd better leave."

Madam turned to regard her. "I thought you got away without notice."

Ari shook her head. "We did. I believe. Still, I'll feel better when I've got another island or two between me and those imperial ferrets."

Madam's smile thinned at the word *ferrets*. Most people did not even know of the existence of the imperial ferrets, and this girl had brushed against them twice. "It is probably wise."

"What I wanted to say is, I like to travel only with what I can carry. You can have my share of the gold. Give it to your mother, or someone who needs it."

Madam contemplated this extraordinary girl who, she felt certain, was going to make a name for herself in the world. If the world didn't kill her first. "My mother is well provided for, but I thank you for the thought. How about this: I will hold it for you, for a small fee. That way, should you ever need it for one of your causes, you will know where to come."

Ari brightened. "I would like that." She made the gallant wanderer's bow.

"Where are you going?" Madam laid her hand on a small stack of sealed letters at the corner of her desk.

Ari had seen those, and assumed they were letters awaiting Madam's attention. But then she understood: these were gallant wanderer letters, waiting for someone to carry them.

"Southwest," she said.

Madam withdrew her hand. "Ayah. All these are going north."

Ari bowed and left, thinking that this was the first time anyone had ever asked — that anyone would entrust her with a letter. As she trod to her room, she felt very grown up.

She thought about being grown up as she got into her Ryu clothes, which she still preferred for traveling. When did people feel grown up, anyway? Was it like opening and shutting a door, or did it come on gradually? Maybe you weren't if you still had to ask.

Lie Tenek came in just as she was winding her hair into her topknot. "Ari?" She glanced at the knapsack on the bed, with the wrapped staff pieces sticking up. "You're leaving?"

"I want to break the trail more." She glanced at the trunk. "I picked out one outfit to take. The rest, the girls here can use more than I can."

"Where will you go?"

"I have a promise to keep." She hesitated, sensing regret, or reluctance, or something akin, in Lie Tenek's averted gaze, and added, "If you want more Redbark drill, I was told that the Blue Hibiscus in Te Gar welcomes gallant wanderers. I believe the proprietor does Redbark drill."

Lie Tenek's quick smile revealed to Ari that she had guessed right.

She slipped away without speaking to anyone else, and headed for the harbor, as copyists were already busy with Rosefinch's story — and I can add here that the bookseller, very well aware that he held the text equivalent of fireworks in hand, was at that moment speaking to his two daughters and a trusty nephew to supervise setting up booths on different islands to sell the books. He well knew that some of those copies would find their way into the hands of other enterprising booksellers, who would then make their own copies, but such was the price of popularity: before that, he meant to put as many out there as he could get made. . .

Ari had a long journey ahead, but would take any sort of ship, as long as its route avoided the imperial island. She knew that it was huge, and full of cities for someone to get lost in, but she was equally convinced that the evil emperor had eyes everywhere. She hoped that Shigan, as an imperial prince, had survived. Goddess of Mercy grant that she'd see him again, someday. But not on the imperial island!

After all these years away from her parents, she was going home to Sweetwater.

Yskanda contrived to stay out of Jion's way until the next morning, when they reached the bay, where the ships to take them to the imperial island lay waiting.

Yskanda had packed his few things in moments, but remained sitting in the airless cubby until Fennel appeared, and gestured to summon him. "The imperial boat is alongside," he said softly.

Jion had remained on deck, watching for Yskanda. He did not want to summon him, which would be a sure invitation to listening ears. In the light of day he felt slightly foolish, and laughed at himself for mistaking an especially vivid dream for an actual occurrence.

But there was no sign of Yskanda until the little boat arrived to take the imperial family from the sampans to the ship for the return to the imperial island. Perforce Jion had to step over; as the boat drew alongside Vaion's sampan, he looked back.

There was Yskanda among the servants clutching bags and baskets. The boats drew apart, the servants to crowd onto the auxiliary ship, and Jion toward the spacious imperial sea-traveler, where hot tea and delicacies on porcelain plates awaited him.

By the time they were underway, expected to reach the imperial city by morning, he had pretty much convinced himself that he had indeed dreamed the whole. After all, if a kraken had really been anywhere near, there would have been noise and alarm to waken sleepers on the next five islands. Instead, all was calm — the ferret couriers had all departed by the time the sun cleared the eastern horizon, haring off to Benevolent Winds fairly close by.

Jion's comfortable conviction remained until they sailed into harbor, when he chanced to look over at the servants crowded at the rail of the auxiliary, waiting for the imperial family to debark first. Dream, he told himself firmly, though why he would dream about Yskanda meeting a kraken, he had no idea. But dreams never made sense, he reminded himself as he watched Yskanda's soberly clad, thin form there between two hatted graywings.

"First Brother!" Vaion called. "Coming?"

Jion was about to turn away when he was distracted by Whiteleaf motioning to Yarrow and Fennel. Yskanda stepped out of their way, his hand lifting to keep his bag of painting supplies from bumping Yarrow as he tried to squeeze by. Yskanda's sleeve fell back.

Jion could see clearly from across the water the marks of his own fingers on Yskanda's wrist.

# FORTY-TWO

WHILE ARI BEGAN HER journey home, her parents went about their daily tasks on Burning Rock Island, where they lived under new guises. Hanu had at first joined the archive as Brother Yan, trading work for a chance to learn deeper levels of Essence manipulation through talismans, specializing in healing.

People had slowly figured out that she was not born a male, but they accepted her as Brother Yan anyway — such was life at Burning Rock. Danno had earned the nickname Brother Brick for his strength in hauling the bricks made by the islanders. It was a gentle tease; no one minded that he seldom spoke. Life had been quiet since Ul Keg had come to tell them Yskanda was alive, but a hostage within the imperial palace, and that he would try to get a message to him that would offer a chance of escape.

Hanu divided her time between the archive and helping at the Sanctuary, where she'd met, and at last was accepted as a student, by a very old, very wise Snow Crane shaman. "But first," this old woman said, her voice a husk, "you must learn through healing those scars."

Hanu had put her hand up to her face. "I . . . did that myself."

The shaman said, not without compassion, "And so very unfilial, to treat your parents' gift of life that way."

Hanu, as Iley, had suffered the pain of those scars for years, thinking them a disguise, thinking them no more than many others endured, but deep beneath, feeling she deserved them. At these words, and the tender touch of that gnarled old hand, it was as if a tight band burst, and she wept.

After that, she began learning a far more difficult and exacting level of talismans while she underwent needle treatment, along with Essence charms and strange-smelling herbs slathered on her face. Danno had been skeptical when he first learned of it, but since then he had to admit that it seemed to work. Each time Hanu returned from one of those treatments her cheeks were inflamed with new skin, which gradually returned to her normal coloring. It seemed that each time the scars had softened a bit more, until they were no more than blotches, from which the old pain was entirely gone.

The slather state required her to endure the stuff burning the scarred skin the first day it was applied. He knew she endured the worst period of it by lying down and reciting sutras and long lists of herbal affinities, while mentally reviewing her talismans.

She had recently undergone a treatment, she said it would probably be the last; this was around the time that Danno got that back-of-the-neck sense that he was being watched. The first time he felt it was while he delivered a load of bricks to the upper level known as the Sanctuary, where seriously ill or injured patients could recover in the quiet air above the busy valley.

He went to see Iley. When he heard her voice whispering a litany, he decided not to disturb her. He did not pause, but kept on pushing his cart down the narrow trail, looking, sniffing, listening. Nothing out of the ordinary: people working their rice early in the day before summer's heat made even breathing difficult; others walking to or from the temple; more sitting under the plantains, drinking tea and talking.

One of the hardest lessons he'd had to learn when they first began life in Sweetwater was the art of small talk. He had been raised to remain silent unless spoken to, and that habit was strong, the more after they arrived in Sweetwater because he'd had so much to conceal. Hanu had been little better—her mother, a renowned scholar on her island, had had little patience with chat. Ul Keg had taught them both how to be part of a community, and though he would always serve as the very opposite of a "five aunts and ten grandmothers" talker, he had developed a small arsenal of compliments and quest-ions that seemed to serve him well.

"Suanek's blessing upon you, Brother Brick! Did you dream well?"

"And to you, Brother Yuneg. Very well indeed? How is that ankle?"

"Nearly as good as new," the old man said, beaming with good will as he patted his crutch.

Two or three more exchanges like that — none of them con-veying anything but a general sense of good will — and that sense of being watched faded. Danno did not quite forget — early habits were too strong for that — but it was no longer in his immediate thoughts as he helped to patch a wall slowly cracking from the spreading roots of an old and much-cherished peach tree.

He had a full day of other repairs, always surrounded by other people. He still caught that sense of a predator observ-ing, which caused him to move with care, and to change his plan of visiting Hanu before he retired to his cottage for the night.

He found an old uncle waiting to discuss some problems having to do with the making of a new set of bricks, and who had the greatest need. What the old uncle really wanted was company — and someone to drink with. He turned up like this once a week.

Danno drank with him until the old fellow slumped over. Danno put a blanket over the old man, and stretched out on his pallet.

In the morning, as usual, he found the blanket folded and the uncle gone. Danno left the cottage, got out his empty wheelbarrow, and started up the back trail toward the brick-yard.

At a sharp turn between an outcropping of rock and an old plantain, he heard a shift of cloth and a soft flick. He whirled around, arm coming up in a block. Twin points of cold pain flowered in his thighs, and his legs gave out. He fell backwards into his own wheelbarrow. A brief glimpse of a face, and another pinpoint of pain — then nothing.

When he woke, his head throbbed viciously. Pain cut behind his knees; how long had his lower legs been dangling outside the wheelbarrow? His body felt extraordinarily heavy, his mind muzzy. His stomach surged unpleasantly, and he lay gazing up at the sky as he breathed against the nausea. Grit ground beneath his head. Dust burned sharply in his nostrils.

Needles — wielded by an expert. It had been nearly thirty years since he had practiced knocking needles out of the air. He hadn't even seen these coming.

When the nausea began to subside a little he tried to rise on an elbow. The rustle of movement caught his attention. A woman he'd never seen before leaned over to study him. Deep brackets either side of a thin mouth indicated someone nearer fifty than forty.

"I wanted you awake," she said, "for this."

Her right hand came up with his hammer, which she brought down with deliberate force on his right kneecap. And when that shattered, taking his breath with it, she smashed the left one.

Then she waved the hammer, smiling. "That was fun. And we'll have a lot more, *traitor*."

He struggled past the pain for breath.

She waited for him to beg, to plead, to cry, but he remained silent. She spoke.

"I am Tek Banu, and when your traitor's head hits the dust in Lotus Blossom Square, I will become his imperial majesty's chief ferret." Still no reaction, so it was time to gloat — to get the reaction of fear and despair that she craved when she meted out justice. "Your trail took a little work. Just enough not to be too boring." She assumed a confiding tone as she raised the hammer again, and hovered it over the ruin of his left knee. "You should never trust your hideout to a monk." She tapped the hammer on one knee then the other, relishing the jolts his body made as agony shot through him: even if a criminal's mind resisted her justice, the body always betrayed them. "Monks don't know the first thing about covert movement, do they?"

Danno's instinct was to cry Ul Keg's name — but he managed to bite that back. If she hadn't used it, that meant she was on a fishing expedition. He was clearly damned, but he would not drag anyone else into the underworld with him.

"Chief . . . Fai?" he asked. It took all his strength to get the two words out. Where was he? The sides of his own wheelbarrow blocked most of his view. Nothing was visible beyond them but the sky.

"The soon to be former Chief Fai is on the imperial island," Tek Banu said. "Ayah! I believe you meant his father. You might see them both before you die. The emperor is waiting for you."

She leaned closer, a sudden darting movement, like a snake. Her laugh was a creaking of glee without a vestige of humor. "Though I hope he won't be in a hurry once we get you there. But before we get on my ship, I need to finish up here by killing the Alk traitor. The emperor, it seems, cares nothing for what happens to her. It's you he wants." Tek Banu held the hammer over his ruined kneecaps. "Where is she?"

"Here."

Tek Banu whirled, a lethal spray of poison needles skimming from her free hand. These tinkled unmusically off the curving side of a cooking pan half a heartbeat before the heavy metal struck Tek Banu's head with a clang.

The ferret staggered, then righted herself — in time to meet a powerful blow straight on the nose from the backswing. She let out a squawk of pain, fell, then began scrabbling in her clothes for weapons, blood blinding her.

With the strength of years of hard labor, Hanu smashed the edge of the pan under Tek Banu's chin, knocking her flat, a poison knife flying from the ferret's slippery fingers. Hanu bent toward a gleaming pinpoint in the black sand: two of the needles Hanu had knocked aside. "Ah." She picked up the needles and jabbed them into Tek Banu's neck. "If the poison on these is a sleep drug, you will wake up," Hanu said. "If not —"

Tek Banu's back arched. She uttered a gargling howl of agony. Greenish foam lined her lips, and she collapsed into a dead heap.

"Killed with your own poison," Hanu said, her voice shaking. She bent once again, and put a practiced finger to the ferret's neck. No pulse. Reaction hit, and Hanu turned aside, retching miserably.

A soft groan of pain from Danno caused her to drop the pan and force herself upright. Breathing hard, she spat on the woman's clothing to clear the acrid taste from her mouth, and bent over Danno.

Despite her body trembling violently, her mind was clear as a day after a rain: all these years, she had imagined every scenario. Never one quite like this. But the aftermath, that she had imagined over and over. They had to get rid of the evidence, fast. If one person saw the dead ferret, whichever ferrets came after would find out, and that innocent person would no doubt die. "Can you bear to wait? I must get rid of the body."

"Do."

She disliked how thready his voice was, but forced herself to take in their surroundings in a fast glance. They were on the shore, utterly alone, except for a small craft bobbing on the sea a short distance away, and a rowboat nearby. Otherwise nothing but black sand, sea, sky.

Hanu slipped the poison-edged knife into Tek Banu's sash, then lifted several sizable rocks and shoved them inside Tek Banu's clothing. She dragged her to the shore a few paces away, and into the water. The shoreline was quite shallow for some twenty paces or so, before a sudden dropoff. Hanu found it somewhat easier once the woman was immersed in the rippling tide. She towed the awkward corpse after her as she moved steadily out, feeling with her feet ahead at each step.

The dropoff was easily discerned by the change of color in the sea around her. She lugged the sinking body to the edge and let go, watching until it vanished into the deep.

She sketched a charm in the air to ward ghosts as she said, "This one is yours, O King of Hell. Hear this unworthy daughter's plea: if you let her cross the Ghost Bridge for rebirth, let it be as a sea worm."

Then Hanu waded back, fetched the pan, and rinsed the blood off in the sea water. Her clothes clung to her, but the late summer sun was hot; as she wrung the worst of the water out, she knew she would be dry before she reached the main path.

Danno had passed out during the interim. She glanced once at his poor legs, then looked away again, fighting against another stomach upset. No time for that. She did not dare touch him lest she worsen the damage, so she tucked the pan in the tool holder, gripped the handles of the cart, and began the arduous trek back across the beach of black sand and glassy clinkers. Midway she heard a moan, and halted.

Danno had woken. His voice was a husk. "Sick? . . . You've . . . seen worse . . ."

She cast an anxious glance at him, wondering if he was delirious, but his eyes, though pain-hazed, were aware. Ayah! Distraction. "It was not the sight," Hanu said. "It was my own weakness, letting the demon free."

"Demon?" His voice was barely audible.

She gritted her teeth and hauled harder, then began talking desperately, willing him to stay with her. Instinct insisted that if he was awake and aware, he would recover. "In my blood," she said. "Why do you think I counseled our daughter to be wary of anger?" A quick glance. "I know you don't believe in anything you haven't faced and fought, but Grandmother Alk was a very truthful person, and always warned us never to give in to rage lest the demon come forth. My sister, the kindest and most merciful of dreamers, was so frightened by the prospect; that's the main reason she went to the temple . . ."

Hanu chattered on until her own voice husked in the punishing heat. It didn't matter if he believed in demons, or even if she made sense. What mattered was keeping him awake and breathing. She counted his every hissing struggling breath, and fought to get the cart to the path.

When she paused briefly, bending over, raw-scraped hands on her knees as she struggled for breath, "You . . . how?" he asked.

"I followed that woman," Hanu said, swallowing in an effort to moisten her dry throat. "You didn't come to visit yesterday. I brought your breakfast this morning and saw her push you into the cart. I hid. When she started up the path I put the food in your cottage and grabbed your cook pot. I kept my steps soundless on the sand. She was so busy gloating she never looked round, though I stayed fifty paces back. I was trying to figure out what to do—whether you were awake—when she picked up your hammer, and then I had to act. I'm sorry it took me so long—I had to make sure she did not hear me coming up behind her. The sand smothered my steps. Bide quiet. Try to breathe slowly. I must get you back now."

At last she saw the main path ahead. The moment the wooden wheels reached the relative flatness, hauling him became marginally easier, and within three steps, here came two temple workers well-known to her.

"Brother Yan! What have you—ayah! What happened to Brother Brick?"

"He went fishing, and fell. Broke his knees."

"Let us help you get that cart up the hill!"

"Sister Lin, you ought to run ahead and fetch a shaman with a portable shrine," the elder urged.

"I can, but why, when we have a temple not a hundred paces from the healer's?" Sister Lin spread her hands.

"Because Brother Brick is far too strong to fall on his knees unless a demon pushed him. The sooner we ward the bad luck, the better chance he has to recover. Brother Yan, you look parched — here is my flask, with fresh gold-tea — that's right, drink it. I can get more."

"Ayah, you are right, and I am no better than a donkey for not thinking. I'm off!"

Danno swam in and out of consciousness as Hanu drained the flask. Then she pulled as the second temple worker pushed, which sped them along.

As she toiled back up the path cut into the ridge, she looked about her, her mind running ahead the way it had for years as she imagined the worst that could happen, and how she must act to protect her family. She had always feared being found by ferrets while in Sweetwater, but somehow she had ceased to worry in this sacred place of peace.

The most important thing was to get Danno to the healers. That, with the help of an increasing crowd, was soon accomplished. She saw him into the hands of those better experienced than she — "That's right, that's right, easy and slow, and give him a stick to hold onto. No matter how he screams and fights, we must straighten those legs and keep them that way. Bamboo strips either side, yes, yes, yes . . ." — as she stood aside, watching in anguish as sweat broke out over his pale face. But accepting pain in silence had been too deeply trained into him in his early days, and he never made a sound other than the hitched breath of agony. It wasn't until he passed out from whatever medicine the old healer slipped between his lips, and went limp, that she could move away.

Then she moved fast: the second most important thing was to remove all trace of that ferret, which meant beginning with the fishing story, suitably embroidered. Danno would have to sacrifice his reputation for sobriety to make it believable.

As the healers set about making Danno comfortable, while taking great care not to move his kneecaps in the slightest, she slipped away and retraced her steps. First to Danno's cottage, where she replaced the cook pot and removed the abandoned breakfast. From there she sped back to the upper path, then around Three Guardians Hill to the black sands shore.

It seemed the ferret had made her task easier by a

determination not to leave traces. Hanu followed the cart tracks to the shoreline, where she felt around until she located all those poison needles. These she wrapped carefully, to be burned in the kiln on her return. She smoothed out the cart tracks, the dried blood, and hers and the ferret's footprints, moving backward all the way to the water. Then she got into the ferret's boat and rowed back around the point, and left the boat in a more secluded spot.

Danno woke the next day.

Hanu made sure she was in the rotation for care. When no one's attention was on them, he gazed up at her, his eyes red, circled with dark skin, but his focus was aware.

Hanu briefly summarized what she had done, then said, "It was her smugness that terrified me. Did you know her? Cross her?"

"No. No," he whispered.

Hanu smoothed back the tangled hair off his face, sweaty from fever and pain. "The most frightening monster seems to be the one whose cruelty is so very self-righteous."

"Yes." Danno struggled up on one elbow, which caused a fresh sheen of sweat across his brow. "Enjai promised to promote her." He struggled to rise, then fell back. "If he found us . . . he can find First and Little Third."

"Yes."

"Holding Second Son . . ." He fell back, sweat sheening his face from the effort he expended to speak. But he had to speak. "Holding him . . . till he has us all?"

"And then kill us all? I thought of that, too; I remember what he did to my mother. Why else would he keep Yskanda, but to kill him and the other two before our faces before he kills us?"

But Danno was done speculating. He had a plan. He had never wanted to leave Yskanda in the capital, but he had seemed safe enough. That was no longer true, now that the ferrets had found him—where there was one, surely more would be coming. "When I can walk again." His tone said *if*. "Rescue Yskanda. Find First and Little Third. Go east. Far as we can." He looked the question he dared not speak: are you with me, or do I go alone?

"I have the little boat secure," Hanu said, her expression resolute. "And I know where that ferret left her ship. It's a single-sail. I can manage, if you sit at the tiller. It will probably

take until the turn of the year for you to heal enough to walk
again—"

He gave his head a shake. "As soon as I can get to that ship.
If I have to crawl. I'll heal while we sail."

# FORTY-THREE

IN THE IMPERIAL CAPITAL, Yskanda made his way to the Court Artist's workroom.

Yoli met him there, smiling with satisfaction. "I saw everything you turned in. The orchids especially — I asked the emperor if we could use it as an example in the flowers class, as there are no figures in it." Because he was in a good mood, he began to tease Yskanda. "I'm surprised there's only the two scholarly gatherings with the first imperial princess." In his experience, the rare times the beautiful First Imperial Princess Manon was seen, the apprentices made endless sketches of her — all of which remained in the archive.

Yskanda smiled, knowing he was being teased. And he had seen the ardency in her admirers' eyes. But he kept to himself the observation that not everyone was entranced with First Imperial Princess Manon. There had been hatred in Ze Kai's face, and Yskanda still remembered the sobbing musician after the second imperial princess's attempt to get a drawing of her dancing to give to her father, that first spring. Beautiful the first imperial princess was, but so much like frost. Sometimes he pitied this person who seemed never to smile though the world was filled with beauty, but he was not the least stirred by her.

That, alas, had happened with someone even more dangerous.

But he knew how to deal with that: there was nothing more effective than work. "I have an idea," he said to the court artist. "Seeing as my painting of the garden in horizontal scroll form was successful, I would like to attempt the Journey to the Clouds in the same form."

Court Artist Yoli nodded slowly. "An idea! We have plenty of very fine vertical scrolls, of course, and your orchids will join those. I have seen one or two attempts, but . . . no, I will not speak, and chance an ill omen. Go ahead. Try it. But first, take an evening of freedom. You worked hard. I worked hard. Our reward will be more work on the morrow, to ready ourselves for the imperial wedding. Let us take our ease tonight, and enjoy being able to breathe freely."

Yskanda thanked him, and was soon at the Ghost Moon temple, where he lit incense and made his bows. The incense here, sublime as always, seemed to clear his head, comforting him. He knelt and soothed his spirit in prayer. But when he rose, the questions crowded back.

He looked up at the serene figure of the god, who was in all places and times, in the world seen and unseen. If any place was the right one for Yskanda's questions, would that not be here?

He was alone except for a temple monk sitting at the side, eyes closed, stick beating slow and steady on the wooden fish. Yskanda approached the young monk. "This seeker apologizes for disturbing your peace."

"Speak, pilgrim," the monk said, his voice unexpectedly high, his chin smooth — either he was younger than at first he seemed, or he was a graywing turned monk.

"I had a . . . perhaps it might have been a vision, or an augury. It's the second. No, third. Each has been successively stronger. I need to learn how to banish them."

"What kind of vision?" the monk asked.

Yskanda looked around again. The temple was still empty. He began to describe what happened that last night of the Journey. When he got to the tentacle touching his palm, the monk's eyes widened, and he laid aside his fish and stick. "Stay. I will go to the abbot."

A very short time later, Yskanda was brought to a plain back room, where a wizened figure with a long white beard sat on a cushion beside a moon window looking out over a red-bark tree-shaded pool. "Sit, child." He pointed to a cushion before him. When Yskanda had finished his bow and knelt on the cushion, the abbot said, "Tell me what happened from the first."

Stumbling over his words, Yskanda described the drawing of three dragons he had made that New Year's Two Moons day, and what the court artist had said before giving him the warding stone. Then he described what happened when he saw what he'd begun thinking of as the fireworks dragon at Spring Festival, after which he detailed his experience with the kraken—and how the vision changed when Imperial Prince Jion took hold of him.

The abbot listened all the way to the end, then said, "First, you must understand that augury is never a sure prediction of the future, as if the future were a single path. From our perspective, there are many possible paths, and they change with every breath we take."

"Pardon this ignorant seeker, but I thought fate was . . . unchangeable."

"Only the gods know our fates, as they live outside of time, that is, in all times. But our perceptions are limited by the river of time, which we cannot escape while in the living world. So, if I lift my right hand instead of my left, that action will change the possible paths toward my fate."

Yskanda bowed from where he sat, more confused than ever.

"Second, it would appear that you have the, ah, attention of the gods."

That startled Yskanda. "The kraken was a god, O venerable one?"

"One might say that the kraken was a creature of spirit or soul, through whom a god might speak." The abbot frowned a little and leaned forward, as if to bring Yskanda into better view, though there was no more than an arm's length between them. "We all have two souls, as you know, or ought to know."

Yskanda bowed in assent.

"There are those who sense the higher soul, and some can even speak one to another, though a hundred islands lie between them. Have you done such?"

"What? No," Yskanda said, considerably startled. Then the usual fear crowded in behind, that the emperor could employ spies to pry open one's mind. "I would not want to," he stated firmly.

The abbot hesitated, then said, "Even so, it is possible you have a gift for that. You said that you were surrounded by water in all forms, while standing on the deck of a sampan. I would venture to guess that you have an affinity for water and wood. Water, in specific, lends itself to spirits communing, as water has no boundaries when left to itself. Your wooden brush is a conduit for Essence."

Yskanda recoiled inwardly. "I don't have any Essence talent. My mother, who did have a measure, said that none of us had that family . . . trait. Which she admitted to my tutor can be indistinguishable from madness. I am *not* mad."

"You are not mad." The abbot smiled. "The truly mad never question themselves. To them, their world is the only world." The abbot could see the knots of fear that Yskanda could not suppress, and said tranquilly, "Let us return to the vision of the kraken."

Yskanda clutched at the ward rock, a gesture that the abbot observed as he went on, "If you wished to speak to an ant, how would you go about it? You could cut a sliver of your fingernail and fashion it into the shape of an ant, and then make it dance and rub its feelers before another ant, but will you and the ant truly understand one another, unless a god speaks through you to the ant? So, perhaps, it is with you and the kraken."

Yskanda bowed again, miserably aware that he was even more confused. And frightened.

The abbot said in an effort to reassure him, "But that is my surmise, as in all my long life, this is a first. Let us move to ground I am surer of. Your studies, while admirable in the perception of the essence of things, have perhaps made you sensitive to Essence. But you do not compass what our novices are taught. We shall be practical. The ward stone, which was kindly meant, acts as a dam to the flow of Essence. I choose the dam image deliberately, as you ought to know how waters build up behind such a structure."

Yskanda blinked. "I really do not have an Essence gift."

"Child," the abbot said gently, "you could not be more wrong about the nature of Essence, which is not measured in amounts, like coins in a bag. You are a leaf upon a deep lake of Essence. Very deep. Infinitely deep. Essence flows through you when you paint." He paused, gazed into Yskanda's stunned expression, then said, "Essence is life. You know that—

you are taught the words from childhood. But many float through life without ever perceiving the lake, any more than they think about the air they breathe. That is as it should be. You know the depth—I suspect have always known it, *and used it.*" He paused there, gnarled finger upraised. "But you did not know how to express that knowledge in words."

Yskanda clutched at the ward stone as he bowed. "What must I do?"

"I will give you some books, and Brother Pine here will make himself available to speak with you when you have questions. But first, we will teach you how to open and close the door to what you call visions, and once you learn it, you must lay that ward stone aside, or the dam will keep bursting. You are an artist, already experienced at looking into the essence of things, so you should find it simple enough to master."

Yskanda found nothing simple about anything he'd heard, but he bowed a fourth time.

"Last is the matter of his imperial highness the first prince. What happened to you on the boat is related to him, or he would have seen nothing, whether he touched you or not. It appears there is an affinity between you. At a guess—from your description of the alteration of the vision—his Essence affinity is of air, and perhaps fire. Very volatile, but his proximity could be balanced with one whose primary affinity is water. Like you. The two of you perceived one vision, one blended of water and air."

"I understand Essence affinities. My mother spoke of those. But I don't understand affinities between . . ." Yskanda looked down at his hands. "People."

"It happens," the abbot said, as tranquil as before. "It is not the same as an inclination, though it can include that, and when it does it can be as deep as the sea, and as everlasting. We've two brothers among us who have Essence affinity for one another. One, Brother Skylark, has led a serenely celibate life for seventy years, and that is unchanged. The other, not much older than you, led a harsh life until he found us, and a sublime partnership with Brother Skylark. They work together to make our incense, which our pilgrims tell us is the finest in the city."

Yskanda nodded in agreement there. He was aware that he was as frightened as he had been since the ferrets first snatched him out of the alley at Imai's harbor. "Thank you," he said.

The abbot signed a blessing over him, Brother Pine gave him the books he'd fetched, and Yskanda left, his stubborn mind lingering not on the kraken from the spirit world, but on those strong fingers gripping his wrist.

Ever since that drunken visit to the entertainment house he had erected a mental wall against desire, fearing that it would be used as a weapon against him in this beautiful prison. But beauty would always be a gate in that wall. And somewhere between the artistic eye noting the casual but devastating line from muscled shoulder down to lean hip, and the intensely devastating grace of a dance in the moonlight, that gate had opened.

He knew what had happened. He also knew all the poetry that likened such emotions to lightning, or fireflies, or roses in bloom — anything that did not last. If he waited, it would fade and vanish.

Yskanda hurried back through the service byways, trying to cope with everything the abbot had told him. Essence! Affinities! Visions were disturbing enough. Whether they were a form of madness or of augury, he wanted to end them. He did not want the emperor finding out about any of this, and forcing Yskanda to be some kind of Essence weapon. He resolved to learn that inner door and keep it shut for ever.

The gate to desire as well.

He reached his building, sighing with relief. He wished for a bath now that he was no longer cramped in that canvas box on the boat, washing out of a basin. But when he arrived at his room, he discovered Fennel there, leaning against the wall, one foot propped behind him to hold him steady.

Fennel looked, and was, more asleep than awake, but at Yskanda's soft step, he opened his eyes and pushed away from the wall, smothering a yawn. "You're to come."

They crossed the entire palace in silence, Yskanda's heart thundering once again as he considered what to say, and what not to say.

As soon as Yskanda entered the prince's manor, Jion looked up from an open scroll on his desk. "What *was* that?" he demanded, and there was the chilling resemblance to his father.

Yskanda stilled. Jion got up from his desk, came around in two strides and gripped Yskanda by the arm. Yskanda tried to pull away, an instinctive movement, but strong as he'd gotten after months of lifting Court Artist Yoli, Jion was far stronger.

Jion pushed back Yskanda's sleeve with his free hand and glared down at the telltale bruises. "First of all, I apologize for doing that. It was entirely inadvertent *when I saw a kraken tentacle higher than a temple roof.*" He freed Yskanda's arm, and moved back behind the desk. "Don't try to tell me I was asleep. You and some kind of kraken . . . shadow, or ghost, because there was no physical presence. I *saw* it. What was it?"

Yskanda reminded himself that this particular matter had nothing to do with The Story, therefore it endangered only himself, and not his family. And once he learned to shut that Essence door, the matter would become irrelevant.

"This ignorant unworthy was as confused as your imperial highness—"

"Please drop the protocol, Yskanda. I beg you."

"—and so went to the Ghost Moon Temple to ask. The abbot was kind enough to see me. He said such visions could be controlled, and he will give me books to learn how to shut the door to them so that they do not turn to madness."

"Madness?" Jion repeated, appalled.

"Yes," Yskanda said, aware he was lying.

Jion said slowly, "I thought it was some sort of augury."

"It is not. Your imperial highness," Yskanda appended quickly. "In any case I will learn how to end them."

Jion said, "I guess I can understand that. Even if it was augury of some kind, I know my father distrusts them, though he respects the geomancers who divine when the dragons beneath the earth will move, and suchlike. Those people, when right, preserve numerous lives. But augury . . . there are too many in history who twisted what they saw in the stars, or in the flight of birds, or said they saw visions in dreams in order to influence events. These last could of course never be proved. That might be why my father hates it so much. He suspects some kind of hidden demand behind every praise of his eternal grace."

"I, too, have read of false augurs in history," Yskanda said, relieved that the prince's thoughts led him in a much safer direction than toward Essence and affinities.

"Plenty of them, starting with Ban Erno the Traitor, whose false auguries brought the end of the Kun Dynasty amid the North Island Wars. But I don't think any of that is relevant here, is it? I *saw* that kraken, or ghost of a kraken, even if I didn't feel it under the boat. And I don't feel that I am venturing into madness."

Yskanda said, "No, your imperial highness."

Jion grunted. "Tell me if you find something enlightening in your abbot's books. I'd like some forewarning if there's a kraken somewhere in the seas that starts spouting dire words." He glanced into Yskanda's face, and added, "You look as tired as I feel. Come back when you've done your reading and I've done mine. We'll play some more Circle and discuss it."

Yskanda bowed, his eyes lowered, and made his escape; Jion watched after, sorry to see Yskanda once again withdrawn behind the invisible wall of rank, but not surprised.

Besides, he had his own problems to mull over.

He had come home from the Journey to the Clouds still convinced that his sister Manon would make a great empress. No one was more dedicated, more disciplined, more loyal. But he was beginning to believe that dedication and discipline and loyalty were not the only qualities of a sage empress — and he was delving into the writings of the first Yslan Empress to prove it.

Manon, he believed more firmly by the day, would enter the ranks of greatness once she freed herself from the mental blinkers of her assumption that merit was strictly confined to the privileges of rank. To disparage the ideas of persons like Afan Yskanda and Scholar Shan Rou merely because of their birth was to forgo the talents that could contribute so much to the good of the world.

He'd decided that the solution was to begin reading in earnest, then talk it over with Ze Kai and some of the other scholars, if Old Zao permitted — and if not, to bring Yskanda to his pavilion, put out the Circle board, and try to recapture the freedom of those nighttime conversations on the boat so that he could test his ideas. Yskanda in a way was even better than the scholars because he was so free of ambition. He, like Scholar Shan, discussed ideas purely for the pleasure of exercising the mind.

Over the following stretch of days, though his intention was laudable, it was surprisingly unsuccessful; it seemed that Yskanda had embarked on another great painting, and what ought to have been his free time he spent in the workshop among the paints and brushes. Even his reading from the monks seemed to lead back into Kanda, and Mana Ta, and the weird world of symbols and sutras. No surprise there, considering it was monks giving Yskanda the lessons.

Of course Jion could summon Yskanda any time he wanted to, but he knew if he did so he'd get the eyes-lowered, non-speaking Yskanda who would stand among the servants until dismissed.

He could wait—he had a lot of reading to catch up on anyway.

The best part of Jion's day began before dawn, when he went to the west court to spar with the imperial guards. After that he had just enough time to bathe and swallow a bun and some tea before he had to attend the school under Master Zao again.

It was slightly less tedious now that they were reading more modern works on the history of court. Master Zao still expected them to memorize great tracts, but that did not prevent Jion from discussing the readings with his cousins and his brother's friends in the imperial garden after the master left—many of whom were going to test next spring, and so were quite willing to share ideas.

He still invited Manon for music or poetry reading, which often devolved into talk—if she came. That was no longer a given. Most evenings Sia Na and the others showed up to entertain him. But on the occasional soft summer night when he was alone, as fireflies wove back and forth in the garden and music filled his head, he danced, his mind invariably turning toward Ryu and the sweet, unconscious freedom of their days together.

When the days turned into weeks, occasionally he continued to hunt Yskanda down, to find Yskanda still deep in his projects and sutras. Jion enjoyed the sunlit workroom, and the smell of paints, as he tried to recapture the free exchange of ideas they'd shared on the Journey. He was most successful when he brought up his own readings; these discussions, short as they tended to be while Yskanda kept working, he treasured up to share with Manon, though there again he sensed that he had lost something.

With Manon the loss reached deeper than regretting the loss of the brief, easy back and forth of conversation aboard his sampan that he'd had with Yskanda. He did not understand what he had done to cause Manon to withdraw; he only knew that he was losing her.

# FORTY-FOUR

MANON HAD HER OWN internal struggles, the most important of which was to find a new project to prove her worthiness to inherit the throne.

It had to impress Imperial Father enough to overcome the disastrous Journey to the Cloud Empire that had been ruined by some criminal *daring* to raid one of the Su family holdings. That was in no way her fault — but the result was just the same: Imperial Father had scarcely said a word to her when the Journey she had worked so hard on ended, but closeted himself with ferrets and ministers. Whereas past organizers had been granted enormous gifts or privileges.

She had not dared to let herself imagine being chosen heir yet, but she had composed a suitably modest speech of gratitude, full of allusive poetry, for a gift that never came. It was clear that the entire subject was done in Imperial Father's mind.

At least she was winning the struggle to overcome that regrettable attraction to low-born Afan Yskanda, helped by his continued absence from the inner palace. Now, whenever she thought of him, the only feelings were a lingering resentment for the impertinence of his indifference, which she attributed to insensitivity —

"Put on a better robe than that." Her mother's voice shattered a reverie she was just as glad to have broken. "My cousin

Afar is on the way."

Manon went obediently to put on her butterfly robe, which was her most flattering, but she took off the phoenix earrings she loved; Aunt Afar was easy-going and pleasant, but quite sharp-eyed, and she would be describing Manon's clothing when she next paid a visit to Su Manor.

Aunt Afar was conducted in by the silent servants, bringing in a musical tinkling of her many bangles, and a waft of magnolia scent. "Elder Cousin," she exclaimed, taking the hands of the second imperial consort, and then she turned to Manon. "Oh, my dear niece, you are more beautiful than ever. I did not have a chance to tell you after the Journey — everyone was so upset over that . . ."

Both mother and daughter scarcely listened as Su Afar chattered on about how very busy she had been; they both knew precisely where Aunt Afar had been in the line — fifth to last — which was only to be expected of someone who had married as indolent a man as Ha Vo of the White Jade Island Has. He easily could have become a part of court and contributed to the Su faction, but no, he preferred to remain home in his enormous manor, looking over his race horses, or spending an entire day clipping three twigs off of one of the miniature trees he so prized.

However, to balance that, Su Afar was the only one of Su Shafar's generation who never gave her a day's trouble. And she always brought entertaining gossip from the city, as well as family tidings. They simply had to make certain she didn't take any entertaining gossip back that they did not want spread.

". . . and oh! Speaking of the latest scandal, have you seen this?" She removed a cheaply stitched book from her sleeve and tossed it down onto the table next to the tea set. "It's spreading all over the city. Grandfather is absolutely furious with Second Uncle Bi."

"Our uncle was always so very greedy." The second imperial consort picked up the book. "*Firebolt and the Mine of Shame*? Disgusting." She threw it down, and held out her hand. A maid scurried forward, head bowed, and gently wiped her fingers with a clean cloth.

Manon picked up the book and leafed through it. Though she permitted no expression to cross her face, she skipped past all the ridiculousness about demons and pigheaded men, and exulted in the thinly disguised description of the ruin of her Aunt Su Suanek's wedding. Manon had never forgiven her Aunt Suanek for her careless laughter and her comment, when Manon was no more than ten, "Why are you blathering on about Kanda's *Conversations*, you silly girl? You'll never sit on the throne. It'll be the boy, because he's handsome, and he rides better than you. You should work on your looks, and marry a prince."

Manon had always remembered that, vowing to visit summary justice on Aunt Su Suanek upon coming to the throne, but it seemed now that fate had got there first. She gloated inside, a delicious sensation, at the fulsomely torrid description of the bridal house in flames.

" . . . and Second Uncle Bi is reputedly working day and night to get his guards to find the miners and return them to work," Su Afar was saying. "After trying to get the garrison to dig it out. But Cousin Suanek's new husband says his company are not bond-servants, they are trained warriors, and our aunt-in-law shouted at Cousin Suanek that the husband she picked is unfilial. Then she turned on poor Suanek and demanded to know why she had chosen such a venomous snake, when she could have any man in the empire."

Su Shafar shook her head. She had never liked her aunt-in-law, who had smirked so knowingly when Su Shafar was overlooked at that demon-cursed consort-competition all those years ago. "She'd do better to smooth everything over as fast as she can," she commented. "Or all three of them might find themselves summoned to kneel barefoot before the throne in white robes and their hair unbound."

"I would die of the shame!"

"Cousin Suanek always maintained she was special among our generation, named for Suanek, whereas we merely shared the 'Ar' generation name. Ayah, it seems she has a special fate indeed, to come to this, after her wedding was ruined and her house burned down."

"Grandfather was heard to say that the three of them must have insulted someone important in a past life."

"In a *past* life?" the second imperial consort drawled, eyebrows lifted. "Uncle Bi has been enough of a curse on the family in *this* life. I suppose he's begging for money — as usual."

"Yes, but the entire family is united against *that*. Your eldest sister told us she bribed Grandfather's latest favorite to remind him how much he's already given Second Uncle to get him out of the trouble he got himself into last time — gold that is taken directly from the inheritance of *our* children."

Su Shafar, and her daughter, were both thinking that any such inheritance would be paltry compared to sitting on the phoenix throne, but it was prudent not to give a hint of such thoughts; Su Afar, seeing them far less outraged than she had expected, was slightly disconcerted.

Su Afar was at heart not a bad person, but she had spent a lifetime struggling to keep her place in a very large and contentious family, first for herself, and now for her two boys. Since she had gotten so lackluster a response, she addressed her niece with a change of subject. "I never thought to live to see my Ysek actually reading, but your brother seems to be making it a fashion." She thought to lighten the atmosphere, remembering that her difficult cousin had always seemed to favor the elder prince. She also knew that her niece and First Prince Jion were as close as her own two boys were.

"Oh?" Manon said.

Su Shafar shot a glance at her daughter, and turned a very false smile on her younger cousin. "It's always a blessing to hear of the young people being studious," she said in a patently false tone.

Thoroughly disconcerted, Su Afar shifted to praising her elder cousin's headdress, and won a more genuine smile. But once compliments on clothing and jewels had been thrashed out, there seemed little else to say, and her cousin seemed to have no palace gossip to offer.

Su Afar finished her tea, rose to make her bows and take her leave, whereupon Su Shafar turned on her daughter.

"What is this? *Jion* is leading that group? Why aren't *you* there leading them? Is Ze Kai among them?"

Manon knew that if she pointed out that the girls had been separated out from the boys by her mother's own efforts, she would get her face slapped hard, so she said, "I thought those gatherings were merely the boys chattering after class, Honored Mother. I did not know they were actually discussing anything substantive. If they are. What Cousin Ysek considers substantive might be the sort of book you gave me to practice my writing from when I was six."

Su Shafar inclined her head at that, the golden chains on her marvelous headdress swinging.

"Also, Honored Mother, it's unlikely to last. Ysek alone will soon be bored. My aunt's own words made it clear it's a fashion, and fashions change with the wind."

Su Shafar knew all this was true. Nevertheless, she did not, at all, like the trend of things ever since Jion's return. She had expended considerable money and effort, to discover what exactly had happened to Jion while he was so unaccountably missing since her daughter unaccountably had not, or would not, find out; from the scraps she had gleaned, it seemed that Jion had been lost among the criminal wanderers. The emperor had to know this. And yet there had been no serious repercussions. That in itself was a very bad sign.

She turned her gaze on her daughter. "You had better find something to do that contributes to your honored father's work, if you expect to be named heir."

Manon had been doing nothing but. She could not go to court without an invitation, or a serious reason; her first, dramatic entry on Jion's behalf had been successful, but a second try, she knew, would not be so well regarded. She would be laughed at if she pretended an interest in martial arts—or she might even risk displeasing Imperial Father, for that edict had not been withdrawn. Instead, and this was a dangerous precedent, it seemed that an exception had been made for Jion.

She had done her very best to indicate to Ze Kai that his suit might be welcome, pending negotiation (first point being, *he* would be consort, and would come to her manor). She was even planning an entertainment for the Easterners, to which the mutt Lily and her rabbit of a mother would be guests of honor—which she had discussed with Imperial Father under the pretense of asking his advice about what Easterners seemed to like to eat.

Perhaps, she thought, it was time for another visit to the bookstore for ideas.

She rose and bowed, thanking her mother for the instruction, and went out.

Su Shafar continued to tap her fingernail on the table, irritated by everyone—until her eye fell on that wretched book, and its reminder of the recent hard blow to the Su clan. She was going to throw it into the fire when her gaze fell on the word "mine." That was a strike at the emperor—or he would take it that way. And this strike, she already knew from gossip immediately after the end of the Journey, had been given by criminal wanderers.

Ah.

She had an idea.

She put it into execution the next time it was her turn to host the after-court gathering of the consorts, which the emperor never failed to attend.

He had not visited Su Shafar at night for years, but she had made sure that at least that was also true of the third consort. She could do nothing about the first consort's visits to Golden Dragon, but those were invariably during the day. Su Shafar was fairly certain it was merely to talk, for far more often favorites were seen coming and going at night.

She had long since figured that she had seriously blundered right after Manon's birth when she found out that one of her own maids — a maid she'd had for seven years — had been to Golden Dragon several times. Of course she'd instantly had the wretch put to death, along with her family — that was longstanding Su family policy. How else could you trust shifty, stupid commoners around your treasures and your very person? You paid very well for silence and impeccable service, but let them know that any betrayal meant not just their death.

The emperor had not been back since. But she still had hopes of finding a way to discredit the other two consorts, so that he would see that she was the only loyal one, as well as the most attractive, by far. She cast a fleeting glance at Manon's chair, and thought, as she had many time, if she could just get a son . . .

With that goal very much in mind, she ordered a new and crushingly expensive hummingbird robe to match a new headdress, brought out all the jewels he had given her after Manon was born, and during the tedium of the after-court visit, as always she counted up how many times he addressed each of them, and how many words in each comment. She got as many addresses as Ran Renyi, and that silly sheep Yu Pirag the least, a very good sign.

As the others finally took their leave, she contrived to let the book accidentally fall within the sight of the emperor, who was about to follow his mother out. He looked — he saw. He bent. "What is this?"

Su Shafar rushed forward. "Oh, do not pollute your eyes

with that offal, Dearest Imperial Husband; my youngest cousin left that, and I meant to have the servants dispose of it."

The emperor was leafing through it, his eyes moving rapidly. She knew how fast he read. He dropped it on the table and took his leave; she continued to apologize, but once he was gone, she smiled, certain he had read enough to be well reminded of the lawless criminal wanderers among whom his precious Jion had wallowed.

The emperor left, feeling every bit as annoyed as Su Shafar had intended — though once again she had underestimated his ability to see behind ruses. That, he knew, was aimed at Jion; what it meant was that gossip about Jion's wanderings, in spite of his effort, had tarnished his son — at least among the Su clan, perhaps in court. The wily old duke surely had whispered in certain ears. That would have to be overcome.

But they did not seem to know *why* Jion had wandered among the criminals — and this was what irritated him. Su Shafar would not have dared to try that ruse if she had sent those assassins to kill Jion — which served as a reminder that they were no closer to discovering the assassin.

# FORTY-FIVE

JION'S NEW SCHOLARLY BENT did not end, to the considerable surprise of many.

It was duly reported to the emperor by Master Zao, by graywings, and tangentially by the ministers whose sons or nephews were involved.

One such report occurred on a cloudy, cool late summer day. The emperor had finished hearing the morning intelligences, and his mood was benign, when Bitternail entered to announce the return of Fai Anbai. The ferret chief had left the Journey to the Clouds the night before its end to sail straight to Benevolent Winds under orders to investigate the conflicting reports sent by the navy, the garrison, and the governor, plus a host of increasingly wild rumors.

"Ah," said the emperor. "At last."

He cleared his schedule in the summary way only an emperor can achieve. When Fai Anbai entered the informal interview room, the emperor noted the thick sheaf of papers carried by the chief ferret. He knew that this case was going to be aggravatingly complex — and he was going to have to force some time for reading that mess.

He said, neutrally enough, "You may pass by my blessed merit, so like the jade-tree of Heaven, and speak freely. A summary first. What will I find when I attempt that book in your hands?"

*Freely*, the ferrets were taught early, was only free to a degree. Fai Anbai had become an expert in not only summarizing what he had, but also how he got it, which was so often the emperor's second question.

"The information I received first, your imperial majesty, was from the governor's people, the garrison commander — who is a second cousin to the governor's wife — and from the ranking naval captain, who ought to have commanded the search of the ships in harbor. But being outranked by Commander Bei, Gold Fleet Captain Gu was confined to trying to capture the escaped criminals, some of whom subsequently blew up the ship they had stolen. There is no way to find out how many of them there were on that ship."

The emperor was still waiting. So Fai Anbai ventured over the bridge of knives in answering that second question. "Of all these reports, your imperial majesty, I found Captain Gu's the most accurate." Implication: he found Garrison Commander Bei's the least.

Fai Anbai paused, looked down at the top of the papers that had taken so many very late nights to compile, rewrite, then copy. But he did not see those. Instead, he saw that man-high word SHAME burned somehow into stone. He had stood there staring up at it, not only surprised to find it, but surprised there had been no mention in Commander Bei's report. If he had not insisted on a personal inspection, wearying as that trip had been, he never would have seen it.

Who was this Firebolt who dared to issue such a profound slap to the face of a very high-ranking army commander — one a step away from a generalship? Moreover, what was Firebolt's motivation?

*Shame*. He looked up at the waiting emperor, knowing that his imperial majesty would take that slap in the face personally. It was in the written report, of course, but he decided not to report it verbally unless in response to a direct question.

Fai Anbai said woodenly, "When my agents went in among the warrens on the north side, they were told absolutely nothing, your imperial majesty. Nobody knew anything about a mine fire, though the stench must have been throat-stinging in the aftermath. Nobody knew anything about escaped bond-miners, though a large number of those miners had apparently been snatched off their noisome alleys.

But when it came to questions about Garrison Commander Bei, it was difficult to get them to stop talking."

"Oh?"

"According to these testimonies, your imperial majesty." Here, Fai Anbai held up the thickest portion of that sheaf of papers. "Every single person interviewed had a close relative, either clan or by marriage, who had been arrested for long-outdated infractions, and sentenced to mine labor. Where the death rate is very high. Even among the guards, who mostly were sent there to work off punishment. The city poor all swore that the patrols were paid by the head when arresting these individuals—always strong in body, and young—for infractions such as walking abroad after Dragon Hour, or a broken cart's wheel rolling in front of a patrol's horse. Except for criminal wanderers, who were taken on sight."

"I care nothing for those. At least they're finally of some use to the empire. But concerning subjects of the empire . . . paid by the head? Do they know that selling people is the very definition of slavery, which is against imperial law? There is proof of actual slave transactions?" He leaned forward.

SHAME. And Fai Anbai had uncovered corruption to a princely degree. But he had to speak carefully, as he was not tasked to pass judgment. "It was called reward money, for turning in criminals. And a crime was entered next to each name, along with the sentence, which was usually ten years at the least."

At that the emperor frowned. "Ten years? Is this city full of hardened criminals, then?"

"Early on—ten years ago, that was true, according to Justice Department records, your imperial majesty, and corroborated in the Department of Imperial Works. But in recent years the crimes were increasingly trivial. One might even say there was something of a joke about them."

One did not joke about imperial law; the emperor's brows snapped together. "Who passed these singular judgments?"

"According to the Justice Department records, the name on just about all of these cases belongs to a rising judge who is a cousin of Ta Fimu—"

"Governor Su Bi's wife." The emperor's frown deepened; this was not the first time Su Bi had been implicated in such schemes. The last time, Old Su had had the upper hand in court, and had promised to see to the matter within the clan.

The emperor had been forced to agree. Su Bi had appeared before the court, and had knelt to beg forgiveness. He had appeared to be thoroughly chastened, but it seemed that appearances could deceive.

Fai Anbai went on, "I can show you a list of the crimes, in order of frequency. Near the top for men are public drunkenness, disturbing the peace, and as I mentioned, being abroad after a curfew has been declared. Apparently curfews are declared quite often. For women, the crimes were related, disturbing the peace most frequent, accusing merchants of theft, and here and there some that, ah, were instituted by someone later removed from office, but the law was never removed from the books, such as wearing the color blue on Fire Wishes Day."

"Someone," said the emperor, "is indulging a taste for whimsy at my expense. Blue is the easiest made, almost ubiquitous, especially among the commoners. It's been that way for at least a thousand years."

Fai Anbai bowed, thinking, here it comes.

The emperor frowned into the distance, then said dryly, "I gather the only interviewees willing to speak were those who had a complaint against Garrison Commander Bei?"

"We thought of that early on, your imperial majesty. But it was either listen to them, and take down what they said, or get nothing."

The emperor was furious—that much complaining from the people too often led to open rebellion.

Fai Anbai continued. "I also have testimonies from the seahorse-level captains on down the chain of command." Fai Anbai hefted a significant portion of the sheaf of papers—many of which were masterpieces of face-saving and mutual blame.

"Duke Su Bi's response? Commander Bei's?"

*And here it is.* "Duke Su was too ill to be interviewed, I was told by his consort. Commander Bei departed the day of my arrival to make a personal inspection of the collapsed mine, but was gone when I went to make my own inspection. He was unavailable during my stay. The captain who oversees the handing of criminals to the bond-service department in Imperial Works refused to see me on the grounds that his rank is above mine. He recently married Duke Su's daughter," Fai Anbai added in his most neutral voice. "I will also add that though he, and his wife, purported to know nothing of the questionable practices in acquiring bond-servants through the method I described in these complaints, it transpires that all their household staff was made up of bond-servants. These servants' crimes are listed here, as are their sentences."

Melonseed took the paper to the emperor, and faded back.

The emperor read it. He looked up sharply. "This sixteen-year-old maid was sentenced twenty-five years for wearing blue on . . . Bitternail!"

"Sire."

"Send an imperial summons to the duke and his entire family, as well as Captain Bei's upper command. I want the chief of the Justice Department in here, too, as well as the chief of Imperial Works," he finished acidly. And to Fai Anbai, "Now we come to the mines. Tell me exactly what happened."

"That, your imperial majesty," Fai Anbai said after a deep breath, "is more difficult to determine. The guards all insist there was an army of disguised wanderers under the command of Firebolt of the Redbark Sect. No report is consistent in the number of attackers. Or how they could have got to the mine without being spotted by the night guard. Or how an army, plus the escaping miners, could have fit onto those few brimstone barges without sinking them."

"And the leader of this invisible army?"

"No two testimonies could describe him with any trustworthy detail, except that he was young. Other than that, he was of medium height and light in build, had a terrifying voice, but sounded youthful, and carried a demon-cursed sword that glowed like lightning."

"A charmed sword?"

"Yes. Many witnesses corroborated it."

The emperor frowned. Swords charmed with Essence did rarely turn up among the criminals, but the holders usually were smart enough to remain on the outskirts of the empire, as such weapons were proscribed by law. A past emperor had been infamous for hunting down and exterminating sects — to the fifth generation — who made such artifacts, as well as the artifacts themselves, until the skills involved had been all but lost.

Since that time, whenever these artifacts turned up, they were confiscated. Only Essence masters could safely wield them, and they were equally rare. So far there was no debate about Firebolt being an Essence master; it seemed to the emperor that his reign was to be cursed with one.

"There was no actual fighting, your imperial majesty," Fai Anbai went on. "Except a single incident. A guard insisted that one of the miners, a pirate, brained him with a rock."

"Insisted—he's not dead?"

"Apparently, your imperial majesty, Firebolt performed an Essence spell and restored the guard to life, though his skull had cracked. It's his description that is probably the most reliable, not that it was very clear, for the man said his sight was blurred from the blow, and the criminal's face was covered with brimstone grit and ash. But the description he gave us was of a very young man—a beardless youth— medium height, no other distinguishing characteristics, who told him he ought to choose better."

"Did you examine this putative skull crack?" the emperor asked. "Was the guard exaggerating to cover for incompetence in arresting the criminal?"

"Yes to the first and no to the second, your imperial majesty," Fai Anbai admitted. "He did have a newly healed scar on his scalp, which my medic said could corroborate a crack. The guards all insist that they were frozen by demon- curse, and thus unable to act."

The emperor dismissed the demon-curse. If there were demons abroad, he would surely know. The Divination Department could be trusted for that. "Ah, now we come to it. Is it possible that there might be another sort of peculation involved, and this whole Firebolt story is a coverup for more enterprise on Commander Bei's part? Or someone in his staff?"

"This is what we thought as well, except that the guards were consistent not only in how they were disabled, but where." Fai Anbai gestured to the center of his chest. "It is part of our training, these acupoints. Which are very difficult to reach correctly, especially if the targets defend themselves. But the truth is, if certain points are struck smartly enough, the nerves will cause the body's muscles to lock up. I doubt any of those guards had enough training to concoct a believable story about that."

"How long were they so conveniently disabled?"

"All night."

"Is that even possible?"

"In my experience, your imperial majesty, the paralysis

lasts no more than ten breaths. Twenty for a powerful, precise strike. Not everyone is able to learn this skill," he added. "But an Essence master could add a charm and freeze them for as long as the charm retains its power."

Fai Anbai was going to move on, but the slant of the emperor's brown deepened. He held up a hand. "Are my imperial guards taught this paralysis?"

Fai Anbai hesitated. "I cannot say for certain, but I believe their training is dedicated to more permanent removal of any threat to your imperial majesty or the imperial family." He made a slight gesture, as if holding a weapon.

"Show me this paralyzing strike," the emperor said, then, without troubling to look, he raised his voice slightly. "Bitternail! Summon a volunteer."

A volunteer meant the lowest ranking graywing on duty, of course.

This individual entered, prostrated himself, and at a gesture from the emperor faced Fai Anbai, who for the sake of mercy did not make the poor "volunteer" wait in anticipation. He took a step, moved sharply from the hip, first three fingers stiff, and struck the graywing in the Gateway point where the ribs come together.

The graywing's eyes widened; he choked on a breath, his entire body unnaturally rigid. No one spoke or moved as the graywing's breath hissed in and out, painfully slow, and presently he swayed then fell in a heap.

He tried to roll over to prostrate himself, his still-locked jaw blurring his words as he attempted to apologize to the emperor for his lack of proper protocol; Bitternail and Melonseed glided in, each took an arm, and they bore their junior away to recover.

The emperor turned back to Fai Anbai. "Interesting," he said, the word drawn out. "I want to be taught that. For now, go on."

"Yes, your imperial majesty. The mine guards all swear they were muscle-locked until dawn. And further, any of their companions visible in line of sight could be seen glowing, as if under a considerable Essence charm."

"You met Firebolt once, did you not?"

"We believe so—when his imperial highness First Prince Jion was taken."

"Does the description—do any of the descriptions you

heard—match this criminal?"

"Not really, your imperial majesty. The one we believe
most likely was Firebolt was quite tall, taller than I am. Very
thin. Said he was a healer. He carried a bag full of herbs."

"That might match up with the Essence charms and the
acupoint."

"Not all healers are trained in such, but we did think of
that as well, your imperial majesty. At any rate, none of the
others questioned that day matched the description at all,
being reported as a half-blind girl, a stocky youth who was
brain-impaired and didn't speak, and a moping apprentice
who could not have been more than twelve or thirteen."

"It occurs to me that my son ought to be able to enlighten
us here," the emperor said, with that slight smile. "I never did
ask about his experiences among the criminals; I felt that the
entire experience could not be forgotten soon enough. I
certainly did not want to encourage any desire to return to that
life by expressing an interest in it. Perhaps this is a lapse we
ought to repair at this juncture."

"We do have the testimony of the Shadow Panthers we
captured, before their executions, your imperial majesty. Some
of them were quite fluent about Firebolt, whom they
considered a traitor."

"Yes, and how trustworthy do you think their words?
Especially as we cannot question them further?"

At one time, Fai Anbai might have thought the words, *And
how trustworthy is your son?* But ever since the revelation up on
the Pilgrims' Path, he had been forced to re-evaluate his
opinion of the emperor's eldest son.

Fai Anbai said nothing. It was not his place to speak, unless
asked. But he wondered why the emperor kept him there, as
graywings ran to summon the first imperial prince.

Fai Anbai closed his eyes and mentally reviewed the list of
matters he had to catch up on now that he was back from
Benevolent Winds. First being to discover whether Tek Banu
had sent even a semblance of a report. At this point it had been
an entire year since her departure—and whatever her feelings
about him, and their relative positions, she was ferociously
loyal. And obsessively observant of the rules. The missing six-
month report could be explained away if she were deep under
cover in a dangerous situation, but not silence for an entire
year.

"Imperial Father? You summoned me?"

Fai Anbai looked up as Jion entered and prostrated himself. The emperor indicated with a finger for him to rise, which he did. Fai Anbai bowed to him, the prince acknowledged him with a respectful dip of the head, and then both turned to the emperor.

In spite of his awareness of Su Shafar's intent at accidentally displaying that wretched book for common consumption, it had after all served its purpose. The emperor remembered Jion's defense of those worthless individuals, and, exacerbated by this news, turned the smile everyone dreaded seeing on his son. "Tell me about Firebolt of the Redguards, or whatever he called his pack of criminals."

"Imperial Father?" Jion said, desperately hoping he did not reveal how painfully his heart was thudding.

"This criminal appears to have raided, then collapsed, one of our chief brimstone mines. You traveled with him, I believe. Escaped the Shadow Panthers, and set fire to their lair together? You must know him. I summoned you to learn what you can tell us."

Jion's mind flitted ahead of his words, barely. "He didn't talk that much, Imperial Father. I didn't either—I didn't want anyone knowing who I was—so I kept to myself. Though we did talk when we were prisoners, planning our escape. He belonged to Redbark Sect. I don't know where they had their headquarters, which in any case was destroyed in a battle with some other sect. Firebolt never talked about it beyond that, and the fact that his weapons master was known as Duin. If that was a clan or personal name, Firebolt never said." Jion watched his father, who nodded slightly at each point: yes, that much he knew.

"What did he look like?"

"He looked much like anyone that age, Imperial Father."

"Which is?"

"Someone Vaion's age, or maybe older, or even younger. I am not good at estimating such things. I don't know—" Jion glanced up, saw the narrowing of question in his father's unwinking gaze, and added, "He was very hairy. Very," he added, thinking of Ryu's mane of curly hair.

"Bearded, your imperial highness?" Fai Anbai asked.

"Just starting," Jion said firmly. "All over his jaw and face."

"Firebolt was not the tall one, your imperial highness?" Fai

Anbai asked, shut his eyes, and recollected the name he'd been offered. "He said his name was Yaso." He had no clear recollection of the face—in any case, his concentration had been on recovering the prince and rounding up the prince's pursuers.

Jion was about to say no, when he hesitated. Yaso had vanished—probably into a bird, although he still had trouble believing that. Yaso had been a whole lot stranger than anyone had believed. And certainly had skills that the others had not been aware of.

One thing Jion was determined to do if he could, which was to avoid betraying Ryu, including tying her to Loyalty—though it would be easy enough to make that connection if they decided to pursue it. But he wasn't going to help them. Too many entirely innocent people might die under questioning, and for what? He did not believe Redbark was any danger whatsoever to the empire. "Yes," he said. "That was Firebolt."

Fai Anbai's lips compressed.

The emperor said, "You have something to add, chief?"

The chief ferret hated finding himself poised between father and son. But duty was duty. "The proprietor of the inn did say that Firebolt left the evening before, which would match up with the time we questioned the supposed Yaso the Healer." He turned resolutely to Jion. "A question only, your imperial majesty. Your imperial highness. Most of the mine witnesses maintain Firebolt was of medium height. Some even said on the short side. I recollect Yaso being quite tall."

"Tall and skinny," Jion said, heart pounding. "Did these guards see him up close? How well are they able to describe someone while in action, or at a distance, without actually measuring?"

Fai Anbai said grimly, "Since almost nothing else in these testimonies matches, I concede the point, your imperial highness. And we did neglect to ask his followers about their leader, not having any idea who he was at the time, so there is no basic information to compare against."

The emperor nodded corroboratively, and Jion realized that the ferrets must have questioned the Redbarks after he was taken away. Questioned them, but let them go, or this conversation would not be happening.

The emperor observed caustically to Fai Anbai, "Firebolt

clearly decamped at the first sign of trouble, leaving behind his followers." And to Jion, "Exemplary leadership."

In spite of his father's sarcasm, Jion found that unexpectedly, he was rather enjoying himself—though it was a very risky enjoyment. But that was part of the fun.

"I want you," the emperor then said, "to summon Court Artist Yoli, and provide a clear enough description for him to draw a recognizable picture of this Firebolt that we can post on the Capital List. With a suitable reward," he added, to Fai Anbai.

The ferret chief assented, hoping the interview was over. He had so very much to do.

The emperor raised a dismissive hand. The two bowed, and began their retreat, when the emperor spoke again, "Stay."

They wheeled and bowed again.

The emperor leaned forward, fingers tapping on the arm of his throne, that slight smile visible once again. "Jion, your improvement this past year has made you a thunder of dragons, as my imperial grandmother used to say. If, by the end of the year, when your sister Lily sails east to begin her new life, the combined forces of the army and navy have not managed to lay this Firebolt by the heels—I know these wandering criminals are like rats when it comes to finding hidey holes—then next spring, I will entrust this matter to you. You have the advantage of being familiar with some of those rat holes. Use this advantage. Find this Firebolt. Bring me back his head, and I will make you crown prince." His smile widened. "Will you do that for me?"

The words were a question, but the tone was an order.

An imperial edict.

Jion bowed, but could not bring himself to speak.

The emperor turned to Fai Anbai. "Chief, you have until that time to select and train a suitable honor guard to accompany my son, and see that he comes safely back."

# ABOUT THE AUTHOR

Sherwood Smith writes fantasy, science fiction, and historical fiction. Her full bibliography can be found on her website at https://www.sherwoodsmith.net.

# ABOUT BOOK VIEW CAFE

Book View Café is an author-owned cooperative of professional writers, publishing in a variety of genres including fantasy, science fiction, romance, mystery, and more.

Its authors include New York Times and USA Today bestsellers as well as winners and nominees of many prestigious awards such as the Agatha Award, Hugo Award, Lambda Literary Award, Locus Award, Nebula Award, RITA Award, Philip K. Dick Award, World Fantasy Award, and many others.

Since its debut in 2008, Book View Café has gained a reputation for producing high quality books in both print and electronic form. BVC's e-books are DRM-free and distributed around the world.

Book View Café's monthly newsletter includes new releases, specials, author news and events. To sign up, please visit https://www.bookviewcafe.com/bookstore/newsletter/

Made in the USA
Coppell, TX
31 October 2022